ELARA

Rage Unleashed

Part 1

H. C. Lopez

Elara: Rage Unleased: Part 1
Copyright © 2025 by H.C. Lopez

ISBN: 9798278776970

DEDICATION

To those who, like me, live with borderline personality disorder.
This book is for you. For every battle fought within, for every moment of doubt, and for the strength it takes to keep going. You are not alone, and your story matters.

TRIGGER WARNINGS

This book contains material that may be distressing or triggering to some readers. Themes and events depicted within the story include:

- Mental health struggles:
  - Borderline Personality Disorder (BPD)
  - Depression
  - Anxiety
- Self-harm
- Suicidal ideation
- Child molestation
- Rape
- Child abuse
- Physical and emotional abuse
- Intense emotional experiences, such as: rage & grief
- Trauma
- Descriptions of violence, including torture
- Blood
- Death
- Guns

Reader discretion is advised. If any of these topics are sensitive for you, please take care while reading. If you or someone you know is struggling, there are resources available. Please seek help from a trusted individual or professional. **Remember, your mental and emotional well-being is important.**

PROLOGUE

The air was thick with the stench of sweat and blood, a suffocating reminder of the battle raging around us. My breath came in ragged gasps as I tightened my grip on the hilts of my katanas, feeling the comforting weight of the blades in my hands. The crimson armor I wore was dented and scratched, but it held firm—a testament to the countless battles it had seen. This was the toughest fight we had ever faced together. It would determine everything—this was the battle that could end it all.

The battlefield was a nightmarish landscape of scorched grass, cracked earth, and smoking craters from elemental blasts. Shattered trees and splintered rocks lay scattered like broken toys, evidence of the brutal force wielded by both sides. The sky overhead was ominous gray, thick clouds swirling in a maelstrom that mirrored the chaos below. Lightning flashed intermittently, illuminating the battlefield in stark, eerie bursts, the rumble of thunder underscoring the sounds of clashing steel and elemental fury.

At the center of it all stood my uncle, the world-renowned human trafficking lord and the epitome of evil, protected by his legion of henchmen. The Vipers—my roommates and the most powerful elemental wielders, Kai, Lius, and Ares—fought alongside me, their powers tearing through the enemy ranks. Sara and Ren, their trainees, were holding their own, their elemental attacks dazzling with raw power and precision. But no matter how many we cut down, more took their place.

My heart pounded as I watched my friends fight. They were more than just teammates—they were my family. We had trained together, bled together, and now, we were fighting for our lives together. I saw Kai take a hit, electricity crackling around him as he staggered back. Lius, ever quick with a retort, threw himself in front of a blade meant for Ares, his fire shielding them both.

I forced my attention back to the battle, pushing aside the fear gnawing at my resolve. I parried a blow, spun, and sliced through another enemy, my movements a deadly dance of steel and skill. But even as I fought, my mind kept drifting back to my friends— the thought of losing them was unbearable.

Ares was battling a hulking brute of a rogue elemental, his earth powers clashing against the brute's sheer strength. He caught my eye for a brief moment, and a silent understanding passed between us: we had to keep pushing. I had to reach my uncle.

"Elara, watch out!" Sara's voice rang out, and I ducked just in time to avoid a fireball aimed at my head. I nodded my thanks to her, my muscles screaming in protest as I surged forward, cutting a path through the enemy ranks. Every step felt like an eternity, my body growing heavier with each passing second.

Ren was a blur of motion, his water attacks creating a barrier around him and Sara. They moved in perfect sync, a testament to their training and bond. But even they couldn't hold off the onslaught forever. Pain suddenly flared in my side, and I staggered, nearly dropping my katanas. My vision blurred, the world tilting dangerously. But I couldn't stop. Not now. Not when we were so close.

"Come on, Elara," I muttered through gritted teeth, forcing myself to keep moving. The thought of my uncle—the man responsible for so much pain, not just for me, but for countless others—fueled my determination. I would see him brought to justice, no matter the cost.

Lius appeared at my side, his typically bright hazel eyes now dark and filled with concern. He was covered in cuts and bruises, but there was no hesitation in his movements. He gave me a brief nod, and together we pressed forward, cutting down anyone who dared stand in our way.

We were getting closer. I could see the entrance to the run-down, abandoned warehouse where my uncle was holed up. It was heavily guarded, but within reach. As we approached, more of his henchmen swarmed us in a desperate attempt to protect their master.

A cry of pain snapped my attention, and I saw Ren go down, a deep gash on his leg. Sara screamed his name, rushing to his side, but she was intercepted by another attacker.

"No!" I screamed, my voice raw with desperation. I pushed harder, my katanas a whirlwind of death as I fought to reach them. But the enemy was relentless, their attacks coming faster and harder, cutting me off from Ren and Sara.

Kai was beside me now, his electrical attacks sizzling through the air. He was panting heavily, his eyes fierce. "We can't give up, Elara! We have to keep going!"

"I know," I gasped, barely able to catch my breath. "But Ren's hurt! We have to protect him and Sara!"

"I will," Ares said, his voice steady despite the chaos around us. "You have to take down your uncle, Elara. He's the key to ending all of this. Go! I'll help Ren and Sara."

I nodded, swallowing my fear and pain. He was right. I had to finish this. With renewed determination, I fought my way forward. Every step brought me closer to the end. I could feel the weight of my injuries and the exhaustion threatening to overwhelm me, but I pushed it all aside. My friends needed me. The world needed me.

And I would not let them down. As we finally broke through the last line of defense, I saw my uncle standing there, a sneer on his face. He was surrounded by his elite guards, but I could see the flicker of fear in his eyes.

"This ends now," I said, my voice filled with fierce determination.

He laughed, a cold, cruel sound. "You think you can stop me?"

"We don't think," I replied, stepping forward, my katanas ready at my sides. "We know."

I charged toward him, with Kai and Lius flanking behind me. The final battle began.

1

Many years ago, when the world was a different place—a peaceful place—a group of miners were tasked with an ambitious project. They were to dig deeper into the earth's core than anyone had ever dared before. The promise of untold riches and resources drove them onward, the leader constantly shouting at the workers to dig faster, dig deeper.

"Come on, you lazy lot! We're close, I can feel it!" the foreman bellowed, his voice echoing through the narrow, dimly lit tunnels. The miners, covered in dirt and sweat, obeyed without question, driven by a mix of fear and hope. One of the miners was on the verge of collapse from exhaustion. His muscles ached, and his vision blurred, but he refused to give up. With one final swing of his pickaxe, he struck something hard. This time, the sound was different–a metallic ring instead of the familiar dull thud. He paused, his heart pounding, and cleared away the dirt and debris.

His eyes widened as he revealed a wall of what looked like a large pink crystal. It shimmered, pulsing with an otherworldly light that cast eerie shadows along the tunnel walls. The other miners gathered around, their exhaustion momentarily forgotten as they stared in awe.

"What is it?" one of them whispered, unable to tear his eyes away.

Driven by curiosity and a need to test its durability, the miner swung his pickaxe again and struck the crystal. The impact unleashed a massive energy wave that swept across the planet, knocking everyone off their feet with its intensity. The crystal shattered into a million pieces, each fragment embedding itself into the earth and everything living on it. The energy surge absorbed itself into all living things, giving them powers to wield the elements of the earth. Some people discovered they could control fire, others water, earth, or air. Some were stronger than others, their powers more pronounced and dangerous. It was a gift, but also... a curse.

In the years that followed, the world transformed. Those touched by the crystal's power became *Elementals*, learning to harness and control the elements. Some used their powers for good, becoming the protectors and healers of the world. But others were consumed by power, driven by a desire to dominate and rule.

Civilizations rose and fell, wars were fought, and the world was shaped by the power of the Elementals. Secret organizations were formed to keep the balance, to ensure that those who sought to abuse their powers were stopped. Among these was the Special Ops 6, a special unit like that of the green berets, known as the Vipers, the most powerful elemental wielders. They were a force to be reckoned with, their skills unmatched, their loyalty unwavering, but even they had their limits. The power of the elements was a double-edged sword, and not everyone could wield it without being consumed. As the years passed, stories of the original miners and the pink crystal became legends, a reminder of the day when the world changed forever. That event is forever known as "The Elemental Awakening."

There were also whispers of a special kind of Elemental, one who could wield all the elements through their emotions. These Elementals were the most powerful and the most feared. So much so that they were executed once they were discovered. The power they held was seen as too dangerous, too uncontrollable. But this extraordinary power brought great fear. Elementals who controlled all elements through their emotions were seen as both the most powerful and the most dangerous. Their unpredictable nature made their powers wildly uncontrollable, prompting a concerted effort to eradicate them. Societies, wary of their potential for chaos, pursued them relentlessly. These most powerful elementals were hunted down and executed on sight, leaving their existence as little more than whispers in forgotten legends. We called them, "E-Level".

Today, E-Level Elementals are believed to be extinct, their presence erased from history. The fear and prejudice against those with emotional power over all the elements, have left a legacy of suppression and eradication. If an E-Level Elemental is ever discovered, the consequences are immediate and severe. Now, I am the unknown descendant of that legacy, fighting to stop a man consumed by power and greed. The blood of those miners ran in my veins, and I would not let their sacrifice be in vain. I would fight, I would win, and I would bring balance back to the world. I am *"E-Level"*.

~*~

ELARA

My name is Elara Blake, and I am 25 years old. I dropped out of high school to dedicate my life to fighting for those who cannot defend themselves. My journey has been shaped by years of trauma inflicted by my family, particularly by my uncle, which ignited a fierce determination in me. This personal history has driven me to protect women and children who face injustice and vulnerability, the way I did. In a justice system often fractured and indifferent, I am committed to seeking the justice they deserve, determined to make a meaningful difference despite the obstacles.

When I was twelve, my uncle moved to town, and my parents decided to welcome him with a special dinner. At that time, I was a happy child living a charmed life as my parents' little princess. We lived in a luxurious house, just shy of being a mansion, and everything seemed perfect. That evening, we gathered around the dinner table: my uncle sat across from me, his eyes frequently drifting in my direction, while my parents were seated across from each other. As we enjoyed our meal, I couldn't understand why this dinner felt so significant. I had never met my mother's brother before, and the formality of the occasion puzzled me. Dressed in my finest dress, with my parents equally dressed up, the evening felt more like a performance than a simple family gathering. The meal had been specially catered, and my mother had emphasized that my uncle deserved nothing but the best. Despite the lavishness, I felt confused and disconnected, unable to grasp why so much effort was being made for someone who was still a stranger to me. I miss being that ignorant, that innocent.

As dinner concluded and we finished our desserts, my father invited my uncle into the study for a cigar and a discussion about business. I glanced at my mother, my eyes full of unspoken questions. I wanted to understand why the evening felt so different, why the formality seemed out of place.

"He has helped our family tremendously, Ellie." my mother said softly. Her eyes carried a sadness and concern that I couldn't quite decipher. In that moment, I chose not to press her further, sensing there was something she wasn't sharing. Instead, I was gently ushered to my room, with my mother saying it was to keep me *out of the way* while the adults had their discussion. As I settled into my room, I couldn't shake the feeling that there was more to the evening than met the eye, but I respected my mother's unspoken request and kept my curiosity to myself.

Engrossed in playing with a new dollhouse my dad had gifted me, I heard the creak of my bedroom door opening. The unmistakable scent of whiskey and cigars filled the air as I looked up to see my uncle stepping into the room. My eyes widened in shock as he closed the door behind him, the sound of the lock clicking into place echoing ominously. A palpable tension settled in the room, making the air feel thick and suffocating. My instinct screamed at me to hide, to escape, but my body felt paralyzed, unable to move despite the urgent plea from my gut. As he stumbled towards me in his drunken haze, I felt a deep, unsettling fear. The heaviness of the situation made it feel as though I was trapped in place, unable to flee. I fought desperately against the invisible force holding me still, my heart racing as he reached out toward me. The dread and helplessness overwhelmed me, each second stretching painfully long as he drew closer, his intentions unmistakable.

~*~

I woke up in a cold sweat, my heart racing as the remnants of the nightmare lingered. Blinking in the dim light of the airplane cabin, I'm reminded that I was on a flight to Tokyo. It was just another haunting dream, a painful echo from the past. I wiped my face with the back of my hand and took a deep breath, focusing on calming my ragged breathing. Looking out the window beside my seat, I let my mind drift back to that night, a night that still haunts me. After the horrific incident, I remember I ran to my parents, desperate to tell them what had happened—what my uncle had done. They dismissed my cries as the fantasies of a child with her head in the clouds. Their disbelief cut deeper than any wound.

In the years that followed, my uncle continued to invade my life, taking more and more from me, slowly eroding my sense of self and innocence. Each visit felt like a piece of my soul piece by piece, I was hollowed out. The torment continued until I was seventeen, leaving me a shell of who I once was. By then, I had become numb, no longer caring about my own survival or what happened to me. That night, something shifted. I finally fought back, summoning the strength I thought I had lost. It was a turning point, the moment I reclaimed a fragment of my power and defied the darkness that had consumed me for so long.

Sitting in my seat, my mind wandered, imagining myself as an elemental–a human with the extraordinary power to control earth's elements. I imagined wielding fire, water, earth, or air with just a thought, a stark contrast to my mundane existence as an ordinary human. Born without such powers, I had always been fascinated by the concept of elementals. The Elemental Awakening, a rare and mystical event from our history, transformed certain humans into beings with control over the elements. This transformation was said to be triggered by intense emotional states–either overwhelming joy or crushing despair. These individuals could harness their emotions to manipulate the natural world, turning feelings into tangible forces.

Without any special abilities of my own, I've been captivated by news stories of the Elementals Special Ops 6–or as we call them, SP6–teams who battle those consumed by their powers. These elite forces fight tirelessly to protect our world from rogue Elementals who have lost control of their sanity from the power. Watching them, I felt both awe and longing. They were heroes wielding incredible powers, while I felt powerless in my own life. After turning seventeen, I resolved that I would never again be at the mercy of anyone, not even my uncle. No one would ever have the chance to harm me or others like he did. I dedicated myself to rigorous training in various martial arts—boxing, taekwondo, karate, and more. My goal was to become as formidable as possible, to be invincible as a mere human, in a world full of other-worldly magic.

My transformation from a victim to a protector took a darker turn following the tragic death of a colleague right before my eyes. This event, coupled with information from Z Group—a covert organization I had been working for—that my uncle had relocated to Tokyo, drove me to leave my home in Arizona. Moving to Japan with a singular purpose: to track down my uncle and end his reign of terror. Back in Arizona, I had become a shadowy figure, earning the nickname *'Crimson Mystery'* in the news. I pursued targets sent to me by Z Group—individuals accused of committing heinous acts against women and children. My efforts, alongside my partner, Trey, led to a significant decrease in such crimes. However, my partner was eventually killed in action, leaving me with a heavy burden and an unrelenting drive for justice.

Now, with my uncle in Tokyo, I am determined to finish what I started. His terror has followed him wherever he goes, and I will not rest until his reign of terror is over. As my plane begins its descent, I have finally arrived. This is my story of how I overcome my past traumas, find love, and become the strongest E-Level Elemental to walk this planet. First, I must settle into my new home in Tokyo and get to know my four new roommates—one of whom, in particular, will prove to be more important to me than I could have ever imagined.

~*~

My taxi from the airport pulls up to a beautiful house nestled amidst the bustling Tokyo skyline. The contrast between the lively city and this serene, elegant home is striking. The house stood two stories tall, a seamless blend of modern design and traditional Japanese elements. Dark wooden beams contrast with sleek glass panels, giving it a refined yet inviting appearance.

The front yard is meticulously landscaped with a small, tranquil garden. A few neatly trimmed bonsai trees add a touch of artistry to the scene. The garden is framed by a low stone wall, beyond which the sounds of the city seem to fade into a gentle hum. I step out of the taxi, taking in the peaceful ambiance that surrounds the house. The driver, a kind older man with a warm smile, helps me with my luggage, his practiced movements show his years of experience. I pay him, feeling a mix of relief and excitement.

As I walk towards the house, the cool evening air carries a hint of jasmine from a nearby bush, adding to the sense of calm. The entrance is marked by a wooden gate with intricate lattice work, which swings open to reveal a well-worn stone path leading to the front door. The door itself is a rich mahogany, adorned with an ornate brass handle that catches the fading sunlight.

Standing there, I take a deep breath and let the reality of the moment sink in. This is it. I'm moving into my new house in

Tokyo, Japan. The initial apprehension melts away, replaced by a profound sense of anticipation. The house, with its blend of modern comfort and traditional charm, feels like the perfect place for the new chapter of my life. The thought of exploring the space, of making it my own, fills me with an excited energy.

I turn to the driver, giving him a grateful nod before he departs, and then I turn my attention back to the house. It's more than just a building; it's the beginning of a new adventure, and I'm ready to embrace every moment of it. Excitement mixed with nerves as I thought about meeting my new roommates. The roommate listing had been up for a while, and even though the specifics about the current tenants weren't detailed, it was affordable and conveniently located in downtown Tokyo, making it perfect for me.

The doorknob was a piece of artistry in its own right. It's an antique brass knob, weathered by time but still gleaming with a subtle sheen when caught by the light. The surface is intricately etched with floral patterns, the delicate swirls and curves telling tales of a bygone era. The base plate is oval, slightly tarnished, with a few scratches and dents that hint at the many hands that have turned it over the years. Despite its age, the knob turns smoothly, a testament to its craftsmanship. The keyhole below is ornate, framed by a tiny, delicate border, inviting curiosity about the secrets it guards. This doorknob isn't just a functional object; it's a portal to the history and stories that fill this house.

2

As I step through the front door, I'm greeted by a spacious foyer that immediately sets the tone for the rest of the house. The floors are polished hardwood, reflecting the warm light from a contemporary chandelier hanging above. To the right, a sleek, modern coat rack is mounted on the wall, with a small bench beneath it for convenience.

Straight ahead, the living area opens up, bathed in natural light from large windows. The color scheme is a soothing blend of neutral tones, with soft beige walls and plush, light gray carpeting. The focal point of the living area is a large, comfortable sectional couch arranged around a low coffee table, with a large recliner to the right of it. A flat-screen TV is mounted on the wall opposite the couch, with a minimalist entertainment unit below it. A large, sliding glass door at the far end of the living area leads out to a small patio, perfect for relaxing outside. The space is well-decorated with contemporary art pieces and potted plants, adding a touch of vibrancy and warmth. My new roommates must have a great decorator, or it could simply just be one of their tastes and preferences.

Next to the living area is the dining area. This space features a modern, rectangular dining table with seating for six. The table is set on a stylish area rug that complements the overall color scheme of the first floor. Above the dining table hangs a sleek pendant light, casting a warm glow over the space. The dining area is open to the kitchen, creating a seamless flow between the two areas.

The kitchen is designed with both functionality and style in mind. It features high-end stainless steel appliances, including a refrigerator, oven, and dishwasher. The countertops are a sleek, dark granite, with ample cabinet space above and below. A large island in the center of the kitchen provides additional prep space and has barstool seating on one side. The backsplash is a modern mosaic tile, adding a touch of elegance to the room. A door from the kitchen leads to a small pantry or utility room, providing additional storage.

Off the foyer, there's a conveniently located half-bath. It's compact but well-appointed, with modern fixtures and a clean, minimalist design. The walls are tiled with light-colored ceramic tiles, and there's a small vanity with a sink and a mirror above it.

A staircase leads to the second floor, its railing a sleek metal design that complements the modern aesthetic of the house. The staircase is centrally located, providing easy access to the second floor while still maintaining an open feel to the space. There are small coats and storage closets tucked into the hallway spaces, ideal for keeping everyday items organized. The first floor is tastefully decorated with a mix of contemporary furnishings and personal touches, such as framed photographs and decorative vases.

I walk into the living room, taking in the space and the people who will be my new roommates. The room was filled with a warm, golden light filtering through large windows, casting a cozy glow on the wooden floors. There were four people in the living room as I walked in, each of them seemingly engrossed in their own activities. A tall lean guy with golden brown hair sat on the couch, absorbed in a book. A cheerful looking guy with tousled hair was fiddling with a guitar. A brooding figure with sharp features, and black hair, lounged in an armchair, looking half asleep. Finally, a guy with an athletic build, dark red hair and blue eyes glanced up from his laptop, acknowledging my presence with a nod.

The living area is comfortably arranged, but it's the people sitting on the couch who immediately draw my attention. The first man caught my eye with his striking platinum blonde hair and lean build. He lounged casually, exuding confidence. At 6'2", his height is complemented by a lean, well-built form that exudes both confidence and strength. His playboy charm is clear in the way he lounges with an effortless grace, but there's a deeper intensity behind his eyes.

Next to him is another man, who seems to be the group's nurturing figure. His light brown hair is slightly tousled, adding to his approachable demeanor. Standing at 6'3", his towering presence feels both protective and reassuring. His posture and the warm, inviting smile he offers conveys a sense of responsibility and care, as though he's ready to offer guidance and support through his golden brown eyes.

The apparent oldest of the group is situated in a position that emphasizes his stoic nature. At 6'4", he's the tallest and his black hair contrasts sharply with his pale skin. His demeanor is calm, almost detached, as he leans back with an air of nonchalance.

Despite his cold exterior, there's something enigmatic about him that suggests hidden depths. His green eyes, though cool, hold a guarded warmth that might reveal itself under the right circumstances.

Finally, there's the youngest of the four, who looks no older than 27. With golden brown hair, bright blue eyes and a height of 6'1", he strikes a balance between youthful energy and thoughtful maturity. His presence is grounded, and there's an almost serene quality to his demeanor that makes him seem like the voice of reason among the group. His calm and measured gaze provides a comforting sense of stability, as though he's the one who keeps everything from tipping into chaos.

As I take in the sight of my new roommates, I sense a complex blend of personalities and energies that will shape my experience in this new chapter of my life. Each individual brings something unique to the table, and I can't help but feel a mix of curiosity and apprehension about how we will all fit together.

I cleared my throat, feeling a mix of anticipation and nervousness. "Hi everyone. I'm Elara, your new roommate." The man with light brown hair, holding a book, looks up, his brown eyes widening in surprise. "Oh, I didn't know we had a new roommate. I'm Kai." The blonde guy puts down his guitar and flashes a friendly smile. "Well hello and welcome! I'm Arelius. But everyone calls me 'Lius.'" The brooding figure, with black hair and matching eyes, in the armchair gave a disinterested grunt directed towards 'Lius'. "I'm Max." The guy with dark red hair, holding a laptop, closed it and gave me a polite nod. "I'm Ares. Nice to meet you."

"There's a room upstairs for you," Kai said, pointing to the stairs.

I nod with gratitude. "Thank you so much."

I turn on my heels to head upstairs, my suitcase rolling behind me. Heading up the stairs to check out the rooms, choosing the only one that was spacious, well-kept and vacant. The room is between two others. It is bright, with open windows letting in sunlight that offers a view of the bustling city below. The bed was made, and the furniture was neatly arranged. The bed sheets felt comfortable and smelled fresh. As I started unpacking, arranging my clothes in the closet and setting up my laptop on the desk, I couldn't help but feel a sense of excitement. This was a new beginning, a chance to explore a new city and make new friends. I wondered what kind of people my roommates were and hoped we would all get along. Just as I was putting away the last of my things, there was a knock on my door. I turned to see the man who said his name was Kai, standing there, with a kind smile.

"Hey, I just wanted to check if you needed anything." He asks.

I shake my head, "No, I'm all set. Thank you, Kai."

"No problem." he replies. "We usually have dinner together. Want to join us tonight?" Kai asked with a smile.

I hesitated, then nodded. "Sure, I'd love to."

"Awesome! Dinner's at seven. See you then." Kai exclaims before heading back downstairs.

I take a deep breath, feeling a mix of relief and anticipation. Tonight, would be the first step in getting to know my new roommates and building a life here in Tokyo. As I finished arranging my room, I felt a renewed sense of optimism. This was the start of a new adventure, and I was ready to embrace it.

~*~

Back in my new room, dinner time arrived sooner than I expected. I could hear the lively chatter and clinking of dishes from downstairs as I made my way to the dining area. The table was set with a variety of dishes, from sushi and tempura to more traditional Japanese fare like miso soup and pickled vegetables. It was a feast, and the delicious aroma made my stomach rumble in anticipation.

Kai was the first to greet me as I walked into the dining room. "Elara, glad you could join us! Have a seat, make yourself at home. We figured some local cuisine would be a great way to welcome you."

I smile in response as I take a seat between Kai and Arelius. Max and Ares were already seated, and there was an easy camaraderie among them that made me feel a little more at ease. As we began to eat, the conversation flowed effortlessly. Lius was telling a funny story about a recent adventure when I noticed something. The way they interacted, the subtle glances, the shared jokes—it was clear they were more than just roommates.

"So, Elara," Lius begins, looking at me with a curious smile. "What brings you to Tokyo?"

I swallow a bite of sushi and take a sip of water before answering. "I wanted a change of scenery, and I've always been fascinated by Japanese culture. Plus, my job had an opening out here and when I was offered to move, it was too good to pass up."

"That's great," Lius says, nodding. "Tokyo is an amazing city. I'm sure you will love it out here."

"What company do you work for?" Kai asks.

"Z Corp. They specialize in cybersecurity for many large enterprises in the area where I'm from and they've branched out to Japan." I say as I take another sip of my water. As the conversation slowed, I set down my chopsticks and asked, "Can I ask you all something? I can't help but notice there's more to you four than meets the eye. You seem really close, like you've been through a lot together or something. More than just roommates."

The room fell silent for a moment, and I could see them exchanging glances. Kai was the first to break the silence. "You've got a keen eye, Elara." He says, leaning back in his chair. "We're not just roommates. We're part of a team, where we work. A very special team."

"A team?" I echo, my curiosity piqued. "What kind of team? Baseball?"

Max sighed, rolling his eyes. "Typical American."

Lius shakes his head, "We're part of an elite task force known as SP6, maybe you've heard of it? We handle special operations that require a high level of skill and discretion."

My eyes widened. "SP6? Wait, your part of Special Ops 6?!" My surprise is clear in my eyes and my voice. "So, you guys are like the alpha team for them?"

"Something like that," Ares says with a small smirk. "We're the top team in the force, actually. We call ourselves the Vipers."

"Vipers…" I repeat, letting the name sink in. I had heard of them before in Arizona. "Wow, that's… incredible. I had no idea."

"We try to keep a low profile," Kai explains. "But since you're living here with us, it's only right that we tell you."

I nod, still trying to wrap my head around it and keep myself from fangirling over them. "So, you guys go out on missions and stuff?" I ask after I get a grip on my excitement.

"Yep." says Max, popping a piece of tempura into his mouth. "And it's not as glamorous as it sounds. It's dangerous work. We're hardly home."

Lius adds, "We trust you to keep this to yourself." His tone became serious. "Our safety depends on our anonymity."

I nod, knowing all too well how important keeping a low profile is. "Of course." I quickly added. "Your secret is safe with me."

"Thank you, Elara." Kai says with a warm smile. "We appreciate it."

As the conversation shifts back to a lighter topic, I couldn't help but feel a newfound respect for my roommates. They weren't just ordinary people—they were heroes, risking their lives to protect others. And now, I was a part of their world, if only in a small way. The thought was both thrilling and a little intimidating, but I was determined to make the most of this unique experience to further myself towards my own end goal, and the true reason why I am in Tokyo.

I help clean up after dinner. I had just dried the last dish, when I heard Lius's voice calling from the living room, "HEY! The new roomie! Come over here!" Finished with the dishes anyways, I walk out of the kitchen to see what he needs.

"Yes…?" I walked towards them, curiosity piqued.

Lius gestured to the couch next to him. "Come sit." Kai and Max were already there.

I sit where he indicates. Lius wrapped an arm around my shoulders and pulled me close. "So, tell us about yourself," he says looking at the side of my face.

I hesitate before speaking. "Well, my name is Elara Blake, as you already know. I just moved here from Arizona. I'm 25 years old and I dislike pickles."

Kai seemed intrigued. "Interesting…"

Max continues to stare but says nothing.

Lius grinned. "And do you have a boyfriend?"

I quirk a brow. "That's an odd question... No, not anymore. I ended a long-term relationship before moving here." I responded reluctantly.

Lius's eyes twinkled. "So, you're single?"

"I guess so... I didn't want to deal with a long-distance relationship since he wasn't willing to move here with me." I look down at my hands as I realize the story I tell people about why my ex actually isn't with me here... How it all actually ended. The memory still haunts me.

Lius leans closer, pulling me from my memories. "So, you're available?" He chuckles and raises an eyebrow. I could tell he was a bit of a flirt, a *fuck-boy* if you will. His question alerted me, filling my gut with unease.

"I guess so... But I'm not really looking for anything right now. If I meet someone, then so be it..." I say as I begin to lean away from him, he's getting too close for comfort.

Lius grinned. "I'm single too." He pulled me closer, his hand settling on my waist, his flirty attitude setting me on edge.

I roll my eyes. "I can't imagine why..." My skin is crawling at his touch. I work to keep my calm when I really want to punch him.

Lius's grin widened. "What's that supposed to mean?" He put his other hand on my other side and gently pulled me onto his lap.

Taken aback, I tell him, "That you seem so modest. How could anyone not have you locked down already?" I taunt as I work to stand up off his lap, very uncomfortable with this situation.

Lius replies with, "I know, I'm a catch." He begins running his hands gently up and down my thighs, tightening his grip on my waist to pull me back down onto his lap.

My heart raced as I pushed his hands away. "Enough," I said firmly, trying to stay calm.

Lius laughs. "Oh, come on… I know you like it." He put both hands on my hips, refusing to let go.

I push his hands away firmly. "Don't… don't do that…"

Lius's smile falters. "Why not?" He starts to move his hands underneath my shirt.

My face turns red with anger. "Don't touch me without my permission!" I shout, slapping his hand away, then slapping him right across his cheek.

Lius looks shocked. "Did you just slap me?"

"Yes! You don't ever put your hands on me without my permission! Shame on you!" I stood up, furious. I glare at the others in the room who are now amused with Lius being slapped.

Lius's face turns defensive. "Whoa! *Relax*! I was just teasing you…"

I was a few feet away from him. "That's *not* teasing! That's harassment!" I glare at Kai and Max. "Do you two think this is funny?" I turn and storm back upstairs to my room, cursing under my breath.

There was a moment of stunned silence before Max muttered, "Damn… she's a feisty one."

I go into my room, tears lining my eyes as I angrily finish unpacking. "How dare he!" I muttered angrily, pacing around the room as I tried to calm down.

~*~

I curl up in my bed, hugging my pillow tightly. Exhaustion and hurt washed over me, my past traumas surfacing like unwelcome ghosts. Rearing their ugly head. I take constant breaths to calm my racing heart in the beginning stages of a panic attack. Suddenly feeling like I'm going to hate living here.

Lius and Kai's conversation continues downstairs. Lius groans. "I just didn't expect her to react so strongly…"

Kai's voice grows sterner. "You need to leave her alone now. She's clearly upset."

Eventually, the house grew quiet. Everyone retreated to their rooms. Even in tears, I finally fell asleep. Succumbing to the peaceful embrace that it brings. I would rather deal with the frequent and familiar nightmares I suffer, than to be groped by my new roommates. Later, I am woken up by a knock on my bedroom door. I sit up and answer.

"Who is it?"

3

"It's Lius…" he says reluctantly through my closed door.

"Come in…" I finally say after a brief pause. Lius pokes his head through the slightly cracked door of my bedroom. "What do you want?" I ask tiredly, with a grumble.

Lius, looking sheepish, "I wanted to talk. Can I come in?"

"Okay, but the door stays open." I sit up completely on my bed, hugging my pillow against me as a shield from him. Lius stepped in, but I cut him off as he unconsciously attempted to close the door behind him. "Leave it open," I said firmly.

Lius walks over to sit down next to me. "I'm sorry for how I acted earlier. I was just trying to have fun… I didn't mean to offend you."

"Consent is important," I say firmly.

Lius lowered his gaze. "I never thought of it like that… I'm just used to acting this way with girls."

I decide to press, "Are they all okay with it?"

Lius seems surprised by my question. As if I have three heads sprouting out of my cranium. He finally nods. "They think it's flattering."

"That's not right," I reply with a slight sternness to my tone as if I'm about to start scolding him. "You need to respect other people's boundaries."

Lius nods. "I promise I will respect your boundaries moving forward."

"Thank you," I replied. "But if I see you do that to anyone else, I won't hesitate to intervene and knock you senseless."

Lius smiles at my warning. "Got it. I won't touch anyone without their permission."

I lower my pillow slightly so that it lies flat on my lap. "Is there anything else you need to say?"

Lius smirked. "You don't need that pillow, you know. You already look cute."

I roll my eyes at his compliment, "I'm not self-conscious. It's a habit. I'm in my pajamas with a man in my room."

Lius leans in towards me. "Are you afraid something might happen tonight?"

I narrowed my eyes on him. "No." My teeth gritted at the audacity of this playboy…

Lius smirks. "Oh yeah? Not even if I ask nicely?"

I shove him away. "Ew. Just don't."

Max knocked on the doorframe. "Everything alright here?"

A look of relief washes over me. "Get Lius out, please." I look at Max as I point at Lius sitting on my bed.

Kai appears suddenly right behind Max, walks in and grabs Lius by the collar, dragging him out. Lius complains the whole way, but Kai closes the door over and looks at Lius, releasing him. "What were you thinking?"

Lius shrugged. "I was just trying to apologize… maybe have a little fun."

"She's not one of your fangirls, Lius. She's clearly not okay with that behavior," Kai said, frustration edging his voice.

Lius protests. "I'm not a perv. I'm a ladies' man."

Kai shakes his head as he pinches the bridge of his nose. "You need to respect her boundaries. She has a right to be upset."

Kai looks at Lius. "She's not going to warm up to you if you keep this up. You need to leave her alone."

Lius sighs. "Fine. I'll back off. But why should I listen to you anyway? It's not like you know what women want, Mr. Celibate…"

"I know more than you apparently. You're a complete idiot and I'm honestly surprised you don't know this already from all the girls you've been messing with." Kai retorts.

"Heyyy… I'm not an idiot and I'm not some player either. Girls are just drawn to me… that's all." Lius complains, still trying to justify his behavior towards me.

Kai gives him a look: "Sure… they like you but from the way you act, I'm guessing that they just like that you're the strongest Viper in the SP6, not you as an actual person."

"You've got that right!" I shouted from my room again. I decided to stand up and walk closer to the door to hear the conversation. I'm nosey, I know… but I had to understand what makes Lou's act like this.

Lius groans, getting truly ticked off at the verbal attacks from Kai and now—me, "Hey! Shut up! I'm having a conversation here!"

I scoff, "Yea… in front of MY bedroom door!"

Lius glances back at Kai, completely ignoring me. He rolls his eyes, "That's not true. Girls like me as a person too!"

I fling my bedroom door open, "That IS true… you have this fake persona when you behave like that. No woman knows who *you* truly are Lius, do they? And if my guess is correct, they don't care and never will. I've known women like that, and they are just infatuated with the idea of being in *your* bed." I cross my arms as I move into my bedroom's doorway, locking my eyes to his. "I bet you never let anyone get to know the real you, do you?"

Lius eyes widened from my sudden appearance. His expression moved to appalled at my shared thoughts of him, "Who I am?! What do you mean? I'm just a fun guy, not some deep mystery. What you see is what you get!"

"That may be, but if all you do is walk and talk like a playboy, that's not the real you. Is it? I could see it in your eyes just now when you were apologizing to me, in there." I gestured to my room. "Before you became uncomfortable with showing any amount of vulnerability and snapped back into being an inappropriate perv." I do my best to keep my tone calm, even with the jab to his made up playboy character. I have been in front of so many different people from all walks of life, so I have come to hone my ability to sense in my gut who someone truly is and if they're wearing a mask to hide their true selves. Whether from being hurt in the past or just how they were raised.

"That's bullshit! There's no secret side to me." He argues. His words may shout in anger, but I could've sworn I saw the slightest glimpse of sadness in his eyes. The eyes always give it away for me. Kai looks at him with a face that tells me *"You're dead wrong mate."*

I pick up on that subtle gesture of Kai's and my hands fling towards him as I tell Lius, "See? That's the actual bullshit…"

Lius is about to boil over with his frustration as he crosses his arms, "And what? You both think you know me better than I know myself?"

I shake my head, "No Lius. I just met you. I'm not saying I know everything about you, but I can see through the fake *'fun guy'* act. You're hiding behind it. You will be very lonely in the end if you keep treating women the way that you do… like they're toys. But… if that's what makes you happy, then so be it. Just leave *me* out of it." I hold his gaze—without blinking—as I say this, making sure he understands that I see right through him.

He huffs out, "Yea well… Sorry for actually having fun with life. I don't get why everyone thinks that I have to be so mature all the time."

"Maturity is relative, Lius. What is considered mature to one person may be childish to another." I replied.

He rolls his eyes at me, "Yea whatever, it's just… it's *fun* to play with girls. Why should I have to stop? When they clearly enjoy it too?"

"If a woman enjoys that behavior from you then she herself has issues of her own to work through. But if that brings you joy, and the female is ok with it then go at it. I just need you to respect the fact that I am not one of them. I never will be." I make sure to scan all three of my roommates to make myself as clear as possible.

Lius huffs again, "Ugh, why are you so stubborn? You don't have to be all high and mighty, I'm sure you'd like it too if you would actually let me-"

I put up a hand to cut him off, "What? Let you grab at me like I'm one of your little fan girls, fawning all over you? *No!* Been there, dealt with that and I will *never* allow that to happen to me again." My hands form fists at my sides as I begin to tremble with anger and fury.

Ares is now in the hall with us, woken up from all the commotion. He leans against the wall of the hallway, listening to Lius and I go back and forth. A smirk on his face, entertained by the situation unfolding before him—Lius getting his ass chewed is his favorite thing to witness. I quickly glance at him and furrow my brow before looking back at Lius.

Lius looks at me with a perplexed look on his face, "Oh come on... seriously? You have one bad experience and you're never going to try it ever again? Because of one bad experience?"

My eyes fill with fury, my fists tightening at my sides. With tears lining my eyes I glare at him, "I will *never* try that again! What happened to me was *not* just a 'bad experience' Lius! I wasn't given the choice!"

Lius looks at me with a bit of surprise at my response, noticing that he seems to have crossed a line with me that he didn't know existed. That maybe, it was more serious than just a bad experience with someone who didn't know what they were doing, that had me so guarded and snarling with offense. His face softens as he looks at my hate filled gaze. "Wait... what happened?"

Keeping my stance, knuckles getting white. "I don't want to talk about it, Lius." I turn to close my door again. Lius grabs my arm to stop me as he notices the tears in my eyes that show the pain and suffering, I seemed to have endured, the memories that were triggered by his words. The tears I refuse to let fall once again over that horrid man, my uncle.

Lius takes in my expression, and how I jerk my arm from his grasp. He looks down at my arm and my reaction to being grabbed. He realizes what could be causing this behavior. "Who the hell hurt you...?"

I hold my arm in my own hand to guard it from anyone touching it again. My skin crawls as the emotional scar in my mind burns with the memory of my past. My eyes snap to his and widen at his clairvoyance at my unspoken thoughts. "I don't want to talk-"

He puts a finger in front of my face in the shape of a one to hush me, "Talk. Who hurt you?" He asks me again but more firmly as a command.

"I don't know you guys well enough to talk about it." I do my best to fend him off. The other three took in my reaction as well, wanting to know more as well.

"No." He commands. "We are going to be living together under the same roof. We might as well get to know each other better. You've dug into my soul, you owe me something of equal girth. Now... tell us... who hurt you." I look down at my feet and then back up at him as I hesitate to speak. He has a point, I guess. I take a deep breath, "My uncle... I was 12 years old, and he was..." I flinch as the memory of that first night floods my memories. I shake the thoughts out of my mind, "That's why I won't let anyone handle me like you did earlier–being touched without my consent, groped or grabbed–never again."

Lius' eyes widened in shock. He reaches out but pauses when I flinch, withdrawing his hand at once. He retracts his hand and clicks his jaw tight. Letting out a sigh of frustration. But not at my reaction, but the reason I react that way. "Wait, wait, wait... hold on. *Who* the *hell* did this to you?! Your uncle? Tell me his name... now." His voice dropped, his eyes dark with rage.

"It won't make a difference... it's over. Done with. What could you even do? If my own father didn't help me, why would I expect you to? I cannot expect anyone to help me, and I won't start now." I explain.

"That son of a- I may have crossed a line, but I'd never force anything on a woman," Lius said, his anger rising.

Kai placed a calming hand on his shoulder, "Lius calm down… you're not helping the situation."

"I will not calm down-" Lius protests.

"Take a breath, you getting angry right now won't help the situation." Kai says as he looks at me. Lius takes a deep breath, trying to calm himself down. It was a few seconds before he could speak again. I hold my gaze on him, watching cautiously.

"He's a bastard, a criminal. He should be in prison for what he's done to you… They don't take too kindly to attacks of that nature on women or *children* around here. You can't just let him continue without reporting him-" Lius continues to say to me.

The last bit of my restraint snaps as I shout out, "I was 12 years old Lius! I was just a child! I told my parents like I thought I was supposed to… and they didn't believe me! Branded me a liar for the rest of my life… My uncle took advantage of my parents blind eye and kept visiting me multiple times after that because he *knew* my parents wouldn't do a *damn* thing… I vowed after that, I will protect and defend all women and children from the real monsters of this world… So please… just… let this go… it's done with… if my parents wouldn't do anything about it… why would the police? I'm here to start over… away from all of that and them." My body begins to tremble.

"I understand that and that's what makes him all the more of an evil bastard. The fact that he hurt someone as innocent as a child is repulsive, not only that, but the fact that he did that to his own kin is even worse." Lius stared at me, his face a mix of rage, frustration, and sorrow. He closes his eyes for a moment. Lius has come off as the type of person who doesn't show or really have a lot of emotions outside of his smug cockiness, for anyone but his own displeasure. But right now… right now is different, I could see the anger in his eyes… I could see his own thoughts haunting him. As if this kind of thing has hurt him in the past. Even though it would appear his anger is directed at me, he wasn't mad *at* me… He was mad at my uncle and what he put a young 12 year old me through. This anger I see in his eyes looks deeper than just me being hurt… he has a personal angst against humans who hurt women and children, it seems. The same way I was hurt.

I place my hand on his forearm to calm him, "Thank you for getting angry on my behalf… but, I really would like to go to bed now… I really didn't want to discuss this right now."

Lius looks at me a moment longer before nodding, "Alright, I'll see you in the morning…" Kai and Max stood listening with their mouths slightly opened, appalled at the information I just shared. The playful smirks that I saw in that hallway have all vanished. Even Ares who kept himself perched against the wall by his room.

I turn around and with one final grim smile and close my bedroom door as all four sets of eyes watch me till the door clicks. I curl up on the floor and lean my back against the closed door, burying my face into my knees.

I hear the knock and stand up from the floor. I take a deep breath as I think it's just Lius again wanting to talk some more and I am so exhausted, "Lius, please leave me- oh…" I freeze as I see Max's towering form in my doorway, blocking the light from the hallway. "Max? What's up?" Max reached out and pulled me into a tight hug, pressing me firmly against his chest. Lius and Kai run up the stairs behind him and freeze as they see Max suddenly holding me in a comforting hug. Max hasn't been one for showing any affection, and the two men are taken aback by the fact that Max is not one to suddenly do things like this. Let alone to a female he just met.

After a moment, Max finally strains to whisper out, "...I'm so sorry kiddo... You should've been protected, and I'm sorry that no one was there to help you when you needed it most..."

"Thank you..." I whisper as I wrap my arms around his midsection, to return the hug.

Max holds the hug, his arms tightly around me before he speaks up again, "I won't hesitate to end him if I ever see him. You're safe now, okay?" His eyes open with anger and sorrow. A sense of sadness in his gaze.

Kai looks at Max, and whispers over to Lius, "I've never seen him this upset... Or react like this."

Lius, still tense, nods. "Neither have I..."

I listen to Max's proclamation, feeling both relieved and exhausted. I hoped that my new roommates would understand and respect my boundaries moving forward. I nod silently against his chest as he continues to hold onto me in his arms before he speaks again so quietly that only I could hear him, "What he did to you was wrong... I will protect you from now on, whenever you need anything, you can come to me alright...?" I nod again as Max pulls away and ruffles my hair, "Get some sleep, kiddo. You need it."

Lius and Kai continue to watch at the exchange as I smile at Max and raise a hand to wave at them and close my door once again. This time I climb into bed finally and silently let the tears fall as I cry myself to sleep, silently. Lius and Kai watch as I close my door again, this time for the night.

As I drift into a restless sleep, the quiet of the night gives way to my mind's torment. Flashbacks creep in, shattering my peace.

I'm 12 again, trapped in my childhood bedroom. His shadow looms, fear choking me as his hand clamps around my wrist. The smell of alcohol lingering in my nose as if it was just this afternoon. I'm 14 and I remember the overwhelming dread of his footfalls approaching my bedroom door. Thinking back to when I was just 17, I recall the desperation of trying to escape his grasp, his words slurred and venomous, leaving scars that still burn my mind every day, right before I swung my knee up, right where it hurts him most.

4

I wake up the next morning slowly, the memory of last night's drama flooding into my mind. I sit up and stretch my arms up as I look outside my window and see it's a gorgeous day... Not just any day either. It's training day! Today is the day I get to meet my new trainer. I jump out of bed with sudden energy from the excitement. I put on my robe to head downstairs for some coffee and to make a protein shake before I get ready and head out to my training session. As I make my way down the stairs, I see that Lius and Kai are already up and, in the kitchen, eating breakfast by the time I make it to the kitchen.

As I enter the kitchen, Lius glances up from his seat at the bar. "Morning. How'd you sleep? Was the bed comfortable?"

As I rub the last bit of sleep out of one of my eyes I nod, "Pretty good, my bed was plenty comfortable, thanks. How about you two?"

Lius nods, "Slept alright"

Kai speaks as he takes a sip from his mug, "No nightmares?" His concern is evident in his eyes as he looks at me.

"None that I can recall. Why...? Did I talk in my sleep or something?" I ask as I tilt my head to the side in question. Lius shakes his head in response. Kai does as well, and the both of them then silently continue to finish eating the breakfast that they have made for themselves.

A few seconds of silence go by before Lius speaks up again, "May I ask you a question...?"

"Coffee first Lius... then ask away..." I respond as I look into the kitchen to see if I can find the mugs and the coffee pot. I have to caffeinate before dealing with his nonsense this morning. I have a feeling that living with him will help me train my patience.

Lius chuckles, "Fair enough." He gets up and walks over to the coffee maker, pulling down a large mug from the cabinet above it, pours me a cup of fresh coffee into it and hands it to me.

I look at him as I raise an eyebrow wondering what he is doing. "Oh... thank you Lius... you didn't have to do that." I take the mug, full of the dark warm liquid, from him. He shook his head, dismissing my comment with a small smile. I press the mug to my lips and sip. I hum with joy at the deliciousness of the first cup of coffee of the day, smiling with joy. "Ok... Ask..."

Lius sits back down on his barstool, "The reason I'm asking this is because of something you said last night... After everything that's happened... you don't trust men, do you?" I silently shake my head. Lius nods at my response, "I thought as much..." I sip my coffee, waiting for him to proceed. He looks at me, trying to find the right way to say what he needs to say next. "I know it might not be simple to answer this next question... and I'm probably going to sound like an asshole for asking, but... was it really because of just what your uncle did to you? Or was it because of other things too…?"

"Well, a few other things too, but mainly that…" I say as I start to coil into myself at his questioning, feeling very vulnerable at the moment. I feel as if this is going to go in a direction that I'm not going to like at all.

"Are you… skittish about physical touch? Even with just friends?" Lius asks. I raise an eyebrow instantly concerned about why he asks such a question, remembering the first night I was here. I nod hesitantly. Lius nods as well, he could understand why. He puts his hands up as if surrendering to make sure I'm able to see where his hands are. "I promise that was an honest question… I'm not trying anything again…" I nod to accept his answer as I increasingly become more uncomfortable which shows on my face. Lius considers what I've been through, it makes sense why I would be somewhat skittish around men and physical touch. I continue sipping my coffee and have a seat at the bar stool next to him, really enjoying the coffee. He watches as I take a seat next to him. "So… that means you're uncomfortable around us?" He asks as his expression forms into concern.

"Not in this capacity. I can be in the same room as men, but… it'll make me really nervous if I'm touched though… anywhere below my collarbone or in any intimate way… which is why I freaked out on you yesterday, Lius."

"But… you didn't shy away from Max hugging you last night?" he asks with confusion.

"No, I didn't… but I was nervous the whole time. And he kept his hands still and wrapped carefully so that his hands rested on my shoulders… No where else. He made sure I didn't feel as if he wanted to do something else. He respected me." I replied. Lius nods, now understanding why I had reacted the way I did when he grabbed at me when I first arrived.

He suddenly had an idea, even if it sounded dumb, "Can I ask something else?"

"Depends on what it is if I'll answer…" I hesitate as to how this has been going.

Lius exhales slightly, hoping that I couldn't refuse, "May I touch your shoulder?" He suddenly sees me tense at the suggestion.

"Why…?" I ask.

Carefully choosing his next words, Lius speaks quietly. "It's so I can test something. It won't take long, I promise."

"Uh… ok." My whole body tenses.

Lius slowly lifts his hand and gently places it on my shoulder, "I'm not going to hurt you, Elara… this is going to sound even weirder, but close your eyes and just focus on the sound of my voice, alright?"

"No." I hesitate at his request. Looking deep into his eyes searching for deception. I glance at Kai who is carefully watching, he nods at me for reassurance. I realize that I don't see any signs of his perviness from yesterday, and more secure that Kai is here to stop the madness if I'm pushed too far, I'm sure. I slowly close my eyes and take a deep breath.

He smiles slightly at my agreement and slowly begins to talk to me, in a calm and even tone. "Okay, I want you to do something for me. I want you to listen to just my voice. Focus closely to where you're feeling my hand on just your shoulder, alright?"

I nod as I swallow down my nervousness.

He notices my nod and my movements from nervousness, "Good, good, that's good… now focus… where do you feel my hand right now?"

I pause to think as I silent the racing thoughts in my mind. I take a deep breath, "On the top of my shoulder joint." I answered reluctantly.

Lius smiles, knowing what he's hoping to achieve might actually work, "That's good. Now, you said you don't like being touched below your collarbone, correct?"

I flinch, "Correct"

His smile drops slightly, noting how tense I have become, but he continues talking to me regardless, "You don't like it when someone touches below your collarbone. So, I'm going to move my hand down to your upper arm, alright?"

I shudder at the thought, "Please don't…"

He pauses for a moment, now curious as to why I got so tense at just the mention of him touching my upper arm, "Keep listening to my words and just focus on where exactly my hand is… I'm going to move it now." He waits for me to agree before he continues. Once I nod, he moves his hand lightly from my shoulder down to the outside of my joint, moving down to the very top of my arm when I shoot my eyes open and move away from him instantly.

"No! Please don't!" I yell, my voice shaking. It feels like I'm shouting not at him, but through him, as if to someone else entirely. I stumbled back away from him. Max rushes down the stairs at my scream, quickly turning me around and pulling me into a protective embrace. I bury my face in my hands and freeze as soon as I realize I've bumped into him–hiding as he holds his arms around me in the same manner as he did the night before.

His face scrunched with worry, concern and fear, "What the *fuck* is going on here?! Lius!"

Kai steps in, "Lius was just trying to work on some touch therapy with Elara. I was monitoring the whole time."

47

Max darts his glare at Kai, "I don't give a fuck! Leave her be… she just met us!"

I look up at Max after a few moments, calming my heart rate and let out a sigh, "It's ok, Max… I agreed to give it a shot." I backed away from him and picked up my mug to sip my coffee.

Lius looks at me, "Who were you screaming at just now, Elara…?" When I don't answer he lets out a sigh and continues. "We now know you don't like your upper arm being touched for sure. Could you tell us why?"

With a solemn look in my eyes, I look into my cup, embarrassed. "Thats… that's how I was held down…" I sigh as I refer to my uncle, and how I was pinned every time he visited… me.

A mixture of anger and disgust forms on his face at the thought of a young 12 year old me struggling for my life. "That's how he…?" Lius' eyes widened in shock.

I nod, "Let's end the experiment here. Now. Please?" I go back to finishing my coffee.

Lius realizes his attempt at beginning my healing failed this time. He watches me continue to drink my coffee, "I'm sorry for that… I was just trying to see if my theory was correct and if I was right about something. I didn't mean to make you uncomfortable or upset you again…"

"What theory…?" I raise an eyebrow.

Lius goes silent at the question, suddenly unsure of how to word his answer. He runs a hand through his hair and sighs, he feels like such a dick for bringing this up, "When you mentioned your uncle doing what he did. I had a feeling that there were probably certain areas of your body that you don't like being touched the most, right?"

"Yes," I answered.

He nods, "I had a feeling the moment you said you don't like being touched that there were spots that were worse than others, right?"

I nod. He replies with his own nod, "Gods, I'm so sorry Elara... I felt like I had to test my theory, and I was unfortunately right... I didn't want to be right. I'm a jackass, I know."

"I agree." I glared at him with hurt swimming in my eyes.

He lets out another sigh, "Are you going to be, ok? I didn't want to bring back those kinds of memories... it was a risk, but I wanted to see if touch therapy might help you."

"I will be fine. Those memories live in my head, playing constantly..." I look into my empty cup, "I will never escape them... I've tried everything I know to do to make them stop."

All three men give me a look of sympathy. Lius' heart suddenly aching for me, "Man... that sounds torturous. Having to deal with those kinds of memories all the time, never being able to make them go away?"

"What was the point of this 'touch therapy' Lius?" I ask, trying to change the subject.

Kai speaks up this time, "Touch therapy could help you because it's a technique often used in trauma therapy to help survivors like yourself, reclaim their sense of bodily autonomy and safety. Lius here was hoping that by gently and respectfully reintroducing you to safe touch, that he could help you begin to dissociate and sensations of touch from the traumatic experiences you endured."

Kai explains that touch therapy is meant to help survivors like me reclaim their autonomy in a controlled environment. It would reclaim my autonomy for me in a controlled environment. As the survivor, I set the boundaries–no touching my torso or arms, for example. I decide what I am comfortable with, helping me regain control over my body. The safe touch reintroduces being touched in a safe, non-threatening manner, helping to rebuild trust in physical interactions.

Gradually, it exposes me to safe, non-threatening touch, reducing the fear and heightened sensitivity that physical contact triggers. Touch therapy will help in managing and reducing the intense emotional reactions that are triggered by touch. It demonstrates that not all physical touch is harmful, which can help in rebuilding trust in others, especially men since my abuser was male. It creates new, positive experiences with touch, counteracting the negative memories and associations from the trauma.

For my emotional healing, it encourages a connection with a trusted person, fostering a supportive relationship that aids in emotional healing, even if it is with someone, I had just met the day before. Lius had hoped to show me I could trust him, despite messing up on the first day. Empowering me by allowing me to set and enforce my boundaries, contributing to my overall sense of safety and self-worth.

"So, as for Lius' approach, he started with non-threatening areas like your shoulder, gradually working towards a possibly more sensitive area as long as you felt comfortable, Elara. This method requires your consent at each step, which helps emphasize your control over the process. His intention was to help you confront and desensitize the triggers associated with your trauma in a controlled and supportive environment." Kai finishes with.

I look back to Lius with my eyes wide with shock as I absorb the depth of his reason behind the shoulder thing… He wanted to build our trust, to help me overcome my trauma. To help heal me from my past.

I finally found my voice again, "I usually just get my touch therapy from boxing, heh." I joke and avert my gaze from them. I didn't know that they were so skilled in this kind of stuff, and it makes me uncomfortable to be called out by them. I look at all three of them and pop up my eyebrow to question the mood they are all serving me right now. "You've all been through stuff too, right? Why's everyone so focused on me? I'm fine."

Kai speaks up, "We aren't focusing on us right now... We are focusing on you. Don't push us away Ellie."

Lius furrows his brow at my attempt to deflect. "Ellie, after I understood the rationale behind touch therapy from Kai here. My concern for you became clearer. I wasn't probing into your history out of just curiosity... I genuinely want to help you heal. My method, though seemingly intrusive to you, was aimed to offer a way to start reclaiming your sense of safety and control over your body, for you. So that you can relax in your own home."

I sigh, frustrated. "I've gotten used to it. I just want to move." Clearing my throat, I try to change the subject. "Well, I need to start my day."

Kai catches my attempt to change the subject since I'm uncomfortable. "We're all here for you Elara. You're not alone in this anymore."

I freeze and lock my eyes onto his. My eyes tear as I nod towards him. "Thank you, Kai... That means a lot to me."

Max gives me a reassuring smile, "We'll help you through it, no matter what." I nod, feeling a sense of comfort and support from my new friends. For the first time in my whole life, I didn't feel so alone.

I turn towards my room and walk out of the kitchen. "Ok guys, I have a training session at the gym down the street to get to. I'm going to go get ready for it."

Lius watches as I walk from the kitchen, happy to see that I look so energetic even though I suffer from such strong demons, even if it is for the gym. "Alright, have fun at the gym. Make sure you stay safe getting there, you're not in Arizona anymore."

"Alright..." I get up to my room and change into my gym clothes.

~*~

As I come back down the stairs, I nod at the guys and head straight for the front door with my gym bag in my hand. "Ok guys, I'll be back in a few hours. Have a good morning." I put my headphones in, and press play on my phone's music app, playing my workout playlist consisting of all my favorite K-pop songs that get my blood pumping. All three men watch as I leave.

Walking to the gym, I think over everything that happened the last 18 hours since I arrived at this house. I walk with haste to the gym, the only therapy I've ever needed when I've been reminded heavily of my past. My resolve strengthened again. I arrive at the gym and head straight to the locker room to lock up my things. I wrap my hands up for my training that I've been taking for years prior, but this is the first time I am coming to this gym that is so highly rated online.

I walk out of the locker room and to the ring where my instructor waits for me, Sensei Hiroshi Tatsuya. I climb in and bow to him as a greeting. "Good morning, Sensei Tatsuya. I'm Elara Blake." Tatsuya gave me a nod of acknowledgement. We began with some basic warm ups, and I feel my muscles loosen, my mind focusing on the movements rather than the memories that haunt me most. As the training progresses, my intensity seems to only grow, each punch and kick delivered with a force that seems almost desperate to expel the shadows lurking in my mind.

~*~

As the session carries on, my instructor pushes me harder, and I welcome the challenge. Tatsuya is testing my progress, to see where I am in my training and where he needs to begin. Each strike, each block, was a way to channel the pain and fear that lingered in my heart. I was determined not to let my past define me, but it was a struggle I fought every day.

"Good, Elara. Keep it up." Tatsuya encourages, his voice steady and calm. "Remember, it's not about physical strength. It's about mental strength too."

I nod, wiping sweat from my brow. "Yes Sensei."

Sweating and out of breath I'm gaining some new moves down with my new instructor.

"Okay. Let's turn it up a notch… you're fighting with some blind rage, and we need to redirect that… you need to hone it into your attacks. Control it, Elara. Own it…" he says.

I nod in response.

~*~

As the training session came to an end, I climbed out of the ring, my body exhausted but my mind a little clearer. I bow to my instructor, "Thank you Sensei. I needed that. See you Friday?"

Tatsuya nods in response to me, "See you Friday. Go home, stretch, and rest. We'll take you where you need to be, Elara. Your progress is remarkable. You had a great teacher in America, and your resolve is incredible. Don't lose that." I head to the locker room to grab my things, and as I walk out with my bag, I'm surprised to see Lius and Max waiting by the exit for me.

"Hey guys. What are you doing here?" I ask as I wipe the sweat from my face with a hand towel I have draped over my neck.

"We wanted to see what your training session was like." Lius replies. "You seemed pretty intense when you left this morning."

I give them both a tired smile. "Yea, training helps clear my head."

Max nods. "We get that. Just don't overdo it, okay?"

I appreciate their concern, even if it felt a bit overwhelming. "I won't. This isn't my first time in a sparring session."

Max smirks and I can see a hint of pride behind his eyes. "Yeah, we can tell."

As we left the gym together, a small sense of relief washed over me. Maybe, just maybe, I didn't have to face my demons alone anymore. With my new friends—Lius, Max, Kai and Ares—perhaps I could start to heal and find a way to truly move forward. But that won't get in the way of my mission… I have to see it through. The walk back towards the house wasn't a long one, but it carried on as I talked with Max and Lius. Discussing different battle and fighting techniques, the guys gave me different tips, pointers and tricks on how I could land my hits harder and faster. The years of combined experience showing through each bit of advice they gave.

As we approach the house and walk through the front door, Lius comments, "Elara, you know you're training with Sensei Tatsuya, right? He was the top trainer for the SP6 Vipers before he retired. We never trained under him, but I've heard about his techniques. You're in really good hands."

"That's why I picked him. I read about him online when I was searching for gyms to work out in." I replied. "I'm going up to shower, that was a rough workout for the first session with him."

Lius noticed how tense I still seemed, far from relaxed–if anything, I was still on edge. His mind instantly went back to the look I held in the ring, and this morning as I left the house, how determined I looked while training, the intensity he saw in my gaze. I headed upstairs leaving the awkward silence coming from the three of them.

~*~

As the days progress, Max and Lius walk with me to my training sessions. Some days they can't attend because of their own work and most of the time it's one or the other who joins me, mostly it's Max who goes with me. I've enjoyed the company. Each time I'm provided feedback on my moves and techniques. Today's session I went on my own and I'm happy about that. Tatsuya is now working on swordsmanship. He wanted me to learn fencing and duel-manship with a sword. It's a wooden one for now but I'm not as bad for my first time as I thought I would be.

I finish my shower after another training session and get dressed for the rest of my day. I have some shopping to do for work supplies, and another errand as I check my phone. I head down the stairs with my things to head out. "Hey guys! I'm going out for a bit to shop for some supplies. Do we need anything here I can grab while I'm out?"

Kai and Max look up as I come downstairs. "No, I'm good. How about you all?" Max answers.

Lius looks up from the couch and lands on me again. That exhausted yet intense look on my face catches his eye once again, and he feels that strange electric sensation run through him, "What, do I look like I need anything?"

"Okay, okay..." I put my hands up in mock surrender, wondering why he's so moody today. "I will be back after a while...Kai? Do you need anything while I'm out?"

He looks up from the couch and shakes his head, "I'm sure we're fine here... Just be careful on the way, ok? Call any of us if you get lost at all."

"Okay, I will. And just text me if Ares needs anything." I add, as Ares is a late sleeper. The three of them all nod in response. They hold their gazes on me as I head out of the house and shut the door behind me.

5

I walk down the street into town and find a little corner store to grab some breakfast and a smoothie to replenish my aching muscles after my intense training this morning with the wooden sword—waking up muscles I've never used before. I walk into the small store and glance around. The store feels quiet, only a few customers milling around, giving me a sense of isolation. I head over to the fridge full of drinks and begin browsing through them. *"Ooooh! Strawberry Banana... I'll take that."* I think to myself. Reaching into the fridge I grab and pull out a bottle of the smoothie I've chosen. As I shut the fridge, I notice a young man standing nearby, leaning against the wall and watching me. I carve the corners of my lips in a *'hello'* expression and look away to continue choosing my breakfast. The man returns the grin with a wide smile. His eyes linger on my toned arms, clearly sizing me up. I can see the interest in his gaze.

I grab the yogurt parfait that I want and head up to pay for the items I've selected. The man continues to watch me as I head to the front to pay for my items. He follows behind at a careful distance, avoiding the attention of the clerk or the few other customers.

He's intrigued by me and wants to see which way I'm heading after leaving the store. I exit the store keenly aware that I am being followed by this man. He follows me discreetly, keeping enough distance not to raise suspicion, but I'm already aware of every step he takes. He continues to follow me until I turn a corner and walk down a more secluded street. It's less crowded here, and quieter, which is perfect for him. He continues to trail behind me down the street, making sure to step quietly enough that I don't hear his footsteps, but I have been honed in on every sound he has made since we locked eyes in the store.

He's close now, just steps away. His smile widens, convinced I haven't noticed him yet. He's oblivious that I already have him where I want him. Just inches away, he finally makes his move. He grabs my shoulder and spins me around, pinning me up against the wall of a building. His other hand comes up and clamps over my mouth to prevent me from screaming, but what's going to cover his mouth to prevent *him* from screaming? I guess I will deal with that in a minute.

"Well, lookie what we have here…" says the creep.

He grins at me, his eyes roving over my body and taking in my figure. He clearly sees me as his next prey for his sick and twisted desires. He is about to find out though… that *he* actually is the prey today. I hold my unwavering gaze on him. Hoping he thinks that he has me in his trap—that he's won—that I am defenseless. He holds his grin at my unchanging expression void of any fear. He thinks that he has me exactly where he wants me, cornered in a secluded place all alone with him.

"You are a pretty little thing, huh?" He whispers in my ear. Running a hand along my side, feeling my body up and down on my side. I feel nauseous under his decrepit touch. I wince at first contact, just enough to make him think I am whimpering with fear, it's what he wants from me. It causes men like him to let their guard down just a little, which is all I need… He chuckles in my ear as he continues to run his fingers along my side.

"Aww, don't be scared, gorgeous… I just want to have some fun. Don't you?" He says in a disgusting coo as he steps closer and pins me harder against the wall, pressing himself flush against my body. Putting both of his hands on my hips, to hold me in place. This perv is really enjoying having me trapped and cornered like this.

"I can tell you're in shape… what, you an athlete or something?" he whispers in my ear.

"Or something…" I snarl through gritted teeth, now that my mouth is uncovered. I calm my panicking thoughts under his touch. Something I've trained throughout the years. In one swift move, I grab his wrist and twist his arm behind his back, forcing him to bend awkwardly. As I shift to his side, I sweep my leg and kick his feet out from under him, causing him to stumble forward. Seizing the moment, I drive my knee into his face, feeling the satisfying crunch of his nose breaking. He cries out in pain and staggers towards the wall he just had me pinned against, throwing a hand out for support. Shaking his head to clear the daze, he looks up to see me already in a fighting stance. My eyes locked onto him with unyielding determination.

Snarling, he lunges at me with desperation and rage in his eyes. "You little bitch!"

I spin and kick back, straight to his jaw forcing his head to launch backwards along with the rest of his body. "What the hell?!" He cries out as he struggles to keep upright and lands back into the ground, right on his ass and quickly looks up at me. I walk towards him and loom over him. I kneel down, gripping his chin to force him to look me in the eyes. His own widens as he feels the ice cold steel of my blade against his throat—the one I keep in a holster on my thigh wherever I go, just in case.

"You stalk and follow women around here, don't you? You know... one of them may be the very one to end that streak of yours. You follow them until you get them alone, huh? Just like you did with me? You paw your disgusting hands all over them, feeling them up, forcing them to submit to do whatever you want. Thinking that they are helpless, vulnerable... That's you right? *Anthony White...*" I coo at him as he begins to tremble under my blade. "Cruising that same store for your next target... right?"

His eyes filled with fear and confusion, he can't believe that this beautiful girl he tried to make today's prey, has suddenly twisted the tables on him and turned *him* into the prey.

"W-What are you talking about?! I'm not... I'm not the one. I was just..." He stutters, unsure of what to say in this situation. He knows that he's been caught, and he's terrified of what I might do to him for his crimes if he were to confess.

"Huh..." I dig my nail into a pressure point near his collar bone, forcing him down further to the ground. I keep my blade held steady against his carotid artery, "I wouldn't lie if I were you... Confess your sins... now..."

The sudden pain and the feel of my blade against his neck that shoots a cold shiver of death down his spine. His fear takes over and moves into panic as sweat drips down his forehead. His mouth begins to open and close like a fish out of water as he tries to find the right words to say, "O-Okay! Please, I'll confess, just don't kill me!" He cries out.

60

"Elara!" I hear a loud voice boom down the alleyway. The creep flinches at the sudden sound of someone shouting my name. He looks towards the end of the alleyway I've pushed us into, fear growing in his eyes as he sees someone approaching. The man's eyes widen as the figure of another person appears from the shadows at the end of the street. He tries to speak up, to call out for help, but the press of my blade against his throat keeps him quiet. The figure gets closer, their footsteps getting louder and louder as they approach. The creep's heartbeat quickens under my finger that is still pressing into his skin, his fear rising within him as he sees this newcomer moving towards him and I. As the figure comes into view, the creep under my blade realizes it's a taller, more imposing man. Now, he's outnumbered.

"Elara... don't..." says Max as he comes into view.

The creep's eyes widen even more as he hears him speak up. He can tell from the tone of his voice that he's someone who knows me and knows what I am capable of doing to him, if this newcomer didn't show up when he did. The creep looks up at me silently begging me to show him mercy and let him go. Max moves closer to me and this creep I have pinned underneath my blade. He can see the situation I have going on and is concerned for my safety and well-being when he should be concerned about this man's life right now, and not mine. "Max, this guy's been stalking women and harassing them. He just tried it with me. I've got this, don't get involved."

Max's expression hardens my words. He looks down at the man pinned beneath me, eyes filling with anger. "This is the one who has been harassing people at that corner store?" He then asks finally. "We've been hearing reports of a man attacking women near here. This is him?"

"Yes..." My glare never leaves the creep's face, ignoring his silent pleas. Max nods, his jaw clenching as he looks down at the man now under my knee digging into his spine. His arm twisted behind his back still, in my grasp.

"I see..." Max's glance looks at my face now, softening his own slightly. He can tell that I am in control of this situation and handling it well. Although he still worries for my soul. "Ok then... just don't kill him, Elara. We will let the police handle this."

I grin widely looking positively haunting, "You got it." I refocus on the man in my clutches again. "Confess... say it... confess your sins you filthy pervert."

Max takes a step back, letting me continue to handle the situation under his observation. The creep trapped under my blade and knee, lets out a fearful whimper and nods. "I-I confess! I've been stalking women in this area and taking advantage of them! I'm sorry! Please don't hurt me! I won't do it ever again! I promise!" He cries out, tears flooding his eyes and falling down his cheeks as he realizes that I will be that one prey who will end his streak, with fearful tears of death.

"Good boy." I patted him on the head and pulled out a rope I saw near some trash cans behind me. Keeping my blade against his neck, I free his hand of my grip but with my knee on his spine he is immobilized. I set the rope down next to him as I pulled my blade from his neck and quickly slammed the butt of my blade into the nape of his neck knocking him unconscious. Once he falls to the floor, I begin tying his hands and feet together rendering him immobile. I ask Max, "Why are you here?"

He sighs, "I remembered hearing about a man following women and decided to make sure you didn't get hurt... Once I saw you exit the store and he was trailing behind you, I followed. But I see that you have dealt with this before. Am I right?"

I nod. "Yes. I began learning how to defend myself in Arizona."

He sighs with a soft chuckle, "I knew from the moment I saw you with that knife and he didn't bleed even a little that you've got experience with this—you were in complete control. And the fact that he was still alive and conscious. You appeared composed and confident in yourself, and I had no doubt that you could handle him on your own. I just had to be sure."

I nod and take out my phone from my pocket. I unlock my phone and dial. The contact shows only one letter: 'Z.' As soon as the other line picks up, I speak. "Z. Target 0568 is apprehended. Yes. Any more news on the bald eagle's location?"

Max freezes as he listens to me, straining to hear the voice on the other end and he can barely make out what they are saying.

He can faintly hear a male's voice on the other end replying, *"Unfortunately, there hasn't been any news about your uncle. We're still looking for him and trying to track him down along with any leads... but so far, we haven't found any solid clues or information leading to his whereabouts. It seems like he's gone off the grid again."*

"Damn it..." I curse under my breath and pinch the bridge of my nose and squeeze my eyes shut.

The voice replies, *"I understand how frustrating it is to not have any more information on the main target. We do know that he is still in Tokyo somewhere. We're doing everything we can to find him and bring him to the police... We won't give up until we find him, I promise."*

"No... bring him to me first..." I interrupt.

Max's eyes widen, the questions he has flooding in his brain over what he is hearing, witnessing, he wonders... *Is she an agent as well...? Did SP6 bring in someone new and not tell us? Is she undercover?* He tunes back in as this *'Z'* person speaks to me again.

"Bring him to you…?" Z sounds shocked.

"Yes, I won't explain further. I have something I need to *discuss* with him first." My face and expression are as cold as the ice in hell would be if it were to freeze over. Max's heart skips a beat with a bit of fear and a chill washes over him as he notices my face change.

"Understood… We will let you know when he shows up. Talk soon." Z says before hanging up the phone to end the call with me. I sigh as I look up at Max who looks so puzzled at everything he's witnessing. I take a deep breath, I have to face this… and with him being a part of SP6's Vipers, I think it will be safe for me to answer his questions honestly. Before that, I have to call the police and leave them an anonymous tip on where this creep is tied up.

I ended the call with the police dispatcher abruptly and put my phone back in my pocket. I look back at Max, "What…?" I finally asked him.

"What the fuck was all that? All of… this? Who the hell are you?!" He gestures with his open hand around me and then at the creep passed out in the alleyway behind me.

I look down at the target and sigh as I look back up at him. He steps back a bit in case I decide to attack him next. I held my hands up to let him know I won't hurt him. "I work with Z Group. I hunt all who hurt and prey on innocent women and children… We protect those who can't protect or defend themselves, to defend their honor and find justice for them. Those whom the system has failed… I hunt targets with their help. I'm an agent for them. They are helping me with locating targets and also helping me locate my uncle." I avert my gaze as I say this next part, slightly nervous at his reaction to it. "Who happens to be in Tokyo. He is the reason

I moved here in the first place." I meet his gaze and await his response.

"So... you're what...? Some kind of vigilante?" His face starts to bunch together as he absorbs what I've just shared.

I shrug my shoulders. "I guess you could say that. The cops do hate me for interfering and handling things the way that I do. Z Group isn't widely accepted by any country's government." I feel a sting on my face as I giggle at my statement. I bring my fingers up to where it is coming from and wince, "Ah..." I hissed. "I have a cut here, don't I?" I look up at Max and tilt my head up keeping my fingers near the area that stings.

He looks over my face where my fingers are touching, "Let me see..." He takes a step closer and reaches out to gently hook a finger under my chin and tilt my face up so he can see better. His eyes scan my face, inspecting the area. He spotted a thin cut on my cheek just near the corner of my lip. "Yeah, it looks like you cut yourself on something. It's not too deep but it might scar if you don't take care of it now and properly..."

"*Shit*... Ok..." I acknowledge, turning to exit the secluded street that the alleyway was connected to. He turns to walk with me to the corner store and helps me pick out some bandages and antibacterial. I walk into the bathroom and clean myself up after purchasing the items. When I emerged, Max was leaning against the wall outside of the bathroom door, his arms crossed across his chest.

His eyes instantly landed on my face, "All better?" He asks, looking at my bandage job.

"You tell me... Is it noticeable?" I touch the bandage.

"Nope. Barely noticeable unless someone is right in your face." He says as he inches closer to my face. "You know we have to tell the others, right? You'll need to–"

"No." I step back, cutting him off. "I work alone."

We walk home in silence and finally reach our house, walking in the front door together. I'm instantly overwhelmed with the sight of my other roommates in the living room, lounging around and chatting amongst themselves as they wait for my return, and I guess Max's since, given their shocked gazes... They didn't know he had left the house.

"Max? Where did you-" Lius pauses as I walk in behind him. All three lock their eyes on me immediately. They all sit up straighter in their seats. Lius and Kai's eyes seem to be inspecting me as I close the door and walk from behind Max.

"Hey guys! Did you all have a good morning?" I smile as I awkwardly try to avoid the barrage of questions I'm about to endure.

They all watch me closely, their gazes roaming over my face and body then looking at Max, as if they've noticed something... or at least searching for something. Max walks further into the house and sits in his favorite chair in the living room to join them in the glaring contest they seem to be having with me—four against one. I look down at my body trying to see what they're looking at.

"What...? What is it?" I ask when I don't see anything.

Max clears his throat, and I shoot him a warning glance. Lius doesn't miss it. "We're just wondering where you've been all afternoon? You told us it was to go shopping..."

A mischievous grin spreads on Max's face as he decides to add to my interrogation. "Yeah, but you return empty handed. Although, as long as you were gone, we suspected you'd return with your hands full." That bastard... I narrowed my eyes on him. He's going to out me right here and now after I told him I work alone. If Lius finds out… I will have more interference than I want.

"I was in town doing some shopping and didn't find anything that I wanted." I shrug as I say this and stop abruptly as I realize that I had strained my shoulder during the scuffle earlier. The pain made its appearance after the adrenaline had worn off, just as my injuries always do after a hunt. All four sets of eyes on my face. Lius is first to tilt his head as he notices the weird way I shrug and the way I subtly wince, I thought I had hid so well.

"You said you went shopping in town? No… trouble at all? Didn't have any issues?" Lius questions.

Max pipes in being the instigator that he is. "Yea… any trouble on your trip into town?"

I stare daggers at Max telling him to shut up. "Nope. Should there have been?"

Lius shakes his head, his eyes narrowing slightly as he studies my face, "No, just curious. You're new in town and we had heard reports of a stalker lurking in the area."

"Umm… nope. There was one creepy guy staring at me at that corner store up the road before-" I stop as I look at their unchanging faces… they already knew, didn't they…? I dart my gaze to Max as my eyes widen. "They already know, don't they?" I asked him.

Max smirks, making a sweeping gesture towards the others, silently telling me to explain. I roll my eyes as Max moves his hands in front of his face to steeple them. He's grinning and not once does his gaze falter from my face enjoying the sight of me becoming uncomfortable under this interrogation in the *'Viper'* pit. He's such an ass…

Lius crosses his arms, his eyes scrutinizing me even more closely now as he sees Max's expression, "So, nothing else happened? You were just browsing…? *'Window shopping'* if you may."

I sigh and roll my eyes again, "Why do I feel like you know something I don't? What is it you really want to say? Spit it out."

Max snorts slightly, his smirk growing on his lips, "I may have sent them a photo of what I saw in town earlier… your little… *activity*…"

My eyes wide with anger. "You didn't…" My face forms into a warning towards him, a warning that I'm going to kick his ass later for that.

"Oh, he did…" Chimes in Kai, holding his phone up with the photo of the man pinned under my knee. "Care to tell us what that was about?"

"Max!   What the hell?! Do you understand what would happen if anyone saw that outside of this house?!" I shouted.

"No one would ever see it outside of us four. Our phones are encrypted. Another perk of the SP6 Vipers." Max replies. "How reckless do you take me for princesa?"

"I am not a princess…" I rebut, quickly turning away from them. "I'm going to make some food…" I walk towards the kitchen in an attempt to get away from the interrogation. "Are any of you hungry?"

Lius, confused by my fleeing, "Hungry? Nah, we're good… but, I think you should just rest after the day *you've* had." I can hear the sarcasm in his voice.

"Lius… it was nothing. That guy followed me, and I just simply defended myself. That's all that was." I look around the kitchen to see what to make. "Let's move on from this, please." I quickly realized that the guys were only sent the picture… it seems they really don't know everything I told Max today. I think I would receive a lot more grilling from them. A hell fire of questioning from them if he did tell them more. The way they are reacting is more in anger at the fact that on my second day here, I've almost fallen prey to the evil that lurks in the shadows in this city. I hear my phone ping in my pocket as I receive a text and quickly check my phone.

Max: *"I didn't give them any context… I'll keep your secret safe for now… you have to tell them though. For your protection."*

Me: *"Why did you take that picture?! Just forget everything you saw and heard today… Or else…"*

I hear him chuckle from the living room as he responds *"As you wish… princesa"*

I cut my eyes to him that are already on me. I put my phone back in my pocket and begin to pull together some ingredients as Lius walks into the kitchen and stands close to me hovering to inspect my body for any injury from the earlier scuffle. I flinch back from him, "Lius, I'm okay. I need to eat more protein after working out this morning. Friday morning Sensei says we're going to take it up a notch, so I need my strength. I have yoga in the morning, and I need to keep up my strength." I finally said to him.

Lius replies, "Yoga huh? I bet you look really good doing all those flexible positions…" He takes a step back from me and leans against the counter. His usual flirtatious demeanor returned. I roll my eyes at his attempt to flirt with me. He replies with a laugh and a teasing glint in his eyes, "I think you look amazing doing all those yoga poses in that outfit I'm sure you always wear… Can't ever go wrong with spandex-"

"Down boy..." I cut him off with a push to his chest to back him away from me further. "Besides... to help that mental image I see you having... Let me share this. My instructor is a man. And yes... he does wear spandex." All four faces twist into small grimaces at the thought of a man in the same yoga outfit that I wear, their imaginations running wild. They all groan and grunt. I giggle at the image I have planted in their heads as a way of payback for Lius' flirting. I lean against the counter laughing at how the four of them react. "Ok guys... I'm going upstairs really quick, to set my things down. I'll be back down in a few to make some food. I will make enough for you all as well."

The four of them nod, watching as I head upstairs. "Yea whatever... Not like I'd eat your cooking anyways..." Grunts Max.

Kai smacks Max across the shoulder with the back of his hand and gives him a disapproving look. Lius laughs. "You can deny it all you want, Max. But I *know* you will scarf down anything she makes in a heartbeat." Kai and Ares silently nod in agreement while Max glares at them all. Lius looks towards me, still smirking, "I know I will..." he watches as I make my way upstairs.

As soon as I close my bedroom door behind me, the rest of the adrenaline begins to wear off. My hands tremble, and I lean against the door, trying to steady my breathing. The room feels too small, closing in around me. I slide down to the floor, my head resting on my knees. The memories flood in—dark alleys, helpless faces, my own screams. My heart races, pounding in my chest. I can't breathe. I gasp, clutching my throat, my vision blurring.

"You're safe. You're safe now." I whisper to myself, rocking back and forth. The words feel hollow, but they're all I have. I focus on my breathing, counting each inhale and exhalation. My therapist's voice from back in Arizona that I had as a child, echoes in my mind, guiding me through the steps. My parents put me in therapy when I made the accusations against my uncle in hopes that my therapist would straighten me out.

"Inhale... one, two, three, four, five... Exhale... one, two, three, four, five..." I replied to her words. I would have constant panic attacks in her office when I was a child. I press my palms to the floor, grounding myself, feeling the cool wood beneath my fingers. Slowly, the room comes back into focus, and the memories begin to recede, like waves pulling back from the shore. I close my eyes, letting the tears fall, releasing the emotional pressure within me. My body feels heavy, exhausted from the fight and the panic.

The comfort of my bed provides temporary relief, but the fear remains, lurking just beneath the surface, waiting for the next fight. My breathing evens out, and the tightness in my chest loosens. I'm safe here, in this room, for now. But the fear never fully leaves. It's always lurking, waiting for the next fight, the next memory. I wipe my tears, resolving to keep moving forward. For the women I protect, for the children I defend, and for myself... I will end *him*... I will save myself from this torment. It will only end when I bring him to justice. And it is now time that this city meets *me*.

~*~

I moved into a shared house in Tokyo, trying to blend in and establish a routine. No one has suspected anything unusual about me. I started my training under Sensei Hiroshi Tatsuya, who is teaching me advanced fighting techniques. He is intense but encouraging, pushing me to my limits. As night falls, I go out on my first mission in Tokyo. Dressed in my crimson armor jumpsuit, I feel a rush of adrenaline as I take down my first criminal. The news networks quickly picked up the story, dubbing me the "Crimson Vigilante of Tokyo," just as they did in Arizona. I returned home exhausted but satisfied, managing to slip back in through my bedroom window, undetected.

I had no idea Max had followed me on my second outing. I didn't sense his presence in the shadows, his careful watch over me. But his eyes were always there, a silent guardian in the darkness. He picked up on a recognizable quality to the "Crimson Vigilante" being shown on the local news network story. He watched. Ready to intervene if things ever went south. His presence was silent and undetectable. I started patrolling more frequently, each night honing my skills further. Max continued to shadow me, his concern growing. He never let on though, maintaining his aloof demeanor at home whenever I, or the others were around. SP6, the elite security team, the Vipers/my roommates, began taking note of the Crimson Vigilante's activities. They started discussing this mystery crime fighter during their briefings, speculating about my motives and background. I listened occasionally as they discussed this during meals we had together, heart pounding but face impassive.

One night, I faced a particularly tough opponent who nearly got the better of me. Max, hidden in the shadows, was tense but held back, trusting me to handle it. I barely managed to win, returning home with fresh bruises. The guys noticed my limp the next day, and the tension in the room grew, but I brushed it off with a casual excuse. I told them I had misstepped off a curb the other day and fell. The media was in a frenzy over the Crimson Vigilante. Tonight's aired story brings up another instance of another similar Vigilante spotted in Arizona—my past. Linking my current activities to the mysterious vigilante who disappeared from there, to now being here in Tokyo. SP6's interest peaked, and their efforts to identify and understand the vigilante intensified. I now have SP6 on my ass along with the local police force. *Great.*

At first, it was just a few raised eyebrows. A bruise here, a limp there. But as my late-night outings became more frequent, the looks became longer, the silences heavier. Lius would catch my eye during dinner, Kai's casual questions didn't feel so casual anymore, and Ares... he was always watching, always calculating. The timing of vigilante sightings was too coincidental to them. They began to suspect but had no concrete proof.

One night, after another particularly brutal fight, I returned home barely able to hide my injuries this time. Max, unable to contain his worry, decides he's confronting me tonight. I stumbled through the door, barely masking the pain from my latest battle. My body screamed for rest, but I couldn't let the guys see how hurt I really was. As I made my way to my room, Max's intense gaze followed me. His eyes spoke volumes, filled with concern and a silent plea for honesty.

I could feel Max's eyes on me as I reached my door. I didn't dare look back as I headed up the stairs, but the weight of his gaze was impossible to ignore. My hand trembled on the doorknob. Just as I began to turn it, his voice broke the silence. "Elara." His tone was soft, but there was no mistaking the seriousness in it. "We need to talk."

I paused, my hand on the doorknob. "Sure, what's up?" I tried to sound casual, but my voice wavered from the pain I was feeling as our eyes met. I looked away quickly, trying to hide the truth from him. "I'm fine, Max. Just a rough day of training, that's all." I can see the concern on his face.

He gently takes my hand into his, his touch surprisingly tender. "Ellie, I've been following you for weeks now."

My heart jolted. "You've been... following me for that long?"

He nodded, his eyes full of unspoken worry. "I couldn't just stand by and do nothing. You're taking too many risks. I wanted to be there in case you needed backup."

I sighed, feeling the weight of my secret pressing down on me. "I have to, Max. These people... they need someone to protect them."

Max's grip on my hand tightened, and for a moment, I felt the strength he was offering me. "And who's protecting *you*?" His words cut through me like a knife, sharper than any wound I'd taken in the streets. I pulled my hand away, afraid that if I held on any longer, I'd break. "You can't do this alone." His voice was barely above a whisper, but the weight of his words lingered. "I thought *I* had to."

I looked into his eyes, seeing the depth of his concern. "I thought I was alone this whole time. I never knew you were there."

He pulled me into a gentle hug, careful of my unidentified injuries. He whispers into my ear. "You're not alone anymore, Ellie. We're all here for you, even if we don't know everything. You need to be careful. We need you now. You're one of us."

Tears welled up in my eyes, but I blinked them away. "Thank you, Max. Please, don't tell the others. Not yet."

He nodded, his embrace tightening slightly. "Your secret is safe with me. Just promise me you'll at least let me help you when you need it."

"I can't..." I whispered, feeling a sense of guilt and fear wash over me. "Thank you, but I can't."

Max sighs as he steps back, giving me a small, reassuring smile. "Yes, you can…" he releases his hands from my shoulders. "Now. Get some rest. We'll talk more about this tomorrow."

I nod, watching him walk away before entering my room. For the first time in a long while, I felt a glimmer of security. Maybe, just maybe, I wasn't as alone as I thought I needed to be. But I can't let anyone else get hurt… Flashes of what happened to my previous partner flood through my mind… I close my eyes and focus on my breathing. The sounds of gunshots echo in my mind. I shake it away and the sight of Max's face just now comes into my mind. His eyes spoke volumes, and it made me smile at the memory. Throughout the following days he kept my secret, respecting my choice to reveal it to the others on my terms.

Later that night, I caught Max watching me with a mixture of concern and something deeper—admiration, perhaps? The pressure was mounting. My body ached from the constant battles, and the emotional toll was becoming unbearable. One night, after a particularly harrowing fight, I broke down in the shower, completely unaware that my sobs were audible to the guys downstairs. They didn't confront me, giving me space, but the air was thick with unspoken words. Max's heart clenched at the sounds, recalling our conversation as he scaled the rooftops alongside me back home.

~*~

"You need to take a break, princesa. You're going to burn yourself out." He pants out as we run along the ledges on the top of buildings.

"No. The attacks don't stop so why should I?" I say with ease, slightly panting myself as we run.

"Please just listen to me, it's okay to rest every now and then. You haven't stopped going on hunts since you got here." He argues, his tone pleading. *"Please... for your mental health if anything!"*

"I'm fine Max. I can't handle it." I finalize as I sprint faster to get ahead of him.

He grunts and picks up his own speed after me.

~*~

As another night arrives, I've finished yet another hunt successfully. I am in my room calming my anxiety attack once again. I get myself together and climb out of my bed after a few minutes, to make my way downstairs to start dinner. Acting as if nothing happened. The guys are all talking amongst each other in the living room as they always do after a long day as Vipers. All four men quickly turn their heads toward the sound of my footsteps coming down the stairs from my room, their faces suddenly becoming serious. They all look a bit guilty, as if they were just caught doing something they weren't supposed to.

I raise an eyebrow at the sight and shake my head, giggling at my fondness for their weird ways. I walk towards the kitchen and start preparing ingredients to cook. They were obviously talking about me again... When will they find something else to focus on... or maybe they're discussing the "Crimson Vigilante" which is also me, and also confidential. The four men watch as I move around the space. They all seem a bit tense and on-edge, sensing that I overheard their conversation. Ares looks especially guilty, which makes my stomach drop as he always keeps a cool demeanor—always in control of the feelings he expresses.

Max clears his throat and leans back slightly on the couch again: "So… whatcha makin for dinner in there princesa?" Max has come to love my cooking nowadays ever since that first week I cooked for them. He could no longer resist after smelling the prepared food. His stomach rumbles, eager for whatever I plan on making.

"Hmmm, I think I'll make a stir fry. With beef and sauteed vegetables. How does that sound?" I say as I tap my chin with a finger as I think about what we have in the kitchen.

All four sets of eyes light up at the mention of stir fry.

Max grins, breaking the tension. "Hell yea! Stir fry sounds great." The others nod in agreement, but I can still feel their eyes on me. The questions are still there, unspoken but heavy in the air.

Lius nods in agreement: "Stir fry does sound great. You're making enough for us too… right?"

"Of course! I thought I would either way because you all *say* you're not hungry… but then you always are once I've made the meal." I begin to grab some pots and pans out to place on the stove.

All four of them chuckle in their own way, realizing I called them out and they know I'm right. Lius grins, leaning back in his seat: "You know us all too well Ellie…"

I grin in response. "Yea… I guess I do…" It's only been a few months since I've met all of them, but I really do feel like I know them well. They are as they seem. Except for Lius–he's being fake majority of the time but, that's a playboy for ya. That is, however, in my experience.

Max smirks and crosses his arms, a smug look on his face: "Just admit it. You love us already and our bottomless appetites!"

I chuckle: "Ok fine, I admit it! I love you all already and your bottomless pit stomachs!" Their laughter fills the room, but even as I smile, my mind drifts to the task ahead, the one I can't avoid. "You know what though, I actually forgot something when I was out earlier…" My tone shifts as I catch Max's knowing glance.

He stands up from his seat and walks into the kitchen, stopping right next to me. "Don't… just take the night… please." He whispers to me.

"I have to" I look at him with seriousness and check the message. I stop the performance and put my phone back in my back pocket to finish cooking. The other three watch as this unfolds and are slightly disappointed when the show ends for them.

Max walks out of the kitchen—disappointed in my refusal to rest for one night. "You know, you don't have to push yourself every night." He mumbles as he walks away. He leans against the doorway, arms crossed. "We could use the company tonight." His tone is casual, but there's an edge to it.

Lius furrows his brow. "What was that about?"

That same look of intent is back on my face as I put together the finished ingredients and plate everyone some food. The men all look slightly confused by my sudden change in demeanor, except Max. They all continue to watch as I finish prepping the food and begin plating.

Kai walks towards the dining table. "Is everything ok, Elara? You seem… distracted."

I look and smile at him "Yes, I'm fine. Food is ready guys, come and get it!" I set their plates on the table and set cutlery next to each plate. All four of them perk up at the mention of food, their stomachs all growling in unison. They make their way to the table and take their seats, eyeing the plates of stir fry in front of them with eager eyes.

Lius sits and admires what's in front of him. "Damn, that looks so good! The food in this place is going to spoil me."

Max sits next. "I'll second that."

"Oh, it's nothing guys... just some cooked items thrown together... Oh and just a heads up... After dinner I'll run out again for a bit..." I give a side glance to Max. He's looking back at me irritated now knowing exactly what I'm pretending to *forget*. The other three pause, their mouths open ready to take their first bites. They look up at me with frowns on their faces.

Max swallows his first bite of food. "What is it you need? Why do you have to go out after dinner?" Holding a glare on me. Trying to egg the others on to convince me to stay home for this one night.

"I just have to go back to the store..." I look at my food to avoid his gaze. The others look disappointed, their hopes of a relaxing night together with me dashed.

Max presses on, his tone sharpening. "Why tonight, Ellie? What's so urgent?"

Lius leans forward, his usual playful grin replaced with a frown. "Yeah, can't it wait? You just got back a little bit ago."

"It can't... sorry guys. And no Max... it can't wait. It's an item I have to get tonight and should've picked up today on my way home from the gym." We held each other's stare, both of us trying to get the other to back down. Kai looks between the both of us with questions. He wants to ask what this stare off is really about... wondering if something happened between us earlier. The guys all glance at each other, silently communicating with their eyes. None of them really want me to leave, since it's now nightfall when it gets even more dangerous in the city. They also don't want to hold me back if I have something I have to do.

Lius pouts. "Are you sure we can't convince you to stay? We can go with you in the morning...?"

"No... but I won't head out till after I've cleaned up the mess I made in the kitchen." I add as I look back down at my food and toy with it a little with my fork.

All the men nod, except Max who keeps his gaze on me.

Kai sighs. "Alright. But you have to promise you'll go straight there and come straight back as soon as you're done at the store ok...? The city is dangerous at night..."

"It's just as dangerous during the day." I protest.

Kai shakes his head. "It's worse at night... I promise you"

"Of course... I'll be careful and come straight back." I reassure them in order to get them to move on.

When I see nods of approval, everyone picks up their forks and beings to eat.

Lius scoops his fork into the food. "Well, let's not let this delicious food go cold. I'm starving!"

"Dig in everyone! Please!" I exclaim with urgency.

They dive into the food, but the usual chatter is quieter tonight, punctuated by the occasional clink of forks against the plates. Even as they enjoy the meal, I can sense the unspoken concern hanging in the air. Max and I make eye contact throughout the meal, as if dueling with each other over his insistence on me taking a break tonight.

Max speaks first to break the tension. "Damn, Ellie! This is really fucking good..."

"Thank you, Max..." I graciously replied.

He grins with his mouth full of food. He swallows before responding. "No, seriously... Since you've moved in, this is the best food I've had in ages. You're a damn good cook!"

"Aww shucks..." I wave my hand quickly at him to dismiss his flattery. Max leans back in the chair, offering a small, resigned smile. He won't push it tonight, but I can tell he's not happy about it. The others all nod in agreement, all of them continuing to devour their food with gusto.

Lius takes a drink of his tea. "Yeah, you've really outdone yourself with this one. I might just have to ask for seconds."

"There's plenty more." I finish my food and start cleaning up the mess I made in the kitchen. Everyone continues eating, each of them silently savoring every bite. Max leans against the counter, his eyes never leaving me, a silent observer as I clean up. I can feel his gaze, waiting for the moment when I try to slip away.

"Ok guys, there's leftovers still on the stove so if you'd like more, please help yourselves. This dishwasher is set, just put your dirty dishes in it please. I can start it when I get back. I'll be right back," I say, forcing a smile as I grab my coat. Max's eyes linger on me, and for a moment, I wonder if he'll try to stop me. But he just nods, and I step out the door, the weight of his gaze heavy on my back.

Kai nods once. "Alright, we'll follow your instructions. Be careful please and come back quickly."

I nod and head out the door. The men watch as I leave, closing the door behind me. They sit in silence for a moment and finish their food.

6

Max, knowing my tendencies, heads straight for the alleyways. He turns the corner of one darkened street corner right into the alleyway—he finds me. He catches sight of me shoving a man down to the ground—he knew it! I came out to hunt a target... not to go to the store again. What he sees next is me behind a man now on his knees, I'm holding his hands behind his back with my blade in my hand wrapped around pressed against his throat.

"Spit it out... now!" I yell as I tug on his hands, forcing his head to fall back towards me more so that I have an easier access point to slit his throat if I so wish to do so. Max's eyes narrowed, his pulse quickening at the sight. He'd seen me in this position before, but something about tonight felt different–like I was pushing too hard. He observes as I hold the man, in the same manner I have done countless times before. I am completely unaware of his arrival, as I tighten in my grip on the man. With my foot holding down one of his legs and my hands on his wrists, keeping them in place, I pressed my blade more against his neck. My target flinches as his face pales with fear.

"I-I'm sorry, ok?! I won't do it again, just please… let me go!" The creep begs.

I press the blade even more into his skin. "You won't do what… I want to hear you say it… or I am not going to let you come out of this alive…" I say through clenched teeth into his ear.

The creep swallows heavily, his eyes wild with panic, darting around nervously. "I-I'll confess! I'll confess! Okay?!" He cries out trembling in fear.

"I'm not a very patient woman… Say the words out loud… Now… Confess what you have been doing!" I snarl right into his ear.

The creep hesitates for a moment, his Adam's apple bobbing up and down as he swallows nervously. He takes a deep, shaky breath and finally says the words I must hear. It isn't a requirement to capture my targets, to hear them say their crimes out loud. Z Group makes sure to gather all of the evidence before sending me after them. Their confessions are for me. "I-I've been stalking girls… following them around, taking pictures, watching them… I've been spying on them for weeks…"

"That's right… good boy…" I say as I would a puppy who's just obeyed a command. I remove my blade from his neck and slam the butt of it right into the back of his neck and tie him up. Just as I always have. Panting I stand up and grab my rope to tie his unconscious body up so that he won't escape, in the event he wakes up. I finally notice Max's figure and I meet his stare… He's leaning against one of the buildings with his arms crossed observing—no, admiring what I am doing. "Shit" I hiss under my breath as I finish tying the man up.

"That's right 'shit'." He pushes off the wall and walks toward me. "I told you I would be here if you needed me, princesa. Especially for someone who's as small as you are." He says as he slowly approaches closer towards me.

My eyes whip to his as if to say 'What the fuck did you just say to me?!' "I train all week, every week. Always perfecting and expanding my skills. Z Group provides me with all the information I need on each target I hunt. They are helping me hunt my uncle down in the meantime. Each target is a step closer to finding him... two birds one stone..." I scoff. "I have been hunting and chasing my uncle down for years now... 'As small as I am'... Sure, keep telling yourself that, Maximus." I fake a full name for him. His full name is indeed Max, but when he annoys me, I make up a fuller name for him.

Max chuckles at the made up full name as he listens intently, his expression hardening back into a frown, "You've been noticed by the roommates... they're out here too. Looking for you. You should be glad that I am the one who found you first."

"Great..." I start removing the bandages I have wrapped around my hands and remove my mask and hood. I pulled out my oversized hoodie and sweatpants out of my bag and gesture for Max to exit the alleyway with me before the cops arrive. Max watches with fascination at how calculated I am about my wardrobe change.

He follows me out of the alleyway, keeping pace beside me, wrapping his arm around my shoulders, as we walk away from the scene. "You know... you're pretty fearless. Taking on all these pervs on your own. I'm almost impressed..."

I run my fingers through my hair to fix it from being in my hood as I scoff. "Almost? Nothing to be impressed with Max. I'm just defending and protecting other women and kids like I promised I would. No one will ever be hurt like I was, if I can help it. Everyone will get their justice…" I continue to walk out towards the main street alongside him as he stops me by grabbing my elbow and turning me to look at him.

His expression is soft as he listened to my resolve. He scans my features, seeing the determination in my eyes, and he feels a strange respect growing for me. "I have to admit, that's admirable. It takes a lot of courage to put yourself in harm's way like that but, don't you ever worry about your own life and well-being? You're just one person, and there's so many of them out there…"

I hold his gaze. "Then I will fight and catch every last one of them until my dying breath if that's what it takes."

Max can see the fire burning in my eyes as I speak. He can tell that I am completely serious, and he can't help but admire my unwavering determination. "You really mean that huh? You're willing to fight and catch them all, even if it kills you…"

My eyes never move from his as they darken. "Yes. I can die peacefully only when I've faced my uncle and taken down every last creep on this planet… They will all pay for what they've done to those who aren't able to defend themselves against them…"

Max nods, understanding the reason behind my stubborn determination. He looks at me with a mix of concern and respect. "I get it. I really do. Still… you should make sure to take care of yourself too. This is your second target today alone. You can't fight everybody right this second. It's not fair for you to shoulder all of the burden on your own, Ellie. Let me help-"

I put up a hand to stop him. "This is my fight Max… I don't want anyone else involved… Tatsuya is the one training me and even that is too many. You are constantly following me on these hunts, there are too many people involved in this. I need you to please… back off."

Max sighs as his expression hardens once again. "I get it, Ellie. Really, I do. But I can't just stand by and watch. You don't have to do this alone." His voice lowered, almost pleading. "Let me have your back. You're strong, Elara. I know that. But even the strongest need backup sometimes."

"Please, Max... don't tell the others," I plead, my voice barely above a whisper. "Lius won't ever let me leave the house again... and I don't want you guys involved in this. You all face enough danger as Vipers as it is. I don't want any of you to get hurt helping me with this..."

Max watched me, torn between admiration and frustration. He could hear the resolve in my voice, but it only made him worry more. He knew convincing me would be a battle on its own, but he was ready to fight it. This battle means more to him than any mission he's fought before-because it's about protecting me. For now, he tells himself that he will keep an eye on me, ensuring I don't face the darkness alone.

Max frowns, a worried look on his face. "I won't tell them, you have my word. You can't keep this to yourself though... You need people you trust and can rely on. People who can watch your back and help you when things get tough... And who better than your roommates, huh?"

"Max... no. In my training I am prepared for just about every scenario possible. I will be just fine." I shake my head lightly at the end to emphasize my refusal.

He lets go of my elbow and nods, his expression tightening. "I know you're strong. And that you've been training hard, I've watched you, seen how you've grown even more since you've got here. Your uncle probably is more dangerous than you or Tatsuya realize. You can't fight him on your own, no matter how prepared you are. You need allies, people you can trust to have your back when shit hits the fan."

"Stop it, Max... I can handle this alone." My voice wavered slightly, betraying the fear I refused to acknowledge. My mind flashes with thoughts of what happened to my last partner... I shake it off the increasing echoes of a gunshot as I notice Max's eyes flicker a bit of hurt in them at my declaration of independence to him.

His expression moves to frustration. "You're a stubborn little shit, you know that...? You should trust what I am saying, if not me then who can you trust to give advice on this?! You need back-up on these hunts you go on. You can't just throw yourself into the fire and expect to come back without being burned!" His hands cup my face to force me to look him in the eyes since I've turned my head away from him to avoid this lecture. His eyes pleading for me to please listen to what he's saying. My expression softened at the worry in Max's eyes, but then I noticed a shadow moving toward us. Lius.

"Unscathed from what...?" Asks Lius as he walks up, hands in his pockets, looking between Max and me. He raises an eyebrow, wondering what is going on between us. I'm pretty sure by the look of his reaction he's heard the majority of what Max and I were arguing about. Shit. I curse to myself. Max glances at him, releasing my face as Lius approaches us.

Max's jaw tightened, but he kept his voice steady. "I was just talking to our princess here about her... activities in the city. She insists on walking around in dark areas by herself, no matter how dangerous it is. She won't listen to reason..."

Lius glances between the two of us, he cocks both eyebrows up. "And...? Care to elaborate on what she's gotten into this time?" He keeps his eyes on me as he asks Max the question.

"Nothing…" I sneer. "Let's just go home…" I can't let Lius see the creep in the alleyway. Or I'm never going to hear the end of it. I think this to myself as I begin to try and walk past Lius, shooting daggers at Max as I pass… if looks could injure… it would be very handy right about now. Max shoots me a glaring look of disapproval back to me, clearly annoyed by my response. Lius—not convinced—looks at me carefully, studying the glance between Max and me.

He knew something was being unsaid. "Are you sure about that? I can tell when someone's withholding information, you know."

"I was just exploring a bit and was in an alleyway, when Max found me… It was nothing." I say as I try to school my expression.

Lius crossed his arms, raising an eyebrow. His expression told me he wasn't buying a word I said. "Exploring huh…? In a dark alleyway… at this time of night? What were you doing there exactly?" He trails after me.

"I was just walking around exploring the surroundings around the house. I got lost and thought I could just cut through it." I cringe as even I know that isn't believable. I stop and turn to face the music that Lius is about to perform and take a deep breath to brace for impact. But he isn't walking towards me anymore, he has turned around and walks back to the alley I just came out of.

"Shit," I muttered under my breath, my heart pounding as Lius spotted the unconscious creep tied up in the alley.

His eyes scan the area, and he freezes as soon as his eyes land on the unconscious body lying in the alleyway. I curse under my breath and quickly walk towards him. I hear police sirens in the distance. And they are heading right this way, my head darting both ways to see which direction the police are coming from.

"What the hell is this?!" His eyes wide, looking at the man then at me with a mix of shock and confusion all over his face. His finger extended towards the man. "Do you know that guy?!"

"No." I say curtly with a straight face as I tug on his arm to pull him away from the area. I walk away from the alleyway, gripping his wrist tightly, towards the main street to get him and myself away from the scene before the cops arrive. Lius shakes his arm out of my grip and runs to jump in front of me, but I do not stop. He reads my face attempting to get a read. He can see that I have that same look of determination and intent in my eyes as I refuse to meet his gaze.

It's the same look that makes him feel as uneasy as it has since the first morning he saw it. He finally speaks. "You did that... didn't you? You knocked him out and tied him up?"

I keep my face void of any expression and don't respond as I stop once we've cleared the corner at a safe enough distance and meet his gaze. He moves more in front of me, putting both of his hands up to stop me from walking any further from him.

"Ellie, just tell him. You can't hide this anymore," Max urged, frustration seeping into his voice. My eyes snap back to him and narrow, telling him to shut up. Lius' eyes narrow as he looks at my reaction to Max. He can now sense he was right, there is something going on that I'm hiding and apparently Max knows what it is.

It makes Lius more suspicious of me. "What aren't you telling me?" He finally asks.

"Not here..." I look around the bustling streets. "Let's get back home and I will tell you... all of you what's going on..." I held his gaze once again.

Lius sighs as he holds up his phone to text the others that I've been located. "Ok... yea... I think we should go back home. We

will have a conversation about this. We don't keep secrets Elara."
He points his phone at me like he would his finger. I wince at him
using my full name. I'm in for it now... for sure... I think to
myself... great.

Max nods in agreement and both are now looking at me with
concern and anger. Oh joy. This is about to be a very fun night...
I roll my eyes at the towering thing they enjoy doing when trying
to intimidate me into bending me to their will. I've never fallen
for it. Why do they have to be so fucking tall...

The three of us head back towards our house in complete
silence, the tension between us is making me sick to my stomach.
The walk back is relatively quiet, with only the sounds of the city
at night providing background noise to our heavy footsteps. Kai
and Ares walk up to us from their respective ends of the street,
instantly noticing the tension between us. Taking note of the very
serious expressions on all of our faces and mine keeping eyes on
the ground like a scolded child.

Ares' eyes land on me, narrowing in question. "What's going
on? What happened?" Ares asks, breaking the silence. Kai begins
to look worried, sensing that something is very wrong.

Lius sighs and looks at me. "We're on our way home to
discuss it... seems like we have some things to talk about..." He
emphasizes each word, leaning closer to my face. I roll my eyes
and look at Kai to try and ask him to get Lius to back off. Max
nods in agreement as he glares at the back of my head. We started
walking again, with the four of them boxing me in. The mood is
tense, and the tension churns my stomach. Feeling short and
surrounded, I feel like I'm the president with her secret service.
We finally made it back to the house, the tension thick. They have
me walk in first, as they follow, settling in the living room. All
eyes on me... Lights, Camera, Elara...

~*~

Lius is the first to speak. "Alright Ellie, explain everything, including what the hell happened in that alleyway."

The room falls silent as I prepare to explain. I look at each of them and finally sigh. "It's me," I blurt out, my voice barely audible. "I'm the vigilante everyone's been talking about. The one on the news. Max caught me finishing a hunt once before… that morning I went to the corner store by the house. Those texts I frequently get are alerts from the Z Group, giving me information on targets to hunt. Tonight's text was one of those. That's why I couldn't wait until morning to go to the store after dinner."

They listen intently. "You're the vigilante leaving tied-up men in alleyways we keep getting briefed on?" Kai asks. "That's why you've been out so late? You've been taking down those criminals?"

I nod. "Yes. Sometimes I run into a target during the day, which is what Max saw that morning. I baited the target into following me out of the store and into an alleyway."

Lius' eyes widened. "Wait… are you saying that guy attacked you and you had to take him down right then?"

I shake my head. "No. I baited him into attacking me. And Lius, the guy you saw tonight is how I leave all of them."

The room falls silent again. Lius looks furious, his face red with anger. Kai and Ares also look angry but concerned at the same time. Lius' tone matches his expression. "He what?! They put their hands on you?!"

"Yes. It's part of my trap to ensure they're the correct target, catch them in the act. Don't worry, I can handle them and stop them before it goes too far." I try to ease the tension. The shock is palpable. Lius looks ready to find these creeps and hurt them further.

Lius speaks again. "You let them do that just to confirm they're as sleazy as you suspect? What happened to not being able to handle being touched below your armpits?"

I glared at him. "It fuels my rage. And… don't bring that up. Yes, sometimes I have to put myself out as bait. It's how I make them think they've caught another prey. It lowers their guard."

Max scowls. "That's a reckless thing that you do. They could overpower you! I hate watching it every time." His voice is low and laced with anger at his recollection of the times he's accompanied me on hunts.

"I'm aware. But I haven't been training under Tatsuya for nothing," I reply, keeping my composure to calm the energy thickening in the room.

Lius runs a hand through his hair. "Training…? Seriously? You're risking your life like that, and you think you've had enough training to handle it all on your own?!"

"I made a promise to myself to protect women and children from those who overpower them. Those who take advantage of them! I won't let anyone go through what I did, walking this earth with their attacker free, just like I do." The blood vessel on my temple rising as I emphasize my words with my finger jabbed into my chest.

Ares speaks up. "I remember reading about a rise in attackers being caught in Arizona, with them found tied-up in alleyways. That was you, wasn't it?"

"Yes… that's where I started this war." I lift my chin slightly, feeling proud that my work is noticed.

"Don't get cocky," Lius snapped, pointing that finger of his at me now–his voice laced with frustration. "You're still reckless for doing this."

I sigh and look down at my hands. "In Arizona… I wasn't on my own though." All four men freeze in place. "That's why I won't take anyone for backup. His name was Troy… he was my partner and… we fell in love. He was murdered during a mission, my final one in Arizona. They caught him and shot him in front of me, execution style. After that, I refused to work with anyone else. Especially you four!"

Max's expression softens. "I guess I can understand that…"

I look at him and nod. "I told you, Max. I'll fight till my dying breath. Isn't that why you've been following me on every hunt? To make sure I don't?"

Lius snaps his eyes towards Max with shock and knows he will definitely deal with that little bit of information later. He throws his hands up. "Great. Now I have to worry about you getting yourself killed. I don't like this, not one bit!"

"Why?! Because I'm a woman?! That's my one leg up in catching those assholes!" I take a step towards Lius, a vein popping out on my forehead even more. I am so enraged at this interrogation this time.

Lius scoffs. "It's because you're a human! It's dangerous as hell, Elara!"

I glared at him. "That's why I train harder than any of you! The end result is to bring down every horrible person who hurts others for their own sick pleasures and gets away with it! I won't rest until they've all paid for what they've done to their victims!"

Lius looks worried but senses my determination. "I respect your determination, Ellie. But you have to be careful. We don't want anything to happen to you."

My eyes soften but don't hide my frustration over this conversation. "I am being careful… as careful as I can be. But I must do this on my own. So please, I need you four to stay out of this."

Lius shakes his head. "You're stubborn as hell. You think you can take on the world all by yourself? This world that we live in now?"

"In this instance… I have to." My voice caught in my throat, causing a forced whisper. "I can't watch another loved one be executed in front of me again. I just can't…"

Max speaks sharply. "Why are you so determined to do this alone? We can help you. We are trained fighters too, you know."

"Because of the reason I just told you! I can't risk any of you getting hurt or killed! Troy was a trained fighter as well! And they still got him because I made a mistake! This is my war." I think about what I would do if any of them got hurt… Lius, Kai, Ares… Max… My heart clenches.

"You're not the only one who's strong. We can handle ourselves just fine," Lius argues in a calmer tone. I stand there, unable to accept their help, refusing to even bend a little to what they are asking of me.

Max walks over to me, stopping just in front of me, his voice is stern. "Enough with this lone wolf act, Ellie. You're outnumbered on this one. If your uncle is as powerful as you've told me he might be, you'll need all the help you can get. Stop being stubborn and accept our help. We are offering it!" I've never heard Max yell at anyone like this. But it wasn't anger behind his eyes that I saw. His eyes softened, filled with a fear I hadn't seen in him before.

I look down in shame at the fact that I am scaring my new found family and shake my head. "Max…" Another tight whisper leaves my lips through gritted teeth as I fight back the tears pricking the backs of my eyes.

Max gently turns me to face him, his grip firm but careful. "Look at me, Elara. You really think you can take on your uncle and all those targets by yourself? You're not doing this alone, princesa. End of discussion." He releases my arm.

"I-" I'm at a loss for words. They are refusing to stay out of this, it seems. I try to gather more reasons why I can't have them with me on these missions when they have their own orders to follow. Their own war to fight against the rogues in the world.

Lius and Ares watch, agreeing with Max. "He's right. You can't do this alone. Even we help each other on missions," Lius says with a calmer tone, helping de-escalate the situation in our quaint living room.

I look at their faces, tears lining my eyes. I sigh with defeat. "The first time one of you gets hurt-"

Max grins and quickly reaches out to me pulling me once again into his embrace. "Atta girl! We're in this with you now. We'll look out for you, okay? Don't worry about us. Just focus on what you need to do."

"Ugh... here's my condition: you all must stay back and hidden from sight unless I need help. Deal?" I counter, although muffled by Max's arms squeezing me hard around my shoulders.

Lius narrows his eyes in thought. "You want us to stay hidden and not intervene unless necessary?"

"Yes. I'll focus better knowing you're out of harm's way. I don't care how strong you are. Stay hidden until it looks like I'm about to lose control of the situation. It's what Max has been doing for weeks."

Max's expression is serious as he pulls back, loosening his grip on me. "Alright. But if you're in over your head, we're stepping in. Understood?"

"Okay. Fine." I sigh. "Anything else?"

They all shake their heads except Max, who adds. "Don't even think you can shake us either. Got it?"

My eyes widened as a thought popped into my head. "That was one time!"

Max nods with a smirk at my statement, reminding him of the time I tried to get him off my trail. "You have to at least tell me when you're given a new target, moving forward." Ares and Kai agree with what's been decided, nodding in unison. My gaze falls on Max, my mouth opens to argue. He holds his stoic expression on me and nods again. "When you're notified about a target, or you run into one, just let me know where you are. I need to make sure you're safe." I nod with hesitation trying to think how that will work. When I'm luring a target, I don't really have time to be distracted by my phone.

I must have this question written all over my face because then Max answers with a hardened expression. He reaches into his pocket and pulls out a black leather smart watch. "I can give you a watch with GPS tracking. All you need to do is press a button and it will alert me. That way it won't take your focus away from the hunt and you can remain focused. So, I will know where you are anytime you press it. You press once to activate, and then again to deactivate." He points to the button on the side of the watch, closest to the wrist strap.

"Does everyone else agree with that…?" I ask the others as I keep my gaze on the watch in Max's hands. As he dresses my wrist with the watch and fastens the band to fit me. My stomach clenches. I hate this… so much. I want to keep denying their requests, well… demands. But I know I am way too tired to try and keep arguing when they're just going to do what they want anyways. The rest of them nod in agreement.

I let out an ineligible grumble. "Okay…" I rotate my sore arm from tonight's takedown, groaning lightly in pain as I limp towards the shower. Slightly relieved that I no longer have to pretend that I'm not injured anymore. "I'm going to go shower now. That last guy actually got a few hits in. He knew a thing or two." I can feel all four sets of eyes lock onto me, noticing my limp and sore arm as I turn to walk away. I do my best to just walk a little normally but with the adrenaline wearing off from the fight and everyone finding out, the injuries I suffered take surface.

"Wait a second… Ellie. Are you hurt?" Lius rushes toward me, concern etched across his face.

"Yeah, just a little. I was surprised this guy knew a few tricks. I have yoga in the morning, so I better go shower and get to bed. If I run into a target, I'll let you all know." I tell them to try and redirect their attention to something else, so I can just shower and sleep.

Max's eyes narrow at the mention of yoga. "Wait, you're still going to your yoga class in the morning even after your take down tonight? Damn… you're either crazy or hardcore."

"I guess both. I can't rest. I refuse to." I say as my eyes darken.

Lius lets out a grunt of approval, impressed with my determination. "You're damn right! But still, don't push yourself too hard, okay? We need you in one piece."

"Okay." I chuckled.

Max's expression softens as he observes my limp, his protective nature taking hold of him. "Seriously, princesa… you need to take it easy." He rushes closer to my side, pushing past

Lius, to inspect the injuries. "How badly did that guy hurt you?" His eyes scan my body as if he has x-ray vision.

"Not too badly. Just a bruise on my arm and a sprained ankle." I chuckled, seeing his concern. His beautiful deep obsidian eyes are filled with worry, giving me that 'you're lying' kind of look.

Lius sighs. "A bruised arm and a sprained ankle are not 'just a little,' Ellie."

"It's fine. It's not my first time getting hurt, and it won't be my last. I just need to shower and ice my ankle. I'll be good as new in the morning." I start to make my way to the stairs, hiding the pain in my ankle as I do my best to walk normally.

Max rolls his eyes. "You say that like it's no big deal. But a sprained ankle is more serious than you think. You need to take better care of yourself."

"I'm doing the best I can. What, do none of you get hurt after a fight? Do you all just lay around the next day over one bruise or a rolled ankle? No. didn't think so…" I cut them off, wanting to end the conversation and get to my shower. I feel like their kid sister trying to prove she can play football with them.

Lius rubs the back of his neck, his frustration clear. "You need to let your body heal."

I stop at the bottom of the stairs, my back to them. "I can't stop… I can't rest… I have to accomplish my goal… I just have to… So, just please stop it. Back off. All of you." The room falls silent, the guys looking at me with concern and sympathy. They know that feeling all too well. Max looks at me with a mix of concern and understanding, while Lius and Ares exchange worried glances.

Lius speaks up. "We know you want justice, Ellie. We know you're determined. But you have to take care of yourself too.

You're not invincible. You can't push yourself to the brink every time you fight."

"How do I get stronger?" I turn to face them. "Hmm? How? If I don't push myself further each time? I'm not even that injured! This..." I gesture to my ankle. "Is nothing compared to what I've suffered before. Just stop it okay?"

Max steps forward closer to me again, his voice firm but caring. "You get stronger by resting and recovering also. You get stronger by taking care of yourself, not by pushing yourself too hard. You think I've never been hurt in a fight before? Of course I have. I also know when to step back and let my body rest."

I pull one last hail Mary to get them off my back–to redirect the conversation away from my stupid sprain. Information I was hoping to keep to myself. I take a deep breath, my heart racing. "There's something else I didn't tell you guys..." I say at an almost whisper. They all perk up, snapping their attention back to my face. "My uncle is in Tokyo... that's the real reason why I moved here. He's here in this city and I have to find him... Max already knew this." The room goes silent, the weight of my revelation sinking in. Maybe they'll redirect onto Max now and allow me to get upstairs quickly and put an end to this lecture. It didn't work.

"Your uncle... is here in Tokyo? In this city?" asks Lius. I nod. Lius's eyes widen, while Kai and Ares remain silent. "Why the hell didn't you tell us that earlier? This is a big deal!"

"Because I was trying to keep you guys away from this!" Max chuckles softly, breaking the tension just a little. "Stop, Max... I wasn't trying to be funny..." I chuckled at his laugh, feeling a small sense of relief.

He snorts once more trying not to burst out laughing. "Your face… you really thought you could keep this whole thing from us…?"

I roll my eyes at him. Lius shakes his head, frustration showing in his voice. "Seriously. You thought we wouldn't have figured it out eventually? What you've been doing every day? We're not a pack of idiots, you know…"

"Yes… eventually… not this soon…" My face falls.

Kai crosses his arms, frowning. "I still don't understand why you were so hell-bent on keeping it a secret anyway. Did you think we were going to go blabbing to people or something?"

"No… I thought this would happen." I gesture to the room, indicating the situation I'm desperately trying to end. "And I was pretty sure Lius wouldn't let me leave the house again."

Lius scoffs. "Excuse me? I'm not that overprotective!"

I giggle and smile at them, shaking my head, dismissing Lius' attempt at defending his ways. "Okay… I'm going to go shower now…"

Max steps closer, his strong arms sliding beneath me before lifting me gently into his hold. "No more arguing," he mutters as he cradles me effortlessly, his expression soft yet firm. "You're not walking up those stairs on that ankle."

"Hey! Max! I can walk! Put me down!" I squirm in his hold.

"Just relax for once and let someone help you… stubborn as always," he mutters, the hint of a smile tugging at his lips.

"Fine! But I'm making it known how much I hate this," I grumble, exaggerating my pout as I cross my arms and legs.

He chuckles, his chest vibrating against me as I feel him shake his head. "Yeah, yeah. You're a real tough one," he says, clearly amused by my exaggerated sulking.

7

Max continues carrying me up the stairs towards the bathroom, each step echoing softly in the quiet stairway. Despite my best efforts to project annoyance, I can't ignore the warmth of his arms around me. The tension in his grip is almost tender, as if he's afraid to hurt me despite my protests. I sit with my arms crossed, a scowl firmly planted on my face, determined to make him understand how infuriating this whole situation is. I hate being treated like this, like I can't take care of myself—damn Vipers. I curse to myself. But as we ascend, I start to notice the little details of his face: the way his jaw clenches with frustration, the gentle steadiness in his breathing, the concern etched into his features. It's clear that his irritation is more about his inability to do anything more right now to help me.

"Put me down, Max," I say, trying to keep my voice steady. "I can walk." He doesn't respond immediately. Instead, he adjusts his hold, making sure I'm more comfortable. There's a moment of silence, punctuated only by the soft creak of the stairs beneath us.

His eyes, which normally carry a mischievous glint, now reflect a deep, almost vulnerable worry.

"This is ridiculous…" I huff out.

"Elara," he says quietly, "I'm sorry. I know this isn't how you wanted things to go tonight. But right now, this is what I must do. It's all I *can* do." His voice is gentle, carrying a sincerity that catches me off guard. It's not what I expected from him, and for a moment, I'm taken aback by the raw emotion in his tone. I soften slightly, the anger melting away as I recognize the genuine care behind his actions. He reaches the bathroom door and carefully sets me down, his hands lingering on my shoulders as if to reassure himself that I'm steady. His touch is light, almost hesitant, as if he's afraid he's held onto me too roughly. I look up at him, the intensity of the situation fading, replaced by a softer, more vulnerable connection.

"I'm really not trying to be a burden," I say, my voice barely above a whisper. "I just—"

He cuts me off by gently placing his index finger on my lips. "I know… And I'm here because I want to be. You're not a burden, Elara. You never are and never will be." His words hung in the air between us, and for a moment, the world outside seems to fade away. I see him in a new light—someone who, despite his flaws, is genuinely concerned for me. It's a side of him I hadn't fully seen before—never thought I would, and it makes the walls I've built around myself start to crack. Max's eyes meet mine, and in the shared look between us, there's an unspoken understanding. Despite everything, there's a deep, abiding care between us that neither of us can deny. It's not the grand gestures or the dramatic confessions, but these quiet, tender moments that reveal the true depth of our connection that has built over the past weeks of him going with me on hunts.

Max lifts one side of his mouth and breaks the tension. "We don't need you falling down these stairs because you're being too stubborn…"

"Wouldn't that be some shit?" I laugh.

Max chuckles, amused by my response. "Yes, it would. And it would be quite embarrassing, wouldn't it? The mighty vigilante Elara, taken down by some stairs." We both laugh as we stand for a moment longer in front of the bathroom door. "You're in a strangely good mood for someone who has a sprained ankle." He adds, clearing his throat.

"I have to see the positive… what I'm doing is scary and difficult… I'd be lying if I said I wasn't afraid every time I hunt a target, but Sensei is helping me hone those feelings into my fighting skills. Use it to my benefit and the greater good."

Max nods. "That's a very wise approach. It's common to feel fear and hesitation in dangerous situations, but what sets you apart is your ability to channel that fear into strength. It takes courage and discipline to do what you're doing."

"Thanks…" I let my hands down, relaxing just a bit.

He smiles gently, "You're welcome. Just take it easy from here, okay? Don't put too much pressure on that ankle." I see the faint glimpse of care and admiration in the dim light of the hallway. I usually tease Max about showing any emotion other than annoyance or nonchalance, but since it's just the two of us, I decide to let him be.

"I won't… thank you, Max." I patted his arm in appreciation and walked toward the bathroom.

He nods and watches me walk into the bathroom to make sure I don't trip. "You're welcome. Just call for me if you need help."

"I won't." I tease as I close the door slowly, holding his gaze for a moment longer. Once the door is shut, I turn on the water to the shower. Max stays a few moments longer at the closed bathroom door, his heart beating as he begins feeling something... something new that he's never felt before.

I climb in and take my time washing, feeling the water fall on my head. I let loose and begin to cry, unaware that the walls are so thin my roommates may hear me. I didn't care... I don't care anymore. The weight of everything I've been holding inside— every fear, every failure—crashes down on me like a tidal wave. I press my face into the warm spray, letting the sobs wrack through me, the tears hidden by the water cascading down my skin. I have to hone my emotions whenever I hunt a target, but sometimes... sometimes I just can't hold it in any longer.

I finish my shower, take a deep breath, and get dressed. After brushing my teeth and washing my face, I exit the bathroom and head to my room. As I step out, the guys all look towards the stairs.

"Ok guys, shower is free." I shout down the stairs into the living room.

"Alright! Thanks for letting us know!" Lius replies loudly back up the stairs.

Max doesn't wait another second before he's up the stairs and at my side again, striding up three steps at a time, looking down at me. "Hey... you, okay? You look a bit... puffy..."

"Oh! Yeah, I'm fine," I smile through my lie and wave my hand. "Some soap got in my eyes, that's all."

Max raises an eyebrow, not convinced. "Soap, huh? Your eyes are quite red and swollen from soap getting in your eyes..." His face softens.

"Yeah, well... what can you do...?" I glance at him from the side and softly grin before hobbling back to my room.

Max's hand shoots out, catching my arm gently. His touch is warm but firm, like he's trying to tether me to the moment.

"Elara... are you sure you're alright? I know you're tough, but...you don't have to be right now. Not with me."

I look down at his hand on my arm. I notice how my skin doesn't instantly crawl from his touch. I look up at him with soft features to let him know that I'm okay. "Yeah, I'm fine, thanks Max. I'm just going to head to bed. Yoga is early in the morning, so I should get some sleep."

Max gives me a kind smile and nods. "Alright, go rest."

"Good night, Max..." I headed into my room and closed the door. Max stands staring at my door for another moment before heading back downstairs to the others.

8

I jog down the stairs, the soft sound of my sneakers tapping on the wood floor as I enter the kitchen. Dressed in my yoga gear, I flash the guys a smile. "Morning, Max. Lius." I smile at them both and walk over to pour myself a cup of coffee and set everything up to make breakfast for the house as I usually do if I notice no one else has made anything. I'm going to make pancakes, eggs, and bacon—the boys' favorite that I've made many times before. I will make myself my pre-workout smoothie to take with me. Lius raises an eyebrow at my appearance, noticing the effort I put into looking nice for my yoga class this morning.

"Morning, sleepyhead. You're up earlier than usual. Got a hot yoga date or something?" Lius teases.

I chuckled. "No, silly. I have just a regular yoga class this morning like I always do on Tuesdays and Thursdays... remember?" I actually have found one of the new yoga mates kind of dashing and have been trying to look cute. I've always kept this to myself as I can't have four humongous men following me to class... trying to intimidate him from talking to me.

Lius grins at me. "How could I forget? You and your daily dose of tree poses, and warrior poses."

"It keeps me limber," I say.

Max grins. "Yeah, keeps you limber. And look at that muscle definition. You're gonna put us all to shame soon with those yoga moves of yours."

I raise an eyebrow at him. "Hey… when I look as buff as you, Max… then I'll stop."

Max chuckles, amused by my response. "Oh, you think you can get as buff as me with all that yoga? Good luck with that, Princesa." He lifts an arm and flexes.

"I don't just do yoga... I lift weights and even have my training with Sensei Tatsuya. He's very built too. I need to keep lean though, for the kind of fighting I do to capture my targets. I can't lure them in if I'm too buff, so I have to stay lean and limber." I say as I sip my coffee.

Lius grins, impressed with my training regime. "Damn… look at you! A regular fighting machine! I like your style, princess. And I can't forget about ole Tatsuya. That guy's got more muscles than a Greek god!"

I spit some of my coffee back into my cup from laughing. "I'm going to tell him you said that!" I laugh harder. "And… Lius… my name is Elara." I corrected him for calling me 'princess'. I don't like it when he does… especially him.

Lius grins mischievously. "Oh yeah, princess? You're gonna tell Tatsuya? Go right ahead, I dare you. Maybe he'll invite me over for a sparring session and I'll show him how a real fighter does it."

I raise an eyebrow. "My name is Ellie or Elara, Lius. Oh… so Max is going to spar with Tatsuya? Because that's the only real fighter I see in the room. I think he would be able to show Sensei anything worth his while. I'll spar with you though! Come on down and let's see what you've got!"

Lius grins, amused with the challenge. "Oh, you're on. Just don't cry when I whoop your ass!"

"Don't *you* cry when I whoop *your* ass!" I squint my eyes at him like they do for boxing matches when the opponents stand face to face for the first time on TV.

Lius laughs, clearly enjoying the trash talk. "Oh ho... princess, I like your confidence. Let's see if you can actually back it up. Come at me, I'm ready..." He tries to egg me on by avoiding calling me by my name, which he knows I don't like. I decided to ignore this one.

"First of all, not in the house. Come by the gym anytime I'm there. My next session is tomorrow morning." I turn and start to make breakfast. "Max, would you like some breakfast too? I'm making pancakes, eggs, and bacon."

Max nods, appreciating the offer. "Sure thing, Princesa. I wouldn't mind some pancakes. And I'll definitely be there for your sparring session tomorrow... can't pass up the chance to see you put Lius in his place."

I turn and grin at both of them. Lius huffs, offended at the implication that I could overpower him. "Hey, I can take her. I'm not worried. Princess ain't got nothing on me..."

"My name is *Elara*, Lius." I corrected him.

Lius nods and corrects himself with a hint of sarcasm. "Alright, alright... *Elara*. But that doesn't change the fact that I can still take you in a fight."

"Bet... we will see tomorrow morning now... won't we?" I taunt.

Lius grins, clearly fired up. "You bet your cute ass we will. And when I win... I'll make sure to rub it in your face!"

I pause, tapping my chin as if deep in thought. "When I win... what should I make you do? Oh, I know. You'll call me *'daddy'*... for a whole year." Max spits his coffee and starts laughing uncontrollably.

Lius blushes, taken aback by my comment. "Whoa whoa! Hold on! You're not seriously going to make me call you *'daddy'* are you?!" His eyes filled with panic.

"Hmm, I guess we will have to see, won't we...?" I keep a smirk on my face as I turn back to working on breakfast.

"You're pretty confident demanding that kind of title. You really think you can take me down and earn that kind of authority over me?" Lius challenges me as he approaches me in the kitchen.

"Yes. I. Do..." I tap his chest with the bottom end of the spatula.

"I hope you know what you're getting yourself into. When I win, you're going to be calling me *'Master'* for a *long* time." He stands close to my side, towering in an attempt to intimidate me.

I ignored his attempt, continuing to mix up the batter for the pancakes. "Oh really...?"

"Yeah, you better believe it! And when I say *'Master,'* I mean it. You're gonna be my little underling for the whole year. Just think of all the things I'm gonna make you do for me..." He has a seductive look on his face.

Max freezes and raises his eyebrows at Lius, glaring at him, watching his every move now. "Excuse me—"

"Don't be gross..." I throw an empty egg shell at Lius, which he successfully dodges with ease, laughing at my response.

"Hey, hey! I'm just messing around with you. Calm down. But if you want to make me, call you *'daddy'* you have to be ready for the consequences. I'm not exactly known for being sweet and gentle, you know…" Lius holds the distance between us, right up against me but not touching just yet.

I ignore his advances. "Then I guess we'll see… won't we?"

"Oh, you better believe I'm going to win. There's *no* way I'm letting you make me call you *'daddy'*. I'm gonna knock you flat on your ass tomorrow." I shoot him an evil glare, narrowing my eyes at the not so subtle innuendo.

I finish making breakfast and serve Lius and Max their food just as I'm finishing up breakfast, Kai walks in, stretching his arms. "Morning, Kai!" I greeted him with a bright smile. "Want some breakfast?"

He nods at me, appreciative of the offer. "Yes, thank you. That would be great. Good morning." He takes a seat at the table, looking over at Lius and Max. "What are you three talking about?"

Max grins, glancing at Kai. "You're just in time. We were talking about a sparring match between our lovely princess here and Lius."

Lius notices how I don't correct Max for calling me 'princess'—just him. It makes him feel a little sad but also very curious as to why. Kai raises an eyebrow in interest. "Oh really? That certainly sounds interesting… I wouldn't mind seeing that myself."

"And when I win… Lius here has to call me *'daddy'* for a whole year." I giggle out.

Lius groans. "Why the hell would you want me to call you *'daddy'* anyway? It's weird."

"Because I know it will torment you. So, if you don't want to call me that… I guess we will have to see tomorrow morning if you can beat me." I tease with an 'eat-shit' grin on my face.

I handed a plate to Kai and got a fresh cup of coffee for the three of them and myself. I start the dishwasher with the current dirty dishes once I've finished making my morning smoothie. "Ok guys, I'm heading out for my yoga class. I made Ares a plate for whenever he gets up. It's wrapped in the oven. "I grab my gym bag, slinging it over my shoulder before turning back to the guys. "See you all later!" I head for the door, feeling their eyes follow me as I walk out.

I make my way to yoga class, music playing softly through my headphones. What I don't know is that my roommates have devised a secret plan to take turns trailing me wherever I go— always ensuring one of them is close by. Today, it's Ares who follows at a safe distance, careful not to let me sense his presence. They all agreed to keep me safe without drawing attention or letting me know. Ares moves quietly behind me, scanning the surroundings for any potential threats.

I reach the yoga studio, blissfully unaware of the watchful eye on me. Ares positions himself outside, vigilant and ready, ensuring nothing goes unnoticed while I'm inside. As I step into class and begin my session, he remains stationed at the entrance, committed to keeping me safe without ever revealing the plan they've put in place.

When my yoga class ends, I walk out of the studio, talking to one of the girls I'm in class with. As I exit the studio, engaged in conversation with my classmate, Ares remains in the shadows, watching intently and listening closely.

"Ok! See you on Monday!" I say to the girl as we part ways. I put my earbuds back in and began to walk home. Ares follows closely behind, keeping his distance as I walk home. He keeps a vigilant watch over my surroundings, ready to intervene if necessary.

I make a pit stop to get an electrolyte drink from the corner store by the house. Ares follows me into the store, watching discreetly from a distance while I browse the aisles. He keeps a watchful eye on my surroundings, peeking up slightly from under the visor of his ball cap, ensuring there are no potential threats nearby. I find the drink I'm looking for, grab it, and head up to the cashier to pay for it. Ares remains a few steps behind as I approach the cashier, casually pretending to be browsing the shelves but keeping his full attention on me. He glances around, ensuring no suspicious characters are lurking in the store. As I pay for the drink and step outside, Ares follows me out, once again keeping a respectable distance as I continue on my way home.

I finally arrived at the house, walking up the sidewalk to the front door. Once I hit the top step, I pause in front of the door. I take a deep breath and remove my earbuds while still facing the door. "Ares... you have to get better at concealing your presence..."

Ares steps out, amused. "So, you spotted me. Guess my stealth needs work."

I chuckle, shaking my head as I look over my shoulder at him. "You did fine, Ares. I just have good instincts." I turn to face him. "I never saw you, but I could sense you."

He nods, impressed with how aware I am of my surroundings. "You have sharp instincts. Most people wouldn't have noticed me unless I was right in front of them."

"I sensed you the moment I stepped out of the house this morning." I add.

He raises an eyebrow, genuinely surprised by me. "Impressive. You're keenly attuned to your surroundings, almost like you have a sixth sense for being watched."

"I have been training for this kind of thing too. Not just to defend myself." I say as I shake my head.

He nods, completely intrigued. "Ah, I see. So, you've been training those senses and not just naturally gifted with heightened senses then? You've put in the work to hone your instincts and awareness."

"One of the many things my trainers have been teaching me." I hold a smug grin on my face.

He smiles and follows me inside the house. The moment I step through the door, Lius is on his feet, his eyes filled with a mixture of relief and residual frustration.

"About time you got back!" he shouts, trying to sound casual but failing miserably.

I smirk, closing the door behind me. "Miss me, Lius?"

He opens his mouth to retort, but Ares cuts in. "She was perfectly safe the whole time. You can relax now."

Max, still leaning against the wall, lets out an exaggerated sigh of relief. "Finally! Maybe now Lius will stop pacing like a caged animal."

Kai folds his newspaper and sets it on the table, giving me a welcoming nod. "Glad to see you're back, Elara. How was your class?"

"It was great, thanks," I replied, setting my gym bag down. "And I picked up an electrolyte drink to rehydrate."

Lius shakes his head, finally sitting down. "Just... glad you're back."

I raised an eyebrow at him. "You're awfully concerned about me today, Lius. You're not worried about tomorrow, are you?"

He scoffs, trying to play it cool. "Worried? About you? Please. I'm just making sure you're in peak condition so I can beat you fair and square."

Max laughs. "Yeah, Lius, keep telling yourself that. We all know you were worried sick."

Ignoring the banter, I head to the kitchen and grab a glass of water. "So, what have you all been up to while I was gone? Aside from pacing and worrying, I mean. And sending Ares to trail me?" I tilt my glass towards Ares who's still lingering by the door, his cheeks becoming flushed.

Kai chuckles. "Not much, just waiting for updates—wait, Ares got caught?"

Ares shrinks slightly, embarrassed.

I nod, sipping my water. Keeping calm because I actually suspected my mother hens to do something like this. "Mmhmm... He sure was. Well, I'm back now. No need to worry anymore." I shoot a warning look at each of them. "And stop following me everywhere I go."

Lius stands, his expression serious. "It's not about worry. I just don't like feeling helpless. You're important to us."

I soften at his words, giving him a small smile. "I know, Lius. And I appreciate it. But you all need to trust that I can handle myself, too. I'm not a damsel in distress."

He nods, his shoulders relaxing a bit. "I know. But that doesn't mean we won't worry."

"Fair enough," I say, patting his arm. "Now, I'm going to head upstairs and wash the sweat off from yoga. When I come back down, how about we do something fun to take our minds off things?"

Max's eyes light up. "Like what?"

I grin. "How about a board game? Or maybe a movie? Anything to keep us entertained until dinner. Or do you all have a *job* to get to?" My grin fades as I try to remind them, they all have something better to do than be my personal security detail.

Lius glances at the others before shaking his head. "Nope. We're all off duty."

Max nods. "Yeah, we've got some downtime. A board game sounds perfect."

Kai sets his newspaper aside, clearly interested. "I could go for a game. What do we have?"

I pull out a stack of games from the shelf, sorting through them. "We've got Settlers of Catan, Risk, Monopoly, and a few others. What's your pick?"

Lius grabs Settlers of Catan with a grin. "Catan. Feeling lucky."

Max chuckles. "Lucky, huh? We'll see about that."

I walk upstairs to take my shower as the guys set up the coffee table for the game. The sound of the shower turning on upstairs cuts through the house, indicating my getting into the shower. Once I've finished and gotten dressed, I head back downstairs and see that they have finished setting up the game. We gather around the coffee table, setting up the rest of the game pieces. The atmosphere lightens as we get into the spirit of friendly competition. As we play, the earlier tension fades away, replaced by laughter and playful banter.

"Lius, you can't just build a road there!" I protest, eyeing his strategic placement.

He smirks. "Why not? It's a valid move."

Max leans over, studying the board. "He's right, princess. It's within the rules. But it's definitely going to mess up your plans."

I narrow my eyes at Lius. "You're going to regret that."

Kai laughs. "This is getting interesting. Let's see who comes out on top."

The game progresses with everyone deeply engrossed. We tease each other over trades, alliances are formed and broken, and the room fills with the sound of dice rolling and friendly taunts. As we near the end of the game, the competition heats up. Lius and I are neck and neck for the win, with Max and Kai close behind, with Ares in last place.

"Alright, final round," Lius announces, his eyes gleaming with determination. "This is it."

I glance at my resources, calculating my next move. "Don't get too cocky, Lius. I'm not out of the game yet."

Max grins. "May the best player win."

Kai nods in agreement. "Let's finish this."

I roll the dice, placing my final settlement. "Game over."

Lius throws his hands up in mock frustration. "No way! I had it!"

Max laughs, clapping him on the back. "Looks like Elara outsmarted you."

Kai smiles, shaking his head. "Good game, everyone."

I bask in my victory, enjoying the lighthearted moment. "Told you I'd make you regret that road, Lius."

He grins, being a good sport despite his loss. "Alright, you got me this time. But next time, I'm taking you down."

We pack up the game, still chatting and joking. As we settle down, I glance at the clock, realizing it's almost dinner time.

"Anyone hungry?" I ask, stretching. "I could whip up something for dinner."

Lius nods eagerly. "I'm starving."

Max grins. "You're always thinking ahead. What's on the menu, Ellie?"

I thought for a moment. "Spaghetti with garlic bread sound good?"

Kai nods in approval. "Sounds good to me. I love Italian."

The game's easy energy follows us to the kitchen. Lius chops vegetables while Max sets the table. Kai scrolls through playlists, landing on a soft tune. As the aroma of garlic and herbs fills the kitchen, I smile at the normalcy of it all. We sat down to eat, enjoying the meal and each other's company. The earlier worries seem distant, replaced by the warmth of friendship and the simple pleasure of a good meal.

After dinner, we fall into the familiar rhythm of cleanup, an unspoken routine that makes everything feel easy. As the evening winds down, a rare sense of contentment settles over me. For once, everything feels calm–no missions, no danger, just us. I glance around at the guys, grateful for their presence. Whatever challenges come next, I know we'll face them together. For tonight, that's enough.

9

The next morning, I came downstairs, dressed in my sparring gear, feeling a buzz of excitement. I glance over and see Lius already at the kitchen table, fully dressed and looking ready for our match. He catches sight of me and flashes a confident grin.

"Good morning," he says, his tone carrying a mix of challenge and anticipation. "Ready for the match of a lifetime?"

I return his grin, my own excitement evident amongst my own tone of voice. "Good morning, Lius. I've been looking forward to this. Let's see if you can live up to all that trash talk."

Lius chuckles, standing up and stretching. "Oh, I'm more than ready. I hope you're prepared to eat your words."

Max and Kai are also already at the table, both observing with interest. Max looks up from his breakfast, a smirk on his face. "You two are up early. I'm guessing this means you're ready to finally settle this?"

Kai, sipping his coffee, nods with a smile. "I'll be interested to see how this turns out. I'm sure it'll be an impressive display."

I grab a quick breakfast smoothie, my nerves buzzing with anticipation. I can't help but glance over at Lius, who is already putting on his gear and warming up.

"So," I say, taking a sip of my smoothie. "What's the game plan for today, Lius? Any special moves you're planning to surprise me with?"

Lius grins, his eyes twinkling with mischief. "Oh, I've got a few tricks up my sleeve. But I wouldn't want to spoil the surprise. You'll just have to wait and see."

Max stands up, patting Lius on the back. "Alright, champ. Time to show us what you've got."

Kai, finishing his coffee, looks at me with an encouraging nod. "Good luck. Remember, it's all in good fun."

I finish my breakfast smoothie, feeling a mix of excitement and determination. "Thanks, everyone. I'll make sure to give it my all."

We make our way to the gym, the tension between Lius and me wafting through the air around us. The gym is quiet and empty, the perfect setting for our sparring session. The gym is a spacious, well-lit area with hardwood floors that echo the sound of every movement. It's equipped with various training equipment, but for today's match, the center is cleared out to provide an open space for the sparring session. The walls are adorned with mirrors, reflecting our movements and adding to the intensity of the moment.

Lius and I start our warm-up routines. Lius begins with dynamic stretches, his movements fluid and deliberate. He executes a series of high kicks and quick footwork drills, showcasing his agility and readiness. I follow with my own warm-up, focusing on flexibility and precision. I perform a few shadow boxing routines, ensuring my form is sharp and my movements are crisp.

"Ready to get started?" he asks, his eyes locked on mine.

I nod, a grin spreading across my face. "Absolutely. Let's do this."

We move to the center of the gym, facing each other. Lius adopts his fighting stance, and I follow suit, both of us poised and ready.

"Remember, no holding back," Lius says, his tone serious but with a hint of playful challenge. "Give me everything you've got."

I raise an eyebrow, my confidence unwavering. "You know I will."

We begin our sparring session. Lius and I move to the center of the gym, the atmosphere charged with anticipation. We adopt our stances: Lius, with a strong, grounded base and a confident expression; and me, with a poised, agile stance ready to counter any move.

Lius initiates the match with a series of quick jabs aimed at testing my defenses. I respond with a series of blocks and counters, moving smoothly to avoid his strikes. We exchanged a few light kicks, each of us trying to gauge the other's speed and strategy. Lius tries to gain the upper hand with a spinning kick, but I manage to dodge it with a swift sidestep. I counter with a low kick to his leg, testing his balance. Lius grins and blocks the kick, retaliating with a rapid combination of punches. As the match progresses, both of us start to show signs of sweat and exertion. Lius becomes more aggressive, launching a series of powerful punches aimed at breaking through my defense. I focus on maintaining my guard and countering his attacks with well-timed strikes.

I execute a quick combination of punches and a spinning elbow, catching Lius off guard. He stumbles slightly but quickly recovers, admiring my technique. He responds with a high kick aimed at my head, but I duck and counter with a swift uppercut that lands squarely on his chin. The intensity of the match escalates as we both push ourselves harder. Lius demonstrates his skill with a series of impressive footwork maneuvers, making it challenging for me to land a clean hit. I adapt by employing a more defensive strategy, focusing on precise strikes and quick movements. Lius attempts a powerful roundhouse kick, but I deflect it with a well-timed block and counter with a series of quick punches. We both exchanged a few hard-hitting blows, each of us determined to gain the upper hand.

By the final round, both of us are visibly fatigued but determined to finish strong. We engage in a rapid exchange of blows, with each of us using our remaining energy to outmaneuver the other. I land a solid kick to Lius's side, causing him to wince slightly. He responds with a powerful punch that I barely manage to dodge. In a final display of technique and skill, Lius and I execute a series of rapid, synchronized moves. We both landed a few hits, but the match ended with a mutual respect for each other's abilities. We both take a moment to catch our breath, smiles on our faces, acknowledging the intensity of the session.

Breathing heavily, we stand facing each other, both of us showing signs of exhaustion but also satisfaction. Lius extends a hand, grinning with a mixture of admiration and relief. "You're pretty damn good. I've got to admit, you gave me a run for my money."

I accepted his hand with a smile. "You weren't too bad yourself, Lius. I'd say we both held our own pretty well."

Max, who has been watching from the sidelines with the others, claps and offers a nod of approval. "That was one hell of a match. I'd say you both lived up to the hype."

Kai, who has been observing quietly as well beside Max, smiles and approaches. "Well done, both of you. That was impressive."

We all share a moment of the successful match, the tension of it giving way to mutual respect and appreciation. The gym gradually returns to its normal state as we cool down and stretch, the sense of accomplishment palpable in the air. I catch my breath and finally break the silence, admitting with a grin, "I guess we tie?"

Lius, still catching his breath, chuckles and nods in agreement. "Yeah, I'd say so. That was a hell of a fight. I couldn't quite get the upper hand, and you were just as relentless."

Max, who's been watching from the sidelines, claps enthusiastically. "I'd call that a draw too. You both brought your A-game. Well fought!" He grins as a proud parent would at a soccer match.

Kai, with a satisfied smile, adds, "It's good to see you both pushing each other. This kind of training is what makes us all better."

Lius turns to me with a playful smirk. "So, what do you think of the sparring session? Do I get off the hook for calling you *'daddy'*?"

I laugh, shaking my head. "You're not off the hook just yet, goose. A deal's a deal, and we'll settle that another time. For now, I'm just glad we had a good match."

We all share a laugh, the tension from the match dissipating into a relaxed, friendly atmosphere. The gym, once a battleground, now feels like a place of shared achievement and respect. As we start to gather our things and prepare to head out, Ares, who had been quietly observing from the corner, steps forward. "Looks like you both did well. I'll make sure to include this match in my report for the day."

I raise an eyebrow, teasing, "And what's the report say? That we're both equally awesome?"

Ares grins, "Something like that. Just remember, next time, you might want to go easy on each other." We all headed out of the gym, chatting and laughing about the match. The morning's excitement has set a positive tone for the rest of the day, leaving us all in high spirits.

We arrive back home, and Lius, ever the gentleman, lets me take the first shower. After freshening up and resting in my room for a bit, I came downstairs to find Lius and the others gathered in the living room, also freshly showered. Lius is wearing a shirt that showcases the bruises from our sparring match, and I can't help but feel a pang of guilt seeing them. I glance down at my own bruises, feeling a mix of regret and admiration for the intensity of our match earlier that day.

Lius notices me and grins. "Looks like someone's ready to take on the day. Are you planning on going somewhere?"

I returned with a smile of excitement. "Yeah, I'm meeting a friend for coffee. Would any of you like to join? She's a longtime childhood friend, and I've told her so much about all of you."

The guys exchange glances, contemplating the offer. Lius is the first to speak up. "Sure, I'll tag along. I'm game for meeting your childhood friend. Plus, I could use a good cup of coffee."

Kai nods in agreement. "Count me in. Meeting a friend of yours could be interesting."

Max shrugs nonchalantly. "Sure, I have nothing else to do. Might as well see what this friend of yours is all about."

Ares smirks clearly intrigued. "Yeah, I'll go too. Wouldn't want to miss out on meeting your childhood friend or getting a chance to talk about how you were growing up."

"Okay then, I'm heading there now if you all are ready?" I head to the little table where I sit my purse every time I come home by the front door.

The guys all rise from their seats, ready to head out. Lius says, "Yeah, we're ready. Let's go meet this childhood friend of yours."

~*~

We arrive at the coffee shop, and I'm acutely aware of the attention our group draws. As we walk in, the other patrons' gazes follow us. Lius, oblivious to the staring, scans the room for who *'Angie'* may be. Max remains unfazed to the surroundings, Kai casts a few disapproving looks at the gawkers, and Ares seems to enjoy the attention. I spot Angie in the corner with a table big enough for all of us. "Elara!" she exclaims, clumsily jumping out of the chair she was sitting in and running up to me.

"Oh my gosh... *Angie*! It's so good to see you finally!" I exclaim, wrapping her in a tight embrace. Angie is a vibrant and energetic woman in her late twenties, with an inviting presence that draws people to her. She stands at 5'4", with a slender yet athletic build that reflects a love for outdoor activities and a balanced lifestyle. Her long, chestnut-brown hair falls in loose waves down her back, catching the light with a natural shine. She often wears it down or in a casual ponytail, accentuating her carefree and approachable demeanor.

Her eyes are a warm hazel, flecked with gold, and they sparkle with a blend of curiosity and kindness as she returns the hug. They are expressive, capable of conveying a range of emotions from deep thoughtfulness to spontaneous laughter. Her skin is a light olive tone, giving her a healthy, sun-kissed look even when she's not basking in the Arizona sun.

Angie's style is effortlessly chic, favoring comfortable yet fashionable attire. She often wears well-fitted jeans paired with flowy tops or stylish blouses, accessorized with simple jewelry that compliments her look without overwhelming it. Her fashion sense is casual but polished, reflecting her easy going personality and confidence—the ying to my yang—or however that saying goes. She's the rainbow to my rain cloud, we are vastly different. Her smile is one of her most striking features—bright and genuine, with a warmth that makes others feel at ease. Her laughter is contagious, and she has a knack for making people feel like they've known her for years, even if they've just met.

Angie tightens her arms around me, beaming with happiness. "Oh, my gods, El! It's so good to see you too! It's been so long! How have you been? How's work and life treating you here?"

Angie showed us to a table she had saved for all of us. We move towards it, and all sit down. I chose to sit right next to Angie while the other four filed around us. As we catch up, the guys sit back, observing our reunion with a mix of amusement and curiosity. Angie's eyes widen as she notices the four tall, very large, and handsome men sitting at the table around us—taking in the sight of them.

Angie lowers her voice "Whoa... are these guys your roommates you've told me about...?"

Max, being blunt as ever, interjects with a sarcastic tone, "Or something like that..."

Lius elbows Max, giving him a warning look before smoothly introducing himself. "Hi there, I'm Lius. Nice to meet you... Angie, was it?"

Angie looks at Max with confusion, then at Lius. "Hello! Yes, my name is Angie. Pleasure meeting you, Lius!"

"These guys are my roommates, yes." I say, giving Max a glare from the corner of my eye. I roll them and look back at Angie.

Angie looks at each of the guys, intrigued. "Roommates? Wow, you must have quite the interesting living arrangement..."

"It's not that interesting. We all have our own rooms. Pretty typical roommate situation." I reply.

Max smirks, adding, "Yeah, just a typical living arrangement. Nothing special about it at all..."

I scoff, giving Max a playful glare. "Max..."

Max grins at my reaction. "What? I'm just saying..."

Lius rolls his eyes at Max's behavior but can't suppress a slight smile at the banter that's surfacing. Meanwhile, Kai lets out a soft chuckle, his stern expression momentarily breaking. Ares continues to smirk, enjoying the friendly banter as well.

I sigh as now my closest childhood friend is going to get a front row seat to what I deal with daily. "Yes, Angie... It's just a typical roommate situation. Just four men and one woman is the only unusual thing about it. We all cook and clean, share the chores, etc. So..." I work to change the subject before these four get too rowdy in this small coffee shop. "How are *you*, Angie? How's the family?" I block the attempt from whatever weird thing Max is trying to start here.

Angie seems a bit taken aback by the sudden shift in topic but quickly recovers with a smile. "Oh, I'm doing well, thank you. Family is doing well. My little brother just got into university, so my parents are pretty excited about that."

"That's incredible! WOW... little Ryan is going into university already? Where has the time gone?" I smile widely with a surprised look in my eyes as I think of the last time I saw Angie's little brother, snot nosed and chasing after us whenever I came over.

Angie nods, a nostalgic smile on her face. "I know, right? It feels like just yesterday he was this little toddler running around, causing chaos. And now he's off to college. Time flies way too fast."

"It really does! So, how's life in Arizona? I do miss it sometimes... The dry heat, the smell of the first rain after a drought—the way the dirt smells when the rain first falls... the Javelinas!" I give her a sincere smile as I'm excited to hear about *home*. My home... as ruined as it was for me now. It was still... home.

"Arizona's great! I can't complain. It's as sunny and vibrant as ever. It's still hot as ever..." Angie chuckles.

"Is your life there going well? Have you given... any more thoughts on my offer to move here to Japan with me? We can get our own place right here, in downtown...?"

"Hey!" Lius shouts as the others shift uncomfortably in their seats as they wait for Angie's response. Each silently pleading with her not to move just yet and take me away from them.

Angie looks thoughtful, a hint of contemplation in her eyes. "Well, I've been thinking about it a lot actually... it's a big decision, you know? Moving to a whole new country, leaving everything behind... I just want to make sure it's the right move for *me*, you know?"

"I agree... just know I'll help you if you decide to. I know not everyone can just drop everything and leave like I did." I look down at the coffee I had ordered as my face falls, remembering why I am here in the first place.

Angie nods. She's touched by my offer of support. "Thank you, Elle... I really appreciate that. And yeah, I know it's not an easy move for everyone. But knowing I have someone like you in my corner makes it less intimidating, for sure."

I reach across the table and take her hands into mine. "How are you coping with..." She hesitates before asking me a difficult question. "With Tr-"

"I'm fine... Angie." The words come out sharper than I intended, but I can't bear the thought of digging up those memories. Even after all this time, just hearing Troy's name feels like a stab to the chest. I turn away, hoping to hide the tightening in my throat, the ache that never quite fades. Talking about him only reopens wounds I've worked so hard to close—wounds I'm not ready to face again. Angie saw me at my lowest point after I lost Troy. She never forced me into ever talking about it. Everyone I came in contact with after his death tried getting me to talk about how I felt. But about my *partner's* death... not the death of my love.

Angie looks down at her cup of coffee and nods, acknowledging I don't wish to discuss this subject. Lius clears his throat after an awkward pause in the conversation, reminding us that the four of them are still present. He curled an eyebrow, glancing between Angie and I with a slight smirk. "We're still here, you know..." The others exchange amused glances but remain silent, keeping the sudden silence in the back of their mind for later.

"Oh! Sorry guys! I just haven't seen Angie since I moved here from Arizona." I released Angie's hands and turned to face the guys.

Lius waves off my apology with a dismissive gesture. "It's all good. We understand. Reconnecting with old friends can be pretty emotional."

Max nods silently, still smirking. Kai offers a small, understanding smile, while Ares glances between Angie and me, still taking in the interaction. Angie looks at them apologetically, feeling a bit embarrassed. "Sorry about that. I tend to get a little carried away when I start talking with Elara here. She's just… home, you know? But anyways, I'm so curious to hear about your life here in Japan! You've been here for a little while now, right?"

"It's been a few months." I remind her.

Angie looks genuinely impressed. "That's right! How's Japan treating you? It must have been such a big adjustment to move halfway across the world like that."

"It's actually been smoother than I originally anticipated." I continue.

Angie seems pleasantly surprised. "Really? That's great to hear! I guess I had this image of you struggling to adjust to the language, culture, and everything. But it sounds like you're thriving here."

"Japan is quite accommodating to English speakers. Plus, my roommates here have been a great help!" I looked over all four of them. The guys seem amused by my praise, enjoying the attention.

Lius rubs the back of his neck, flattered by my praise. "Well, we do what we can."

Max crosses his arms across his chest as if he's a peacock showing off its feathers. "Yeah, we're pretty great roommates, aren't we?" I roll my eyes at his dramatic display, but it still brings a smile to my face.

Kai and Ares just nod, both trying to suppress smiles.

We finished our visit with Angie at the coffee shop. I stand with her as we stay in a hug with each other for a few moments longer. Taking in the feeling of home… Oh how I miss her. I break the hug with tears in both of our eyes as we say our goodbyes. My roommates and I departed from her to head back home. As we walk together, the atmosphere is oddly quiet, each of us lost in our thoughts. Lius occasionally sneaks glances at me with a small smile. Max seems contemplative, his eyes drifting to the sky. Kai silently observes our surroundings, ever vigilant, while Ares steals quick, lingering glances my way.

After a few moments of this uncomfortable silence, Lius breaks it, as he often does. "So… that Angie. She seems nice."

"She is…" I smile, a hint of nostalgia in my tone.

Lius nods, curiosity in his voice. "You two seem really close. How long have you known each other?"

"Since we were ten years old. We lived two houses down from each other in Arizona."

Lius raises his eyebrows in surprise. "Wow, that's a long time. You practically grew up together."

"Yeah… I would run and hide at her house when things started with my uncle and all that…" Lius's expression turns more serious. He gives me a sympathetic look, but remains silent, allowing me to continue. "She saved me so many times… hiding me from my dad when my uncle was 'visiting' my dad…" Lius clenches his fists unconsciously, his jaw tight. His expression is a mix of understanding and anger, directed more towards my uncle than me. "My dad would always come to her house and drag me back home whenever my uncle was over… telling me to quit being so disrespectful towards my family." I sigh. "Angie was my peace… I miss her so much. I told her she should move here with me and she's considering it. Her job is a dead-end, and she could get a great job here with her credentials."

Lius nods, his expression softening. "A fresh start in a new country with a better job opportunity. Sounds like a smart move."

"I agree... anyway, she doesn't know about my vigilante work, and I plan on keeping it that way." I look at each of them, pleading they too don't tell her if she moves here. The guys all nod in understanding. "Thank you..." I smile at them with gratitude.

Silence falls between the group again as we continue walking back home. The guys are all lost in their thoughts, but it's a comfortable silence, each of them now aware of a part of my past that I've never shared before. Lius looks like he wants to say something several times, but he just purses his lips and stays quiet, walking closely beside me instead.

Eventually, as we all approach the front door of the house, Lius finally breaks the silence. "Hey, if you ever... need to talk. A-About anything... just know I'm here for you, alright?"

I smile at him and nod: "Thank you, Lius."

Lius returns the smile, his eyes soft as he holds my gaze for a moment longer than necessary. The others watch the exchange, each of them sensing the subtle moment between the two of us. Max raises an eyebrow, a smirk forming on his face. Kai gives Max a warning look, knowing that Max's expression could make Lius very uncomfortable, prompting a smug smirk from Max in response, he's itching to ruin the moment. Finally, as we all step inside the house, Max can't help but tease Lius, his smirk growing wider.

Max does a mock cough as he blurts out. "Whipped."

"And what do you mean by that, Max?" I ask as I cross my arms and glare at him.

Max grins, feigning innocence. "Oh nothing, just saying that Lius here is whipped."

Lius's ears burn red as he glares at Max. "Max, shut it. We're not having this conversation right now."

Max laughs, enjoying Lius's reaction. "Oh yes, we are. You're just mad because you know I'm right. And I'm calling you out in front of her this time"

Lius rolls his eyes. "I'm not whipped. You're completely misreading the situation here."

"Doesn't being *'whipped'* mean he'd have to be in a romantic relationship with me? How could he be whipped then?" I ask, annoyed at Max's jabs at Lius and me.

Max grins wider at my question: "Who's to say he isn't? The way he looks at you, talks about you, always concerned about you... Sounds like a relationship to me... and Lius is whipped right up in it."

I raised an eyebrow at his response. "Wouldn't I have to be aware of such a relationship, Max?"

Max chuckles at my expression "Come on, you can't deny it's true. Lius here is smitten with you princesa. He's just too chicken shit to admit it." He attempts to pinch Lius' cheek.

Lius scoffs and swats Max's hand away, his face still red. "Shut up, Max..." He snarls.

I turn to look at Lius. "Is it true...?"

Lius sputters for a moment, caught off guard by my question. "I... uh..." He shoots a quick glare at Max, silently cursing him in his mind. Max just grins, enjoying the sight of Lius flustered. Kai and Ares remain silent, watching the interaction. Lius finally collects himself enough to stutter out a response: "It's... uh... it's not that simple, okay? I just care about you... a lot." Lius says quietly. He looks away, avoiding eye contact, his flushed face betraying his words. I placed my hand on his forearm.

"I care a lot about you too, Lius… about all four of you…" I look at each of them. "You four are my family now…"

A mixture of emotions flitter across each of the guys' faces as I say this. Lius seems the most touched, his eyes meeting mine again with a softer look. Max looks a bit taken aback, but he quickly covers it up with a smirk. Kai lets out a quiet exhale, his expression a little gentler. Ares… well, his expression is still difficult to read.

Max is the first one to speak, breaking the brief silence with his typical swagger. "Of course you care about us. We're awesome." Lius shoots him a glare but can't help a small smirk from forming.

Kai sighs quietly, a hint of a smile playing on his lips as well. "You know, if you keep feeding his ego like this, his head will become even more insufferable to deal with."

Lius feigns hurt feelings, placing a hand over his heart. "Hey! I have the perfect amount of ego, thank you very much." Max bursts out laughing.

Ares, who's been mostly quiet this whole time, chimes in with a smirk. "Perfectly inflated ego, you mean."

Lius shoots Ares a mock offended look. "Oh, hardy har har. Very funny, Ares…"

Kai rolls his eyes, while Max is still laughing. Ares's smile only grows wider. "I know. I am quite funny. Unlike some people." He glances at Lius, prompting that now famous scoff from Lius.

Max laughs once again. "Hey, don't worry, you'll always be funnier than Lius, Ares. That's not hard to accomplish."

I chuckle and walk out of the room to head upstairs to my room. "I love you guys…"

10

It's a warm summer night tonight. I'm hanging out in my room when I begin to feel hungry and emerge from my solitude to head downstairs to start preparing dinner for everyone. I spent time in my room just hanging out reading in the little nook I've created in my room. The house is eerily quiet, a stark contrast to the earlier commotion. As I look around, I realize the guys aren't home. There's no note on the counter or anything to indicate where they might be. I pick up my phone and text our group chat:

Me: *Where did all of you go?*

Almost immediately, my phone pings, alerting that I've received a reply.

Lius: *We had some stuff to take care of for work. We'll be back soon. Don't wait for us, birdie.*

Me: *Ok, be safe.*

I smile at the new nickname that Lius has seemed to have favored for me recently. I remember the first time he called me that...

~*~

"During one of our intense sparring sessions—the gym echoed with the sound of our movements. Sweat dripped down my forehead, my muscles burned with exertion, but I was determined to give it my all. Lius and I had been sparring for almost an hour, and I was trying out a new aerial attack technique I'd been working on with Tatsuya. I took a deep breath, gathering my energy, and launched myself into the air, executing a series of flips and kicks that felt almost like I was flying each time. My movements were swift and fluid, each one perfectly timed to keep Lius on the defensive.

After a particularly graceful maneuver that ended with me landing lightly on my feet, Lius called for a break. We both took a moment to catch our breath, leaning against the padded walls of the gym.

"Not bad, Ellie," he said, a grin spreading across his face. "You've really got a knack for those aerial maneuvers already."

I smiled back, feeling a sense of pride. "Thanks, Lius. I've been working hard on them."

He nodded, wiping sweat from his brow. "You know, you remind me of a bird when you fight. The way you move through the air, it's like you're gliding through the air. Like an eagle."

I tilted my head, curious. "A bird?"

"Yeah," he said, still smiling. "You're so quick and agile, it's like you're gliding through the air. I think I'll start calling you 'birdie.' It suits you."

I laughed, shaking my head. "Birdie, huh? That's a new one."

Lius chuckled, his eyes twinkling with amusement. "Trust me, it fits. You're like a little bird, soaring through the sky, graceful and unstoppable."

I felt a warm blush rise to my cheeks, but I didn't think it over too much. "Well, if you say so. Just don't expect me to start chirping."

He laughed again, the sound echoing in the gym. "Deal. Just keep on flying though, birdie."

From that day on, the nickname stuck. Every time Lius called me "birdie," it reminded me of that moment in the gym, and the sense of freedom and exhilaration I felt when I was in the air. It became a symbol of my strength and agility, a reminder of how far I'd come in my training. And every time I heard it, I couldn't help but smile a little.

~*~

The phone vibrates once more immediately after I send that message:

Lius: *We will. See you soon, birdie.*

No other messages are sent after that, leaving me alone in the quiet house. I decided to take this opportunity to blast my K-pop music loudly as I start to make myself something to eat. The house fills with the sound of upbeat music, and I lose myself in cooking and singing along to each song. It's relaxing and freeing, not having to worry about disturbing anyone with the volume. I finish preparing my food and sit at the bar counter to eat. The kitchen is quiet again, the only sounds are the hum of the refrigerator and the soft ticking of the clock on the wall.

I take a few moments to sit and eat in silence, the earlier liveliness having faded into a peaceful stillness. As I eat, I decide to pull out my phone and browse social media, keeping half an eye on the door, waiting for the guys to come home. Time seems to pass slowly in their absence. The house feels much emptier without them here, picking on each other. Browsing my social media feed, a news post with a video pops up that catches my eye. It's a breaking story about a recent villainous attack in the city. Curious, I click on it to read further and watch the video. The news report details the attack currently in the heart of Tokyo, describing how a group of criminals have caused chaos in the city. People are getting injured, and buildings are being destroyed. The whole place is in a frenzy. Police and Special Ops Six are on the scene trying to contain the situation and minimize the damage by rogue elementals. As I continue reading, I realize that Special Ops Six units are all present, including my roommates—the Vipers. My heart sinks as I play the live news broadcast. "Vipers…" I whisper.

As I switch to the live news feed, the image of destruction and chaos fills the screen. Fire flickers as buildings burn, smoke billows into the air, and frightened civilians run for cover. Special Ops Six units and police are visible in the midst of the chaos, battling against the elementals that have swarmed the city. My heart sinks as I search for footage of my roommates fighting on the scene. The news reporter's voice carries over the chaotic sounds of the city, detailing the situation with a sense of urgency. But I barely hear them, my mind occupied by the thoughts of my roommates—Lius, Kai, Max, and Ares—battling amongst the rubble and flames. I struggle to hold back a growing feeling of worry. These guys are strong, but against that large of a swarm… the thought of them being injured… or worse… sends a chill down my spine.

In the video, I notice a human man among the rogue elementals assisting in the chaos. I put my fork down and looked closer. There are humans helping the elementals! I stand up and decide I'm going to help. Humans have never worked alongside rogues before now. As I observe the news report closely, the seriousness of this situation sets off alarm bells in my brain. I can't just sit by and watch while my roommates are fighting elementals and even regular humans.

I quickly change into an armor jumpsuit with a hood and mask to conceal my identity. I've been saving it for the day I finally face off with my uncle to make him pay. I usually go out in a cotton jumper when I hunt targets... This suit... was specially made for me in Arizona. The suit is sleek and form-fitting, made of a durable, flexible material that allows for a full range of motion—protecting my body from any flesh penetrating wounds. The hood covers my hair, and the mask conceals my face, leaving only my eyes visible. The suit is designed for both protection and agility, with reinforced padding in critical areas. It's lightweight, and breathable fabric elsewhere.

I ran out the front door, heading toward the chaos, ready to fight. As some time passes—and I've sprinted down a few blocks—I arrive at the scene. I see a man holding tightly onto a woman's wrists. He laughs as he pulls her flush against him. Without a second thought, I darted straight for him, jumping up and sending the bottom of my foot into the side of his head. He releases the woman upon impact and falls hard against a nearby car. I felt the force of the kick reverberate through my leg as he slammed into the car. The man—caught off guard by my sudden attack—looks around in shock. He loses his balance and falls against a nearby car with a loud crash, after he attempts to stand back up. He looks up at me with a mixture of anger and shock, not expecting someone to intervene.

"Are you okay?" I ask the woman. My eyes wide with fury

The woman looks up at me, her eyes wide with fear and uncertainty. She nods shakily, still visibly scared from her encounter with the man. She glances at me, taking in my imposing appearance.

"Can you walk? You need to get away from here now!" I urged her.

The woman nods again, her legs still trembling slightly. With a shaky voice, she responds, "Y-Yes... I... I can walk..." She glances back at the man who's starting to get up from the ground, his eyes narrowing in my direction. I stand between the woman and him, shielding her.

"Go! Run! I'll hold him off!" I say to the woman. I already knew I had redirected his attention off of her.

She looks at me, gratitude and a hint of concern in her eyes. She takes a deep breath, steeling her nerves, before nodding firmly. "O-Okay..."

The woman quickly sprints away, disappearing away from the chaos of the city. The man snarls as he watches her escape. He turns to face me, his expression full of anger and irritation. "You little brat... who the hell do you think you are?!"

"I think I'm about to be your worst nightmare!" I cringe internally and make a mental note that I must come up with more clever lines.

The man scoffs, his expression turning from irritation to disdain. "A nightmare, huh? You're just a kid playing hero! You have no idea who you're dealing with..."

"I'm not a kid..." I say through a snarl, being mistaken for a kid has my blood pumping for this fight. I'm taller than the average female dammit!

The man's expression falters slightly, taken aback by my unexpected assertiveness. He sneers at me, his eyes narrowing. "Even worse... an overconfident adult playing hero... Pathetic."

"Who told you I was playing? I just saved that woman from your slimy, disgusting grasp. Preying on innocent women is what's truly pathetic."

The man glares at me, his expression hardening. "And you think you're some kind of hero to her? Playing the knight in shining armor, coming to the rescue?" He laughs bitterly. "The fact that you're even here in the first place shows how deluded you really are! You're just as delusional as the rest of Special Ops Six, thinking you can make a difference in this world."

I smirk at him. "Fun fact! I'm not SP6!" The taunt hangs in the air between us like a loaded weapon. His eyes narrow, his lips twitching into a scowl. For a moment, he hesitates, thrown off by my confidence, but then his face darkens, frustration flashing across his features.

"You think that matters?" he spits, fists clenching at his sides. His posture shifts, bracing himself for a fight. I can feel the tension building in the space between us, thick like static before a storm. I step into a fighting stance, my eyes locked on him, daring him to make the next move. He glares, but now there's a flicker of doubt. He wasn't expecting resistance. And that doubt? That's what I'm counting on. He looks me over once more, taking in my armor jumpsuit and the mask concealing my face. A smirk then appears on his face. "You're just a nobody. A little insect who thinks they can play hero…"

"Again, who said I'm playing?" The last few words are dripping with venom as my face hardens.

The man scoffs, his smirk fading into irritation. "More bravado. You think you can actually fight me?" He moves closer, a menacing glint in his eyes. "I may not have any special elemental abilities, but I'm still powerful in my own right. And I sure as hell don't mind making a point to some pathetic worm who thinks they're tough and wants to play *hero*!"

"Alright then... let's dance, Fred." His name probably isn't Fred, but it feels like it fits.

He grins menacingly, enjoying the way I challenge him.

"With pleasure..." He lunges at me, faster than I anticipated, and swings a punch aimed square at my jaw. With all the years of training I've endured, I dodged the hit. The man's punch misses, his eyes widening in surprise as I dodge his attack. He growls in irritation and quickly adjusts his stance, preparing for another strike. I get back into my defensive position, ready for his next move. The man seethes, his eyes narrowing as he assesses my stance. He circles me, trying to find an opening. Then, without warning, he launches another attack, a swift kick aimed at my leg. I jump straight up to dodge it.

His kick misses once more, and his irritation visibly grows. He grunts, clearly not used to being dodged like this. Sensing my agility, he switches tactics and decides to throw a nearby trash can at me. I throw my hands up in an "X" formation in front of my head and block the trash can, pushing my arms out with all my strength, sending it back at him. The man is caught off guard as I am able to block the can and push it back toward him. It slams into his chest, causing him to stumble backward a few steps. He grunts in pain, his arrogance momentarily replaced by surprise. He glares at me, clearly not happy with my quick reflexes and countering ability.

"Damn you... How are you so fast?!" He composes himself, his expression regaining that smug look. "You can't dodge everything I throw at you..." Without giving me a chance to regroup, he throws several more items of rubble and trash cans at me in quick succession, attempting to overwhelm me with the barrage of projectiles. I jump straight up and land on every single one of the projectiles thrown at me, while they're in the air, running towards him—closing the distance between us. The man looks stunned as I jump on top of the trash cans, using them as aerial stepping stones to charge toward him. His surprise quickly turns to annoyance, and he hurriedly backpedals in an attempt to keep the distance between us. "What the-? How the hell are you doing that?!" He shouts.

I land in front of him. "Training."

The man is on the defensive now, his confidence shaken. I can see his attempt to regain his composure, straightening up and glaring at me. "Training, huh? Who the hell trained you? A circus clown?!"

I chuckle, and we begin our hand-to-hand combat as I swing a hooked punch towards his jaw. He dodges and throws a counter punch. I bob and weave around his attempted hits, landing my own strikes into his ribs several times. The man is visibly frustrated by my constant dodging and counterattacks. He is slowly wearing down. "Damn you! Stop dodging and let me hit you! Sit still!"

"Now why would I do that?" I sneer through a smug grin.

The man growls in frustration, his attacks becoming more frantic and desperate as my counterattacks wear him down further. "Because I'll... I'll knock some sense into you if you'd just let me land a single hit, you little bastard!"

I dodge another one of his blows. I crouch down, shooting my foot up into his chin with all the force I can muster, feeling the satisfying impact as he stumbles back and crashes hard against the pavement. I pressed my blade to his throat, my fingers tightening on the handle. It would be so easy. So easy to end his miserable existence. But... was I any better than him if I did? *Dammit.* I pulled the blade back, throwing his head down instead.

"Stop!" I hear a voice from behind me. My focus is torn from the man on the ground as I hear a voice from behind me. My heart was racing, but I couldn't afford to be distracted. I turn my head around to see a slender figure standing in the shadows, their voice firm and authoritative. It's a young woman, no older than 18, with shoulder length deep red hair, sharp features, and a calculating expression in her gray eyes. She looks at me with a disapproving scowl, her hand gesturing for me to lower my blade. She appears to be a part of SP6, given her outfit. I sheath my blade back into my thigh holster and throw the man's head back down to the ground.

"Who are you...?" I asked her with a scowl as she had just interrupted my final step when dealing with this particular low life of a human.

The young woman steps out of the shadows, her eyes scrutinizing me intently. She studies me for a moment, her expression unreadable: "My name is Sara. I'm an SP6 Viper Trainee... And who are you...?" She looks down at the man on the ground, her scowl deepens mixed with suspicion of me. "You were about to kill him... weren't you?"

"Yes." I hiss through gritted teeth. She's interfering with my goal for the night.

Her expression hardens even further, a flash of anger crossing her face. "So... he's a criminal... but you were about to kill him, just like that?" She folds her arms, staring me down almost as if she's searching for something in my eyes... a sign of recognition if possible.

"Yes." I hold her gaze, unwavering.

Sara doesn't falter, her eyes narrowing slightly. "You don't hesitate to play judge, jury and executioner, do you? Killing without a second thought..."

"Only when it comes to confirmed creeps, Sara..." My jaw clenched with annoyance.

She continues to scrutinize me, her expression now stoic. "Confirmed, huh? So, you've made a habit of this?" She glances back down at the unconscious man before looking back at me. "How many more have you killed, exactly...?"

I pause briefly, resistant to answer this particular question. "Three... all three I caught in the act... with children..."

Sara's expression softens just a fraction at my response, a hint of understanding in her eyes. She holds my gaze for a moment before letting out a sigh. "Three..." She steps closer to me, her gaze intensifying: "And do you not feel the slightest bit of remorse for taking those lives?"

"All the time." My eyes show how haunted I've been. The eyes of those three people flash through my mind. I never enjoyed killing. Not even those creeps... but with them, it was necessary. I justified this to myself every time I remembered or had a nightmare about them.

"Hey! Sara!" Another voice calls out who seems to be familiar with her.

Sara's head snaps towards the source of the voice, a hint of recognition lighting up her eyes to confirm what I suspected. "Ren...?"

I hold my gaze on Sara as this new arrival, *Ren*, walks up.

Sara's attention shifts to him momentarily as he approaches, but her eyes soon return to me, her expression still wary. Ren then appears beside her, taking in the scene before him with a concerned expression. "Sara... what's going on here?"

Sara turns to him, her expression serious: "I was just having a conversation with our mysterious friend here." She motions towards me, gesturing for Ren to look at me. As he does, his eyes roam over my armored jumpsuit and masked face. His expression remains neutral as he looks me over, his eyes taking in my concealed appearance.

"Mysterious, huh...?" Ren looks back at Sara, raising an eyebrow. "Do you know who this is?"

Sara shakes her head, her expression forming with the annoyance she feels with her own reply. "No. I have a nagging feeling like I should know who this is, but I'm not sure yet. I was just about to get answers out of her when you arrived."

"I am standing right here guys..." I scoff as I cross my arms across my chest and lean onto one leg.

Sara turned back to me. "And we're aware of that. That doesn't change the fact that I caught you in the act of a crime." Ren tilts his head in question, his gaze flicking over me again.

I glance towards the chaos, making sure none of my Viper roommates appear. "Ask your questions and make them quick... because there's a battle going on, in case you've forgotten."

Sara and Ren exchanged a quick look to each other, their expressions filled with curiosity and a hint of caution. "Alright. First, who are you?" Sara fires the first question with her eyes boring into mine.

"I'm no one you know" I reply

Sara's eyes raise. "Why don't you let us decide that...?"

Ren's eyes widened: "Wait... could you be...?"

"You and I have never met Ren." I snap, to throw him off. I began to fear that he may actually know who I am through my roommates... Maybe one of them has mentioned me around the station...

Ren looks conflicted, as if he wants to say something but holds back. "... but there's a mutual friend between us isn't there...?"

"That's a very broad statement..." I begin to tap my foot with impatience.

Sara glances between Ren and I, her curiosity growing.

Ren snaps. "Answer yes or no"

"Yes" I say quietly... *dammit*

Sara's expression shows a hint of surprise. "Who are they?"

"Now if I told you that you'd figure it out for certain. And they don't know I'm out here..." I gesture to my uniform. "I want to keep it that way."

Sara looks intrigued yet frustrated at my refusal to give a straight answer. Ren, meanwhile, seems deep in thought, trying to piece things together. "And they don't know about..." She gestures to all of me. "*this*?"

"No. And I would like to keep it that way. Now there's some criminals I need to deal with if you don't mind..." I look over towards the chaos again.

Sara hesitates, her mind appears to be torn between continuing to interrogate me and letting up to allow me to go perform my duties and they can also get back to theirs. Ren, sensing her internal conflict, steps forward and glances at Sara, his expression calm before turning to me. "You mentioned criminals... as in humans?"

"There are humans here helping the elementals fight against SP6, and to overpower the innocent humans... I'm here to protect and defend the innocent humans..." I say as I drop my hands and straighten my stance, looking towards the chaos, anxious to get out there. I dart my gaze back to the two of them.

Sara's eyes widened in shock, her expression turning dark. "Humans... are *helping* the rogues?"

Ren looks equally surprised, his eyes darting between the unconscious man on the ground and me.

"Yes… and *that* man over there was one of them…" I point at the man on the ground. "He was assaulting a woman when I arrived on scene."

Sara and Ren exchange a grim look, the gravity of the situation sinking in. Sara's face hardens with determination, while Ren's eyes narrow as he processes the information. They both seem to understand the complexity of the situation and the urgency to act quickly.

Sara takes a step closer to me, her tone softer but still firm. "I see... You're here to protect the humans, just like us. But we need to work together, not against each other."

Ren nods in agreement. "We can't afford to be divided, not with the elementals and their human allies causing this much chaos."

I keep my stance defensive but relax my shoulders a little, sensing their willingness to cooperate. "Fine. But we need to move fast. There are more of them out there, and they won't stop until they get what they want."

Sara nods, her expression resolute. "Agreed. Let's go. We need to find and stop them before more innocent people get hurt."

Ren glances at me, his gaze now piercing through me. "We'll trust you for now. But know this: if you cross us or endanger anyone, you'll have to answer for it."

"I wouldn't expect anything less." I reply, my voice steady.

The three of us move out, ready to face the chaos and protect the city together. As we run toward the heart of the conflict, I can't help but feel a sense of unease. Working with SP6 is not something I planned, but for now, it seems like the best course of action. We weave through the city streets, the sounds of battle growing louder as we approach. The air is filled with smoke and the acrid smell of burning debris. Civilians are huddled in corners, trying to stay out of harm's way, their faces etched with fear and desperation. We reach a particularly chaotic scene where several rogues and their human allies are wreaking havoc. Sara signals for us to split up, each of us taking a different approach to flank the enemies.

I move swiftly, my senses on high alert as I navigate the battlefield. Spotting a group of humans assisting a rogue. I rush forward—taking them by surprise. They barely have time to react as I engage them in combat, my training kicking in. The rogues are formidable, not like anything I've faced before. With precise strikes and agile movements, I'm able to dodge their earth, wind and fire attacks, buying time for Sara and Ren to handle their targets. As the fight progresses, I notice Sara and Ren fighting with impressive skill and coordination, their own elemental powers astounding. They work seamlessly together, a testament to their training and experience with SP6. For a moment, I feel a pang of envy at their teamwork, but quickly push it aside—focusing on the task at hand.

We fight with everything we have, slowly but surely turning the tide of the battle to our favor. The rogue elementals and their human allies begin to falter under our relentless assault. I catch glimpses of civilians being led to safety by other SP6 members, their faces filled with gratitude and relief. After what feels like an eternity, the last of the enemies are subdued. The city falls into an uneasy silence, the aftermath of the battle hanging heavy in the air.

Sara, Ren, and I regrouped, breathing heavily but victorious. We share a brief nod of acknowledgment, the tension between us momentarily easing. For now, we've managed to protect the city and its people. Sara looks at me, her expression thoughtful. "You fought well. Thanks for having our backs. Maybe we can trust you after all."

I nod, hiding the flicker of surprise at her praise. "Understood. For now, let's make sure the city is safe, and the people are taken care of."

Ren adds, "Just remember, we're all on the same side. Let's keep it that way."

As we begin the process of helping the injured and assessing the damage, I can't help but wonder what the future holds. For now, though, I'm content with having made a difference, even if it means working with SP6 a little—alongside Sara and Ren, that is. The night is far from over, but for the first time in a while, I feel a glimmer of hope. Together, we might just be able to protect this city and the people we care about. I maneuver through the field while my eyes dart around so that I may avoid my roommates... I doubt they are still floating around to help with the aftermath. The battle may be over, but the night is far from quiet. Sara, Ren, and I move through the city, our presence a shadowy vigil over the recovering populace. Emergency lights flash in the distance, sirens wail, and the scent of smoke lingers in the air as rubble continues to burn. The streets are littered with debris and the wounded. The people of this city are resilient, they will come back from this.

We work efficiently, checking for stragglers and hidden threats. Sara and Ren's familiarity with the city's layout and its people make them invaluable guides. We assist wherever we can, from evacuating trapped civilians to providing first aid to the injured. I move with caution to avoid being spotted, ducking behind debris and around corners to hide in the shadows if anyone approaches us. Around midnight, we find a group of rogues attempting to regroup near a factory. Sara signals for silence and we approach with caution. The elementals are distracted, discussing their next move, unaware of our presence. With a silent nod, we spring into action.

Sara takes out the leader with a swift, precise strike of her lightning power. Ren engages two more, his movements fluid and deadly as he takes control of the earth's core around us, bringing forward the force of his water power. I focus on the remaining rogues, my blade a blur as I cut through their defenses. Within moments, the threat is neutralized. We tie up the unconscious elementals and leave them for SP6 reinforcements to handle.

As the hours pass, we encounter more small groups of enemies, but each time we are quicker and more decisive. The elementals are clearly disorganized, their plans falling apart under the relentless pressure. By the early hours of the morning, the city is mostly secure.

Sara, Ren, and I find a brief moment of respite on a rooftop overlooking the city. The first light of dawn is just starting to creep over the horizon, casting a soft glow over the skyline.

Sara breaks the silence, her voice thoughtful. "Tonight was... unexpected. I didn't think we'd be working with an unknown ally." Her attention moved towards me.

Ren nods, looking at me with a mixture of respect and curiosity. "You proved yourself out there. But I still want to know who you are and why you're doing this."

I lean against the railing, my gaze distant. "I'm here because I care about this city and its people. That's all you need to know for now."

Sara sighs but doesn't press further. "Fair enough. But if you ever decide to join us officially, we'd welcome someone with your skills."

I give a small nod, appreciating the offer but unsure if it's the right path for me. "I'll think about it." I hesitate. They could help, but… no. My secret is mine to keep, for now.

As we prepare to leave, Sara and Ren turn to head back to their base. I watch them go, a sense of mutual respect having formed between us during the night's battles. I slip through the city's streets, careful to avoid being seen by my roommates. They have no idea I was out here tonight, and I intend to keep it that way. When I finally reached our home, I climbed up to my room and quietly let myself in.

The house is quiet, my roommates still have not returned it sounds like. I change out of my combat gear and into my usual clothes, hiding my weapons and armor in a secret compartment I've built in my closet. As I lay down in my bed, exhaustion finally takes over. I close my eyes, replaying the events of the night in my mind. Despite the chaos and danger, I'm satisfied in knowing I made a difference tonight—more than I normally do with hunting targets. The adrenaline I feel when fighting an enemy with powers is intoxicating. I want to feel this rush again. The city is a little safer, and for now, that's enough for me.

This is just another beginning. The rogue elementals won't give up easily, and there will be more battles to come. I can feel in my gut that there's more than meets the eye, the increase in attacks from large groups of rogues—the increase in rogues. As I drift off to sleep, I resolve to be ready for whatever comes next, protecting this city and my friends from the shadows, lurking around the corners.

11

I had been running alongside Sara and Ren every time there was a call to battle with SP6 for the following months. I purchased a burner phone for them to text me anytime there's an attack— keeping my identity a secret from them a little longer. The three of us had developed a seamless rhythm, our movements synchronized through countless skirmishes. We became an unofficial trio, fighting shoulder to shoulder under the radar of SP6, our trust in each other's abilities growing with each rogue confrontation. I had to be cautious to ensure my roommates never caught wind of my nightly escapades, often slipping out undetected and returning home before dawn, whether the battle was over or not, my heart racing with the thrill and danger of each encounter. Sara and Ren became used to my disappearance each time the sky started to brighten with the rise of the sun.

There were times I went into battle alone, the adrenaline coursing through my veins as I faced the enemy without my comrades. On those nights, I pushed myself to the limit, only focusing on enemies without any elemental powers. My body a blur of motion as I dodged and struck, mind laser-focused on the task at hand. It was during these solitary missions that I felt most alive, the world around me a cacophony of sound and chaos, my purpose clear and unwavering. Yet, I always had to maintain the facade of normalcy at home. I would pretend to be tired, claiming the day's events had worn me out, and retreat to my room, feigning exhaustion. I had let Z know that I will hunt targets mainly through the day. If there was one, I could only hunt in the night, I would capture the target then head towards the larger battle with Sara and Ren. My roommates seemed to be none the wiser, accepting my excuses without question, their trust in me coming through as unwavering. It made the guilt of hiding this from them gnaw at me from within.

Tonight was a particularly rough night. The city was under siege, the rogues more ferocious and relentless than ever before, the humans just as vicious. Flames licked the sides of buildings, and the air was thick with smoke and the scent of burning debris. The attacks have been so frequent I felt as if we were in a war zone–no rest for anyone. We have to put a stop to this. Civilians screamed and ran for cover as we battled to protect them, each move calculated and precise from everyone present. Sara's sharp commands cut through the chaos, guiding us as we fought to push back the tide of destruction. Ren was a whirlwind of strength and precision, his every strike purposeful and deadly.

Despite our best efforts, the enemy was overwhelming. For every rogue elemental we defeated, it seemed two more took its place. I found myself separated from Sara and Ren, my back against a crumbling wall as I faced down a particularly vicious elemental after tying up its human companions to be apprehended. Its eyes burning with an otherworldly fire, its movements a blur as it lunged at me. I dodged to the side, my blade slicing through the air, it was faster than I anticipated. Its claws raked across my side, and I gasped in pain. The searing sensation exploded in my ribs as I gasped for breath. I stumbled but regained my footing, determined not to let the pain slow me down.

The fight continued, each movement a battle against the burning agony in my side. I pushed the pain aside, ignoring it as if it weren't there. I managed to land a series of blows, my blade finding its mark as the elemental screeched in fury. With a final, desperate strike, I brought it down, its body disintegrating into embers of ash at my feet. I stood there, panting, my vision swimming as the pain threatened to overwhelm me. Blood oozed from the gashes on my side, soaking through the fabric of my armor suit, but I couldn't afford to stop. Not yet. Thank the gods I chose crimson and black as my jumpsuit's colors to hide when I bleed. It was an idea I got from one of my favorite movies. I placed a hand to my side in an attempt to stop the bleeding from continuing.

Rejoining Sara and Ren, I saw their worried glances, their eyes lingering on my hand where they could see the blood shining in the fire light. They asked if I was okay. Once I convinced them I was, we fought on, our movements slower from exhaustion but no less determined. By the time the battle ended, we were all battered and bruised—but alive. The city was a smoldering ruin around us. We had managed to save countless lives. As we made our way back to the rendezvous point on a nearby roof, every step sent a jolt of pain through my body as the adrenaline from fighting for my life wore off. I gritted my teeth, forcing myself to move, my mind already concocting the excuse I would give my roommates–how I would hide this.

When we finally reached the safe location, I could barely stand, pale from the blood loss. Sara and Ren offered their support, their concern evident in their eyes, but I waved them off, determined to maintain my independence. "I'll be fine," I said, my voice hoarse with exhaustion. "Just need some rest. It's a flesh wound." I lied.

They nodded, though I could see the doubt in their expressions. "Take care of yourself, Lady Red." Sara said, using the name her and Ren had been calling me. It had become a term of endearment among us, a reminder of the bond we shared on the field. The corner of my mouth lifts at the name, successfully keeping my identity concealed from them—for now that is.

I nodded and made my way home, every step a battle against the pain. When I finally slipped through the door, the house was dark and quiet. I crept to my room, grateful for the cover of night, and collapsed onto my bed. My body screamed in protest as I removed my jumpsuit, the wounds throbbing with every heartbeat. I bit back a cry as I cleaned and bandaged myself up, not wanting to alert my roommates to my condition, in case they happened to be home already. I don't recall seeing them out in the living room when I crept by the windows. I bit on the arm of my jumpsuit to muffle my grunts in pain.

As I applied each bandage, my mind drifted back to the battle, the faces of the people we had saved, and the determination in Sara and Ren's eyes. We had fought hard, and we would continue to fight, no matter the cost. For now, I needed rest. I closed my eyes, willing the pain to fade, knowing that tomorrow would bring another battle, another challenge. I was ready. I was *always* ready.

~*~

The next night was heavy with the aftermath of battle, the air thick with the acrid scent of smoke and the distant wails of sirens.

Tonight, my roommates had been on the front lines, and the battle had been more brutal than any before. The enemy was relentless, their attacks fiercer than the nights prior, their numbers seemingly endless. We fought with everything we had, pushing back with sheer determination and grit. Sara, Ren, and I moved as one, our coordination honed through months of fighting together. But the rogues were relentless, and in the chaos, I sustained several more severe injuries. My bandages over the gashes on my side loosening over the night's activities. Being only human definitely has its downfalls when in battle. Sara had offered to use her lightning power to cauterize my wound, but I refused. It would mean she would see the tattoo on my side just under it, an identifiable mark if she were to look further into it.

My side throbbed with the deep gashes from the previous elemental's claws, the blood seeping through my uniform despite my makeshift attempts to keep it bandaged. I fought through the pain, my movements slowing, my vision blurring. The adrenaline that had kept me going began to fade, leaving me acutely aware of every injury, every bruise, and every drop of blood I had lost. When the battle finally ended, I could barely stand. Sara and Ren gave me concerned looks, their faces mirroring the exhaustion and worry I felt. "You need to get that looked at," Ren said, his voice firm but laced with worry.

"Why did you come out here tonight, Lady Red?" Sara runs to my side and inspects my injuries.

"I'll be fine," I lied, as I waved her off. My voice is barely more than a whisper. I couldn't let them see how bad it really was. I needed to maintain the facade, to protect my secret. "I just need to get home." They exchanged a glance but didn't press the issue. We parted ways, each of us heading back to our respective safe houses. The run home was agonizing, every step sending jolts of pain through my body that I ignored, gritting my teeth at the jolts of pain. By the time I reached the door, I was barely holding on, my vision darkening at the edges. I fumbled with the key, my hands shaking, and finally managed to open the door. The house was quiet, my roommates likely still out or asleep. I slipped inside, hoping to make it to my room without waking anyone. I chose to use the front door instead of climbing up to my window, to help ease the pain in my body. But as I stumbled down the hallway towards the stairway, the pain became too much. I collapsed against the wall, my breathing ragged, my vision swimming as I grunt upon impact with the wall.

"Elara?" a voice called from the living room. I turned my head, seeing Max standing there, his expression shifting from confusion to alarm. "What the hell happened to you?!"

Before I could answer, the rest of my roommates appeared from their spots in the living room, their faces etched with concern and shock at my appearance in the armor jumpsuit. Lius rushed to my side, dropping to one knee. His hands hovering over my wound, his eyes wide with panic as he looked up into my eyes under my hood and mask. He quickly stands and removes them to see my face clearer. "We need to get you to a hospital," he said urgently. I see his restraint in yelling at me and lecturing.

"No," I gasped, shaking my head. "No hospital."

"You're seriously hurt! This is no time for your stubbornness!" Lius protested.

"I can't," I insisted, my voice weak. "They can't know... what I've been doing. I'll be found out."

Kai knelt down on my other side, his eyes filled with fear. "Elara, what are you talking about? What have you been doing?!"

I took a shuddering breath, knowing I couldn't keep it a secret any longer, cursing myself internally at my mistake in taking the front door this time just for a bit of comfort. "I've been fighting... with you all and the SP6," I admitted, my voice barely audible. "I've been helping... against the rogue elementals you guys have been fighting lately." I braced myself, fearing their reaction, but I had no choice. They needed to know the truth. I knew I needed help with this injury that just wouldn't quit.

The room fell silent, my roommates staring at me in disbelief. "You... you've been fighting *with* us out there?" Max repeated, his voice incredulous.

I nodded, wincing as a fresh wave of pain washed over me. "I couldn't just stand by and do nothing," I said, my voice strained. "I had to help."

"Why didn't you tell us?!" Kai asked, sounding more like a command than a question, his voice breaking.

"I didn't want to put you in danger... by distracting you," I said, my eyes meeting his. "I didn't want you to worry... By... being distracted by my presence."

"You should have told us!" Lius shouts, his voice catching in his throat. A mixture of anger and concern. "We could have helped you." His fists clenched at his sides, knuckles white, as though he was holding back more than just his words.

"I'm sorry," I whispered, my vision growing darker. "I didn't want you to get hurt by... losing focus out there." I said, my voice barely more than a whisper. Silence hung in the air, thick with disbelief. Before I could say anything more, the world tilted, and everything went black.

~*~

When I came to, I was lying in my bed, my wounds cleaned and bandaged, my jumpsuit removed. My roommates were gathered around, their faces a mixture of relief and worry. "You're awake," Max said, his voice soft, as he gently brushed a stray hair out of my face.

I nodded weakly, my throat dry. "Thank you," I whispered.

"You scared the hell out of us!" Lius shouts, his voice shaking. "But… you're going to be okay. We called in a favor with a doctor who works with SP6. You're safe. They promised to keep your identity a secret."

"Yea, because Kai threatened to ruin them if they told anyone." Max chuckled out.

Tears filled my eyes as I looked at my roommates, their concern and care overwhelming me. "I'm sorry I didn't tell you," I said, my voice breaking. "I just wanted to keep you focused."

"We're a team, Ellie." Kai said, taking my hand on the other side of my bed. "You scared us. It's not just about the missions, we care about you. We're here for you, no matter what. Don't ever forget that."

I nodded, the weight of my secret finally lifted. I knew the road ahead would be even more difficult with them knowing. As I lay in bed, and my wounds tended to, my roommates' concern carried its weight on me.

Kai's voice cut through the silence, his tone a mix of curiosity and disbelief. "So… you're the mystery *'Lady Red'* that Sara and Ren have been telling us about…?" Kai's eyes were sharp, studying me with a look of disbelief and intrigue.

I sighed, nodding slightly. I sit up to talk with them more, the movement sending a twinge of pain through my side causing me to wince. "Yes. I'm the one they've been working with."

Max's fists clenched as he paced. He looked at me with a mix of frustration and concern. "I don't know whether to be impressed or furious, Elara. You've been fighting alongside Sara and Ren all this time, and you didn't think to mention it? We're supposed to have each other's backs. You could've gotten yourself killed!" His voice booming against the walls of my room.

Lius, sitting on the edge of my bed, his face pale with worry, chimed in. "Why didn't you tell us? We could've helped, or at least we could've known what you were putting yourself through."

I took a deep breath, wincing slightly from the pain. "I didn't want to endanger any of you. The less you knew, the safer you'd be."

Kai raised an eyebrow, his expression skeptical. "So, what exactly have you been doing? Fighting against rogues? What. Did you get bored with just hunting targets? What's the story here?"

I looked at Kai, meeting his gaze steadily. "Yes, I've been fighting rogue elementals *and* humans. They've been causing more havoc, and I couldn't just stand by. I started working with Sara and Ren to stop them and protect the innocent people caught in the crossfire. I didn't want to drag your focus from your own missions to worry about what I was doing. I have a great partnership with Sara and Ren… They are incredible agents by the way. You should be proud of your trainees."

Ares, who had been quietly observing from my bedroom's doorway, spoke up. "You should have trusted us, Elara. Keeping secrets like this—especially when it puts you in danger—wasn't fair to any of us."

I nodded, feeling the weight of his words. "I understand that. I thought I was protecting you by keeping this from all of you." I look down at my bandages. "I just didn't want you guys to be in danger from being distracted by me…"

Max ran a hand through his hair, frustration evident in his voice. "We're not just roommates, Elara. We're a family. We should be allowed to handle whatever you're dealing with, *with* you."

I met his gaze, my eyes filled with remorse as he called me by my name. He only does that when he's truly unhappy with me. "I know, and I'm sorry. I was trying to keep you safe and focused, but I see that my actions only caused more worry for you all, which I was trying to avoid."

Kai leaned back, his expression thoughtful. "So, what happens now? Do you keep fighting, or are you done with this vigilante stuff?"

I looked around at my friends, their concern and support clear in their faces. "I don't know what the future holds, but I understand I need to be more open with you all moving forward. If I'm going to continue fighting, I need your support and understanding. I know for certain that I will still hunt targets. That much hasn't stopped and won't stop."

Max nodded, his eyes tinged with determination and disappointment. "We'll support you, Elara. But you need to be careful. We don't want to lose you. Look at the state you're in... How old is that wound?!" He points to the large gashes covered with gauze on my side from a rogue elemental a few nights ago that seemed to be having trouble healing.

I look down at the bandages that cover the injury. "I got it a few nights ago..." I admitted quietly, the memory of the fight flashing in my mind. The cut hadn't healed as quickly as I'd hoped, and now it served as a constant reminder of how close I'd come to being killed. I felt a deep sense of guilt and gratitude as I looked at each of them. Their support, despite my secrets and mistakes, meant the world to me. "I promise to be more honest from now on. I couldn't have asked for better friends." I said softly.

Kai's expression softened, a small smile appearing. "Just make sure to stay out of trouble, okay? And if you need help–tell us."

I nodded, feeling hopeful and determined. With these four in my corner, I knew that the challenges ahead, I would no longer face them on my own. I fell back asleep after a while of being questioned and lectured by them, about how reckless I was.

~*~

After a week of bedrest, I finally heal and am well enough to get back out there. With my roommates unaware once again. I keep a low profile each time and don't go out as much, so I don't raise suspicions. Ever since my injuries they've been even more watchful of my every move.

The days following my roommates finding out what I've been up to, were a whirlwind of adjustments. My roommates were now more vigilant than ever keeping an eye on me. Their scrutiny intensified anytime I had even a paper cut or bumped my elbow on the counter. Every move I made seemed to be under a magnifying glass. They kept asking questions every time I went out of the house, their concern becoming a tad too much, but their frustration with my former secrecy remained in their eyes whenever I would tell them I'm going out. I knew I had to tread carefully, balancing my responsibilities as a friend with my need to protect the city. I was well aware that at least *one* of them was following me wherever I went—the gym for training, the yoga studio and even the coffee shop when I just needed a break from them.

To manage this delicate balance, I devised a few strategies to keep my double life under wraps. Creating diversions became essential. I started taking up new hobbies—long evening walks, late-night yoga sessions, and occasional visits to local events, all along with my regular training sessions with Sensei Tatsuya. These activities provided me with legitimate excuses for my absences from the house and helped me blend into my normal routine. Whenever I needed to slip away for a night patrol, I'd use these hobbies as a cover, leaving detailed notes about my plans to ensure no one suspected anything.

I also developed a more structured routine. By setting a consistent schedule, I was able to get the four men to predict when I'd be at home and when I'd be out. This predictability allowed me to manage my time more effectively, making it easier to explain any unusual behavior as part of my *'normal'* life. I made sure to stick to this routine as closely as possible, so any deviations wouldn't raise red flags. Technology became my ally in maintaining my secrecy. I set up fake social media posts to create the illusion of my presence elsewhere, and I still used a burner phone for communication with Sara and Ren, who I've made promised they wouldn't discuss my involvement each night with them letting them know a little about how my family suspected something was up. These measures ensured that my real activities remained hidden, even when I was in constant touch with my allies.

I also made it a point to strengthen my alliances outside of my immediate circle. Sara and Ren, with their experience and understanding, each became crucial in my operations. They helped me navigate difficult situations and provided the support I needed to carry out my vigilante duties effectively. Their assistance also gave me a buffer to manage my activities discreetly and would distract my roommates if they were to get a little too close to us while fighting.

To enhance my methods of concealment, I upgraded my armor and took extra care to hide any new injuries I sustained. The new gear was designed to be less conspicuous and more effective in protecting me during confrontations with elemental attacks. I also came up with new ways to mask my injuries, using makeup and strategic clothing choices to keep my roommates from noticing anything out of the ordinary. Gradual trust-building became another critical strategy. I knew that if I wanted to maintain my cover, I needed to earn their trust again, even though I was already breaking the promise I made them. I began being more open about my daily activities, sharing details about my routine and showing increased commitment to their concerns of my safety. My efforts were aimed at demonstrating that, despite my occasional absences, my focus remained on our shared well-being. There were some nights when I would refrain from leaving the house and just sit in the living room if one or more of them was home.

Finally, I kept a close eye on my roommates as well, carefully monitoring their reactions and any signs of suspicion. Their heightened vigilance meant I had to be even more cautious and adapt my strategies as needed. If I sensed that they were becoming more wary, I would ramp up my tactics to divert their attention, ensuring that my vigilante activities remained hidden.

Despite the challenges, I remained determined. The balance between my two worlds was delicate, but with careful planning and strategic maneuvering, I managed to keep my double life intact. My commitment to protecting the city remained unwavering, and with each successful mission, I felt a renewed sense of purpose and hope.

As I continued my work with Z Group, the strain of juggling my dual life became increasingly evident. Max, who shadowed me for extra backup on hunts, was proving to be a valuable asset. His presence provided the reinforcement I needed during particularly challenging missions, but it also brought its own set of complications.

Each night after the battles, I found myself struggling to hide the injuries I sustained. The cuts and bruises from skirmishes with elemental rogues were becoming harder to conceal without the ability to heal them on my own. Max's perceptiveness only added to my growing anxiety. I could sense that he was beginning to question my increasingly erratic behavior during hunts.

During our downtime between missions, I took extra precautions to manage my wounds. I became adept at using first aid techniques to minimize the visibility of injuries and employed a combination of makeup and strategic clothing choices to mask any remaining signs. Despite my best efforts, there were times when I couldn't avoid Max's scrutinizing gaze.

His growing suspicion was becoming a heavy tension in our interactions with one another. He would often linger a bit longer than necessary when assisting me, his eyes probing my every move. His questions became more pointed, and his attempts to catch me off guard were subtle but persistent. I knew that if I didn't address this issue, my secret might be exposed. Not to him... I couldn't let him, of all people, find out I've been continuing on missions with Sara and Ren, when I told them I wouldn't without telling them. My desire to keep them focused and safe was stronger than the guilt I felt in my heart.

To counteract Max's suspicions, I began to adopt a more defensive posture. Whenever he asked about my injuries or questioned my whereabouts, I would deflect with plausible explanations or shift the focus to our shared mission. I carefully crafted stories about minor accidents or harmless mishaps that could explain the bruises or cuts.

Additionally, I used misdirection to keep Max's attention away from my nighttime extracurriculars. I fabricated stories about minor skirmishes or encounters with minor criminals that could be the source of my injuries when he wasn't around me. I even said that most of the bruises happened during training with Tatsuya. By steering the conversation towards less significant matters, I hoped to redirect his focus and alleviate his suspicions.

In our moments of downtime, I made a concerted effort to maintain a friendly but guarded demeanor. I continued to engage with Max and the rest of the roomies in a way that reinforced my commitment to our shared goals. By building rapport and demonstrating reliability, I aimed to keep Max's attention on my contributions to the team rather than my personal secrets.

Despite my efforts, I remained cautious. The tension between us was a constant reminder of the fragile balance I had to maintain. Every encounter with Max was a potential risk, and I needed to be more vigilant than ever to protect my double decker missions. The challenges were daunting, but I remained determined. My commitment to both protecting the city and maintaining my cover was unwavering. With each successful mission and each day that passed without detection, I felt a mixture of relief and apprehension. I knew that the stakes were high, and every decision I made had to be carefully calculated to ensure my continued secrecy and the safety of those I cared about. It was regretfully thrilling to keep moving under their radar.

The house was quiet as I pushed open the front door, the cool air brushing against my newly bruised ribs from tonight's endeavor. Every step felt heavy, each movement a challenge with the pain of a possible rib fracture. The thought of a cold Dr. Pepper in the fridge was almost too tempting, but my main concern was slipping inside unnoticed.

I made my way through the foyer with as much stealth as I could manage, eager to get to my room and tend to my injuries in private. The house seemed still, the absence of my roommates giving me a false sense of security. But as I moved down the hall, I noticed a light turn on suddenly in the living room. I froze, my heart racing as I peered into the room. The sight before me stopped me in my tracks. There, sprawled on the couch, were my roommates—Kai, Lius, Ares. Max is standing leaning against the wall as always. Each of their eyes were already on me. My expression moved to that of shock as they glared at me. *Dammit...*

Lius was the first to react, his eyes widening. "*I knew it!*" he exclaimed, his voice cutting through the silence like a knife.

"*Shit...*" I cursed under my breath, my heart sinking. I had hoped to avoid this confrontation a tad longer, but the cat was now out of the metaphorical bag.

Kai's eyes widened in disbelief as he took in my battered appearance. "You're still going out and fighting on SP6 missions?! You said you would tell us before you did! We knew something was off with you lately!" His voice was a mix of shock and anger.

I tried to steady my breath, forcing myself to stay calm despite the pain radiating from my ribs. "I-I can explain," I started, but my voice faltered.

Ares stood up, his expression a blend of concern and frustration. I've never seen him like this, even when facing a particularly difficult target when he's had to step in. "Explain? You've been sneaking around, again!" My expression falls as my mouth drops open at Ares showing emotion and a strong reaction for once.

Max's gaze was fixed on me, his eyes drilling a hole into mine with a mix of suspicion and worry. "So, it's true then. You've been out there, fighting on your own, again?! After *everything*?" His voice lowered into a dangerous growl... he was *pissed*. More pissed than I've ever seen him at me.

Lius's voice was firm but laced with a hint of empathy as he paid attention to how I'm holding my side. "You're hurt again, aren't you? You need to sit down then."

Without waiting for a response, Lius stands up and walks towards me, gently guiding me to the couch where he was sitting. His touch is careful despite the urgency in his movements. I winced as I sat, the pain from my ribs making every movement excruciating. Kai quickly moved to get the first-aid kit from the cabinet, while Ares and Max watched with a mix of concern and confusion. Max looked more pissed than Ares, but what else was new?

Lius took the kit from Kai and opened it to begin cleaning and bandaging my wounds with practiced hands. "We need to know what's going on with you. You're working with two Viper Trainees. Which means you are unofficially working for the SP6. We need to be aware of that as their senior agents, at least." His voice was steady as he worked, his eyes laser focused. "But for now, let us take care of these injuries."

As Lius worked to assist me in removing my jumpsuit's top half, exposing the sports bra tank top that I always wore under it– now shredded. I looked to the other roommates who were exchanging worried glances as they saw each cut and scratch. Every bump and bruise. Even a few burn marks from the fire wielding rogues. Kai's expression softened from shock to a deep concern, while Ares looked like he was trying to piece together the pieces of a puzzle. Max's eyes were still skeptical, but there was that lingering undercurrent of worry in his eyes.

Max finally spoke up, his voice low but tense. "Why didn't you tell us? Why go through all this? Why do you continue to lie to us? To *me*?" The hurt in his eyes almost knocked the wind out of me.

I took a deep breath, the weight of the situation pressing heavily on me. "I didn't want to worry you anymore than I already have. I can handle it on my own. I can't be a distraction to you guys... I stand by that. Sara and Ren have my back out there, and I have theirs."

Kai shook his head, his voice tinged with frustration. "Handle it on your own? You're putting yourself in danger, and we're just left in the dark. You work with Viper *trainees*, which is our department in case you've forgotten. We have the right to know!"

Ares nodded in agreement. "Elara, we're supposed to look out for each other. You should have told us what was happening. That you're still going out there on top of your own hunts. Are you even sleeping?"

I felt a wave of guilt wash over me as I looked at their concerned faces. "I wish I could say I was sorry... I apologized, yes. But I would honestly do it again. I stand by my reasoning to keep you four from knowing." Even if it tore me apart to see the hurt in their eyes, I couldn't let them know the truth. They were safer that way.

Max shouts with frustration. He always growls like that when I'm being difficult in his opinion. Which is always... at least that's what he tells me every day. Lius finished bandaging me up and looked at me with a mixture of relief and determination. "We need to talk about this, but for now, you need to rest."

I nod with confirmation. As the room fell quiet, the tension gave way to a somber understanding, I felt myself growing more at ease emotionally, despite the pain. I decided to allow myself to be cared for as my way of pacifying them, knowing that the conversation about my secret affairs was only just beginning. They won't let me off *that* easily. After a while of continued questioning and lectures about how reckless I had been, and the Viper's protocols, exhaustion took its toll. I finally fell asleep on the couch, the sound of my roommates' voices, as they discussed how to handle this situation with SP6, fading into the background as I drifted off, knowing that the days ahead would be filled with more discussions and decisions about my extracurricular activities.

I stirred, groggily becoming aware of the gentle rocking motion. My eyes fluttered open, and I blinked slowly, trying to make sense of my surroundings. The pain in my ribs was still there, but it seemed to have receded to a dull throb, likely due to the first aid Lius had administered earlier. To my surprise, I found myself being carried upstairs. I glanced up and saw Max's face, his expression focused but soft, as he carefully carried me up the stairs. His arms were strong and steady, providing a sense of security despite my discomfort.

I tried to speak, my voice barely a whisper. "Max...?"

He looked down at me, his eyes showing a mix of concern and determination. "Oh. You're awake. We're almost to your room."

I nodded weakly, feeling the warmth of his body and the steady rhythm of his steps as he ascended the stairs, rocking me back to sleep. The sound of his footsteps echoed softly in the quiet house, and I could hear the faint hum of the air conditioning working in the background. When we reached my room, Max gently eased me into my bed, his movements careful to avoid jostling me too much. He adjusted the covers around me, making sure I was comfortable before sitting down in a nearby chair.

"How are you feeling?" Max asked, his voice low and measured, though there was an edge of concern in his tone.

I took a deep breath, trying to assess how I felt. "A bit sore, but better now. Thanks for carrying me up."

Max gave a small, reassuring smile. "Don't mention it..."

I glanced around the room, noticing the concerned faces of my other roommates peeking in from the doorway—Kai, Lius, and Ares. They were waiting, their expressions a mix of relief and worry.

Kai stepped forward to enter my room, his voice gentler than before. "We've been talking, Elara. We need to figure out how to handle this situation and how to support you better. How to keep you from hiding this from us. And how to keep leadership from finding out. SP6 does *not* take kindly to civilians butting into their affairs. Insurance and what not..." He waves his hand in the air and rolls his eyes to dismiss the politics of it all. The four men are soldiers... front linemen. They despise the *"business"* side of being a part of SP6.

"We're sorry for not realizing it sooner. But now that we know, we'll do everything we can to help you trust us... to rely on us. Understand that we all look out for each other out there. Let us help you... and in return. You help *us*." Ares added, his tone a mix of frustration and care.

I looked at each of them, feeling a swell of gratitude and relief. Despite the pain and the challenges ahead, I contemplated their pleading with me to allow them to help *me* help *them*.

Max sat quietly on the edge of my bed, his gaze now appearing thoughtful as he looked at me. "We're going to figure this out," he said softly. "But for now, get some rest. You need it."

I nodded, feeling my eyelids growing heavy. The combined warmth of my roommates' support and the comfort of my bed were working their magic. As I sank down into my blankets and bed, I drifted back to sleep, not caring that my roommates were still there. I was too tired to care. The room fell into a calm silence, broken only by the soft sound of my breathing as I fell into a sound sleep, surrounded by those who cared deeply for me.

~*~

When I woke up hours later, I opened my eyes, the chair in my room within my line of sight. I see Max sleeping peacefully sitting up in my chair, next to my bed. I go to sit up, groaning slightly as I do, trying to stay silent so I don't wake Max up.

"Don't…" I heard him whisper. His eyes slowly open and land on mine. "I'll help you."

12

My eyes snapped to his, a mix of shock and confusion on my face. Was he here all night? "Okay…" I huff out. Either I allow him to assist me, or he will just pick me up and carry me there. He seems to forget that my legs do in fact work–even in this state.

He stood up from the chair and made his way over to me, his eyes studying my expression. He offered me his hands to help me sit up. "Take it slowly. Don't push yourself too much. We don't need you in more pain."

I took his hands with my own and slowly sat up, wincing from the massive bruise on my ribs. It was tightly and neatly covered up thanks to Lius' handy work. He guided me gently, supporting my weight as if I were delicate china. Noticing the grimace on my face, he gave my hands a reassuring squeeze. "I know it hurts, but you're doing well. Just take your time."

I nodded, my face scrunched in discomfort. Once I was fully sitting up, Max stood beside the bed, one hand on my back to steady me. His eyes were filled with concern. "How's your pain level this morning? You look like you're in quite a bit of discomfort."

"I am… But I just woke up, so that's normal for me." I shifted a bit so that my sitting position is more stable.

Max nodded in understanding, his eyes scanning my face. "I figured as much. It's to be expected. I've had my fair share of bruised ribs. Can you walk? Do you need me to carry you?"

I shook my head. "No. I just need to go to the bathroom, Max."

Max nodded again, his hand still on my back as he helped me stand. "Alright, let's get you up and moving then. Just lean on me, I've got you."

"I've had bruised ribs before, Max. I'll be fine." I held onto him, regardless as he assisted me in walking towards the bathroom. Just as we approached my bedroom door, I heard the other three roommates running through the hall to investigate the commotion. It didn't sound like they had known Max was already in here helping me. I couldn't help but grin a bit at their caretaker's concern at my grunts as I moved. I was actually enjoying not having to keep it hidden from them, but this was over kill. After months of tending to myself after battles, having this kind of care was oddly enjoyable, especially from Max, whom I had come to bond with deeply over the months of hunting my targets with him.

Lius burst into the room before the others, eyes wide with concern. "What the hell happened? We heard you—"

Kai quickly cut him off with a swing of his arm in front of him, realizing the situation. "She was just standing up. Max is here helping her."

Ares narrowed his eyes at Max. "You were in here already? Were you here the whole time?"

Lius's eyes darted between Max and me, worry etched in his expression. "Why didn't you say anything to any of us?"

Max met each of their gazes with a touch of irritation. "She needed to use the restroom, and I was already here, so I helped her. I didn't think it warranted an alert to the house, Arelius."

Kai gave Max a disapproving look. "She's injured and should be resting, not getting up and moving around yet. You shouldn't have helped her sit up on your own. What if you made her injuries worse? You should have gotten us to help you lift her or carried her yourself."

Max rolled his eyes at Kai's words, not appreciating the tone in his voice nor his implication that he would hurt me further. "I am capable of helping her. I was being careful with her. Besides, the stubborn ass here was getting up whether I helped her or not."

"Guys... please... I will piss my pants if I have to stand here any longer... Max, please... let's go." I groaned out. "Like I told Max. I've had bruised ribs before. You all are overreacting."

Lius chimed in, trying to deescalate the situation. "See? Even she's saying to get moving. No need to stand here arguing about how to help her *Kai*."

Kai sighed in resignation. "Fine. Just... be careful with her."

"Quit talking about me like I'm not right here!" I snarl at them. I begin to walk normally past them, attempting to prove to them that I'm not made of fucking glass.

Max nodded slightly, acknowledging Kai's comment. He resumed his supportive grip on me and carefully guided me the rest of the way into the bathroom, making sure not to let me strain the muscles around my ribs. When we reached the bathroom door, I sighed, preparing for a bit of a battle.

"Umm... Max? I've got it from here," I said firmly, meeting his gaze.

Max looked at me, a bit of frustration crossing his face. "I know this isn't ideal, but you're going to have to let me help you—"

"No... I draw the line there." I press a hand to his chest to stop him.

Max clenched his jaw but then nodded and backed away from the bathroom, closing the door behind him. "I'll be right here if you need me. Just call out when you're done, and I'll come back in to help you back to bed."

I nodded as he exited, waiting for the door to click shut. The other three waited outside the door, their voices hushed. I rolled my eyes and turned towards where I urgently needed to be. I begin to hear their voices come through the door as I try to focus on completing my task.

Ares's voice came through first. "What's going on in there?" Worried as to why Max wasn't with me.

Max responded calmly. "She's just using the bathroom. She can do at least *that* on her own."

Lius's voice, filled with a mix of irritation and curiosity, followed. "Why are you the one helping her, Max? We're here too. Couldn't you have gotten one of us to help, too?"

Max smirked, a hint of amusement in his eyes. "Maybe she just likes my company best. Can't blame her, I'm pretty great. I'll be her hero all she wants." He teases. Lius rolled his eyes, and crossed his arms with a pout, looking towards the closed door. Max continued his torment, further explaining his presence in my room when I woke up with a sigh. "It's because I was already in her room. I told you all that, and I didn't see or do anything I wasn't supposed to."

The others exchanged glances, skeptical of Max's explanation. Lius's expression grew even more skeptical than the others. "You expect us to believe that you were just sitting there, watching over her, and you were a complete gentleman the entire time?"

Max rolled his eyes. "Yes, I treated her like I would my own flesh and blood. I'm not some kind of pervert like *you*, Lius. I don't find the need to grope a woman anytime I'm within reach of them."

Kai interjected, his tone serious as he scolded the two. "It's not about being a pervert. It's about respecting her as a person and her boundaries when she needs us most."

Lius added, "Yeah, speaking of boundaries… How exactly did you end up in her room in the first place? Did you wake up super early and go check in on her or something?" His smile returned.

Max lets out another sigh, only this time out of frustration. "I was already in her room, watching over her, okay? When she woke up and started to sit up, I helped her. That's when she told me she needed to use the bathroom. You all came in right as I was helping her stand up. End of story."

The others, processing the information, exchanged looks. Lius seemed still unconvinced. "You were just sitting there, watching her sleep?"

Ares raised an eyebrow, amusement playing on his face. "That's a bit odd for you, Max. Why were you in there watching her like that? Were you being creepy…?"

Kai seemed to agree, studying Max intently. "Yeah, it does seem a bit strange for *you*. Were you really just there to monitor her?"

Max sighed, clearly irritated by their line of questioning. "I was there all night in case she needed something. That's all. And *strange…?*"

The conversation left a charged atmosphere as the roommates processed Max's explanation, with varying degrees of acceptance and skepticism, questioning the typically aloof man's actions when it came to me.

Lius snorted with a hint of mockery. "You stayed in there the whole night? Keeping watch over her like a guard dog? That's pretty damn dedicated of you."

Max clenched his jaw, his frustration evident. "I wasn't watching over her like a *guard dog*. I was just there in case she needed something or help getting up. To ensure she didn't hurt herself by being stubborn. You can't tell me *none* of you have ever had your ribs bruised? It hurts like hell to even *breathe*."

Kai interjected, trying to calm the heating situation. "You could have just checked on her periodically instead of sitting by her bedside the whole night."

Ares, narrowing his eyes, added. "Yeah… and since when did it become your job to be her caretaker? We're all perfectly capable of taking care of her too."

Max glared at them, feeling defensive. "I wasn't implying that you guys aren't capable. I just wanted to make sure she was comfortable and resting. The poor girl is really banged up, if you haven't noticed."

Lius smirked, sarcasm dripping from his next set of words. "Right, because watching her while she sleeps is definitely the best way to ensure her care."

"I didn't see any of you come in and check on her, now did I? I had only closed my eyes here and there. I never fell fully asleep. Not *once* did I see *any* of you come in and check on her." Max shot back.

The others exchanged glances, realizing Max had a point. None of them had checked on me after my pained vocalization the first time.

Lius, however, couldn't reveal his true night-time endeavor to the others. "Well, we were all pretty tired last night. And it's not like we thought she would be waking up throughout the night needing anything. I gave her a pretty strong pain reliever that would help her sleep."

Kai frowned. "Regardless, you could have given us a heads-up that you were going to be in there watching her, so we didn't run to her room in a panic at the sound of her cries as you helped her up, this morning."

Max raised an eyebrow, challenging Kai's criticism. "Why?"

Lius huffed, impatience showing. "Why? Because it's common decency to let us know if you're going to be in a room with an unconscious woman who is vulnerable and hurt during the night, so we don't bolt out of a dead sleep to come help her. Made me nauseous…" He mumbled.

Just then, I open the bathroom door, my voice carrying a mix of frustration and annoyance at the four sets of eyes huddled around the hallway. "Max…?" I look at him.

Max's attention snapped to the bathroom door as I spoke. "Yeah? What is it?" He sounded as if I interrupted him and annoyed him.

I ignore his tone as I know Lius was probably giving him a hard time. "I'm done," I said, leaning against the sink to relieve some tension off of my torso.

Max's concern was immediately directed at me again as his face softened from its earlier scowl. He steps in and walks to my side. "Alright… just be careful with her, Max," said Lius, stepping back slightly to give us room to pass by.

I looked at the group, my patience wearing thin. "I need you all to clear the way now. Please."

The other three shifted their gaze to Max, who nodded and extended a hand out in front of me, his other near the small of my back. "Alright," he said. "Let's get you back to bed."

As Max helped me out of the bathroom, Lius mentions. "Alright, now that that's taken care of, can we go downstairs and eat? I don't know about the rest of you, but I'm starving."

I glared at Lius, my irritation peaking. "Max... please just take me back to bed...?" I said, my voice carrying a hint of exasperation with the situation and the conversation I overheard through the door. I wasn't hungry and was oddly more irritated with Lius this morning. Could be because he's given Max a hard time who's just trying to help me out, since he knows how it feels to have deep bruises wrapping around each individual rib.

Max guided me back to my room, his presence a comforting contrast to the bickering of the others progressing behind us. As we made our way back, I felt grateful for his support, even if the others were still grappling with their feelings about the reason for his behavior towards me. There was a pause as Max considered my request, the others listening to our exchange. Lius broke the silence. "You sure you want to just go back to bed? You haven't eaten anything yet."

"He's right. You should eat something before going back to sleep." Kai added.

I sighed, feeling a mix of irritation and fatigue. "Okay... fine. I'll go downstairs." I turn quickly on my heels. I was so annoyed that I forgot for a brief second about half my body, basically being one giant bruise. I stumbled a bit from the sudden movement.

As I started to push away from Max, he gently but firmly blocked me with his hand out in front of me. "No... I will make you something and bring it to you. She's going back to bed, fellas." He points a glare towards Lius and Kai.

The others fell silent, their expressions shifting to guilt as they watched me attempt to head towards the stairs on my own. The last thing they wanted was to see me painfully navigating the flight of stairs to the kitchen.

Lius suggested, "We could just carry you down—"

Max cut him off with a firm tone, "I said... I will make something and bring it to her." He shoots his glare at Lius, making it clear he wasn't open to negotiation.

Kai reluctantly agreed. "Alright... Max will help her back to bed. Max, make sure she eats something."

I snapped back, "Just go away, you three. Go do something else." I am so tired of them talking about me as if I'm not right next to them. The backside of my ribs was becoming aggravated by how I was standing in the hallway.

Lius's irritation flared at my sharp response. "Oh, so now you're giving us orders? You gotta learn some respect, birdie. I'm getting a little tired of the 'tude..."

Max growled, his new found protective nature over me kicking in. "Lius... *back off*. She's in enough pain. Come on, princesa... let's get you to bed." My heart flutters at his protectiveness over me. Never before have I had anyone be so... territorial over my well-being. It was refreshing coming from him. The bond between us certainly has grown over the past year. I've grown fond of this man, he's my best friend, even more than Angie has been these days.

Lius rolled his eyes, realizing Max was now acting like a protective guardian. "Alright, alright... I'll back off." He crossed his arms and glared at Max and me, annoyed that it was Max helping me and relied on him, rather than himself. He quickly masked his frustration before anyone could see it.

Lius grumbled under his breath, "I don't want to hear any complaints from you later, birdie... So, you better eat all of your food..."

Max carefully guided me back to bed. The process was painful, but it was more manageable with his support compared to when I had done it alone in the past. He helped me lay down gently and fluffed my pillows to help me get comfortable. I chuckled at the gesture. Concern etched on his face, he asks me. "Are you doing alright? Is anything hurting more than it did this morning?"

I managed a small, quick smile. I shake my head. "No... I'm okay, Max." He nodded, relieved that I wasn't in more pain. He glanced at the others, who were still hovering by the doorway.

Lius finally spoke, "So, we're just going to go make something to eat. We'll be down in the kitchen if you need us." The three of them filed down the hallway, albeit reluctantly leaving the two of us.

I reached out and placed a hand on Max's arm as he began to turn and walk away from me to follow them. "Thank you, Max... It means a lot to me. You're such a gentleman..."

Max couldn't help but smile at the compliment, never meeting my eyes. He looked down at my hand and gave it a reassuring squeeze with his own. He finally looks back at me. "No problem at all... You get some rest, and I'll be back with some breakfast, okay?"

I nodded in gratitude. "Okay."

Max lingered by my bedside for a few moments longer, his gaze fixed on my face, trying to gauge my condition and if I was putting on a brave front. After a moment, he released my hand and headed towards the door. He paused and turned back to me. "Would you like coffee as well?"

"That would be great… thank you," I replied with a smile.

He gave one last smile before heading out the door and closing it softly behind him. Alone in my room, I rolled painfully to my side facing my bedroom window and I allowed some pent up silent tears to fall. I felt defeated, my body betraying me after a single battle gone awry. I was too weak to face my uncle and longed to be back in training. My pride was hurt, and my resolve was fraying. My world is crumbling around me. The sight of my overly protective roommates discovering my more minor injuries has shaken me. I thought back to when they had all begun to show their care and concern for me, especially during one of our weekly movie nights when I felt a profound sense of wanting to keep them all in my life, even if it meant making sacrifices to ensure their safety while they worried about mine. We had become one massive family, willing to do anything for each other. Being the smallest and a female among these traditional men, I felt as if I was treated like the queen of this Viper Den.

As the tears flowed down my face, once I was alone, gripping my pillow. A mix of pain and frustration overwhelmed me. The physical agony merged with an emotional storm, tearing at the resolve and pride I once held so high. I hated this feeling of vulnerability, this sense of helplessness. My pride was battered, and my resolve seemed to crumble into ash. I buried my face in my pillow, muffling my sobs as best as I could to avoid alarming my roommates. The last thing I wanted was for them to worry more, though I couldn't deny how much it grated on me that they were so protective–making me feel even weaker.

I struggled with the feeling of being constantly mother-henned, especially when Kai treats me like a child with his

189

lectures. But deep down, I know he's right—I was inexperienced compared to them. I desperately needed to become stronger. The silence of the room only heightened my sense of isolation and frustration. Memories of Kai's words echoed in my mind, serving as a harsh reminder of my limitations.

~*~

I had just returned from another fight alongside a powerful target who turned out to have elemental powers. Max didn't make it with me on this one because of his own duties. After being stopped by my roommates as soon as I entered the front door, I'm in the middle of being lectured yet again about my actions tonight. Max had just taken another sip of his drink, his casual demeanor at odds with the seriousness of our discussion. "I'll bet it still felt good beating their asses, though, right?"

"It was amazing!" I couldn't hide the excitement in my voice, the thrill of the fight still fresh in my memory.

Kai's response was immediate and stern. "No... do not encourage her... do you have any idea what you were doing out there?"

Lius, being the more supportive one tonight, chuckled at my enthusiasm. "You look like you've been having the time of your life out there! I bet you gave that creep a good thrashing!" He enthusiastically punches the air in front of him.

Kai's glare was intense as he turned his attention back to me. "Yes, do you even realize the danger you put yourself in by going out there alone each time...? Especially after we explicitly told you not to get involved with elementals anymore?!"

"You four don't want me fighting at all, Kai! But I couldn't just sit back and do nothing! Do you have any idea how many of

my targets are out there still?! And yes! Sometimes I face off against one who is an elemental!" My face is burned with rage.

Kai's expression was resolute, his jaw clenched at my argument. "We understand your desire to help, but you're not part of SP6... you're not properly equipped to go into these battles with an elemental! You don't possess the power required to take on these enemies, let alone an elemental one. You're putting yourself in unnecessary danger by involving yourself in these battles!"

"Do you see me standing here, Kai?!" I challenged, my frustration bubbling over. "That's because I can fight! Do you know how many women and children I've saved during these fights...?"

"Just because you've managed to survive so far, does not mean you have the skills necessary to fight these enemies consistently. You're relying solely on your strength and martial arts, and that's not enough in our world. Elemental enemies come in all shapes and sizes, with various strengths and abilities. You're putting yourself in serious danger, Elara, by thinking you can handle them all on your own!" Kai's gaze was unyielding, his stern disapproval clear, he was not letting up this time.

"And what exactly do you think I do when I'm training?! I am trained for this! How will I ever know where I'm at in my training if I never use it...?" My anger made my voice tremble, and I fought to keep the tears of rage at bay. I didn't want them to think I was someone who cried over everything when my emotions were heightened.

Kai's expression softened slightly as he saw my emotional struggle, but he remained firm. "Training is one thing. Real-life battles are another. You may be capable of holding your own during practice. But you're not prepared to handle the real danger *that comes with battle. I understand your desire to test your limits, but you can't learn to swim by jumping into the deep end."*

"That's how I was taught! To jump right in! No... to be thrown *in without any choice in the matter! Only* now, *I can defend myself!"*

"Regardless, you still went out without our knowledge. You put yourself in danger and potentially risked everything you've worked so hard to build." Kai's gaze remained unwavering.

"Wait... do I need your permission?! *No... I don't think so..."* *My eyes burned with anger at the notion of needing their approval for anything I do with my life.*

"Yes, you do. Moving forward. SP6 is going to take over your targets. You're not just risking your own safety when you interfere out there. You're risking all of our lives and the lives of those around us by getting in the way. We care deeply about you like family, and we can't just sit back and let you endanger yourself without our knowledge. Now that we know about you and your antics... we will be distracted, ensuring you're safe out there. Rogue elementals are-" Kai's gaze becoming more intense.

"Performing human *crimes!" I cut him off. "How do I endanger you further?! Huh?! How?! These are* my *hunts! I never know what powers they wield! If any at all!" I take a step toward him. "And you forget Kai... I've been hunting targets for* years *before I even met any of you! So, to question my experience with battle is insulting."*

"That's not the point and you know it! What you did in America may have been ignored there. But here *you're a liability to the SP6 when you fight against* anyone *with elemental powers. We have powers and abilities that allow us to fight against elementals. You, on the other hand, are a human civilian with no powers." Kai's irritation grew.*

"I can't believe this. Then fine… I retract what we agreed to… when I'm out hunting for my targets… you four do not get to come along to have my back if I need help. You also are a liability to me… and my mission." It was a childish retort, but it was the only thing I had in my arsenal to use against him.

"Wait, what??? What do you mean we can't come along anymore?!" Lius's smirk faded, shock crossing his face.

"You think we'd just sit back and let you face danger alone?" Max, who had been quiet until now, spoke up–his mouth lifting in a sneer, dismissing my retraction. He's still going to accompany me whether I like it or not and I knew that's what he was saying, given the look he was giving me.

"If you get to fight your battles without me, then I will fight mine without you." I stood my ground, meeting Kai's gaze with a burning determination.

"You can't be serious. You're being really childish right now. You can't go out there alone, potentially fighting enemies with powers. It's suicide." Kai expresses firmly. I see a flicker of unease in his eyes.

"If I encounter an elemental… I let the SP6 know after the fact like I do the cops." I continue to reason with Kai. Hoping to find a middle ground and end this so I can go to bed.

"And what if you don't have time to alert the SP6, they break free, and you have to engage with them? You're putting yourself in needlessly dangerous situations." Kai sighed in frustration.

"Then I fight. I was serious when I said I would fight till my dying breath for what I have to accomplish. I will protect all from the creeps of this world…" I stand tall with my arms tight at my side, taking another step forward to hopefully show him I mean what I've said.

Lius's expression hardened, a cold intensity in his eyes as he stood up and moved to face me at Kai's side to cut into the conversation. "I understand your desire to take down your uncle, birdie. But you can't do it alone and you can't keep shutting us out from it. You don't know what you're up against… it's too dangerous and you know it. We're not trying to keep you safe because we think you're helpless, we're trying to keep you safe because we care about you. You have no idea about the bigger picture here!"

"And I care about you four also! I want to help protect you too! By continuing my work, alone. I understand that something bigger is going on, Lius. And I am working diligently to get it under control!" My voice is becoming hoarse from straining as I fight back the angry tears itching to break free of their cage.

The room fell silent as they exchanged glances, unable to deny my point. I took a deep breath, the pain in my gut becoming more pronounced. The earlier shots from the target's electrical attacks. I clutched at my stomach, trying to calm and mask the pain. When I see that the guys won't back down, I do my best to put an end to this conversation.

"Ok… I need to go shower now and go to bed." I turned and headed for the stairs, wanting to escape the tension and the physical pain that was catching up to me as the adrenaline from the fight wore off.

Kai watched as I walked away from him, his expression a mix of frustration and concern. Max's voice followed me towards the stairs. "What, you're just going to drop this bombshell on us and walk away just like that?"

"I have an early session, Max… And what bombshell? You all already figured it all out, right? Need to tell me more about what I'm going to do like I'm some pet?"

Max gave a sly smirk to my sarcastic remark. "You've declared that you're ditching us the next time you go out on a hunt. I'd say that's a pretty big bombshell."

"Well, I feel it's only fair. I can't gain the experience and get stronger to complete my mission if all that you four do is keep me in a bubble..." I fling my arm as I speak, not sure what else to do to get through to them. To get them to back off.

"It's not about wanting to keep you in a bubble, Elara. It's about wanting to keep you alive, for heaven's sake!" Kai's frustration was felt through us all in his words. He always has to have the final say.

"By not letting me learn at all? By having me sit back like some helpless maiden in distress while my four big strong heroes fight my battles? No! I will fight my battles alone*! Without any of you! Without anyone's help!" I scream through the ragged sharp edges forming in my throat. I've had enough of this horrid scolding every day.*

The room fell silent again as my declaration hung in the air. Lius's gaze was icy, and it sent a chill down my spine. Tears lined my eyes. Their silence was my only answer. As I turned and made my way up the stairs, the pain in my body grew sharper, but I fought through it. I couldn't let them see how much it hurt. I needed to be strong, to prove that I could handle this—no matter the cost. Any sign of weakness—like crying—in front of any man in power, no matter the situation, will give them the upper hand instantly. It's what my mother has always told me whenever I would cry as a child. It invalidates anything you say from then on out. Even in today's progressive times.

~*~

Lost in my turmoil of the memory, I heard the door creak open. Lius stepped in, holding a cup of fresh steaming coffee. He halted at the sight of how I was lying. His expression softened as he placed the cup on my bedside table. "Hey... you, okay?" he asks gently.

"No..." I sniffled, feeling too raw to deny it any longer, let alone hide it from him.

Lius's face contorted with a mix of sympathy and concern. He moved closer to the bed, as his shoulders lowered, his gaze fixed on me. "I figured you weren't, but I thought I'd ask. You're really going through it, aren't you?"

"Yes... A battle goes sideways, and now my body is bruised and weakened. I'm still too weak. I have to get stronger... I *have* to..." A tear slipped down my cheek.

"Hey, hey, don't be so hard on yourself, alright? You took on some powerful foes, from what I hear from Sara. That's more than any other novice fighter can say. What you do is admirable. What you *continue* to do is as well. You put yourself out there and fight despite the odds and the injuries. That shows great courage, not weakness." His expression softened as he listened to my frustrations and fears. He moves to sit on the edge of my bed behind me, his voice steady and reassuring.

"But you four all scrutinize and yell at me for it every time... for doing it behind your backs or at all. I kept it a secret because I knew you'd all react that way... to try and stop me. To intervene. I can hold my own in a fight. I can defend myself... but... then my body just proves you all right..." I buried my face in my pillow again, lifting it up to my face as the tears flowed freely. I couldn't hold them back any longer.

Lius's expression turned guilty, understanding the conversation we'd had on previous occasions. He rubbed the back of his head sheepishly. "Yeah, about that... Look, we are all just worried about you, okay? We know you can fight. You held your own pretty well during our sparring sessions. But you need to understand that you're still very inexperienced, compared to us. We're just trying to look out for you."

"I know... I will always be inexperienced next to you all... I'm so angry that I made you all worry even more... Can you all please just stop always worrying about me? Treat me like you do each other for once?" My breathing began to slow as I calmed down from his words of comfort.

"Hey, it's okay. You don't mean to make us worry. We care about you and want to protect you, that's all. That's why we are so harsh. We don't want to see you hurt like this. Just take a deep breath, alright? You're doing great. Just relax a bit." He reached out to caress my shoulder, his touch warm and soothing. His fingers gently ran through my hair, calming the storm inside me. The tears gradually subsided, and my breathing returned to normal.

"Are you okay?" Max's voice cuts through as he enters my room, taking in the sight of Lius's comforting gesture. "Are you in worse pain than you were leading us to believe again?"

Lius turned to Max, his concern still evident but a little more relaxed. "She's okay. She just needed a moment to let it all out."

Max walked over to the bedside, holding a tray of food. He glanced between Lius and me, questioning what had happened. "What happened here? What did you do, Arelius?"

"Nothing... We were just talking." I said, my breath catching in my throat one last time.

Max's face softened as he looked at Lius, who gave him a reassuring nod. He searched my face for any sign of hidden discomfort. "Are you sure you're, okay? You're not in more pain, right? I brought you some breakfast if you'd like to sit up and eat?"

"I'm okay. There's no new or worse pain. I would love to eat what you've brought... That's very kind of you." I lifted my arm to reach for a pillow to prop myself up.

Lius noticed and grabbed my wrist quickly, but gently. "Hey, don't do that... I got it."

"Umm..." I release the pillow to let him help, allowing him to adjust the pillows and lift me carefully.

Lius finished adjusting my pillows and said, "There... all set."

Max placed the tray of breakfast on my lap. "Is that comfortable?" He asked, observing the tray of breakfast foods, making sure everything was placed perfectly.

"Yes... Thank you, Max... did you make all of this yourself?" I looked up at him with an expression of gratitude.

He shook his head and gestures to Lius. "We all did."

"Thank you..." I looked at both of them with deep appreciation.

Lius gave a small nod. "No problem. We just want to make sure you're comfortable and taken care of." Max patted my leg softly, his expression warm. They stayed by my side while I began to eat, making sure I was settled and pleased with the food they've prepared.

Once I nodded and smiled with a small hum of approval, Lius nods with pride at my approval. The two of them headed towards the door telling me to enjoy the food and reminding me that they were just downstairs if I needed anything.

"And no crying. It freaks us out." Max paused, turned back to add. Teasing me with a wink and a half smile.

I managed a weak smile at his playful comment. "I'll do my best..."

"Teasing you is just too easy, princesa... I love it." Max grinned, pleased to see me smiling, even a weak one. My cheeks heat at the endearing nickname he's adopted onto me.

~*~

Once Max and Lius left, I finished my breakfast. Max came back into my room after a while, looking as if he had something to say, but upon seeing the empty tray next to me, his expression showed he had changed his mind.

"Done already? Are you still hungry?" He asks, picking up the tray and setting it on my nightstand. I smiled, feeling fortunate to have such caring roommates. Max pulled up a chair and sat beside me. We talked, and soon Kai, then Lius, and finally Ares joined us. My room was filled with chatter, laughter, and warmth, a testament to the strong bonds that we shared.

13

Days passed, and I was finally healed enough to return to training. At least enough to gain my roommates approval without argument. The guys insisted on coming with me to the gym, under the guise of observing, but I knew it was their protective nature at play. They wanted to make sure my trainer went easy on me for my first day back. Last time he was too rough for their liking when I basically crawled home afterwards. They were going to observe and make sure he took it easy on me this time. Stepping into the ring, I could feel their eyes on me, their concern barely concealed.

~*~

Tatsuya and I were in the middle of a sparring match, working on easier moves to assess my current capabilities and my range of motion after healing from injury. I grunted as Tatsuya landed a hit on my still-healing ribs. It wasn't enough to cause any new damage but just enough to test my pain threshold.

"Get up! Do you think the enemy will care that you just recovered from an injury?" His voice was stern, almost harsh. He charged at me again, not allowing any time for me to regain my bearings. The guys watched from the sidelines, their hands were all clenched into fists, faces etched with a mixture of worry, anger, and admiration. They tried to remain composed, but it was evident how torn they were between wanting to intervene and letting me push through this on my own. I dodged the next set of attacks, but he swept my legs out from under me, sending me crashing to the floor with a loud thud and a grunt.

Tatsuya's voice was unforgiving. "You can't stop! No giving up!" I felt the familiar sting of pain and exhaustion, but I couldn't afford to let it show. His brutal training was something I had requested. I required it. And now, the men were witnessing it firsthand. As Tatsuya went for his next attack, their faces were a mixture of admiration and concern. With each hit, my body screamed in pain, but I pushed through, biting down hard to keep from wincing. I could feel all of their eyes on me, Lius's jaw tightening with every blow I took. Max's hands curled into fists at his sides, itching to jump into the ring, but he held back—barely. Ares' fists were balled in frustration. Kai remained calm but his eyes spoke volumes of his concern. Each blow I took made the men flinch and wince silently.

"*Gods dammit!*" I slammed my fists into the floor of the ring after the last hit slammed me into the floor. Ignoring the pain, I jumped up instantly and took a defensive stance. Tatsuya smirked, showing he was pleased with my fighting spirit.

"There she is! That's what I want to see!" He praised me as he prepared for my counterattack.

The men continued to watch anxiously, their eyes glued to the scene unfolding in the ring. Lius' fingers twitched with the urge to join in, but he held himself back, knowing this was a test of my endurance and mental strength. Not just another training session. Sensei flips me out of the ring, and I land flat on my back with a hard thud. The wind knocked out of me, and the four men flinched at the sound.

They all began to rise to help me, but I quickly shouted, *"No! Don't help me!"* With anger and frustration on my face, I leaped up, flipped back into the ring, and resumed my assault on Tatsuya. My anger fueled my motivation.

"That's the fire that every strong fighter needs!" Tatsuya seemed taken aback by my sudden burst of energy, but he quickly regained his composure and defended against my attacks. He continues to encourage me as I continue to get back up after each fall. The men watched from the sidelines with admiration. Despite my apparent exhaustion and pain, I pushed myself further. After a while, I finally landed a hard punch to Tatsuya's jaw. He stumbled back, rubbing his jaw and a look of surprise at the power behind my blow for my first day back. The men looked on with pride, their respect for my strength and perseverance evident-the proud mother hens that they are.

"You're getting stronger." Tatsuya says, his smile widened, providing me with his approval as he straightened up. The men applauded from their seats, their faces filled with admiration and respect for my dedication.

"Okay…" I took a deep breath, heavy with exertion, and took my fighting pose once more. "Let's go…"

Sensei shook his head. "Nope, that's our time for today, Elara…"

I glanced at the clock and saw he was right. "Oh… thank you, Sensei, for training me today…" I bowed to him in gratitude.

He gave a small nod, his satisfied smile conveying his approval. "You've worked hard today. Your progress is impressive. Keep up with your training, and you'll be a force to be reckoned with, once again, in no time. Just remember, true strength isn't just about physical power; it's also about mental resilience."

As I exited the ring, the men approached me, showing how concerned they've been during this session. Their eyes roved over my body's condition after sparring with Tatsuya. Lius spoke first, his hands clenching and unclenching at his sides. Something he does when he's calming himself down, I've noticed. "Damn... you took some serious hits there, birdie... Are you ok?"

"Yes, I'm fine... I need to make sure my body never breaks again... I asked him to be that relentless while training me. Even after a recovery." The concern in their eyes became clearer at my statement, but I could see their admiration too. I was grateful for their support, even if it meant enduring their worried stares.

Max, ever the protective one, stepped closer to me with a small frown on his face. "That's enough for today. You're still recovering. You need rest, not more training..."

"I've recovered enough, Max. I need to get my body back in shape." He gave me a look that showed his concern and disapproval, but he didn't argue further.

Lius cuts in. "But you need to listen to your body and rest when it needs it. Overdoing it could cause more harm than good."

"Why do you think he stopped our session just now? We usually go over our scheduled time, but today... he didn't." I scoff.

"He knew you'd pushed yourself as far as you could, today. Any more training and you'd be at risk of further injury... Right?" Kai answers, as perceptive as ever, understanding immediately.

"Correct…" I pulled out my water bottle and took a swig from it, resting on my knees sitting on the bench, the men circled around me. They were struggling with their protective instincts, wanting to comfort me while also respecting my independence.

"You know, that was some brutal training you just went through, princesa. How are you still standing after all that?" Max asked me as he looked upon me with a mix of concern and even curiosity.

"I won't let myself give up…" I proclaim.

"Hm… You're one stubborn little thing…" Max's tone carried a hint of admiration despite his attempt to sound mocking.

I dug into my bag and grabbed a pair of leggings, slipping them on over my spandex shorts that I always wear to train in. The men's eyes followed my movements, their gazes lingering as I slipped them on.

"Those… ahem… leggings look good on you, birdie…" Lius comments, his voice huskier than usual.

"Down, boy…" I snap.

"I can't help it if you look so damn good in those leggings." He grinned through his words, unashamed of his eyes roving appreciatively. The other men rolled their eyes at his shameless flirting but seemed to agree with his sentiment.

"Okay…" I gathered my things ignoring Lius' comments. "Ready to head home, guys?"

All four heads nodded in agreement.

"Yes, we are ready." Kai answers out loud for everyone,

"Need help walking, birdie?" Lius teased as he slung his arm around my shoulders, pulling me close into him.

"No, I'm good, thanks." I laughed, teasing him right back as I pushed him away with a playful shove.

"Ouch, rejected. You wound me, birdie." Lius pouts dramatically, pretending to be offended.

The other men chuckled at our banter, amused with our dynamic. Max, as usual, stayed silent, brooding over the interaction. His expression stern as his eyes darted between both Lius and I. Kai shook his head at Lius' antics, and Ares just smiled, accustomed to our playful exchanges, adding his own quips here and there. As we walked out of the gym, Max trailed slightly behind the group, his eyes fixed on the back of my head. He placed his hands in his pants pockets, and with his shoulders slightly slouched forward. His brows knitted together as he looked away towards the sky, unable to look at the exchange any longer.

"Come on, Max… you, okay?" I looked back at Max and extended my arm towards him.

"Yeah, I'm fine." He stopped in his tracks, surprised by my gesture. He glanced at the rest of the men, who were still ahead of him, and now me, before hesitantly taking my extended hand into his. I can sense his inner turmoil brewing behind his eyes.

"Want to tell me about it?" I ask him as I release his hand and loop my arm around his.

Max stayed silent as we walked, his shoulders tight, his jaw clenched. I could feel the tension radiating off him, but he wouldn't look at me. Finally, after what felt like an eternity, he let out a heavy sigh. "You and Lius… it's irritating how close you two are." He muttered, still refusing to meet my gaze.

I look at him with concern. "I'm sorry to hear that it bothers you… I feel like I'm close to all of you, each in a different way."

Max let out a reluctant sigh. "Yeah, I know you are. It's just…" He paused, struggling to find the right words. "You two just have this… annoying banter thing going on. It's like he's always teasing you, and you just go with it."

"That's just our thing, Max… You always cheer me up when I'm sad and take care of me when I'm sick or injured. That's our thing." I caress his arm to help soothe his inner raging storm.

"Yeah, I guess so. I know I'm good for cheering you up. I just don't like seeing you all chummy with Lius." Max grunted, his expression a mix of annoyance and sheepishness.

"Oh…? And why is that, might I ask?" A sly grin spreads on my face. Ready to tease him without mercy.

"I just… I don't like the way he flirts with you and teases you constantly. It irks me." Max looked away, avoiding eye contact.

"Max…" I released his arm and wrapped it around his waist, pulling him into a friendly, comforting embrace.

"What…?" he asked gruffly. He appeared surprised by my affectionate gesture but didn't pull away, begrudgingly allowing me to pull him closer.

"Does it bother you more that he flirts with me or that he teases me?" I tilted my head, wondering what he's thinking.

"Both. You're too good for his stupid-ass flirting. And his stupid teasing is just irritating in general." He lets out a huff.

"Yeah… it can be at times." I sigh out in agreement.

"So… why do you play along with it? With his teasing and flirting?" He grumbles, still a bit peeved. He was quiet for a moment before speaking again.

"Eh…" I shrug. "It's funny when I get the best of him and make him mad as payback."

Max smirked slightly, amusement flickering in his eyes. "Oh, so you like getting one over on him, huh? Making him mad is your game?"

"Yep. I get under his skin, and it's hilarious!" I giggle.

A small chuckle escaped his lips at the thought of Lius getting riled up. "I gotta admit, I do enjoy seeing that. Lius getting all riled up because you've outsmarted him."

I grinned at Max, elbowing him lightly. "And when I finally beat Lius in a sparring match, he'll be calling me *'daddy,'*" I teased.

Max chuckled softly, shaking his head. "You're ridiculous," he muttered, but the smirk on his face showed he didn't mind my teasing. "I'd pay to see that." he added, a flicker of amusement finally crossing his features.

"But Max... Do you want me to stop going along with his flirting and teasing?" I look up at him quizzically.

His expression softened slightly as he looked down at me, his jaw set tight. "I... I don't know. On one hand, I don't like seeing you play along with his games. But on the other hand, it's almost funny to see him get all riled up when you get the best of him." He paused, searching for the right words. "I guess I just don't want you to get hurt or for him to cross any lines."

I gave his waist a reassuring squeeze. "Thanks for always looking out for me, Max. I'll keep that in mind."

Max's expression eased as he nodded. "Alright. Just... don't let him get away with anything too ridiculous."

"Got it." I nodded in confirmation. We walked on, the playful banter and Max's protective streak making the late morning livelier. I looked up at him with remorse. "I'm sorry that you've felt I wasn't as close with you as I am with Lius... but hey... wanna know something?"

He looked back down at me, his expression a mix of curiosity and reluctance. He nodded slightly, gesturing for me to continue speaking.

"You're the only one allowed to call me princess… Did you ever notice that? Nobody else is allowed to." I squeezed his waist in comfort. Max's eyes widened momentarily in surprise at my revelation. He looked down at me, taken aback by my words. After a brief pause, a small smile tugged at the corner of his lips.

"Heh… really? I'm the only one allowed to call you princess, huh?" he said, seeming a bit pleased with this newfound knowledge.

"Yep… just you. That's *your* thing with me… no one else's." I smile at him. The reaction he gives at my words makes butterflies form in my gut.

Max's smile turned into a smirk, a hint of pride and satisfaction showing in his expression. "Well, good. I like having something that's just ours. Makes me feel special, y'know?" He reached down and ruffled my hair affectionately.

I giggled. "Hey… my legs are a bit tired after training today… mind if I have a piggyback ride the rest of the way home?" I added a coyness to cheer him up. He may be prideful at times and nonchalant the most… but even Max needed to be reassured at times.

Max chuckled at my request, a look of mock annoyance on his face. "You want a piggyback ride…? Seriously?" He feigned reluctance, but I could tell he was amused by the idea. I grinned up at him. He rolled his eyes melodramatically before letting out a resigned sigh. "Fine, princess. I guess I can give you a ride on my back the rest of the way home, just this once." He motioned for me to climb onto his back, still grumbling a bit for show.

"Thank you, Max…" I said in a loving tone.

His grumbling ceased at my tone, and he let out a soft huff, a hint of a smile on his face. "Yeah, yeah, whatever. Just get on already." He bent down slightly, waiting for me to climb onto his back. I clambered on minus any grace whatsoever, giggling at his obvious fake reluctance. He steadied himself, securing his arms under my thighs and wrapping them around my legs and under my knees to hold me in place. Despite his earlier grumpiness, a hint of playfulness was evident in his expression as he started walking with me on his back. I placed a hand on his head and ran my fingers through his hair as a small way to thank him. My other arm draped around his shoulder, my hand resting on his chest where I gently rubbed as if to soothe an ache I thought might be brewing beneath. I didn't have to hold on too tightly since his arms held me up with surprising ease. He let out a low chuckle, enjoying the feeling of my fingers running through his hair and the affectionate touch of my hand on his chest. He kept walking, his steps steady and firm, as if my weight was practically nonexistent. He stole a glance back at me, a fond smile on his face. "You're enjoying this, aren't you, princesa?" he asked, his tone teasing.

I chuckled lightly. "Yes, I am actually." I squeezed his head in a hug and kissed his cheek gently. "Do you feel better now?"

Max nodded, his smile widening at my affection. "Yeah, I do. Being the only one allowed to call you princess definitely makes me feel better. Plus, I always like it when you get clingy like this... it's usually only when you're sick or tired, but it's nice." Max continued walking with me on his back, enjoying the feeling of my arms around him. He turned his head slightly to look back at me, a small playful smirk on his face. "Y'know, most people would probably say that I'm whipped for letting you use me as a human horse like this."

"Haha! Probably... and weren't you teasing someone else for being whipped just the other day...?" I tease him with a poke to the cheek.

He grinned, remembering the incident of him giving Lius a hard time. "Yeah. You've got a memory like a steel trap. I was definitely making fun of Lius for being whipped by you... Guess that makes me a hypocrite."

"Only slightly. But it's okay... this can be our secret. I won't tell the others how *whipped* you are..." I grinned, teasing him further with another poke to his cheek.

He chuckled, his eyes narrowing slightly in jest. "Yeah, yeah, you better keep your mouth shut. Last thing I need is people thinking I'm just some big softie who lets his woman boss him around. You've already got me wrapped around your little finger, princesa."

"Awww... but you like this finger, huh?" I wiggled my pinky finger in front of his face, teasing him further that is quickly turning into some light flirting. I completely overlook the way my heart clenched at his words of referring to me as *'his woman'*. I want to squeal.

He rolled his eyes, attempting to hide a smile. "You're such a smartass." He grabbed my wiggling pinky finger and gently tapped it within his own hand. "And yes... I do like that finger. Only because it's attached to you." I blushed, glad that he couldn't see it. He continued walking with me on his back but noticed the slight change in my demeanor.

"You're quiet all of a sudden. What, did I embarrass you?" He grinned, enjoying teasing me. I laid my head down on his shoulder, hiding my face, nodding. His chuckle was music to my ears, amused by my reaction.

"I knew it. You're too easy to mess with sometimes, y'know? Just a compliment and you get all shy and quiet." He held his grin, silently relishing having this effect on me. I blew a rush of air in his ear to get back at him. Max flinched slightly at the unexpected gust of air in his ear, his ear twitching from the sensation. He let out a small laugh, caught off guard by my retaliation.

"Playing dirty now, are we? I see how it is." He gave my thighs a gentle squeeze with his arms in response while continuing to walk. I squeaked with delight. Max grinned at my reaction. He adjusted his grip on my legs slightly, his hands strong and firm around my thighs.

He enjoyed the knowledge that he had made me slightly flustered. "You really are just too cute sometimes, princesa."

"Well, so are you, Max…" I hugged him around his neck with both of my arms this time.

Max rolls his eyes at my teasing response. "Oh, come on, I'm not anywhere near *cute*. I'm rugged and stoic, remember? A badass through and through."

"Oh yes… so *stoic*… tough man…" I lowered my tone to taunt him with my impression of his voice. "Not at all my *sweet* and *caring* Max."

Max bristles at my comment, he doesn't seem to be used to being called *'sweet.'* "Oi, watch it. Don't get too cocky or I'll drop you right here on the street." He grumbles slightly, his tone trying to maintain a measure of toughness. But secretly, he loves the way I tease him. He has always told me that he finds it endearing.

"Oh well… I guess that's one way to go. *Roadkill*." I chuckled.

Max snorts with laughter at my morbid joke. "Roadkill. You're twisted, I'll give you that. Don't worry, I won't actually drop you. At least, not on purpose." He gives my thigh a reassuring squeeze this time, indicating that he's definitely not going to let me fall.

"I know you won't…" I ran my fingers through his hair. He lets out a sigh of content through his nose, enjoying the feel of my fingers in his hair. He tightens his grip on my legs, holding me a bit closer to him, appearing to almost melt at the motion.

He seems to almost sag slightly, comforted by my touch. "You're going to put me to sleep like that. It's very relaxing…"

"Well, don't fall asleep yet. I wouldn't look good as roadkill." I stop my hand and rest it back around his shoulder.

He snorts again, still keeping up his tough exterior despite getting drowsy from the earlier head rub, he clicks his tongue. "Tch. As if I'd fall asleep with you on my back. Don't worry, princesa, you're not going to become roadkill tonight… at least, not by my hands."

The rest of the way home, we continued to tease each other. We chat, banter back and forth, and enjoy each other's company. Max seems to relish the feeling of having me on his back and the way I lightly touch and caress his head every now and then. He keeps a strong grip on me, his arms firmly wrapped around my legs as he walks. I think of how he has been the only one who's been allowed to touch any part of my arms, my legs... anything below my collarbone. I trust him enough not to hurt me... abuse me... or go too far. His touch doesn't trigger my traumatic memories. I realize that I care about him the most and even more than the other three.

In the beginning, I couldn't stand anyone touching me below my collarbone. After everything with my uncle, it felt like every touch was an invasion. But Max… Max was different. From the first day I met him, his touch was careful, never too much, never too close. With him, there was no fear. Only comfort. He was the only one I trusted like that.

Soon, we reached our house's front yard and walked up the path to our front door. Max slowly lowers me from his back, steadying me with a hand on my lower back, holding on for a moment longer. As we stand in front of the front door, I raise my eyes into his. My heart does a somersault as his hand moves to my waist as he takes a step back. He looks back at me with a soft and warm expression, as if reluctant to let me go. Despite his best efforts, his eyes give away a hint of tenderness.

He finally lets go, though he looks down at me with a small smile. "Didn't exhaust you with that little ride, did I?"

"Not at all. Thanks for the lift, it really helped." I blink and finally break my stare, looking down as a faint blush paints my cheeks. I twirl my ponytail around my finger. My legs still ached from the training earlier, muscles sore and heavy as if they could give out at any moment. The evening breeze was warm, but a soft, cool edge crept through the air as twilight deepened, brushing over my flushed skin. The street lights flickered on, casting a soft glow over the quiet neighborhood.

Max notices the faint color on my cheeks and chuckles softly, his voice lowered as he teases me on the fact. "You still get embarrassed so easily. You'd think after all this time, you'd be more used to being teased by us. But somehow, you still get all shy like a little rabbit whenever *I* tease you." He steps a bit closer, his hand brushing a stray strand of hair from my face.

"Yeah, I guess that's another one of our little things, huh?" I release my ponytail to rest over my shoulder.

We stand in front of the house, the quiet evening air wrapping around us. The sky is a soft canvas of twilight, with stars beginning to peek through. The street is calm, with only the distant hum of city life providing a backdrop to this now intimate moment between us. My cheeks are still tinged with a faint blush, my heart fluttering from our close parameter. I look up at him, my eyes soft and sincere. The silence stretches between us, filled with the gentle rustling of leaves and the distant sounds of the city.

Max looked down at the ground for a moment, hesitating. He shifted his weight and let out a small breath before lifting his eyes back to mine. "You know... it's not just teasing. I... I really care about you, Elara. More than I ever thought I would."

My heart skips a beat at his admission. I search his eyes, looking for any hint of doubt in him, but all I see is sincerity. I take a small step closer, my hand finding his at his side. "Max... I care about you too. I've been trying to figure out my feelings, and... well, they're stronger than I realized."

Max's expression shifts from uncertainty to a warm, hopeful smile. He gently squeezes my hand as he briefly looks at our hands and intertwines his fingers with mine, his voice low and earnest. "I've been trying to keep things light and playful, but the truth is... I've fallen for you, Elara. I couldn't help it."

My eyes wide, shine with emotion as I look up at him. I squeeze his hand in return, my voice trembling slightly with the excitement I want to unleash. "I think... I'm falling for you too, Max. I didn't want to admit it at first, but... being this close to you, sharing these moments, it's made me realize how much I care for you. More than anyone."

Max's smile widens, and he pulls me closer by the waist, his arms wrapping around me with a tender strength. I melted into his embrace, my cheek pressed against his chest as I leaned in closer to him, closing the distance between us. The world seemed to fade away around us, leaving only the two of us in our shared, intimate bubble just big enough for two.

"I'm glad you feel the same. I was afraid that I'd push too hard or mess things up." I hear him say through the rumble in his chest. I can hear how quick his heart is beating against my ear.

"You didn't. You've been perfect. I wouldn't have it any other way." I grip him tighter, my hands on his back pulling him closer to me. We stand there for a moment longer, just holding each other, savoring the closeness and the effect of our confessions. The sun continues to shine over the horizon, witnessing our heartfelt admission to each other. He leans back to look at me after a few moments.

Max's eyes flicker with uncertainty, though his arms tighten around me, seeking reassurance. I feel my heart pound as the silence stretches between us. His gaze lingers on my lips, and I realize he's waiting for a sign. I nod, almost imperceptibly, but it's enough. Slowly, he leans in, and I close my eyes, feeling the warmth of his breath. The kiss starts soft, tentative—like we're both afraid to break whatever fragile connection we've just admitted. It's a kiss that speaks of our affection, our joy, and our hope for the future with one another. When we finally pulled away, he rested his forehead against mine, our breath mingling in the warm early evening air.

Max finally sighs, breaking the silence of our tension. "So, what now?" He whispers, as if afraid to ask the question.

My eyes twinkle with warmth and affection. "Now... we enjoy this moment and see where it takes us. Together. No pressure, just a day at a time."

Max grins, pulling me closer and pressing a gentle kiss to my forehead. "I can't wait." We stand there, wrapped in each other's arms, ready to explore what comes next with the strength of our newfound affections. The front door creaks open, and Ares steps outside, his gaze landing on Max and I and the pose we are in. Our little bubble pops at the sound.

Ares' eyes widen slightly in surprise as he catches us in the intimate position. "Oh. Sorry, I didn't mean to interrupt."

We pulled away from each other, our faces flushed with a mix of embarrassment and surprise. I quickly stepped back, my heart racing. Max's expression shifts from contentment to one of mild annoyance at the interruption.

"Ares, um… hey." I squeak out, bringing my fingers up to cover my lips. The feel of Max's lips lingering on mine.

Ares gives us a sheepish smile, as he's realized that he's walked out on something private. He scratches the back of his neck, his expression a mix of awkwardness and concern. "I just came out to check on you all. Didn't mean to… well, you know." He waves his hand at us, gesturing at the moment Max and I had shared on our front porch.

Max clears his throat, trying to regain his composure. He places a reassuring hand on my lower back, his voice steady and a hint of defensiveness. "It's fine, Ares. Do you need anything else?"

Ares nods, his gaze flickering between Max and me. He can tell from our expressions that something significant has just happened. He raises a single eyebrow. "Right. Well, I didn't mean to intrude on… whatever this is." He wiggles his forefinger between Max and me. "If you need some space, I can head back inside."

Despite the interruption, I'm still feeling a warm glow from Max's earlier confession. "No, it's okay, Ares. We're just coming in." I reply as I turn to fully face Ares.

Ares gives a nod of understanding, his expression softening. He seems to sense the genuine emotion between us and gives a small, encouraging smile. "Alright then. Just wanted to make sure everything was okay."

As Ares turns to go back inside, Max looks at me, his smile returning as he takes my hand again. "I guess the moment got a little bit of a detour."

I chuckled. "Yeah, but it's okay. We still have plenty of time to explore this." We share a knowing look, the earlier intimacy still presents despite the interruption. Ares heads back inside, leaving us standing outside, alone, once again. Our connection is stronger and more meaningful than ever before.

Max gently pulls me closer, his voice low and sincere. "We'll have our time, princesa. And I promise, I'll make sure it's worth the wait."

I smiled up at him, my heart full. "I'm looking forward to it."

We walk towards the front door, knowing that our feelings have finally been confirmed and that this is just the beginning of our journey together. As we walk into the house, Max's hand is firmly on my waist, a silent declaration of our new closeness. Inside, we notice Lius lounging on the couch, flipping through a magazine. He glances up as we enter, his eyes immediately fixing on where Max's hand is resting around me.

Lius cocks an eyebrow, his gaze flickering between the two of us before closing his magazine and leaning back with a smirk. "Well, well, well. If it isn't the two lovebirds…"

"For the love of the gods… Don't start Lius." I roll my eyes, bringing my fingers to my forehead. I'm getting a headache already, before he even begins his annoying torment.

"As soon as Ares mentioned what he saw outside our front doorstep, I had to come out here and witness it for myself." He looks over at Max and me, his eyes resting once again on Max's hand on my waist.

"What you really mean is he saw us through a window and then ran to tell you about it? What… So, Ares made up a reason to come out and interrupt us, huh? You two are rude." I cross my arms and narrow my eyes at him. It is definitely something the two peas in a pod would do.

Lius feigns innocence, his hand dramatically coming up to his chest in mock surprise. "What? Me? Interrupt the two of you? Never... I would never purposely try to stop one of my best friends from having a nice little make-out session with a pretty girl." His eyes flicker with mischief, indicating otherwise.

Max is not buying Lius' act. He tightens his grip on me, pulling me closer as if to make a statement. "Yeah right. You just couldn't resist sticking your nose in where it doesn't belong, could you, Arelius?"

Lius, enjoying the way he gets under our skin as always, leans forward on the couch, resting his chin on his hand. "Oh, come on. You can't blame me for being curious. It's not every day that I see my cold-hearted emotionless friend going all soft and gooey over a girl..."

Max grew impatient with the needling. "Shut up, Arelius. I just... happen to have a soft spot for *her*, that's all."

I can feel his body tense and see his eyes lock onto Lius' face. I rub the back of my hand on his chest lightly to calm him down and show my gratitude for his sentiment. I look up at him and smile, letting him know it's okay and to just let his teasing slide this time. His expression softens slightly at my touch, and he lets out a small sigh, relaxing a bit. He gives me a small nod, appreciating my attempt to calm him down, but his eyes flick back from me to Lius.

Lius watches the exchange with a smirk, picking up on the subtle change between us. "Wow, look at you, Max. Going all soft under her touch. She really has you whipped, doesn't she...?"

"That's enough, Arelius..." I shoot a warning glance at him. Picking up the sense that Lius seems to be angry... And I might have a good idea as to why, but now isn't the time to talk it over with him.

Lius holds his hands up in surrender, though his grin reveals he's not done. "Fine, fine, I'll back off. Just making a statement of my observation, that's all."

"And you've made your point. We get it." I snap. My own protective instincts over Max kicked in.

He laughs at my comment, amused by my annoyance. "Hey, can you blame me? It's not every day I get to see Max here go mushy over a girl. I have to take advantage of the situation whenever I can."

"Okay, but if you keep poking fun…" My eyes darken, my voice becoming sharper with warning. "I won't stop him next time."

Max shoots a glare at Lius, liking the idea of not having me intervene next time Lius decides he's going to poke fun at him. "Watch yourself. You wouldn't like the outcome if you upset my girl too much."

Lius laughs again, his smirk widening. "Oh really…? And what's she going to do…? Hmm? Yell at me? Send me to the *'naughty corner'*?"

"Wanna find out…?" I lower my hands and start to walk towards Lius, my hands in fists.

Lius' smirk falters slightly as I approach him. "Woah, easy there, birdie. I was just joking around. No need to get all feisty. Wasn't trying to offend you or Max, just having a little fun."

Max watches the exchange with a mixture of amusement and pride at how protective I became over him. He appreciates that I'm standing up for myself as well, but remains a bit on edge, wary of Lius' tendency to push things too far with me. I turned back to Max, grab his hand, and lead him upstairs. He follows willingly, intertwining his fingers with mine. As we walked up the stairs, I let out an annoyed breath.

Max notices my expression and squeezes my hand gently. "Relax, princesa. You know Lius is just teasing."

"I don't mind it when it's directed at me... it's when it's directed at you..." I squeezed his hand.

He couldn't help but smile slightly at my protectiveness. He tugs on my hand to stop me, he reaches up to touch my cheek with his free hand, his thumb brushing against my skin. "C'mon, princesa. I can handle myself. I'm not some delicate flower that needs protecting, you know."

"I understand that... but still..." I instinctively leaned into his hand against my cheek.

He chuckles softly, his smile softening. "I appreciate your concern. I can handle Lius' teasing. He's just being his usual smart-ass self, that's all. No need to stress about it." I lean into his touch as his hand cups my cheek, his thumb continuing to brush against my skin. He looks down at me, his expression tender, a hint of a smile tugging at the corner of his mouth. I've never seen him look at anyone like this.

Max grins softly, his thumb brushing my cheek. "You know that look makes it hard for me to hold back..." His voice is a low whisper, almost teasing, but I can hear the depth of his feelings in the way his breath hitches slightly.

"Well... we were interrupted earlier..." I lead him into his room since it's closer, and close the door, locking it behind me.

He grins. There's a sense of anticipation in his eyes as he looks at me. "That we were. Can't let Lius and Ares ruin our fun again, can we?"

"No, we can't." I answer as I walk closer to him.

Max pulls me close, he grips the nape of my neck, the other hand resting on my hip, as he leans down to kiss me. The kiss is slow and tender at first. But it quickly deepens, fueled by the emotions we've both kept hidden for so long. His hands move gently, almost reverently, as if afraid to break the spell we've cast around ourselves. I lose myself in the kiss, my hands tangling in his hair. The warmth of his lips sends a shiver through me, a soft heat spreading from where we touch. His hand is firm on my waist, pulling me closer until I can feel the steady beat of his heart against my chest. The world around us fades, leaving only the taste of his breath, the warmth of his skin, and the rhythm of our breathing, falling in sync. The world outside fades away, leaving only the two of us in this moment back in our little bubble built for two. We break apart briefly, both of us out of breath, our foreheads resting against each other once again.

Max's playful smile fades into something more serious as he brushes a strand of hair behind my ear. "I've waited so long for this, Elara," he whispers, his voice raw with emotion. There's no teasing, no banter—just him, and me, and the closeness we've both longed for.

"I think I have some idea. I've wanted this too, Max. Ever since you took care of me when I bruised my ribs…" I think back to how my heart would flutter each time he gently reapplied my bandages, the warmth of his fingers brushing against my skin, or the way the soft clink of the teacup at night became a comforting routine. It wasn't just the way he cared for me, but the way he saw through my defenses. How he knew when the weight of my emotions became too much, and without hesitation, he'd climb into bed next to me, wrapping me in his arms, as if he could quiet the storm inside me just by being close.

He smiles, his eyes full of warmth and affection as he looks at me. "Good. Because… I'm not letting you go now."

I smile back at him, feeling a sense of contentment and happiness I haven't felt in a long time. "I wouldn't want you to."

His smile warms me from the inside, and as our lips meet once again, it's not just a kiss; it's a promise—of comfort, of love, of something we've both been waiting for. His lips move against mine with a gentleness that makes my heart race, and as his arms pull me closer, I know with certainty—I am home.

14

I wake up to Max no longer in bed with me and sit up to look around, confirming he is not in his room somewhere. The sun is shining brightly, and I look at the time—it's early. I get up and head towards the bathroom to shower and get ready for my yoga class that starts in a couple hours. The grin I'm sporting is cemented to my face this morning at the memory of what just transpired. I have Max now.

As I make my way to the bathroom, I hear the sound of voices coming from the living room. One of the voices is Max's, the other is one I don't know and have never heard before. I can't make out what they're saying, but the tone of the conversation sounds agitated. I decided to get my coffee first, and find out who's here, if Max is okay. In one of Max's shirts and my spandex shorts, I head down the stairs to the kitchen to see what all the commotion is about and maybe greet our visitor.

As I enter the living room, I see Max standing in the middle of it, his body tense and his face twisted into a sneer. The same expression he makes when he's fighting against an enemy.

He's facing another man whose back is to me–I don't know who this other person is. The conversation seems to be heated, and it's obvious that there's no love lost between the two of them. I stop behind the unknown man and look past him and up at Max with questions on my face, but I stay silent so as to not interrupt.

Max glances at me as I enter the room, his expression softening slightly when he sees me. The unknown man doesn't notice me standing behind him yet, his attention solely focused on Max, and he seems torn, like he wants to say something to me but doesn't want to show weakness in front of this other man. This has me really concerned as to who's in our living room right now. The unknown man continues to argue with Max, his voice getting more and more aggressive with each passing second. Max keeps his cool, his arms crossed over his chest and his expression neutral, but I can tell he's growing restless, like he's just itching for a reason to let loose—to throw the first punch.

Finally, the unknown man seems to push Max a little too far, and he snaps. In a blur of motion, Max lunges forward, grabbing the man by the throat and slamming him up against the wall next to him, away from me.

"Hey! Whoa!" I shout and charge towards Max, I notice he doesn't weaken in front of this man as I place a hand on his arm. I play along to keep his secret from this man for him. "Take it outside Max!" I scold even though I would love to get this stranger in a chokehold for upsetting my Max.

Max's grip on the other man's throat tightens briefly before he lets go, letting the man drop unceremoniously to the floor with a loud thump. He doesn't look at me, his gaze still trained on the other man, but he can't deny the effect my voice has on him.

He takes a deep breath, trying to calm himself down, before reluctantly stepping away and heading towards the door. "Fine. We will take it outside." The tone he uses towards me makes my heart sink. He's mad that I've intervened with whatever business he has with this man.

"No fighting in the house! Max, you know that!" I shoot a glance at the unknown man who is now rubbing his neck to soothe the pain from Max's grip. I straighten and lower my hand to fully face the unknown guest. "Welcome to our home sir. I apologize for my outburst, but I do not permit fighting inside the house. If you want to start shit with one of us living here. Take it outside…" I take a quick look out the side of my eyes at Max. "Who are you by the way?"

The unknown man picks himself up off the floor, still rubbing his throat where Max's grip had left marks, his eyes narrowed into a glare directed at me. He looks at me with a mix of surprise and annoyance, as if he's not used to being spoken to like that by a woman. "Who the hell are you?! Don't you know who I am?!" Max lets out a low growl at how this man addresses me.

I shake my head and proceed. "I'm Elara. I'm Max's roommate. You're in my house, no… I don't know who you are. Answer my question… who are you?!" My voice firm and my glare locked onto him.

The unknown man's expression shifts from annoyance to confusion as I speak, surprised by my confidence. He seems taken aback by the fact that he can't intimidate me, and he glances at Max, as if expecting him to jump in and correct me for my behavior towards him. When Max doesn't say anything, the man looks back at me, his tone becoming more insolent. "You really don't know who I am? Really?"

"Really. Who are you? That's the final time I will ask nicely." I hold my gaze on him. Not showing an ounce of fear or backing down. I live with four very large Vipers. This man's little attempt at intimidation isn't going to scare me nor make me submit. If I can handle my roommate's rage fits, I can handle this idiot.

The man huffs in irritation, I can tell he's not accustomed to being questioned like this. He sizes me up for a moment before replying, his tone dripping with contempt. "Tch. You really don't know who I am? I'm Max's fucking brother."

My expression relaxes and my eyebrows rise. "Oh... ahem... Hello Max's brother. Brotherly quarrels are handled outside when they become a physical altercation." I look over at Max. "What are you two fighting about anyways?"

"None of your business, Ellie. Mark... watch how you talk to her." Max's words are sharp and cold, his jaw tight with irritation. It's clear that he really is unhappy about my interfering in his business, especially in front of his brother, Mark. Mark glances at him, a smirk on his face as if he's enjoying the display.

I turn and head towards the kitchen. "You're right... Just don't make a mess." My tone is sharp as I really don't appreciate how Max just spoke to me, but he must have a reason, and I will ask him about it later. Max can hear the annoyance in my response. He understands that I'm mad at his snap at me. I walk to the coffee maker and pour my coffee into my favorite coffee mug that I've had for almost 10 years. It's a twenty ounce light blue cup with a cartoon donkey on the side of it. I got it when I went on vacation with my mother to Los Angeles. It's been my only coffee mug ever since. I took my cup filled with just the right amount of coffee, milk and sugar, and headed back upstairs, without saying anything further to Max or his brother, nor looking at either of them. I headed into my room and slammed the door shut. Max listens as I walk away, the sound of the door slamming shut ringing in his ears, making him flinch slightly at the sound. He feels a pang of guilt at the coldness of his words towards me, knowing that he's hurt my feelings in some way. But he can't afford to show weakness in front of his brother. Why did his words cut so deep? I had heard him snap before, but this was different. It wasn't anger—it was something else, something distant. Something that made my stomach twist in ways I wasn't ready to confront.

I emerge from my room and head back downstairs dressed in my yoga gear. "Ok everyone. I'm headed to yoga." I say to the room without looking at any of them. My anger is still evident at Max's earlier curt words. I grab my things and head out the door. Lius–who had come downstairs with Kai and Ares to investigate all the commotion–and Max shot a sympathetic glance my way as I stormed out the front door, clearly sensing that something was off. Kai and Ares watch as well, their expressions neutral, but they're confused about the tension in the room and why I seem to be upset. Mark, on the other hand, just laughs, enjoying the display of expressions of the four men towards me, their roommate. How I seem to affect all of the men that live in this house has piqued his interest.

~*~

The coldness in Max's voice stung more than it should have. I wasn't just mad—I was hurt. And the worst part? I had no idea why he was pulling away from me, just when things between us were finally starting to feel real. I continue to walk to the yoga studio when I summon Ares to walk next to me as I know he's close by, following me to class as always. "Ares...? Could you walk with me please?"

Ares steps from out of the shadows silently, falling into step beside me like a natural shadow. "Yes?"

"What's the deal with Max's brother?" I ask as I keep my walking pace.

Ares glances at me as he walks beside me, his eyes continuing to scan our surroundings almost unconsciously to ensure there isn't any danger. "The Rossi brothers... they're both very difficult men, but Mark more so. Those two were always competitive growing up, never quite getting along. They were always trying to outdo each other in everything... fighting, money-making, even in women..."

"Women...? Hmm, so that explains why Max was pretending that we're just roommates to each other in front of Mark. Huh... okay. What else should I know?" My brow furrows as I understand the situation that unfolded earlier in the living room.

Ares pauses for a moment, considering his next words. "Mark was always the favored one growing up, the one who was supposed to inherit the family wealth and power. Max, on the other hand, was seen as the disappointment of the family. The one who never quite lived up to the family standards."

Sadness strikes my heart. "He's not a disappointment... that's awful..." I comment with a low tone of sadness for Max as it takes over my heart along with it. His family sees him as a disappointment...? How could they?

Ares' expression softens as he sees the sadness on my face, touched by my unwavering belief in Max's worth. "No, he's not. But that's how their family always saw him. And that's how Mark still sees him."

"Then why is Mark here?" I quirk and eyebrow in question and now suspicion.

Ares' expression becomes more serious as he considers my question. "It's hard to say for sure. But I have a feeling his visit has something to do with the fact that Max left the family and its influence behind. The Rossi Family is very old fashioned, very traditional in their beliefs. Max and Mark are the ones meant to lead the next generation. But Max renounced that life, and it's something Mark hasn't forgiven him for."

"Oh… so what does he want from Max?" I begin to put the pieces together but still cannot understand why Mark has come to our home to cause trouble for my sweet Max. I hope he fills me in on everything later.

Ares pauses before carefully sharing the information as to not say too much without Max's permission. "It's not just about what Mark wants from Max. It's about what their family, as a whole, wants from him. They see Max as a wasted opportunity, a chance to regain their lost pride and power. Max, however, wants nothing to do with that life, with the violence and greed that comes with it."

"That's admirable." A small grin spreads across my lips. Proud of Max for his decision to leave his family in the rear view mirror.

Ares nods in agreement. "Yes, it is. But his family doesn't see it that way. They see Max's rejection as a snub, a betrayal of their ways. And they may try to force him back into the fold, willing or not."

As Ares spoke, a chill ran down my spine. Max had always been so protective, but now I wondered—was he protecting me from something bigger than just his brother's arrogance? Was there more to this than he'd let on? Mark didn't just want to rile him up—he wanted to pull him back in. Max's defiance was a stain on the Rossi legacy, and Mark was here to clean it up, one way or another.

Ares stops as well, seeing the worried look in my eyes. He understands my fears, the dangers of the situation I find myself in. "Take a deep breath, Ellie. It's going to be alright. Even if they want him back, Max is one of the strongest elemental wielders there is, no one can force him to do anything he does not want to do."

I nod once and begin walking again. "Ok good... I hope that they don't tear up our house while we're out..." I mention this as we arrive in front of the yoga studio.

Ares chuckles at my comment, he is amused as he listens to my concern for the state of our house more than anything else. "I'm sure they won't fight that hard... if they do, you let me know and I'll do a little renovation on their faces."

"Thanks..." I chuckled. "Ok, thanks for walking with me. I've gotten used to you following me to yoga. It's nice to have someone to walk and talk with... I'll see you afterwards."

Ares nods, a soft smile on his face. "Of course. It's what we do. We look out for each other. Try not to worry too much about Max, okay? He will be fine. We won't let anything happen to him. We won't let anything hurt you, physically or otherwise. Never have and we never will."

I nod in a firm affirmation and enter the studio. Ares watches as I head into the studio, keeping a watchful eye on me until I'm inside. The studio is a place known for its tranquility and relaxation, a stark contrast from the situation unfolding back at the house. Inside the tranquil yoga studio, the class begins shortly after I arrive. The soft lighting and gentle music create a peaceful atmosphere as the instructor leads the group through a series of poses and movements, guiding them to find their center and their breath. As I flow through the familiar motions, I can feel my body slowly begin to relax, the tension and stress in my muscles gradually melting away with each inhale and exhale. I go through the moves effortlessly all while thinking about what must be happening at the house right now. Despite my best efforts to focus on the class, my mind keeps wandering back to the house, wondering what's going on between Max and Mark. Are they still arguing? Has the situation calmed down?

~*~

My class ends and I walk out to meet Ares so we can walk home. He is waiting patiently outside, leaning against a nearby wall as he scans the surroundings, his sharp eyes constantly watchful for any potential threats. As I walk out of the studio, he looks over and nods in greeting. "Finished?"

"Yep. This class was intense. My muscles are still a little tight from when I was injured but… I feel better now. Shall we?" I gestured for us to head home. Ares nods, falling into step beside me as we begin our walk home, his demeanor calm and watchful as always. He knows my muscles are still healing, and he's careful to keep a close eye on my movements, making sure I didn't strain something. As we walk, we talk about different things and laugh as we crack jokes and make jabs at each other. My friendship with Ares is different than it is with Max, or the others. We understand each other, both have suffered traumas in our past and we know just how to help each other through our bad days. We can share anything and everything with each other and know that neither one of us will judge the other.

I freeze in place on the sidewalk as I feel the hairs on the back of my neck stand up in alert. Ares notices the change in my demeanor, and he stops as well, his eyes sharp and alert as he glances around the area. "What is it?" His voice is sharp as he searches for what he now can feel too.

"We're being watched... I can't tell where though..." I whisper to him as I begin walking again at a slow leisurely pace as I scan our surroundings without moving my head too much so that whomever—or whatever—is watching us doesn't catch on that I've sensed them. Ares follows my lead, continuing to walk alongside me, keeping his guard up. He's always trusted in my instincts and knows that I'm rarely wrong about these things.

A quiet moment passes as we both walk, and then Ares speaks up quietly. "I feel it too. But if it's someone with hostile intentions, why haven't they attacked yet?"

I hum in acknowledgement. "I think they must see you and are being cautious."

Ares nods, his expression darkening as he considers my words. Whomever is watching us is wary of him, but that doesn't mean they won't attack if they feel desperate enough. "Hmm. They're either waiting for an opening, or they're gathering intel."

"I think waiting for an—" I'm cut off as the source of my alarm lands from above, right in front of us. A rogue elemental.

Ares tenses as soon as the rogue lands. He lunges an arm out in front of me. "Get behind me. Now." He steps in front of me, his eyes locked onto the rogue, analyzing its form and potential abilities. We didn't need to speak; we both knew what it meant to face demons, both literal and metaphorical. His presence grounded me, even in the face of this monstrous threat. The rogue gazes at both of us, its expression almost... human.

It smiles, revealing rows of sharp, jagged teeth, and its voice is surprisingly soft. "Well, well... look what we have here." Its eyes flicker over both of us before landing on me. "You. You're the one, aren't you?"

"The one what...?" I tense as it addresses me. This one can talk?! I have yet to encounter an elemental rogue that can speak, hinting to me that it must be very strong.

The rogue laughs, the sound cold and hollow. "Don't play dumb with me, girl. You know exactly what I'm talking about..." It takes a step forward, its eyes locked onto me.

"I'm not playing dumb... I don't know what you're talking about," I say through gritted teeth. This rogue is after me, it seems. Possibly sent by my uncle... Did he figure out that I'm the vigilante getting in the way and ruining every plan he's been attempting to accomplish since my arrival? Did this rogue figure it out? Or is this thing after me for another reason...? A lump forms in my throat. Its smile widens as it notices the increased tension.

It seems amused by my confusion, though whether it's genuine or just cruel taunting is impossible to tell. "Oh, you don't know? Or you just don't want to admit to it in front of your friend here?" The rogue takes another step forward. Its form seems to waver and flicker, as if it's not fully solidified. Ares moves further in front of me to shield me.

Seeing Ares move more in front of me, the rogue's smile turns to a sneer, its eyes narrowing. "Ah, so that's how it is. Protective, isn't he?" The rogue refers to Ares, its eyes never leaving mine as it speaks. It takes another step forward in challenge, its form becoming slightly more stable as it eyes Ares up and down, assessing him as a potential threat. Ares doesn't respond to the taunting, his gaze locked on its form, ready to react at a moment's notice. His body is tense, every muscle coiled for a fight. "You think you can protect her? You have no idea what you are up against." The rogue's voice is now mocking. Its eyes flicker between me and Ares as it steps closer once more. It seems amused by the situation, enjoying the fact that it's got both of us cornered.

"State your purpose, rogue." My body is tense and fists form as I ready myself to react if it decides to attack.

The rogue laughs again, the sound harsh and grating. "My purpose? Oh, I have a very specific purpose in being here." It takes another step forward, now close enough that I can see its true form more clearly. Its body shifts and flickers, taking on an almost human appearance at one moment, then a twisted, misshapen form the next. Ares tenses more, staying firmly between me and the rogue. His expression is cold and unreadable, but I can feel the tension radiating off of him in waves. He's ready for a fight, the earth rumbling beneath us as he readies for a fight, his eyes never leaving the rogue's shifting form. "I'm here to make a little... trade." Its tone is almost casual now, as if it's discussing something as mundane as the weather. It glances over at me, its eyes filled with an unnatural gleam.

The word 'trade' sends a shiver down my spine, and I can feel Ares tense even further. He's definitely on high alert. "What kind of trade?" Ares finally speaks up in a low and dangerous tone. His eyes permanently locked onto the rogue's form. He doesn't trust its intentions and he's not going to give it an inch without knowing exactly what it wants.

The rogue grins, the expression even more menacing in its shifting form. "It's simple, really. You see, I have a... special interest in your friend here." Its eyes shift over to me again, its gaze predatory, like a lion sizing up its prey. Ares stiffens even more, his hands clenched into fists at his sides.

Ares is furious at the rogue's tone, at the implication that I'm some sort of prize to be won or an object to be traded. "And what exactly do you want with her?"

The rogue chuckles again, the sound dark and menacing. "Oh, I think you know what I want with her. She has a very... special kind of power. One that I've taken quite an interest in." It circles around us, its form still shifting and flickering as it moves. It seems to be sizing us up, trying to figure out the best way to get what it wants. I hold my stance, keeping my eyes on the rogue, never letting it out of my sight. I feel Ares grab my wrist as he reaches for my watch. He presses the button on it to alert Max of our location, indicating that we're in trouble and need backup. Ares keeps his eyes locked on the rogue as he presses the button, while it continues to circle us. Noting the subtle movement of its form and trying to detect any potential weakness. He keeps his composure as he presses the button again, despite the danger we are now in.

Ares' hand tightened around my wrist, his thumb brushing the watch's button again. "Where the hell is Max?" His voice was tight, the seconds feeling like hours. His only goal right now is to get me out of this situation alive and unharmed.

"You're quite perceptive, aren't you? But you both are out of your depth here. Neither of you can handle taking me on..." The rogue laughs again, the sound dark and mocking. It stops its circling, standing directly across from us, its eyes locked back onto me. I hold its gaze, refusing to back down even as I feel the weight of its malice bearing down on me. I really wish I had my Katanas with me right now. Every instinct screamed at me to grab my blade inside my gym bag, but Ares' voice echoed in my head—'Never take on an elemental alone.' As much as I hated feeling powerless, I knew this was his fight. For now. Ares remains a solid presence beside me, his body tense and ready to act.

"You're a tough one, aren't you? Most people would be begging me for their lives by now…" I hold its gaze, unwavering as I stand ready for anything. It grins, enjoying my defiance. It's so close now that I can feel its cold presence in the air. "Oh, how I do enjoy a challenge. It will make the victory so much sweeter."

It reaches out a hand, its long, bony fingers almost brushing against my cheek as it moves closer. Ares pushes me back, away from its touch. "Do not touch her…" He snarls.

Its eyes gleam in amusement, looking at Ares, enjoying just how protective he is being. It's relishing the challenge. "Oh, come now, don't be so stingy… I just want a little… taste of that power." It senses Ares' tension and aura giving off a deadly warning. It straightens up and sighs as if annoyed. "Your power… it's not just yours, is it? There's something ancient inside you, something that's been waiting to awaken. I can smell it." It stops and closes its eyes as if aggravated by an invisible interruption. "It seems as if we have company…" It looks up towards the roof of the building behind us.

I look up and see that Lius is crouched down, ready to pounce, perched on the building's ledge as he observes the scene unfold below him. His eyes meet mine, before darting between Ares and the rogue elemental. The rogue scoffs, "Looks like your knight in shining armor has arrived… Isn't that right, Arelius Blackwood?" The rogue addresses Lius, whose expression doesn't waver as the rogue addresses him. He stares down at it, his eyes locked on its shifting form.

Ares and I don't waver or show a reaction to Lius' arrival. My body relaxes slightly as I know Max will also arrive soon, since my watch alerts only him. The guys told me to never take on an elemental on my own since I don't have any powers to wield myself. I'm relieved that Ares was with me for this one. Its power is unfathomable, and I would have never been able to take it on my own. Now that Lius is here, the other two should arrive any second.

The rogue maneuvers in a fluid and quick motion as it gets between Ares and I, looking down at me, backing me against the wall. Ares' eyes widen with alarm as the rogue appears behind him, quickly turning around.

Lius' eyes darken as he sees the quick movements of the rogue, his knuckles white as he tightly grips the ledge of the roof. He begins to calculate the best way to intervene, without harming me or risking the rogue grabbing me and taking off. The monster reaches out and grabs my chin as soon as it is in front of me, it's cold, slender fingers gripping tightly on my chin as it looks down at me. The rogue's form flickered again, shifting between human and something monstrous. Its face distorted into a grotesque smile, as if it were toying with us.

I hold a hand up to stop Ares from acting too recklessly once I see him tilt his baby to lunge towards us. I meet its gaze. "What is it you want with me? What's the trade you seek?"

The rogue chuckles again, its fingers digging into my chin as it roams its eyes over my face, a sick sinister look in its eyes. "Your power, girl... It's buried deep, but I can sense it. That ancient energy locked away. It's only a matter of time before it awakens, and when it does... you'll be mine."

"No. I don't know what you're talking about." I snap.

The rogue snarls at my response, becoming annoyed at my ignorance. Its grip tightens on my chin, painfully. "You're playing dumb, aren't you? You know that you're something... special. Something valuable."

"No... I'm just a human..." I don't react to the searing pain from its claws digging into my skin. Why me? What did it want from me that others didn't? Could it be connected to my uncle, or was there something deeper at play?

The rogue's eyes narrow as it looks me over, taking in my words. "Oh, you are more than just a human, pet." It shifts slightly, its form flickering in and out of solidity as it considers its next move. It finally releases its grip on my chin and steps back. "But enough talk. I will get what I came for. One way or another..."

The rogue's sneer faded for a brief moment as its gaze shifted upward. Lius stood like a shadow, his aura brimming with lethal intent. The rogue licked its lips, as if savoring the challenge. Ares stays tense, waiting for its next move. Lius doesn't react, but I can see the tension in his body. He's ready to strike once there's a sure chance that I won't be hurt in the crossfire. The rogue's form begins to flicker again, and I realize it's preparing to make a move. I brace myself, ready for whatever comes next. But then, before the rogue can act, there's a blur of motion as Max and Kai arrive, their forms flashing as they land between me and the rogue. They quickly stand ready to intervene. Max holds his arm back touching mine as reassurance I am within reach of him, safe. I look down at his other hand and notice he has two long and slender rods in his grip—my katanas. The rogue's eyes widen in surprise, and then narrow in anger.

"Well, well... it seems the rest of the welcoming committee has arrived... SP6's Vipers are here." It sneers, looking between

Max and Kai. The two men stand tall and confident, their eyes locked onto the rogue's form.

"You're not taking her," Max says, his voice firm and unwavering. Kai nods in agreement, his gaze equally intense. Max grabs my wrist quickly and turns with me walking away from the beast, leading me to a safe distance. He hands me my Katanas and gives me a knowing smirk. He's seen what I can do with them, and I will have to inevitably fight as well.

The rogue growls out. His voice's bass echoing off the walls of the buildings around us. "You think you can take her from me? You think you can protect her? You're not as strong as you think you are, Viper! I'll get to her sooner or later! Just wait and see!"

Max's grip on me moves around my waist, shielding me completely from the rogue. His grip tightens slightly at the rogue's words, his expression becoming more and more frustrated. "Shut the hell up you low life rogue! You're not getting anywhere near her!" He bites out.

"You don't get to decide that Viper... I will have her... I will take that power she possesses, and you all will be powerless to stop it!" The rogue shouts at Max and I as we continue walking away.

I feel Max's grip grow even tighter as his expression is now bordering on outright rage. He starts to shake against me. I graze the back of my hand on his stomach to calm him. I don't look back at the rogue again to avoid encouraging him to attack, but I feel Max's body jolt and tense under my touch, his expression relaxing for a moment before the sound of the rogue's roar rips through the air towards us.

Max snarls. "Dammit!" His grip on my waist tightens again as he begins to turn around to face the charging beast, throwing up a shield of spinning flames in front of him and I. Shutting us away from the rogue's attack. Kai, Ares and Lius are now in front of it, holding it off. They finally found their moment of opportunity, Lius' eyes locked onto Max and me.

Lius shouts, "Don't worry, we've got this. Focus on getting her out of here!"

Max hesitates for a moment, his eyes darting between the rogue and the others. "Are you sure you can handle this?"

Lius scoffs as he fends off the rogue's attacks. "Are you kidding? We've handled worse than this thing before!"

Ares chimes in. "Don't worry, we'll hold it off. Just get Elara to safety Max! Go!"

Max nods and he turns to guide me away from the scene, his body taut with tension. As he leads me away, the sound of the rogue's roars and the sounds of the others battling it grows fainter as we quickly walk away.

The rogue scoffs. "We shall see about that…" Its form flickers again, and it lunges forward, attacking with a burst of speed and force. Ares and Kai move to intercept, their forms blurring as they engage the rogue in a flurry of movement. Max pulls me into a jog, gripping my hand tight, ensuring I'm out of harm's way as the battle unfolds behind us. The rogue's form flickers and shifts as it fights, its movements quick and unpredictable. But Ares, Kai, and Lius are well-coordinated, their attacks precise and powerful. Max stays close to me, ready to protect me if the rogue manages to break through their defenses. We tuck into an alleyway, I peer around the corner as Max blocks me while the battle ensues.

"Max… let me go help them." I grab the hilts of my katanas, one in each hand. I fling them down and out, removing their sheaths. I take a step forward intending on charging into the battle.

"Over my dead fucking body will I let you go out there, princesa…" Grits out Max. "They've got it… stay here." His arm out to his side to block me from leaving, this time instead of shielding me from being taken into that thing's custody. I look at him with a scowl at being denied my request to go help. I wanted to fight. Every instinct screamed to join the battle, but Max stood firm, and for a moment, I felt a flicker of resentment. I wasn't some fragile thing to be coddled, but his protectiveness had always been one of the things I admired most about him.

The battle is intense, with the rogue using every trick and ability at its disposal. But the three men are relentless, their combined efforts gradually wearing it down with combined attacks of earth, lightning and water, encapsulating the rogue without mercy. With a final burst of energy, the rogue is subdued. It collapses to the ground, its form flickering and unstable as it struggles to maintain its shape. The rogue's claws scraped against the earth as it lunged again, but Ares was faster, raising a wall of stone between them with a deafening crash. Dust clouded the air as Kai's lightning flashed, striking with a force that shook the ground beneath our feet.

Lius steps forward, his eyes locked onto the rogue. "You're done. Leave now, and never return…" His voice is cold and commanding, leaving no room for argument. The rogue glares up at him, its eyes filled with hatred. It knows it's been defeated, and any wrong move could result in its demise. With a final flicker, it disappears, its form dissipating into the air.

Ares, Kai, and Lius stand tall, their expressions determined. They turn to me, relief evident in their eyes. Max looks back at me. "Are you okay?" I step forward, my heart still racing from the encounter as I pick up my katana guards and I insert them, tucking them under one arm.

I nod, taking a deep breath to steady myself. "Yes. Thank you. All of you…" My eyes shift to Ares, Kai and Lius, who both nod in acknowledgment. Max offers me his hand so that we can step out from the alleyway. I take his hand and walk out from being tucked behind the corner of the building. "Great job everyone." I exclaim even though I'm bummed I couldn't join in on the fun.

Max smiles at me, his fingers intertwined with mine as he pulls me closer to him. Max's touch calmed the storm in my chest, but deep down, I couldn't shake the unease. What did the rogue know about me that I didn't? And why did it leave me feeling both safe in Max's arms and... stifled? He pulls back and looks at the small cuts on my face with concern, taking his other hand to lift my chin turning my face side to side to get a better look at them. He looks into my eyes. "Do those hurt?"

My own expression softens as I shake my head slightly and smile in reassurance. "No. I'm ok." I muttered out. He caresses my cheek with his thumb.

He smiles lightly. "Good... I can't have my girl getting seriously hurt again now, can I?"

I giggle at him calling me his girl… it warms my heart out of its downtrodden fit from him keeping me back from fighting. I look behind him and see the other three walking towards us. As they approach, they take a moment to catch their breath and compose themselves. All three look absolutely exhausted but smile with pride as they come to a stop in front of Max and me.

Lius huffs. "Well, that's one rogue taken care of."

Kai applauds. "Thanks to Max for getting Elara away from the scene so we didn't have to hold back."

Max grins at the compliment from Kai, his chest puffing out slightly with pride. "Just doing what I need to, to protect my princesa here."

Lius rolls his eyes at Max's cocky response, but there's a hint of jealousy in his eyes. "Oh, look at you showing off... You love doing that don't you?"

I patted Max on his chest. "I love it when he shows off..." shooting a glare at Lius out from the corner of my eyes.

Max grins at my words, his hand covers mine on his chest. He gives me a quick wink as he looks over to Lius. "See that? Even the lady loves it."

"Let's get out of here," Kai says, his voice calm but firm to put a stop to an inevitable fight that is sure to ensue between the three of us—Lius, Max and me. We start to head back towards our house, our steps quick but cautious. Max walks to my side and grabs my hand as we walk.

I look around as we walk back and notice that Mark is not around. I look up at Max. "Where's Mark?"

Max huffs at my question. "He took off once he saw the rogue we were facing. He's such chickenshit. Typical Mark. Full of bravado when it came to taunts, but when faced with real danger, he always fled." Max had been right—his brother was a coward.

The adrenaline is still coursing through my veins, but I feel a sense of relief knowing that we're safe for now. So many questions are swarming through my mind... Powers? What powers? We made our way back, and I can't help but feel grateful for the support and protection of Max and my friends.

We walked into the house, and I walked to the middle of the living room. Once they've all filed in, I turn to look at all four of them. "What power was that beast talking about? The one he wanted to steal from me?"

Lius, Ares and Kai all exchange glances that have me suspicious and nervous. Their expressions are serious and contemplative. It's clear that the rogue's words about my power have caught my attention and have made me uneasy. Lius shares, "It's hard to say really. Elemental Rogues have a habit of talking nonsense to try and throw us off. But the fact that it specifically wanted your power... is concerning." They exchanged glances again—glances that made my stomach twist with uncertainty. I may have been human, but something about the way they looked at me now suggested that they knew something I didn't. Something important.

"I know. I don't have any powers, I'm just a human..." I ponder as we all sit there and think over the day's events. The men all listen patiently as I speak, their expressions becoming more and more serious as their own minds wander. "I may just ask Tatsuya... he may know something... or I'll reach out to the Z Group and see if they know anything."

The men nod, as they absorb my thoughts. "Tatsuya may have some idea of what the rogue was talking about. But reaching out to Z Group is a good idea too. They have a lot of information that they could share. It's worth a shot."

I nod. "Okay... that was enough excitement for one morning... I need a shower." I turn and head upstairs. As I stepped into the shower, the cool water washing away the grime of battle, my thoughts kept circling back to the rogue's words. Power. I had always thought of myself as just a human, but if there was something more buried within me... what would that mean for all of us?

15

It's been weeks of my continued training regime, and bliss with Max as we explore our relationship with each other. Our bond grows as he trains me separately to work on some maneuvers against someone who harnesses elemental powers. Every night Max and I spend together is heaven on this earth, my affections towards him deepen. I've continued to get stronger with my training each day. Instead of the guys all taking turns walking with me anywhere I go, it's mainly been Max, and the others take turns when he can't come with me. I've taken down many targets as Max still shadows, he's only had to step in and help me a couple of times as my targets have gotten stronger and more difficult to overpower on my own.

I still sneak out of the house and join them on their missions when rogues are running rampant, to protect the humans from the criminals assisting them, the men always find out afterwards. Kai lectures me without mercy each time until Max steps in and carries me upstairs, ending the conversation which infuriates Kai without fail. This has soon become our new normal. The men now expect me to show up during their missions. Kai has backed off of his lectures since I'm not listening anyways.

On one particular night, I'm running towards a group of rogues and criminals, Sara and Ren running alongside me. They've become my two battle buddies that I can rely on to have my back when things get rocky. I haven't been severely injured again since the first night I met them. The gashes have scarred and are something I'm actually quite proud of. Tonight, however, I got a little too cocky.

The guys are focused on taking down the remaining rogues when suddenly something catches Max's attention. Something's wrong and he feels the gnawing in his mind. He glances around, his eyes scanning the area until he notices me off in the distance, the shine of my katana blades reflecting the light of the ignited rubble around me. His heart stops for a moment as he sees me fighting off a group of humans. My movements are sloppy, and I'm taking hits that I shouldn't be, that I normally wouldn't allow. It's clear that I'm getting tired and more reckless. Max's eyes widen as he watches me, a feeling of dread pooling in his stomach. He turns in my direction and starts to run to me, he can see that I need help. His heart clenched tighter with panic at each step.

My katana sliced through the air, but my arms felt heavy— each swing slower than the last. A punch landed square on my jaw, the impact jolting my head back as stars burst behind my eyes. I stumbled, struggling to stay on my feet as the world swayed. I'm up against a group of six elemental wielding humans when one of them gets another good solid punch to my jaw and my mask flies off of my face, as I slam to the ground, revealing my face to them. They now see I'm the same human that the rogue was after weeks ago and who they were supposed to be searching for tonight. I scramble back up and take my defensive stance in preparation for them to attack again. They slowly walk towards me, closing me into their circle. Max watches in horror as they close in around me. He starts to run faster towards me, his eyes locked onto my form. He can see the humans realize that they recognize who I am. He sees the fear in my eyes, but also the determination to keep fighting. His heart sinks as he can see how exhausted I am and seem to have suffered a lot of strikes, the odds are not in my favor.

I brace for impact, watching every one of them get closer to me. I attempt to raise myself up off the ground to get a better stance, but I'm too slow. They advance quickly towards me. Max curses himself as he breaks into a sprint, for not realizing sooner that something was wrong, to look for me knowing I was for sure going to be out here, just like all the other times. He glances around quickly searching for anyone who may be close enough to help me. He notices the other guys are still busy fighting their own foes, unaware of what's happening with me. He looks back at me as he hurdles over large fallen debris, his heart racing with panic, seeing how dire this situation is. He has to get to me in time... he just *has* to. He looks up and sees that Sara and Ren are racing towards me as well, on their way down to help me. He feels as if he's been running to get to me for miles.

His eyes widen as he sees one of the guys throw a brick down at my head and I collapse back down to the ground, no longer moving. My vision blurred as I felt the cold ground beneath me. Pain throbbed in every inch of my body, my mind sluggish and fading. Somewhere in the distance, I thought I heard Max's voice calling my name, but it felt so far away, as if I were sinking into darkness. The men stand up straight, relaxing as they've finally got the infamous *'Crimson Vigilante'* down on the ground. They are talking amongst each other as one of them kneels down at my head and removes my hood while another inspects my mask in his hands. A fist full of my hair in one of their hands as they pull my head up for all of them to get a better look at me. My face was swollen, bloody and bruised. Max's heart sinks as he sees me collapsed on the ground, my head in their grasp. His blood boiling with rage as he charges towards them faster. Sara and Ren are also going as fast as they can to get down to me, hopping amongst the rubble of nearby buildings and cars.

Max races towards the men, his eyes fixed on their faces as they hover over me. He can see my face more clearly, dirt stained, bruised, swollen and bloody. It only fuels his anger more. He's determined to save me from further damage, no matter the cost. Sara and Ren aren't far behind but they're still a few feet away. Max gets closer, his heart thundering in his chest as he closes in on the men. He can hear them taunting me, their words making his blood boil over. His jaw clenches and his hands that have formed fists tighten as he continues to sprint.

He's almost there, he can see the men's hands on me, their fingers in my hair, one of them reaching down to my katanas in my hand. Max's anger reaches its breaking point. He's ready to rip them apart for touching me, for hurting me. He finally closes in and looks at Sara and Ren who are shocked to see him running in as well. "Sara, Ren—get her out of here. Now!" His voice was tight, strained with barely controlled panic, and they didn't need to be told twice. He slams into one of the men, knocking him away from me into a wall behind him. He towers over the men, his presence imposing and menacing. The men look up at Max, their faces paling as they realize who he is. They had heard rumors about him, and now they're face to face with the legendary mercenary, and former assassin Viper of the SP6.

Max's eyes are filled with fury as he looks down at them, looks down at me. His heart wrenches at the sight of me on the ground, bloodied and bruised as Sara and Ren slide to my side. The men attempt to back track, realizing that they are in way over their heads. They try to make a run for it, but Max isn't letting them go that easily. He grabs one of them by the collar of his shirt and pins him against the wall. The other men freeze in their tracks, their fear visible on their faces. The desire to rip them apart surged through him like wildfire. His fists tightened around the man's shirt, his knuckles white. It would be so easy to snap his neck, to make them pay for what they did to me. But he couldn't—he had to stay in control, for me. As Max takes care of my attackers, Sara gets to me and assesses the damage to my body.

"Ren... we need to get Lady Red out of here..." Sara says with a shaky voice. Her face is horror stricken as she kneels in a small pool of my blood.

Ren nods, his eyes widening in horror as he takes in the sight of me. "Oh, my gods... she's really banged up, Sara. We need to get her back to the Vipers Den as quickly as possible."

"I know... I'm afraid to move her though... if she gets hurt even more from one wrong move, Max will surely kill me." Sara strains to say through her own sobs threatening to burst out.

Ren nods in agreement. "You're right... Plus, we don't know how badly she's hurt. If there's any internal damage, moving her could make it worse."

Sara is torn on what to do. Ren notices her hesitation and places a reassuring hand on her shoulder, "I know it's a tough call, but we need to do what's best for her... We can't risk making her injuries worse. We'll just have to wait for Max to finish up with those men, and then he can carry her to the house... For now, we have to stop the bleeding to her side here... and her leg. She will bleed out before long." Ren hunches down and places a hand down on my side where I'm bleeding most, using cloth from his pants that he quickly rips off. Sara nods in agreement, she reaches a hand to my wrist and squeezes it with two fingers to check for a pulse as her other hand presses down on my leg wound. She waits a moment, feeling for a steady heartbeat. She feels the steady rhythm of my pulse against the pads of her fingertips, letting out a small sigh of relief, I'm at least alive, even if my heart rate is slowing by each second. Ren lets out a sigh of relief as well once he hears Sara's, knowing that me having a pulse is a great sign, but they're not out of the woods just yet.

Ren sends up a shield of water around us as more rogues close in towards us, the way they attack makes it seem as if they're trying to get to me only. The beasts don't seem to care about who they eliminate out of their way. Max finishes the last guy in the group and walks back towards where I am with Sara and Ren. He shoots off fireballs towards the rogues to get them away from us as Ren holds his shield up. Once the final rogue is gone, he strides over to where Sara and Ren are kneeling next to me. He nods at Ren to release his shield around us, his eyes narrowed as he takes in my battered form. There's a mix of anger and fear on his face, his jaw tense as he assesses the damage. He kneels down next to me, gently taking my face in his hand. His touch light and careful as he examines the rest of my injuries, his fingertips tracing over every bruise on the skin of my face.

Max's heart clenches at the sight of me, as tears begin to line his eyes. He can see the pain etched in my unconscious features, and it only refuels his anger. He glances at Sara and Ren, nodding to them, thanking them for attempting to help me. He looks back down at me, his expression hardening as he gently scoops me up into his arms, cradling me against his chest. He stands up, holding me tight in his arms. His grip is firm but gentle as he adjusts my weight against him. Every bruise, every drop of blood, felt like a knife to his chest. How had he let this happen? He was supposed to protect me, keep me safe, and yet here I was, broken and battered in his arms. He turns to Sara and Ren, his voice gruff as he speaks. "Let's get back to the den. She needs medical attention... now."

Ren and Sara nod in unison, acknowledging Max's instructions. They both stand up and fall into step behind Max. They all head back towards the location of the den, also known as our house. The tension is heavy in the air. As they walk, Max keeps his gaze fixed on my face. His heart is still filled with a mixture of anger and worry, his arms tightening around me as he holds me close with one hand strategically placed on my leg gash and he uses the pressure of his body to stall the bleeding to my side. He can see the ragged rise and fall of my chest with each shallow breath, a constant reminder of the extent of my injuries. He picks up the pace, wanting to get me back to the house as quickly as possible. He hears Sara calling for a field medic to meet us at the house to tend to me. He hears her voice and the confirmation through his connected earpiece, as she and Ren continue to follow close behind him. They both notice the worry on Max's face which makes them worry even more, seeing how concerned he is about my current condition.

After what feels like an eternity, they finally reach the house. Max carries me inside and lays me gently on the table in the dining room, his eyes never leaving my face. Sara and Ren follow Max into the room, hovering nearby as he carefully lays me down on the dining room table, treating it like an operating table. Their eyes flick from Max to me, sensing the intensity in the air. Max takes a step back, his eyes taking in the full extent of my injuries. He is drenched in my blood. The sight of my battered form fuels his anger, and he clenches his jaw, his hands forming tight fists at his sides. He feels as if he let those six bastards off too easily tonight, letting them live just barely... but letting them live at all. Sara and Ren watch as Max gazes down at me, his eyes filled with a mix of anger and remorse. Max swallows hard, trying to control his emotions. Each second felt like an eternity. Max stood over me, watching the slow rise and fall of my chest, praying it wouldn't stop. Sara kept pacing, her eyes darting to the door, while Ren clenched and unclenched his fists, helpless to do anything but wait. He turns to Sara, his voice raw as he speaks. "How much longer till the medic is here."

Sara meets his gaze. "He will be here in five minutes."

Five minutes. Five minutes until help arrived. Until then, it was just Max, his fear, and the woman he loved, lying broken in front of him. He swore to himself, then and there, that he would never let this happen again. Max shakes his head. "That's too long. Get me the first aid kit. I need to start cleaning and bandaging her wounds. We have to stop this bleeding."

Sara turns. "I'll get the kit. Ren. You can assist Max with removing her armor suit. We need a better look." Ren looks at Max for his approval.

Max nods in agreement, his eyes back onto me. "Do it. But be careful, we don't want to make anything worse..."

Ren responds. "I will be as gentle as I can. We may have to cut it off of her though. I think she may have a broken bone or two... Removing the clothes the traditional way will make them worse."

Max swallows hard at Ren's words, his stomach churns at the thought of cutting my jumpsuit off. I love it so much more than any other accessory I own. He thinks to himself: '*I will buy her a new one.*' He knows that Ren is right, however. "Do what you have to. Just… be careful."

Ren swiftly pulls out his blade and cuts through the tough fabric of my armor and removes the clothing till all I'm wearing is my sports bra crop top and spandex biker shorts that I always wear underneath my armor, to get a better view of all my injuries. The extent is so much worse than they thought. There's even evidence of old wounds that hadn't finished healing mixed up with the new ones. It's apparent how hard I fought for my life tonight. Max's eyes widen as he takes in the full extent of my injuries. The mixture of old and new wounds is overwhelming, and he can hardly believe that I was able to keep fighting through such pain.

Max's chest tightened with every bruise, every cut he found on me. He'd been with me on the battlefield, training me, shadowing me—but this? This felt like failure. And failure wasn't something he was used to. His fingers trembled as he brought my hand to his lips, kissing my knuckles. "I'm so sorry, princesa… I should've been faster. Gods… how did you even stay standing with all those wounds, my love…? Ren…" He mutters out. "What the *fuck* happened out there?! *Why was she alone? Where were* you two!?" He questions Ren, as his tone sounds like a lion's growl.

Ren snaps out of his daze of shock as he stares at my wounds to Max's threatening glare. "We were fighting some rogues who were closing in on some innocents when Lady Red took off towards a group of humans who were taking off after some innocents, Sarge. We didn't realize she was in danger until we got to her and saw her on the ground just like you did…" Ren looks back at the door as it flings open.

The other three Vipers return home. They ran here once they heard the news over the radio that Max had taken a badly injured human off the field and the call for a medic to the Viper's den. They walk in the door to see what's going on. They approach the dining room and stop in their tracks as they take in the scene before them.

Lius angrily asks through gritted teeth. "What the hell happened?!"

Kai's eyes widen as he sees the extent of my injuries, his normally stoic expression faltering for a moment. "Dear gods... is she alive?!"

Ares' eyes widened at the sight of me on the table, his mouth dropping in shock. "What the hell?! What happened to her? Max!"

Lius eyes widen and lock on to Max as he hovers over me, his expression neutral but curious and concerned. His eyes flicker from me to Max, a mix of anger and concern on his face. "Max... you wanna explain what the *hell* happened?"

Max's eyes are fixed on me still, his hand grabbing mine gently into both of his, bringing my knuckles to his lips again as he speaks low against them. "Some assholes attacked her on the field... They had her down and it looked like they were about to kill her when I got to her."

Lius' eyes darken at Max's recount of the attack, his anger building up inside of him. "Who were they? And how did she get this banged up? Haven't you been training with her?! How could this happen?!"

Max's grip on my hand tightens, his jaw clenching at the memory of what he saw. "I don't know who they are... they were just some lowlife elementals who wore the SP6 crest. They were toying with her... They had her surrounded, raining blows to her body. One of them threw a brick at her head... She put up one hell of a fight... but there were too many of them... she was outnumbered. They used their powers against her. They knew she was human. They definitely intended on killing her tonight."

Lius' eyes flash with a deeper rage as he listens to Max's recollection of what happened. "Those bastards… I'll tear their damn hearts out when I find them."

Kai nods in agreement, his face set in a stoic expression. "This is completely unacceptable. They should've never attacked her. It's a miracle that she's even breathing right now…"

"Who would even want to hurt her? Especially in the unit?" Ares' eyes flicker between Max and me, his expression neutral but observant.

Max's voice is laced with anger and protectiveness. "I don't know. But I'm going to find out. And when I do, I'm going to make sure they suffer for what they did to her."

Sara walks back into the room with the first aid kit. All eyes fall on her as she approaches with the kit. Lius blurts out. "Finally, we can start patching her up."

Kai nods as his eyes continue to assess my injuries. "We need to act fast. The longer we wait, the more damage her body will sustain. She's already too pale from blood loss"

Lius takes the first aid kit from Sara's hands and walks with it over to the table. He stands next to me. "Alright, let's get to it. We need to clean and dress each wound one by one… It's going to be a long night guys. Someone hand me their belt… we have to stop her leg bleeding."

The others nod silently in agreement, their eyes fixed on me as Lius begins to clean and dress my wounds. There's a mix of anger, concern and determination in their expressions as they all walk up to dress and clean each wound. Each of their faces firm and brows knitted as each wound is worked on, they all silently vow to get revenge on whomever did this to me—for me. As everyone works on a different wound, Max keeps his gaze locked on my face as he works. He looked at me with tears lining his eyes, wishing I would just wake up. Even if I cried out in pain… he just wanted me to be alert. As each stitch he pierced through my skin, it felt as if he was piercing his own heart. *'I'm so sorry princesa… I'm so sorry.'* He thinks as he works.

The next morning, sunlight streamed through the window, gently caressing my face. I slowly begin to open my eyes, wincing slightly as the pain in my body begins to throb. It takes a moment to adjust to my surroundings, but I quickly realize that I'm lying on the dining room table in my house. It's eerily quiet, the only sound coming from the ticking clock on the wall. I look down to see I'm now in one of Max's shirts and still have my spandex shorts and tank top on from the night before. I look over to the side and see that my armor suit is lying shredded on the floor. One of my arms is in a cast and sling, hinting to me that I must have broken it. I stare at the ceiling as I try to remember what happened last night. Once the memories flood over me I try to sit up to look around and to get off of this table. The table is lined with bloodied sheets from the overflow through the bandages on my cuts. There's a folded towel under my head as a makeshift pillow.

As I attempt to sit up, a sharp pain shoots through my body, causing me to flinch and cry out. I manage to push through it, propping myself up on one elbow as I look around the room. The evidence of last night's events is everywhere. The destroyed armor on the ground, the remnants of the first aid kit scattered all around the base of the table, and the general stillness in the air. I look around the room searching for any sign of Max, all I see is a messed blanket on a chair close by as if someone slept there. Just as I'm starting to get my bearings to swing my legs over the side of the table, I hear footsteps coming down the stairs. Max appears in the doorway of the dining room, wearing a pair of loose sweatpants and no shirt. Looking as if he didn't get any sleep last night, my face falls with relief as soon as I see his face, but also a pang hits my heart with worry as I see the dark circles under his eyes.

Max's eyes widen when he sees that I'm sitting up and awake. He quickly crosses the room in long strides right to my side. He stops inches in front of my face, his eyes roaming over me as he takes in my current condition. I lift my arm, which is not in a sling and cup his cheek, smiling at him. It hurts to even smile but I push through because of how happy I am to see him, to try and calm the worry I see painted on his face. "Hey…" I breathe out, my voice rough as my throat is still raw from all the yelling I had done during the fight last night.

Max's expression softens as he feels my hand on his cheek, a mix of relief and concern in his sunken eyes. He leans into my touch, gently taking my hand in his own. "Hey there… how are you feeling?"

"Not the greatest…" I chuckle but the pain shoots through me and as I wince, I grip my side with a hiss.

Max reaches out to steady me, his hand gently resting on my shoulder blade. "Easy killer… don't move too much. You took quite a beating last night. You need to let your body rest for real this time."

I let out a sigh once the pain calmed. I look down at his hands and see the cuts and bruises around his knuckles and fingers. I caress a finger over each mark, my heart clenches as I realize what he must have suffered during this battle as well. With a serious look I met his gaze. "Get Lius, Kai and Ares... I need to speak with all of you. I remember who my attackers were. One of them was a target that Z sent me."

Max's expression hardens as he listens to my words, his eyes narrowing. He nods in understanding, "Alright, I'll get them in here. You sit and don't move too much. I'll be right back."

"Okay..." I whisper out as I move to sit up fully. Max nods and quickly leaves the room. I take in the sight of my blood dried on the sheet that was draped over the table. It seems my roommates have turned our dining table into an operating table for the evening. I rub a hand over one spot and lean over to look at a large bandage on my leg. I wince as I lift the bandage slightly to see what's underneath. I whimper at the sight of the stitched up flesh below it. I place the bandage back over it and do my best to look over my body. Lifting the collar of the shirt I am wearing and seeing the bruises and bandages that are more than likely covering even more cuts.

A few moments later, Max walks back into the room with the other three close behind him, their own expressions neutral but alert. They glance over to me on the makeshift hospital bed and their eyes flicker with surprise and joy as they see me sitting up and alert. Max walks closer and takes his spot next to me with a hand on my back to steady me.

Lius tried to keep his voice light, but the smirk on his lips didn't quite reach his eyes. "Damn, birdie, you gave us quite a scare." His fingers flexed as if itching to punch something, his anger barely contained.

"I guess I was kind of tired..." I grin as I hold back a laugh.

Kai crossed his arms, his face unreadable. "You're still too stubborn," he muttered, though his usual sternness had softened, replaced by something deeper—concern, maybe even guilt.

Lius steps closer into the room next to Max, his arms crossed over his chest. "So, we heard that you remember who those bastards were that attacked you. Care to share?"

I tell them the descriptions of each one, the names I heard each of them called and all of the information of my target since the Z Group sent me his information. As I speak, the men listen intently, their eyes each widen at different times as each of them begin to realize who I'm describing. I see four sets of eyes become darker and more serious as I share the details of the SP6 members who attacked me. "That's all that I can remember…" I started coughing from talking so much, my throat dry and scratchy. I grip Max's side to hold myself steady, and for comfort as my lungs scream with the sharp pain of each cough. Max leans lightly on the table next to me immediately, his hand gently resting on my back as I cough. He watches me with a mix of concern and worry in his eyes, his jaw tightening at the sight of my pain. Max's hand lingered at the small of my back, steadying me with the gentlest touch. He didn't say a word, but in that moment, his presence was enough. More than enough. Max's stomach churned as he replayed the fight. SP6 crests on their jackets. His mind raced—who would have dared betray them? And why me?

"Okay. I'm good." I wince once I finish coughing causing my sore and tender muscles to contract then release. "I'm sorry. I still have some dried blood in my throat I think." I've been through worse, I told myself, but the ache in my chest—the pain from more than just the bruises—told me otherwise. I hated feeling this weak, this exposed. But with Max by my side, I let myself exhale, trusting that just this once, it was okay to not be strong. The pain was a sharp reminder of how close I'd come to death. Every movement sent a wave of agony through my ribs, my leg, my side.

But what hurt most was knowing I hadn't been strong enough to take them all down.

Lius steps closer to me, he leans down to assess me further. He places a hand on my shoulder, ignoring Max's snapping glare, giving my shoulder a gentle squeeze for comfort. "Don't push yourself too hard birdie. You need to rest and let your body heal. We will handle things from here."

I nod as Kai cuts in, his eyes locking onto my face. "And don't apologize for anything. You don't have to be sorry for getting ambushed by a bunch of lowlifes who didn't fight fair."

"Yeah, they cheated for sure. Too scared to handle fighting me like men..." I huff out a laugh. "There isn't '*fair*' in the art of war. So I'm only surprised that they were SP6 members."

Max grins at my snide comment, his eyes gleaming with pride. He nods in agreement, his hand still gently rubbing my back. I hide that it hurts so much as he does. "Damn straight. Those cowards knew they didn't stand a chance against you in a fair one on one fight, so they had to resort to dirty tricks."

"Mmhmm" I strain out to hide the pain I'm feeling, not wanting to hurt his feelings that his touch is hurting me this time... as he tries to comfort me. Lius sighs as his eyes roam over my body taking a moment on each bruise and wound. I can see the sorrow in his eyes as if he blames himself. I furrow my brows as I look down where he's looking. "Lius..."

He glances back up to me and lets out a sigh as his eyes finally soften and he straightens back up, crossing his arms across his chest. "Well, now that we have the names of those bastards who did this to you, we can take care of them. You can count on us to make them pay."

I sit myself up a bit more, leaning forward from Max's arm for support. "Bring them to me first... here."

The others jolt and fall silent for a moment, taking in my request. Lius and Ares exchange a glance and Kai's jaw clenches at the thought of me going up against my attackers in my current state. Max, on the other hand, just nods in agreement. "You guys heard the lady. She wants first dibs at those assholes. We will bring them to you, princess." He presses a kiss to the side of my head, gripping my opposite shoulder to pull me closer towards him. The whole ordeal shooting sharp jabs of pain throughout my body.

Lius looks at me for a moment, his eyes narrowing slightly as he considers my request. He knows that I will try to fake being fine as I face the assholes, and he really hates the idea, but he also understands the fire burning within me for justice. He sees it in my eyes. Lius lets out a sigh, "Fine. However, you're in no condition to fight right now. You can have first dibs on them, but we're still going to be the ones who actually capture them."

"I agree." In my mind they are running around free, unaware that after I was knocked out cold, Max ripped them apart within an inch of their lives. "Bring them to me restrained." My eyes darken as I look up at Lius.

Lius takes in the darkness in my eyes, a mix of respect and concern on his face. He's intrigued by my request and simply nods once. "You got it, birdie. We'll bring them to you, gagged and bound as per your request. They'll be yours to do with what you wish."

"Thank you" I start to push myself off the table to stand up, but Max stops me with his hand gently pressing on my arm.

Max gives me a pleading look, "Stop..." He stands up, puts an arm out to support me. He helps me stand and then picks me up bridal style. "Where do you need to go?"

"I was going to get into bed…" I lean my head against his chest as I pant from the pain of being moved.

His arms hold tightly, "Sure thing baby. Let's get you upstairs to bed. You need some rest." He walks with me up the stairs as the others observe, standing in their places in the living room. Max makes his way up the stairs, making sure his grip isn't too tight on me but tight enough as to not drop me. He can see the pain and exhaustion I'm experiencing all over my face and how my body lays against him. We finally reached my room, and Max carefully laid me down onto my bed. He lets out a sigh of relief that he didn't even know he was holding in. He helps me get into bed. He stands over me watching my expression, searching my body for any aggravated cuts. I pat the bed next to me, inviting him to lay next to me. He catches my small gesture, and a small smile tugs at the corners of his mouth. He understands what I'm asking for and obliges. He slowly climbs onto the bed, being careful not to jostle me too much.

"Thank you…" I whisper as I slowly move towards him. He pulls the blankets up to cover the both of us, gently wrapping his arms around me, waiting for me to get comfortable.

His arms close in around me, pulling me close to him in a protective embrace. "No problem, baby… You just rest. I'll be right here with you." I let out a sigh of relief and exhaustion, closing my eyes and falling asleep. He watches as I fall asleep in his arms, his gaze softening as he takes in how peaceful I look under the cuts and bruises on my face. He strokes my hair and whispers softly in my ear. "Sleep well, princesa. I'll be here when you wake up." He lays there with me for a while, listening to the steady sound of my breathing and feeling the warmth of my body against his. Thankful that I am alive, his mind filled with the thoughts of revenge against the bastards who attacked me as he quietly continues to stroke my hair. As Max laid by my side, the weight of his promise settled heavy in the air. "We'll find them," he whispered, more to himself than to me. But deep down, he knew—this was just the beginning of something far more dangerous.

~*~

The lights dim and the atmosphere quiet. I'm still asleep in my bed where Max left me, as the men quietly exit the car and grab each perp out of their cars and approach the house, their steps careful and deliberate. Max drops the guy in his grasp on the hardwood floor of our living room before looking towards the stairs. He heads up towards my bedroom, his footsteps careful and silent. As he reaches my bedroom door, he pauses for a moment, listening. He hears my soft breathing, a reassuring sign that I'm still asleep. Taking a deep breath, Max slowly opens the door wider and steps into the room, his eyes falling on my sleeping form in the bed. He approaches the bed, a mix of relief and worry coursing through him as he sees me lying there. He reaches out and gently brushes a strand of hair away from my face, his touch tender and gentle.

He studies my face, he can see the signs of my injuries— the bruises and cuts that mar my skin under the late morning sunlight shining through my bedroom window. Max's heart clenches in his chest as he looks at me, his hand lingering on my face, a million thoughts and emotions running through his mind. He stands a moment longer, watching over me and making sure I'm not experiencing any discomfort while I sleep.

Lius walks in, interrupting his thoughts that were quickly spinning out of control. "Hey... are you done? Let's get this over with. Wake her up."

Max turns to Lius. "Chill, I was just making sure she was okay. And I will check on her as much as I'd like to, for however long I'd like to. Now what do you want?"

I stir awake at the sound of their voices, groaning lightly in pain as I move my stiff muscles and look at the two of them with a confused look on my face. Both men look at me instantly as I stir awake, their faces filled with relief.

"Hey, hey, easy there princesa... You're okay. You're safe. I'm right here." Max coos as he rubs my hair away from my eyes. They both move to stand on either side of my bed, their eyes roaming over my body, surveying the damage still wrapped in bandages.

"Did you find the assholes yet?" I clear my throat to ask and snap them out of their *mother hen* tendencies before they get carried away again. I can see that Max is fully dressed, indicating he left the house recently. They both seem to have been in a scuffle as I see the dirt they've tracked in all over their boots and clothing. I am more irritated that they have their shoes on in the house than the dirt now in my bedroom. Oh, they will definitely clean this house later...

Lius and Max exchange a look before answering, noticing how I'm glaring at their dirty boots and clothes. "Well, we found four of them..." Answered Lius first.

Max cuts in. "We're still searching for two of them. But the other four are tied up in the living room now, waiting for you to deal with them sweetheart. Tell us what you'd like us to do."

My eyes widen and I look at Max, my heart thunders and I shift to get up using the non-casted arm to sit up, wincing and hissing in pain the whole way. I seem to have napped hard as every muscle screams from being stiff and in one position for so long. Both Max and Lius notice my struggle, their eyes widening in alarm as I start to sit up. Max lunges towards me. "Whoa, whoa, easy there killer. Let me help you up."

Lius shifts to my other side to assist. "Yeah, you need to rest and recover first. You are in no condition to deal with those assholes right now. We can-"

"Yes. I. Am... They need to see that *nothing* anyone does to me will get me to stay down. They need to see I will still cause them pain, even when they think I'm broken." I say through gritted teeth as Max helps me swing my legs over the side of the bed to a sitting position. Max and Lius exchange a look, their conflicted expressions evident. They see the determination in my eyes, but they also know that acting rashly in my current state is not a smart idea.

Max lowers his tone as he speaks while assisting me off the bed. "I get that you want to show them you're not weak, but you're too injured to even sit up on your own, let alone walk down there in front of them. You can't do anything like this."

"Yeah, you trying to get up is just going to make things worse and slow your healing. You need to rest and let yourself heal more before you try to do this." Lius agrees.

"Stop..." I threw my hand up. "They're gagged and bound right? Then let me see them." I push off the bed and slowly stand up breathing through the pain so I don't faint. I stand still with my eyes closed for a moment as I gain my bearings, waiting for the room to stop spinning. Both men watch as Max holds a hand out behind me in case I lose my balance. They worry over the pain they see me in but admire the strength and determination in my eyes.

Max lets out an aggravated sigh. "You're stubborn as hell, you know that?" He mumbles.

Lius shakes his head. "Yeah, but you're not going to be able to walk all the way down to them like this. Sit back down before you hurt yourself even more."

I glare at Lius as I take a couple of steps, to show him that I will walk to them on my own whether they like it or not. Lius watches as I take a couple of steps, a smug smirk painting his face as he respects the attitude I'm giving off. He can see how determined I am, but he's very worried over my stubbornness worsening my condition. He lets out a heavy sigh. "Damn... you're tough as nails." He takes a step closer, ready to help Max catch me if I stumble. I walked past him and out of my room. Both men quickly chase after me, watching as I hobble out of the room.

"Hey, slow down. You don't have to prove anything to us right now." Max runs up and hovers his hand behind my back for support if needed.

Lius walks along my other side. "Yeah, you should really take easy slow steps at least, birdie." They both try to keep pace with me, ready to catch me if I stumble or lose balance. I continue to ignore them as I walk towards the top of the stairs. Max and Lius exchange a worried glance as I continue to ignore their advice and move toward the stairs. They now know they can't stop me, but they continue to try by pleading with me to go back to bed and rest as I continue towards the stairs.

"Hey, maybe you should let us carry you down the stairs. It'll be easier on your injuries." Pleads Max.

"Yeah, you're going to hurt yourself if you try to take them on your own like this." Begs Lius.

I grab onto the railing and take the first step down, breathing through the pain I feel as I steady myself. I will walk down these stairs on my own, I now have to prove a point to these worrying warts behind me. They watch as I grab the railing and take the first step down, I hear their hearts racing as they ready themselves to grab me if I trip.

Max places a hand around my hip as he steps down beside me. "Be careful, princesa. Just take it slow and easy. One step at a time."

Lius holds his breath. "Yeah, don't hurt yourself further please…"

I take each step one at a time breathing through the searing pain with each step that I hide from the two of them. The two men remain around me, Max to my side holding onto my waist as Lius is behind me, his hands hovering out behind my shoulder blades to balance me if needed. "You're doing great. Just a few more steps." He cheers quietly.

Max looks at my face, searching for any overextension of my energy. "Take your time. We're right here with you."

I stop on the next step, halfway in the stairwell, both men notice that I've paused on the stairs, their eyes quickly scanning my face and body for signs of distress.

Max's concern deepens as he asks in a panic. "You, okay? Need to take a break?"

I let out a huff of air through my nostrils. "Please stop babying me guys… both of you… I know you're worried and I'm ignoring your advice. Now's the time to put on our brave faces before I walk into that room and face the dirtbags." I snap at them. They look at each other, their expressions harden as I speak. They understand what I'm asking, and they appreciate my need to face the attackers head-on without any sign of the pain I am in.

Max nods and raises a hand up in submission. "Alright… We will stop babying you."

Lius cracks his knuckles. "Yeah, it's time to teach them a lesson."

"Thank you…" I continue to slowly walk down the last few steps and walk into the living room where Ares and Kai are standing behind four men, hands tied behind them and tape over their mouths as they sit up on their knees, ready for their execution. I walk in with my head up with confidence, emanating power over them. Flanking behind me, Max and Lius walk into the room as my eyes are glued to the four men sitting on their knees on the floor. Their wrists and ankles are bound with ropes, their mouths gagged with clothes covered with tape. They are all conscious and their eyes widen with fear and shock as they see me enter, my injured state standing tall and powerful over them.

"Hello gentlemen… remember me?"

16

The men's eyes widen further as they recognize me. Their expressions moved to terror, realizing their mistake in attacking me. They try to speak all at once, but their words are all muffled by the gags in their mouths.

"Good boys…" I say with a devilish grin. This is a side of me that none of my roommates have seen before—except for Max during my hunts for targets. I avoid looking at their reactions.

Max and Lius watch me with a mix of awe and concern, Max is the one more concerned since he knows what this persona I'm exuding means. They've seen glimpses of my fierce and strong side before, but never like this. Not at this magnitude. I'm protruding an unmistakable aura of power and dominance, a side of me that's cold, calculating and unapologetically ruthless. The men bound in front of me, their fear grows with every moment I am in front of them. I look down at the tools I asked Ares to prepare for me, sitting on the coffee table in front of the men. I chose not to ask anyone else to get these ready for me, as I knew none of the others would agree with the methods I was about to use. Ares and I always understood each other, and he understood why I was planning what I had for this retribution of mine. I pick up one curved blade from the table of choices, I spin it in between my fingers as I admire it.

All the while, I grinned with pleasure, then averted my eyes to the four captives. "Okay now... who would like to play a little game? Anyone want to volunteer to go first? Or do I have to choose...?"

The men look between each other, fear and terror taking them over. They all look like they want to be anywhere but in front of me right now. They make pitiful pleas for mercy, but their words are once again muffled by the gags in their mouths. I get down low and kneel in front of the first guy and lean close to his face.

My leg is shooting strikes of protest throughout my body, as my legs lower. I steady my voice to mask the pain. "Now for everything you did to *me*... I will do it to you..."

The man looks at me with wide, terrified eyes, his body trembling in fear as I point at him with my blade. He tries to speak, garbled by the gag. His eyes full of pleading and remorse, that he will do anything to escape this situation, but I know that he deserves whatever I'm about to do to him. I lift up the curved blade to pull down his gag from his mouth, wanting to hear his pleas for mercy. To hear the sweet sound of his begging.

The man looks at me as his gag is pulled away from his mouth, the tape ripping his facial hair, his eyes pleading with me as he speaks. "Please, please don't do this! Please don't hurt me! I'm sorry, okay? I'm so sorry for attacking you! I was just following orders!" He sputters out.

"Sorry isn't going to heal my broken bones any faster now is it...? Now, who's in charge of this little... group of yours? Is it your friend over there-" I point with the blade to the man next to him. "Who gave you orders... to kill me?"

"W-we don't know his name! We never directly spoke with him! He contacts us through texts from an unknown number. I swear! That's all I know!" The man I'm in front of me shouts as tears of dread line his eyes. He looks over at Max momentarily as if asking him to please step in and save them. I use my blade to redirect his gaze back onto me. Lius catches the look from the culprit, and looks at Max as well, raising an eyebrow. My head is now filled with so many questions about the connection between the mercenary Viper and this asshole. I will have to deal with this later. Right now, my focus is on the men lined in front of me.

I press my blade against the man's throat as I continue to ask him questions of why I was targeted. The man grimaces and whimpers as he feels my blade press against his throat. "A-All we know is your name, your face... and t-to bring you in alive... We were never told why you were a target! I swear!" All four of my roommates glance at each other with concern as they observe this side of me. They won't let me go as far as to kill these creeps, but they'll let me mess with them for a while, for as long as I can handle it. Max watches me closely, his eyes following my every move. I can see the worry on his face as I stand back up slowly to grab another tool from the table. These Vipers–that I now call family–know I'm in excruciating pain and am doing a very good job of hiding it. I won't let myself be vulnerable in front of these heathens.

The captives start to all whimper as I approach the table of tools, ready to toy with their fate, anxiously waiting for what I'm going to do next. I decide on a tool and turn to provide each of these men with an injury similar to the ones they each gave me, including ones that their two absent friends gave—for extra measure—in a slow torturous manner that once the third guy loses consciousness, Kai decides he's seen and heard enough of this show I'm putting on in front of him, shifting uncomfortably in place. Max sees how pale I've become during this whole ordeal as my hair sticks to my face with sweat. They discreetly look at each other and decide to step in and stop me as this new look of wild malice in my green eyes grows.

I overhear Lius whisper to Max. "She's starting to look really bad…"

"Yeah, she's pushing herself too hard… The pain must be unbearable. We have to stop her-" Max whispers back.

"That's enough, Elara." Kai, having watched silently, can't stay quiet any longer. He steps forward towards me and speaks up, cutting Max off.

My eyes flick up to Kai as I'm panting, my eyes wild with rage. "I've only just begun, Kai."

"No, you've gone far enough. You have pushed too far. These idiots aren't worth your energy… what little you have." Kai grips onto my gaze with his stern one, showing me, he is serious, but his expression gives way to his concern.

Max walks up and kneels down next to me, prepared to catch me in case I fall over. "He's right princesa… You need to stop… They've had enough."

Panting and sweating from over exertion, I stand up away from the men, and Max. I look at the last one still consciously on the ground, peering through his non-swollen eye at me. I look down my nose at him.

"Now you…" I point with my blade at his face. "You are a strong one huh? The only one who didn't pass out from the pain I've inflicted onto you. Everything I've done to all four of you is *everything* you *six* did to *me*… and I am still standing. Now I'm going to leave you with these guys. They are better people than *I am...*" I snarl, causing the man to whimper further. I leaned down towards him again. "And they may show you mercy... or they won't. But know this... remember *this*... you may have beat me down, but I will still stand and fight." I bit my teeth at his face. "Until my dying breath against lowlife humans... so piece of *shit* scum, like *you*... stay *out* of my way!"

The last man looks up at me, his face pale and his body shaking violently with a mixture of what I presume to be fear and pain. He can see the pure anger and determination shining in my emerald eyes, and the realization that I'm not going to give up or stop fighting, no matter how much I am beaten down.

"Please, *please* just let us go... We won't do it again, I promise! I swear!" He begs and pleads for his life, the fear swarming in his eyes as he looks around the room to his comrades.

"That is up to these four friends of mine. One of whom..." I use my blade to point at Max. "Is my lover... and you've hurt his lady... so keep that in mind, while begging *him* for forgiveness."

The man looks at Max, his one good eye growing even wider than it already was. Max's towering stature and intense gaze only make the man more scared, genuinely scared for his life. He seems to shrink and let out a sigh of realization, as if he knows exactly how badly he screwed up messing with someone Max cares deeply for.

"Please... please have mercy on me! I had no idea she was *your* woman, Max! I won't do it again I promise!" He chokes out, begging for his life. He cries out with the realization as Max's eyes darken as he looks upon the man on the floor.

I jolt as my eyebrows raise up in shock as I look at Max who keeps his stoic expression as if to not be bothered by the man calling his name, I look back at my attacker. My stomach begins to churn, and my head begins to spin, I suddenly realize that I have to get out of here, *now*. Or I will vomit all over the living room floor.

"Ok… I'm bored with you weaklings." I stand back up and turn to gracefully walk away towards the back porch, keeping my composure till I am out of sight.

My head is spinning, and I feel the pressure rising up my esophagus, my vision blurring. I hear the man begin to panic as Max looms towards him. I step through the sliding glass door to get some fresh air. I walk to the side and fall to my knees, feeling the cold concrete slam against my knees and my hands, as I vomit in the bush we have just to the side. All the pain I've fought against finally breaking through and my frayed nerves come stampeding to the surface.

The men watch as I walk away and the moment, I step outside Max stalks closer towards the one still conscious man with a smug smirk. Lius keeps his eyes on me and once he sees me fall to my knees at the bushes, through the back door, he rushes out to my side. Once he gets to me, he immediately drops next to me, steadying me as I retch in the bushes.

He uses one hand to hold my hair away from my face. "Dammit birdie… you pushed it too far."

"I'm fine…" I say in between retching. "My body will get stronger after this…" I pant out. "I can handle this…"

"You're not fine… You've overdone it again." He says with a soothing tone.

Kai walks out to the patio. "You need to rest now and recover, Elara. Your body is telling you it *can't* keep up with what your stubborn mind wants to do. Pushing yourself like *this* is reckless and will only prolong your healing."

"I am not in the mood for your lecturing right now Kai. Besides... I think I made my point with those guys..." I smirk as I chuckle.

Lius rolls his eyes. "Yeah, you definitely made your point, but at what cost? Look at you, you can hardly even stand anymore. You need to take it easy from here on out."

I sigh as I wipe my mouth with the back of my hand as the dry heaves finally subside. I can hear the shouts from the man I left with Max back in the living room. The sounds of screams and grunts are what I can only think are the sounds of Max having his way with him. I look back towards the sliding door, "Is Ares in there managing that?" They both nod. If anyone was going to end the lives of these lowlifes... it will be *me*. I won't let Max carry that burden for me. But a part of me knows that he wouldn't feel guilty if he were to take the life of that man. And not just because I know he's taken a human life before, but because of the demons he carries from last night.

Lius moves his hand that was holding my hair back to rub between my shoulder blades. "Don't worry about those idiots. They're being handled. Ares will stop Max before he goes too far."

Kai continues his *'mother hen'* scolding of my choice to face these men and handle this in my current state, so soon in my recovery. I scared all of my roommates with how close I danced with death. I hear it in his voice when he speaks. "We are more concerned about *you* right now. You need to get back into bed. You've probably injured yourself further after putting yourself through that display in there."

"My enemies must never know when I am weak... even when they are the ones who've done the beating and bruising... I refuse!" I strain out as another dry heave takes over my body. I grip my ribs as the motion sends a shockwave through me.

Lius nods as he rubs his hand gently on my back in soothing circles. "We know, we know. You're tough and fierce," His voice gives off a slight mocking tone. "...but even the strongest people have their limits. We refuse to let you do anything stupid like that again."

Kai sighs. "It's not about being weak or strong and you know that, Ellie. It's about being smart and strategic. Overdoing it will only hinder your recovery. Why is it you can't get that through that thick skull of yours?" I can see the frustration in his eyes as he taps a finger to his temple, how completely over my stubbornness he's become.

"Then I guess that makes me a masochist..." I finally stood up but my legs give out, they have met their limit of me today too.

Lius grabs my arm quickly to steady me, as Max finally walks out, wiping off his hands and face of what appears to be blood splatter, with a paper towel. He sees what's going on and the prideful smirk he was sporting vanishes as he runs to my side to steady me with his hand on my lower back and the other in front of me. "Whoa, whoa, easy now."

Lius helps him support me. "You're not walking anywhere right now. You can barely stand."

I huffed out in acknowledgement. Max wraps his arm that was on my back around my waist to support me. "Come on, let's get you inside and up to bed."

I don't walk forward as I look up to Max with pain and pleading in my eyes. My legs won't move and I'm not putting barely any weight on them as I lean against him. He notices my pain and pleading look in my eyes, immediately understanding what's going on. "Don't worry, sweetheart. I got you." Without hesitation, he effortlessly scoops me up into his arms, lifting me off my fatigued, worthless legs and holding me against his chest.

I groaned as he adjusted me. "Thank you." I whispered out.

Max holds me close, his grip firm. "No problem, princesa. Just try to relax. I've got you." He carries me inside and up the stairs into my room. He lays me down on my bed helping me get comfortable. "There we go. Just relax and let me take care of you, okay?"

Kai and Lius enter the room shortly after behind us. Lius walks closer to adjust the pillows around me to be sure I have plenty of support. Max looks at him with a warning for him to watch where his hands touch, his protective and possessive nature taking over his mind. Kai exits the room momentarily and returns with a Ziploc bag of ice wrapped in a towel, he places a pillow under my ankle and carefully places the ice pack on it. I furrow my brows at them, I hate it when they hover like this, it makes me feel even weaker. That they will only ever see me as someone who needs protection. This is why I do my best to hide when I'm hurt as best as I can. Every cut, every bruise I receive. Even the ones that are just from me being clumsy, they freak out over. Why are they so hell bent on treating me like I'm made of porcelain? I am too tired to argue and fight against them this time. So exhausted and fatigued that my voice box doesn't want to assist me in protesting. Seems as if my body is also sick and tired of my stubborn mind.

Max notices my expression, "What's that look for? We're just trying to help you, sweetheart."

My breathing quickens as I wince at a sharp pain all through my chest, I can feel I'm about to pass out again and I try to fend it off. My face pales and my head bobs as I place my hand to my forehead. "Ok guys... I need some-" I slump over and pass out, losing my battle with consciousness.

~*~

Hours later I finally stir awake, I find myself lying in bed as Max has me wrapped in his arms, sound asleep. The early evening sunlight shining through my bedroom window casting a golden glow, highlighting every detail. Max wakes once I stir, his eyes lighting up with relief as his eyes land on mine. "Hey... You're finally awake. How do you feel?" He whispers as he scans my face, searching for any more signs of pain.

"I'm okay. I feel much better." I whisper back as I wince from shifting slightly to get into a better position to feel more comfortable.

Max jolts with worry at my wince and moves to help my shift. "Shhh... It's okay. I've got you, I'll take care of you. Show me what hurts."

I gesture to my whole body with my one good hand, to answer him. I then tap a finger to my temple, indicating that my brain hurts. Although it isn't a headache that I'm indicating, it's my emotional state as I remember that one man knowing Max's name... The memory of one of them looking to him to save them like he was a comrade to them. The memory creates more questions and panic in my mind. Max looks at me with concern, and all he wants to do is alleviate my pain and discomfort. Holding me gently he asks, "You're hurt all over still huh? I'll get you something for the pain, my dear."

I nod as he moves to carefully climb out of bed, but not before he places a kiss on the temple that I tapped. He exits the room, and I lay there staring at the ceiling thinking of how I should approach this subject with him. I hear a faint knock on the ajar door and see as Lius walks in. "Hey... I thought I heard voices in here. How are you holding up?"

"Hey Lius. I'm alright. Just sore. Are those four guys gone?" I ask quietly as my throat hurts from being so dry.

He walks towards me and sits in the chair by my bed, scooting it closer. "Mmhmm. We cleared them out while you were asleep. Where is Max going?"

"I was just getting her some water and painkillers. She's hurting a bit." Max says as he re-enters the room.

"Well, we will do whatever you need to feel better, birdie." nods Lius.

Max hands me the water and pills. I take them instantly, drinking the whole glass before setting it down on the bedside table. "There you go... That should help with the pain. They should kick in soon." Max says as he moves to the side of the bed and sits back down.

"Well..." Lius breathes out. "You look really tired. We should let you rest some more."

I give a thumbs up as I lay down in the bed again, grimacing at the discomfort I feel as I do. I tug onto Max's shirt to have him stay behind, stay with me. He immediately understands what I'm asking and lays down with me as he waves a hand to shoo Lius out of the room. He understands my need for comfort and closeness to him right now.

"I've got you princesa... you just rest." I snuggle closer to him as he wraps his arms around me, where I feel the safest. Even with hesitation at his possible involvement with all of this... I feel the safest in Max's embrace. I let out a sigh of contentment and closed my eyes. He tucks me in against him, rubbing soothing circles on my back, "There you go. I'm right here with you. Just rest." He whispers to me as he runs the other hand through my hair gently. "Let yourself rest. I've got you. You're safe now." Max holds me close, his arms a protective barrier around me.

~*~

The next morning, I finally stir to the sound of the men chatting in my room, through poor attempts at whispering. I don't think they have the capability *to* whisper. I keep my eyes closed as I listen to what they are discussing that can't be discussed elsewhere. And also, because I know that once I open my eyes, they will all immediately jump to *'mother hen'* mode.

Kai's voice comes through first. I can hear the strain in his voice as he tries to control his anger. "She needs to take better care of herself. She always puts others before herself, and it's not healthy."

Next is Max, I feel the vibration of his voice as he is laying reclined back next to me, against the headboard. "Yeah, you're right. She's just too damn stubborn and independent, she refuses to ask for help or admit that she needs a break. It's like she thinks she has to handle everything on her own."

"Not everything..." I finally croak out as I stir to alert them, I'm awake. I've heard enough and know that this will be just another berating discussion of how careless they think I am when it comes to my own well-being.

All four men startled at my voice, caught off guard that I spoke. With my eyes still closed they aren't sure if I'm awake or just talking in my sleep. Max shifts to place a hand on my head, rubbing his thumb across my hairline. "Sweetheart, did you say something?"

"Yes. I know that I can't do everything…" I breathe out and slowly peel my eyes open. The four of them let out a collective sigh of relief as I watch their shoulders collectively sag, they all look happy to hear my voice. That I'm conscious and responsive.

Max looks at me with a soft smile. His voice matching. "Hey, you're awake. We are just discussing how we can help you stop before you overexert yourself like that again."

"I know. I heard" I shift and sit up. Letting out a sigh of aggravation at the discomfort of sitting up. My muscles are tight from laying down for so long once again.

Max shifts quickly to help me sit up. "Hey, be careful. Don't move too much or you'll end up hurting yourself more."

"I can't keep lying here anymore. I need to get up and move around." I grumble.

Max clenches his jaw, holding back an argument as he nods and gets up on his knees to assist me into an upright sitting position. "Is that better?"

"Yes… thank you." I smile softly towards him. "Don't you guys have work or something?" I reach for my phone on the bedside table to check the time. "I don't want you guys missing work because of me… that's a bit excessive."

Lius shakes his head. "Nah, we're taking the day off today. Nothing needs the Vipers' attention at the moment."

I nod as I unlock my phone to check it. I can see different missed calls and texts from Z, Angie, my parents and Sensei Tatsuya. I pressed the most recent call to return Tatsuya's. "Sensei…" I greet him as soon as the line picks up on the other end. He instantly began to scold me. My face falls as I begin to answer his barrage of scolding. "I was blindsided… no… I did do that… but the-… *sigh* I understand… yes Sensei… understood…

yes Sensei..." I hand the phone out to Max. "He wants to speak with you..."

Max takes the phone from me, a small bit of confusion on his face and concern as he brings it to his ear. "What can I do for you Tatsuya?" He listens to whatever it is that Tatsuya has to say, a frown slowly forming on his face. He nods along as if in agreement with whatever is being said, occasionally making affirmative grunts. "Yeah, I understand. We will take care of her. I'll make sure she doesn't do anything reckless." He winks at me as I cross my arms and look away with a pout. Max listens a little longer before replying with a note of finality in his voice. "Alright, I'll let her know. Thank you, Tatsuya. Goodbye." He hung up the call and handed my phone back to me.

I grab my phone and slam my hand with it on the bed. My face contorted with anger and sorrow like a child who's been heavily punished. All four men realize that something must have been said on the phone call that has upset me. Lius speaks first, his dislike for drawn out silences seems to always make his skin itch like wool against skin. "What's wrong? What did the old man say to upset you like this?"

I look down to my feet, my face contorted with rage and annoyance. "First... I'm not allowed to step back into the ring at the gym until every single injury is 100% healed and approved by a doctor of *his* choosing. Second, he's really ashamed of me for losing control of the situation like that... and third... those men who attacked me... were ordered by my uncle... which means... he knows now that I'm the vigilante... he must've known the whole time... someone's reported the information to him." I bury my face in my hands and sniffle as the tears of frustration spill over. The mention of my uncle feels like a punch in the gut. He's been controlling my life for as long as I can remember, and now...

he knows about the vigilante. My secret. Panic rises in my chest as tears burn my eyes, the weight of his shadow suffocating.

Max glances up at the other three as he moves closer to my side and places a hand on my back. "Your uncle did this? He ordered those men to attack you?" Max's stomach bottoms out with fear staining his voice at this realization.

"I'm not surprised… he has eyes everywhere…" I breathe out as I wipe the tears away. "Control… he has to have control of me… he must be trying to *'put me back in my place'* as he used to say to me when I was a kid…"

Lius' eyes darken. "He thinks he can control you, does he?" His voice is laced with venom as he glares at Max.

I take a deep painful breath. "When Tatsuya lets me back in the ring… I think it's time I start training with all four of you…" All eyes fill with a sense of surprise at my statement. They had not expected me to bring up the idea of training with them, but now that I have, they could see that same stubborn determination returning in my eyes.

Max nods slowly. "Are you sure about this princesa? Training with all four of us will be intense…"

"That's why I said I want to train with all of you… once Tatsuya lets me…" I snapped back, holding his gaze.

"Understood. In the meantime… you need to rest and focus on getting better, alright?" Max places a hand on my arm sling.

"Fine… what else do I have going on at the moment…? But can I at least get up and get out of bed? All this lying around is driving me crazy." I debate with my four rather large mother hens.

Max gently pokes my cheek, a small smile playing on his lips. "It's only been one day, princesa. And you have plenty going on, darling. You have a handsome man who is taking care of you. Does that not satisfy you?"

"Of course it does…" I caress his cheek softly with the back of my hand, giving him a loving stare as I look over his features.

Lius makes a mock gagging motion at our exchange. I look over at him and laugh as I move to stand up with Max's assistance. We all exit the room and Max assists me with walking down the stairs and helps me sit on the couch. As I watch TV, the guys go into the kitchen to fix some.

17

Months have passed by and although I'm only 60% healed, according to Tatsuya's doctor. I'm able to do regular things on my own again. I spent the majority of my time spending each moment with my four roommates, bonding and getting to know them better–mostly with Max. When he's not at work or out on personal business runs–as he calls it–he's by my side. My being able to do regular things on my own again was a huge step in my recovery. Not just physically, but emotionally as well. Max was especially protective and attentive during my recovery, always making sure I was taken care of and healing properly. Lius and Kai tended to me too, mostly in his absence since Max did not let anyone near me when he was around. Not even the guys. They helped wherever they could.

It was a relatively peaceful time, the five of us spending time together and enjoying each other's company. There was a hint of underlying tension, particularly between Lius and Max. As usual, Lius would playfully flirt with and tease me. The flirting had ramped up a bit more since Max's possessive nature was made known and Lius seemed to thrive in getting Max to show his true nature around me. Meanwhile, my patience was wearing thin with Lius' constant flirting. I knew it was all just a game to him, but I was getting tired of it. Max would grumble and glare at Lius, occasionally pulling me closer to him to make his claim in front of Lius. I would always put a stop to it as I knew what he was doing and suspected why. It was so aggravating how they bickered like a puppy trying to take the older dog's favorite chew toy.

Kai would always have to get Lius away from Max and I so that the house was not torn apart, or I was caught in the crossfire. He was used to Lius' playful flirting and Max's possessive behavior, but he also knew that it occasionally got out of hand. He would step in and diffuse the tension occasionally as well. Keeping the two of them from getting too heated. However, as the tension continued to build, Lius' flirting became more and more intense. He seemed to derive some sort of pleasure from riling Max up, enjoying the way Max would get defensive and possessive over me.

One day when Max wasn't home, Lius got braver with his flirting and decided he would touch me. His sly grin widened as he took advantage of the moment while Max was not around, out on personal business again. He walks towards me as I stand in the kitchen, making my morning smoothie, and leans in. His hand reached out to touch my arm, or perhaps my waist, or any other part of my body he could reach—he couldn't decide. His eyes sparkled with mischief at his options, knowing full well that his actions will set Max off in a nuclear way if he finds out. He decides to snake his arms around my waist from behind and hug me, pulling me close into his chest. He nuzzles his face into the back of my head, and his body pressed against mine. "How about a little *'touch therapy,'*? Just friends helping each other, right?"

My eyes widened and I threw my hands up in the air, dropping the knife and fruit I was cutting up. "Get off of me Lius…"

Lius tightens his grip around my waist, holding me tighter against him. "With Max not here, how about we work on some of your issues with touch?"

"Lius… get off…" I say through gritted teeth. "I am supposed to be willing as well and I am *not*!"

Lius doesn't budge, his arms still wrapped around my waist. "Birdie… It's just a hug, from a friend. We need to work through this."

My body tenses the moment his hand brushes below my arm. A surge of anger and panic coursed through me, the unwelcome touch triggering a flood of memories. My skin crawls, and my mind reels, the sensation pulling my mind back to places I don't want to remember.

"You know exactly what you're doing, Lius… " I snap, my voice trembling with a mix of fury and fear. My body shakes, every nerve ending on high alert. I close my eyes, trying to steady my breathing and calm the storm of emotions crashing through me. '*One… Two… Three… Four…* ' I count in my head just as my therapist taught me to. The memories threaten to overwhelm, but I force myself to focus on the present. The violation, the unwanted touch, fuels my determination to get away from him.

"Get away from me!" I shout, my voice a mix of anger and defiance as I'm frozen in place.

Lius doesn't budge but notices my reaction and a pang of guilt causes him to loosen his hold slightly. "Focus, Ellie… on my voice. You can push through this."

"Get off me… *now!*" I hold my position as my muscles tense further.

Lius' smirk falters as he sees my expression. He starts to feel awful that he's triggering me this profoundly this time, even if his intention was to just mess with me playfully. "Hey... focus on where my hands are right now. I'm not moving them." He moves his face out of my hair and steps back a bit so that he's not pressed against me. Alleviating some of my emotional pain.

"Get off me..." I repeat as my voice shakes. "Please..."

"Focus on my voice and where my touch is. I mean no harm." His voice moved to a more calming tone. Trying to calm the storm that he's caused.

"She said... *no...*" I look over and see Max leaning against the door frame, who's watching the encounter.

Lius' eyes widen as he sees Max standing there. His famous sheepish expression returned to his face. He's been caught red handed. "Max... hey man. This is not what you think-"

"It is what you think it is..." I cut him off before he could try and lie his way out of this again. Rage crawling all over my face. "I'm sick and tired of you *just having fun* while harassing me, Lius!" I turn and punch him square in the jaw with my once broken arm. It isn't a hard strike, but just enough to make my point.

Lius' hands go up to his jaw, his eyes wide with shock as he takes a few steps back, taking a defensive stance, and releasing me from his grasp. His expression growing serious as he realizes that he's royally fucked up. "Alright, alright, I get it! I know I've pushed the limits this time and I know I've upset you. But it wasn't like I had malicious intent or anything. I was just... I figured I would use this opportunity, while Max was out, to work on some touch therapy. I didn't think you would take it so horribly."

"Yes, you did..." I storm out of the kitchen and to my room slamming the door, leaving Lius to face Max, alone.

I walk further into my sunlit room when a dark figure darts out from behind my door and grabs me from behind. I feel the cold sensation of steel against my throat. I fight against the man's grip around my shoulders.

"Ah, ah, ah... shhh... Don't want to cut off that gorgeous head of yours..." The intruder whispers into my ear. "Call your man in here... now..."

"*MAX*?!" I shouted from my room without a second thought. This guy is done for once Max gets in here and he's *asking* for me to bring him in here? What is this man's motive? Is he another one of my uncles thugs? Or just someone who has a personal vendetta against my boyfriend?

"Yes darling?!" I hear his response back from down stairs.

"*Max!* Please bring me a banana!" I respond, using a secret code phrase that only he and I know. It's for me to indicate to him that there's danger. I am in danger.

The intruder chuckles at my choice of reasons to bring him in here.

"On it! I'll be right there princesa!" I can hear the urgency and understanding in his voice at the reason for my strange request.

I hear two sets of footsteps running through the house to the stairs. I hear Lius shout. "Wait, something's wrong. I'm coming with you."

His voice low and commanding, I hear Max tell Lius, "No. You stay here. Let me handle this."

Lius reluctantly obeys Max's instructions. "Fine. Just... be careful..."

Max heads up to my room. I'm sure he knows that the situation is tense and potentially dangerous, but I trust his skills and experience to handle the intruder. I'm waiting anxiously for

Max to arrive, the intruder tightens his choke hold on me, his presence an ominous threat over me, the cold steel of his blade against my throat making me afraid to even swallow. Max arrives at my doorway, his eyes landing on the situation I'm in. His eyes widened slightly, taking in the dangerous situation in my bedroom. Rage and protectiveness fill his features as he stands in place, taking a moment to assess the situation and plan his next move.

The intruder sees Max's presence and tightens his grip on me, the blade pressing against my skin. The tension in the room rises as the intruder speaks, his voice cold and menacing. "Well, well, well. Look who decided to join the party? He really does come whenever you call... doesn't he?"

Max keeps his voice steady, despite the anger bubbling underneath the surface. "Let her go. *Now*"

The intruder chuckles, thinking he has the upper hand in this situation. "Oh yeah? And what are you going to do about it Max? Rip me to shreds just like you did the others?"

My eyes widen and I freeze as I look at Max, realizing he's talking about those other four men who attacked me. I knew this intruder sounded familiar. Max's gaze sharpens as he takes a step forward. "You really don't want to find out. Let her go, and you might walk out of here with your life. Keep pushing, and I guarantee you won't."

The intruder smirks, still holding me firm. "Heh... *he* was right. You have finally developed a weakness and fallen off the path... haven't you? But I do know you don't want anything to happen to your precious little human here... do you?" He caresses the flat side of his blade against my cheek. "If you take one more step, I promise you, I will repaint this room with her blood." His breath stuck to the skin of my cheek like swamp water–smelled like it too.

"Max? Can I take it from here?" I raise an eyebrow and smirk at him. I can see in his eyes that he picks up what I'm truly asking him. He locks eyes with me, understanding my request. Despite the danger, he can see the look in my eyes. He knows I'm itching to defend myself, to once again handle another creep.

He gives me a slight nod, a subtle gesture of approval. "Go for it, princesa." The corners of his mouth lift as he readies his own stance in case this goes south.

The intruder's arm tightens around my neck, but I force myself to stay calm. I take a deep breath, centering myself and focusing on the training I've had. I twist my body to the side, using the momentum to break free from his grasp. His surprised reaction gives me the opening I need. I follow up with a swift elbow strike to his ribs, feeling the satisfying impact as he gasps in pain. He swings at me blindly, but I duck under his arm, moving with the fluidity and precision of my training. My mind is clear, my focus razor-sharp. As he stumbles back, I pivot on my heel and deliver a swift kick, catching him off guard and sending him stumbling back. I rush forward, grabbing his arm and twisting it behind his back in a painful lock. He struggles, but I press my advantage, slamming him down onto the floor with a thud. I pinned him there, my knee pressing into his back to keep him immobilized. His breaths come in ragged gasps, and I can see the fight draining out of him.

Max steps forward, ready to assist if needed, but I hold up a hand to stop him. "I've got this." I say firmly, my eyes never leaving the intruder. I lean down, my voice cold and steady. "Who sent you?" I demanded, pressing my knee harder into his back. He groans in pain, but I don't ease up. "Talk!" I command my patience wears thin.

He coughs out a response. "I-I don't know! We were just given orders to capture you. That's all I know!"

I glance up at Max, who nods in approval. "Good job, princesa," he says softly.

I release my hold on the intruder, standing up and stepping back. My muscles are screaming out with soreness at my sudden movements that I haven't done in a long time. Max moves in to restrain him further, ensuring he's no longer a threat. My heart pounds in my chest, but I feel a surge of pride and confidence. Despite my injuries not being fully healed, I proved to myself and to Max and this man on my floor that I'm not to ever be underestimated.

Max looks at me with a proud smile. "You did great, sweetheart." As the adrenaline begins to fade, I realize just how much I still have to learn and control. But at this moment, I know that I can still face whatever comes my way, even at 60% recovery. Max takes the man's knife as he ties up the intruder to restrain him even further, tucking it into his belt.

The man looks back at me and grunts out, "He will catch you... eventually he will have you in his grasp again... Mark my words-" Max punches him in the face, breaking his cheek bone from the sounds of it, knocking him out.

My eyes narrow at his words as Max meets my gaze and stands to walk towards me. "You fought well, but we need to be careful. You're not fully healed yet." His tone is light.

"According to the doctor I'm not..." I stretch my arms out in front of me, hands intertwined together with my palms out.

Max's face forms into a wide grin with pride. "I gotta say... I'm impressed. You've got a hell of a right hook on you."

I smile with joy, my whole body shaking with the residual adrenaline. "Gods that felt good…"

Max chuckles, entertained by my enthusiasm. He walked closer to me, pulling the knife from his belt, handing it to me. "You sure showed him who's boss. I've never seen someone enjoy a fight quite as much as you did just now."

I chuckled and took the knife. Max looks down at the unconscious intruder on the floor, shaking his head in amusement. "Look at him, all beaten up and out like a light. You really did a number on him, princesa. I have to admit that was rather badass."

I bounce up and down a bit like boxers do to loosen up their muscles, getting ready for a match. "It was entertaining from this point of view too."

His eyes follow my movements with a hint of admiration. "High spirits I see? I'm impressed with how well you held your own there."

"Lius! Could you come here please!" I call out over my shoulder as I know he's been waiting just below the stairs. He must've heard the commotion.

Lius peers around the corner, looking slightly nervous. "Yeah? What is it? Everyone, okay?"

I point to the unconscious man on my bedroom floor. "Not exactly…"

Lius' eyes widen as he sees the intruder laying knocked out on my floor. "Whoa, what the hell?"

Max crosses his arms, a smug smile on his face as he proudly adds. "Ellie took care of business. She handled an intruder that was trying to hold her hostage, like a boss."

Lius holds his surprised expression on the man. "She… she took him out? But she's not even fully healed yet." He looks up at me with a smirk. "Damn, that's impressive. That's some serious skills you've got there, birdie."

"Well thanks… This guy is the fifth attacker from that night…" I gesture back to the man on the floor.

Max sighs, "One more to go… Lius, we need to find that final guy asap. End this once and for all. These guys are only set on one mission."

"To capture me… according to this guy, they're to bring me in… to my uncle I assume." I say with bated breath as my nerves start to close in on my throat. I've always imagined the day when I would face my uncle, but after so long. Why now? What is it he wants with me?

Lius' eyes widen as he takes in what Max and I both share what we've learned. "So, one more of your attackers is still on the loose?"

I let out a breath that I wasn't aware I was holding in. "Can we cross that bridge when we get to it? For now, Lius, can you please help Max get this guy out of my room."

Lius raises his eyebrows slightly at my request. "Yeah, no problem. I'll help take care of this guy." He turns his attention to the unconscious intruder grunting as he picks him up and carries him out of the room. Max follows behind him, as I sit on my bed and flop back to think over all that has happened with these six shady agents and the five we've captured. My head is filled with so many questions. It's time I started investigating this further.

As the first rays of sunlight begin to filter through the curtains of my room, Max begins to stir slightly, groaning as he's pulled back into consciousness. He slowly opens his eyes, blinking a few times as he adjusts to the light. He looks down at me, still asleep in his arms and takes a moment to appreciate my peaceful expression. He watches me sleep for a few more minutes, appreciating my soft features as I rest. Eventually, he decides to wake me up, not wanting to let me sleep too late into the day. He caresses my cheek. "Hey, princesa, wake up. It's morning."

"Mmm... five more minutes..." I grumble and nuzzle closer to him.

He chuckles at my groggy protest, finding it endearing how resistant I am to waking up, this morning when I'm usually up before dawn. Eager to head out and explore the city—to keep my mind busy from the fact that I can't train, nor hunt targets for the time being. He tightens his arms around me, pulling me closer against him. "Come on... you can't stay in bed all day. We've got a few errands to run."

I open one eye and look up at him. "Mmm... morning, darling..."

Max grins down at me, his warm and affectionate expression peering at my groggy gaze meeting his. He reaches to brush my hair out of my face, his touch gentle. "Morning, sleepyhead. You're finally awake, huh?"

"Mmhmm..." I grunt. I scoff and cover my face as I look towards my window and see the sun. I also hate when he sees how I look when I first wake up. I'm always able to wake up before him and clean myself up before he can see the mess that I am the first thing in the morning. "I'm all gross... don't look at me like that."

"You're not gross... You look absolutely stunning. With your messy hair and sleep in your eyes. Trust me, I've never woken up next to anybody that looked as good as you do right now." He coos.

"What do I have to do today…?" I asked with a pout. I have to know what's so important that I have to wake up right now when I am so comfortable.

"Well, we have to shop for some groceries–it's my turn. And you need to stop at the bank to handle some paperwork. You're the one who told me to make sure you got that done today. After that… we can do whatever, you want. Okay?" He says as he rubs a finger over the cloth of my night shirt, along my spine.

"Gross… the bank…" I groan.

We make our way downstairs, and we see the other three men look up, their eyes immediately noticing my outfit for the day. They've been so used to my casual attire since I've been on rest and recovery the past few months. Kai is the first to greet us. "Well, don't you look nice today, Elara."

Lius whistles appreciatively. "Damn birdie! You fill that top out nicely! I forgot you had those kinds of curves." Yes. He still flirts whenever he sees the opportunity to. At this point I've come to understand that, it may be *flirting* to me… but Lius may just talk that way. Maybe just who he is.

I don't acknowledge it anymore with the irritation it causes… just eggs him on more. "Thanks guys… We're heading out for a while. We will get groceries while we're out. Do you all need anything that wasn't on the list?"

Kai speaks up. "Actually, there are a few things we'd like you to pick up. Can you grab some extra snacks and some more liquor? We'll be needing them for movie night later."

Lius jolts straight in his seat. "And get some of those extra strength painkillers, too. You know how *some* of us tend to… overdo it." He gives *me* a pointed look. In the past I have taken it too far while playing drinking games with the four of them. I do my best to keep up with them and I *always* seem to black out first.

I cut loose like that only here, in the safety of our home. It's always awful the next day... especially with Kai's nagging about how alcohol affects the liver.

I raise my hand in admission. "Yup... I'm one of them. Ok we will make sure to grab those things too. Text me if you think of anything else. See you all later." I wave my hand to say bye. The three men wave back as they watch Max, and I head out the door.

A while later, I'm laying with Max tracing patterns on his chest, I let out a sigh as I'm lost in thought and blurt out. "I love you Max..." My eyes widened, *'Did I just say that out loud?!'* I wince as I brace for his reaction. It's as if my mouth decided it was going to share this bit of thought, without allowing me to think it over first!

Max freezes for a moment as he hears my words, his expression one of shock and surprise. A slow smile spreads across his face, a look of tenderness in his eyes as he gazes down at me. "Did you just... say you *love* me?"

Still in shock at my word vomit, I finally snapped out of it at the realization he was asking me to repeat what I just said. Did he not hear me? Should I play it off as I said something else? When I can't think of anything to say, to clean up my word vomit, I take a deep breath. "Yes..." I let out a sigh. "I love you... Max. I've known that I've fallen in love with you for a while now..." I look up to meet his gaze reluctantly, scared of what I may see in his eyes. All I can see when I look up at him is a smile across his face, his eyes soft as he absorbs my words. There's a look of wonder and disbelief on his face, as if he can't seem to believe what I've just said.

"I can't believe you said it first, princesa. I've been wanting to tell you for a while now, but I was afraid I was moving too fast. I love you... so *damn* much." His voice wavering slightly, filled with the emotions I've always seen in his eyes when he looks at me.

A smile crosses my face, relief mixed in and tears start to line my eyes so fast they spill over before I get the chance to stop them. "Y-you... do? Really?"

He locks onto my eyes, reaching a hand to my face, cupping it in his hands, wiping away the tears running amok across my cheeks with his thumbs. "Of course I do. I've known I was falling in love with you for a while now. I just didn't want to rush you. But hearing you say it... it's the best damn thing I've ever heard. I love you, Elara Vivienne Blake... More than you could ever know."

"I love you too, my darling Max Drake Rossi..." I lean my face into his touch. "I can't imagine living this life... fighting this war with anyone else by my side... you're the first man I've ever trusted to touch me the way that you do... and I wouldn't change a fucking thing..."

His eyes widen in surprise and tenderness at my words, his hold on me becoming even tighter, as if he's afraid to let me go. "You mean that?"

I nod my head. "Yes."

He lets out a shuddering sigh at my response. "I'm honored... to be the one you've chosen to trust with your body. I'll never take that for granted... I promise."

I smile as I study his face. "I know you won't..."

~*~

The two of us head back downstairs, walking into the living room where the others are already gathered and have all the snacks laid out on the table, ready for the movie night. Lius looks up at the sound of our footsteps descending the stairs. "Hey! Look who decided to finally join us!" He teases as he eye's Max and I up and down, his tone playful and suggestive. "So, what were you two doing up there this whole time?"

Kai glances over his shoulder. "It's about time, we thought you guys were never going to come down here."

I scoff and roll my eyes as I walk into the living room while holding Max's hand. "What movie are we watching Kai?" I ignore Lius completely, not giving him the satisfaction of getting under my skin. I lead Max to sit in the recliner, as I sit down on the arm of the chair next to him.

Lius pouts as I ignore him, looking like a petulant child denied a treat. "Aw come on, birdie… I just wanna know what you two were up to."

Kai watches the exchange, he smirks "We are planning on watching a horror movie tonight. Is that okay with you two?"

"I'm good with that. Babe? Sounds good to you?" I continue to ignore Lius as I'm dying of laughter on the inside from how pitiful he looks right now.

Max smiles at me in response, enjoying me perched next to him. He wraps an arm around my waist and pulls me down onto his leg, closer towards him. "Yeah, princesa. I think we can handle a little horror. But I doubt it'll be as scary as when you're mad at me." He teases.

I giggle at Max's comment that I scare him more than a horror movie could when I'm mad at him. Max grins back at me, his eyes sparkling with tender affection. He plants a soft kiss on my forehead.

"Okay Kai… horror is good with us." I say as I close my eyes and relish his touch. Kai nods and picks up the remote for the TV.

He presses play on the remote and dims the lights. "Alright then, let's get the movie started."

As the movie plays, I lay my head back onto Max's shoulder and get comfortable. We play quite a few drinking games that involve what we see in this classic horror film. Our laughter and shouts fill the house late into the night. I drank way more than I should have, once again, since I felt safe at home and that Max was right beside me. The men become rather amused at the sight of me getting increasingly drunk as the night progresses. Shouting comments at the characters in the film, calling them names when they made a dumb move that inevitably got them killed. After a while—and too many shots later. I get so drunk that I black out and fall into a drunken coma, collapsing onto Max's lap, snoring which interrupts the rest of the movie for the others just before the ending.

I stir awake as I feel something wet, hard and even squishy beneath me. My eyes are heavy and my whole body hurts. I can smell dirt, mud and motor oil all around me. It's dark out, or at least around me as I can't see any light trying to pierce through my eyelids.

"SHE'S HERE!" I hear someone shout. I know that voice. Lius. I hear two sets of feet running through gravel and puddles of water. I work to open my eyes and to move my body. The liquor must have paralyzed me because I can't seem to move. I'm trapped in between the conscious and the unconscious. I hear Lius and Ares voices as they kneel down closer to me, "Why is she lying in an alleyway? Her clothes are a mess and torn…" I appear to them still passed out cold on the cold wet ground of the alleyway, a new busted lip stings my face with blood smeared along my chin–I so badly want to wipe it off… to wash this dirt and grime off of me. I hear another set of feet arrive at the end of the alleyway. It must be Max arriving at where Lius and Ares are, I've heard his run many times in the past as we ran to and from hunts. I can faintly hear how his heart slams into his chest at the sight of me in such a state.

He blurts out as he runs towards me, kneeling beside me. He hovers his hands over me, not sure where to inspect first. I can feel their warmth close to my cold skin. "What the hell happened to her…?" I can hear the fear and pain in his voice.

Ares' voice is just above a whisper. "We found her like this. She seems a bit roughed up, but she seems to still be breathing, thankfully. Did she go on a hunt and not tell anyone?"

Lius reaches a hand out to gently shake my shoulder. "Hey, wake up. Birdie… can you hear me?"

My eyes pop open at Lius' touch and I stop as soon as I see my roommates surrounding me. I let out a sigh of relief that I finally was able to move. I sit up and clear my throat, wiping the mud off of my face. "Oh… sorry guys…" I look down at my clothes and my surroundings realizing more clearly what's going on–what they were talking about. I place my hand on my forehead, down over my eyes and swipe my hair out of my face. "Oh no…" I quickly rose to my feet, adjusting Max's now shredded shirt on me, and straightening the shorts of his I was wearing as well, which are also torn. I took a look at the clothing as these were not what I was wearing to movie night. I pull the collar of the shirt out and look down my front and can see evidence… I was assaulted… for the first time since I was 17. Only this time… I can't remember a thing. I look at Max as maybe the evidence I see is from him and I. "Max... did we... have an intimate moment after I blacked out during the movie?"

Max is relieved to hear my voice and that I'm awake and standing. His relief is quickly replaced with confusion and worry as he notices my disoriented state and the implication of my words. "What are you talking about? We didn't... I just carried you to bed and went to sleep. Why do you ask?"

My eyes widened as the air in my lungs rushed out at the realization. "I need to go to the hospital... now... May I use someone's phone? I think I was attacked..." I glance around at the guys to see who may have brought their phone with them.

Max's face pales, his eyes wide with disbelief. None of them look like they can believe what they're just heard me say. "Wait... what?! Are you sure? Were you really-?" Max finally breathes out.

"Yes, I'm sure... no one touch me... I'm now a crime scene..." I hissed and touched the bottom of my lip, flinching as I felt the sting of the cut. "Ugh... and they were rough too. Is my head bleeding?" I ask as I touch a sticky liquid at my hairline in the middle of my forehead. None of the men answer me, they seem to be frozen in place.

"You have a busted lip as well... and a gnarly bruise around your neck..." Lius looks at me as if I'm a puppy that was just abandoned on his doorstep. He then digs into his pocket, grabbing his phone and hands it to me. "Here you go. You can use mine."

I take it from him as I dial a call and hold the phone to my ear, listening to it ring. Max nods as he looks to see if he can locate the bleeding on my head, his fist clenching as he resists the urge to touch me and clean up my wounds. He will find whomever did this to me and make them suffer for it, I can see it in his eyes.

The phone rings, the sound seeming to echo loudly in the tense atmosphere of the alley as it's pressed against my ear. The line picks up as Z voice answers. "Hey it's me... I've been attacked... run a perimeter for me please... yea... yep." I look down at myself. "I'm not sure how long ago or how long I was out here... yup... I *was* pretty shit faced... Okay, thanks... oh and go ahead and alert the police of the search and of the attack, let them know I don't have a description to give of my attacker... Thanks Z... yea, I've got the guys with me... mmhmm... okay gotta go." I hang up the call and hand Lius his phone back. "Thanks, Lius."

All four men listened silently as I talked with Z. Max's heart sinks as he hears the details of my attack, anger rising within him. "Who were you talking to? Z?"

I nod as Lius takes his phone back from me, as they all anxiously wait for me to explain. "Yes, that was Z. He's going to try and locate the attacker. Alright... could one of you drive me to the emergency room please? I need them to do a test kit on me before the DNA dries, absorbs or rubs off..." I'm met with momentary silence as the guys digest what I've just said.

Max grits out. "I'll take you. Come on." He reaches out to grab my waist, to lead me to his car, which is back at the house. I flinch back away from his hand.

His eyes fill with hurt as I've never flinched away from him. He looks so hurt as he retracts his hand back towards himself. "I'm so sorry darling... You can't touch me right now... not until the hospital collects all of the... *evidence* off of me..." I look away from him, ashamed and embarrassed. How could I let myself get so drunk as to not remember what happened here?

His heart clenched as he retracted his hand, my own heart whimpered as I saw the hurt in his eyes. He seemed to understand as he stuttered out, "R-Right, right. I'm sorry... I forgot for a second." His helplessness and frustration showed on his face, hating that he can't do anything to comfort me right now. We get to his car, and he opens the door for me as I climb in and buckle myself up. Keeping his distance so that he didn't accidentally bump into me. Once we arrive at the hospital entrance, Max shifts the car into park before rushing out of the driver seat to open my door for me. I walk quickly in through the automatic doors, straight to the check-in desk of the emergency department. The sounds of my sandals hitting the floor, that I grabbed out of Max's car, echoing off the walls of the entrance hallway. I must have startled the night nurse managing the desk, since she jumped up out of her seat behind it. I firmly believe it is due to my appearance more than just my unexpected arrival.

Nurse's voice comes out urgently as she scans over my clothing. "Oh, my goodness… Are you alright, Miss? What happened?"

"Hi, yes. I'm alive so I'm good enough. I've been attacked and need a rape test kit done right away… These guys behind me are my roommates. This one…" I gestured to Max. "Is my boyfriend so he's safe to be in the room with me during the examination if he wants to."

The nurse's expression immediately turns serious as she registers what I'm saying. She nods and quickly grabs a clipboard and some paperwork from the filing cabinet stationed underneath the desk that held the computer screens. "Of course. We'll get you taken care of right away dear. Your boyfriend is welcome to follow, the other three will have to wait here." She looks at Lius, Kai and Ares who all nod acknowledging what the nurse is instructing. The nurse walks from around the desk and waves a hand at Max and I to follow her past the double doors down to a room. Once we enter the vacant room she has chosen, she closes the door behind her. "Ok dear… I need you to get into this gown and strip all of your clothes off and put them to the side so I can bag them… Are you comfortable with that?" She pulls out a hospital stock gown and sets it on the bed, careful with her movements. I can see that she's had to handle these situations many times before, sadly. She waits for my answer with calm and caring eyes. It throws me off that she isn't concerned at how professional I am about all of this right now. I must not be her first victim that has behaved this way. The thought makes my blood boil.

"Yes. You have my permission to do what you need to." I meet her gaze, holding a professional tone as I try to just keep this business going as quickly as possible. I look over at Max. "This is going to be rough… not just for me… but for you as well… The doctors and nurses are not hurting me." I fill my gaze with pleading need for him not to let his protective instincts take over as I'm examined.

Max lets out a deep breath, trying to calm his racing mind, and nods in understanding. "I… I know. I'll be alright." His jaw clenches, bracing himself for the emotional toll ahead. The nurse steps out for a few moments and I begin to remove my clothing as soon as the door clicks shut. Max's eyes water as he sees hand prints on my body. He's never left handprint bruises on me during our intimate moments and now… he knows he never will after the sight of the asshole's handprints on me. The nurse returns to the room after a gentle knock to continue the procedure with another nurse following behind her to assist. She collects samples as the other documents everything meticulously. Max stands beside me, his eyes never leaving me as his heart aches for everything I'm going through. The room is filled with a tense silence, broken only by the sounds of the medical equipment and my whimpers and hisses as the nurse gives instructions of what she's going to do next.

The entire process feels like an eternity. It seems to last forever, each swab and sample seeming cruel and violating as I bite back any further sign of my discomfort. I just want this all over with and to shower. Max keeps his composure, following the nurse's instructions and staying up by my head, his presence, a silent reassurance of his unwavering support. Finally, after what seems like hours, the nurse finishes the procedure and takes the final picture of my marks from the attack. She looks at the both of us with sympathy and compassion. "Okay, dear. That's everything. We'll have these samples sent to the lab. We'll need to keep you a little bit longer for further observation. Is there anything else I can get for you?"

I nod as I adjust the hospital gown back on me. "Yes, please... is it ok if I ask you to get me a change of clothes...? I'd really appreciate it... If it has to come from the gift shop that is perfectly fine. I don't want to take any clothes from the hospital's stash of clothes for victims... Charge it to the card on my file? Please?"

The nurse nods and makes a note on her clipboard. "Of course, dear. I'll arrange for some clothes and shoes, and make sure it's charged to the card on file. I'll be right back. In the meantime, try to rest. You've been through a lot, and we'll take great care of you. If you need anything else, just press the call button."

"I will... thank you so much nurse." I give her a small, weak smile in gratitude. This kind of kit can be tough for them to do as well. The thoughts that go through their heads while they swab the victims that come through here. I can empathize as I've brought my fair share of victims here to support them through this process. I also understand a bit of what Max must be feeling through all of this too–the helplessness, the anger building within.

The nurse gives me a final reassuring smile before leaving the room, closing the door quietly behind her. Max lets out a long, shaky breath, his tough demeanor faltering for a moment as he sinks into a nearby chair. "You did so well, you know that? You're so fucking strong..."

"This isn't my first time going through this..." I keep my eyes on the door after the nurse. "I've come here with other survivors to help them get through this..." I turn to face him. "You're okay to touch me now... She got everything that she will need..."

His heart sinks at my admission about it not being my first time witnessing this process. But he quickly shakes off his sadness and anger, moving closer to the edge of his chair. "Ah, so that's why you're handling this so... so... calmly?" He reaches a hand out to take mine into his, intertwining his fingers with mine. His touch is tentative, as if I might shatter under his fingers, but his grip is firm, grounding me in the present.

"Yes... it is still difficult to go through though... Even though I know what the process is." A tear slips from my eye, and down my cheek as I stare down to the floor. "What the *fuck* did I drink last night?" I say in between small sniffles, full of frustration for losing my memory. Losing control of my senses and leaving the house, in this vulnerable state. Tatsuya will most definitely give me an ear-full over this. Not to mention how much of that ear-full will come from Kai and Lius once we leave here.

Seeing the tear fall down my face nearly shatters Max to pieces. He tightens his grip on my hand to snap me out of my turmoil. "Hey, don't blame yourself... this wasn't your fault. It's that asshole who decided to take advantage of you in your vulnerable state. Don't you dare blame yourself... Not even a little, Elara. Alright?"

309

"I know it's not… What I'm upset about is that I am a trained fighter… I apparently didn't defend myself well enough… all because I had no control over my senses." I shake my head as I keep it low, facing the floor.

Max's jaw clenches at the thought. "I get it… I really do. But being a trained fighter like you doesn't make you immune to everything. You had your guard down it seems… You are allowed to enjoy a night of fun in your downtime… Then some bastard takes advantage of you. Sadly, it happens. You might be a tough woman, but you're still human." His gut clenched as he tried to say the right thing. I listen to his words and know that he is doing his best. "I… I should've been more prepared to keep you from leaving the room… from the house. I am so sorry, Ellie…"

My eyes snap to his as tears fall, and I shake my head. "No… it is *not* your fault Max… don't you *ever* blame yourself… I got carried away… I know better than to do that without taking precautions." I squeezed his hand.

His heart aches seeing me cry like this. He swallows the lump in his throat and stands up to walk closer to me. Using his free hand to gently comb through my mud caked disheveled hair, as he leans onto the top of my head. "Hey… shh, it's okay. Just let it out. You don't have to hold it in, you hear me? You are safe here… You can cry."

His gentle words and touch break the dam I've been holding back. The sobs come stronger, each one releasing the pain, as I sink further into his comforting embrace. My arms wrap around his waist, and I squeeze as hard as I can. He feels helpless, watching as I cry and fall apart against him, not knowing what else to do to help me. I hear his heart race, and his muscles tighten beneath me. "Just let it out… it's alright baby… I'm here… I'm here." His whisper is shaky.

There's a knock at the door of my hospital room. I immediately stop crying and lift my head away from Max and wipe my tears away quickly, schooling my expression immediately. "Come in." I call out once I've cleared my throat. The door to the room slowly opens, the same nurse from before enters with a change of clothes and a pair of shoes in her hands. She smiles politely and looks between the both of us. "Here you go, dear. I've brought a change of clothes and some shoes for you." She places the items on the edge of the bed, next to me.

"Thank you. Am I ok to take a shower now?" I want to wash away this whole night, send it swirling down the drain and away from my life.

The nurse nods in response. "Yes, you're free to shower if you'd like. Just be gentle with yourself... You've sustained some damage down... there. Let me know if you need my assistance."

"Thank you, I think he can help me if I need it." I smile softly in gratitude for her kindness, pointing a thumb towards Max. I never did like the feeling of medical staff touching me. I hate the feel of their latex gloves, the smell of the sanitizer that's always used in hospitals and sadly... they always smelled like it. I get that they can't help it... but I try to limit my exposure as much as possible. It always sets off a panic attack within me whenever I'm in a hospital. It's something that I've always tried to get over... but never could.

The nurse glances over at Max, then back at me, understanding my request. She nods reluctantly and understandably so. "Alright then. Just press the call button if you require anything else." She leaves the room, closing the door quietly behind her.

"Thank you..." I look back to Max. "Ok, the next hard part... the shower."

Max nods, without hesitation, letting out a sigh. "Of course. Do you... need my help?"

"No... I think I'll manage. I appreciate the offer. I just didn't want her to help me..." I walk into the bathroom with Max staying in the room behind me. Once I close the door behind me, I remove the hospital gown and walk into the shower, turning the water on to just the right temperature. As I stand in front of the mirror, my heart tightens as I take in my reflection–my body, marked with bruises, scratches, and bite marks. Each one is a reminder of the moment I lost control. The anger rises, mixing with the guilt that's already festering inside me. *'How did I let this happen?'* My stomach churns at the thought of my vulnerability. I tell myself it wasn't my fault, replaying Max's words, but the shame clings to me like the dirt on my skin.

I step into the shower, letting the hot water wash over me. The water stings, but it's nothing compared to the heaviness in my chest. I scrub harder than I should, trying to erase not just the physical grime but the helplessness. Every bruise, every bite mark reminds me of my weakness. I bite down hard on my lip, the taste of metal filling my mouth. *'Why couldn't I have been stronger?'* I flinch at my own touch as I continue scrubbing, as if I can wash away the self-blame and guilt that cling tighter than the dirt ever could.

Max's voice echoes in my head: *'It wasn't your fault.'* But the guilt doesn't listen. It's easier to blame myself than to accept how powerless I felt. I continue with the cloth, gently washing my back as far as I can reach, the suds hiding the evidence of my assault if only briefly. I'm methodical, making sure not to miss a single spot. I wash my hair and rinse all the soap off of me. I turn off the shower and dry myself off with the towel. I can still feel all the grim, dirt and idiocy of the night in me.

After I dried off, I put the new clothes on and walked out. I exit the bathroom and am met by Max's gaze. I can see the trouble brewing beneath his eyes. The hospital door opens as three figures enter through the door. Three sets of eyes looking right at me as soon as they enter, taking in my condition. The nurse must have allowed them to enter since I've given permission during her examination of me, that they are allowed in for a visit and are welcome to stay with me during my time here. I told her that they are my brothers. It made me chuckle slightly at her face as she looked at the three of them, not believing for a second that we were siblings because of the vast difference in appearances. I look at them as I towel dry my hair, walking back towards the bed. The men all stop close to my bed. I can see all the questions they are dying to ask, swarming through their eyes. After a moment of awkward silence, the reality of the situation hung heavily in the air. They see the signs of my assault more clearly now that I've washed all the dirt off of me, none of them know what to say. They look confused and concerned, unsure what to do or how to help. I watch as their eyes lock onto each visible cut, bruise and bite marks on my skin.

As I sit on the edge of the bed, I take another quick glance at their faces. Taking a deep breath I answer their unspoken questions, cutting the silence. "I know about as much as you all. I don't remember anything... so all I am feeling right now is pissed."

They all looked at each other, at Max then back at me. Lius clears his throat and steps towards me, always to be the first to speak and break the awkward silences we always seem to find ourselves in. "Ellie... are you... how are you feeling right now?"

I shrug. "I just said I'm angry. I was so drunk last night that I couldn't defend myself. I'm trained for this shit, *for fucks sake...*"

I gasped. "Oh… Lius, may I see your phone again? Mine is still at home." I only ask him because he is the only one of the four of them who always has his phone with him.

Lius jumps a little, startled by my sudden request, but he quickly pulls his phone out and hands it to me. "Yeah, sure. Here you go." Curiosity appeared on his face as to why I needed it right *now* of all times.

I dial Z's number again. The phone rings once, twice and then I hear the empty air as Z answers the call. Z's voice comes through, sounding groggy. I think I woke him up. "This better be important."

"With me it always is. Sorry to wake you Z, but who was the last target you sent to me?" I ask with a small chuckle at the sound of his groggy irritated voice. I know I'll be lectured for that later.

Z pauses a moment, surprised by my sudden question, I can hear the rustling of him sitting up to be more alert. "Ah, Elara. Straight to business, I see… Alright, the last target I sent to you was a man named Tomio Kawachi. Why are you asking about this *now*?"

"Look into his location history, please. In my drunken stupor I may have gone… hunting. If he was anywhere near where I was attacked, that may be our guy. Notify the police please?" My tone is sharp as I begin to piece everything together. At this point it is all speculation and assumptions but… my gut is telling me I'm right about this. And if I am in fact, right. That is going to make me feel way worse… I was careless with a *target.*

Z's voice sounds more alert now. He starts tapping away on what sounds like his laptop, presumably searching for more information. "Hold on a sec… I'm checking his whereabouts now… Got it. Looks like he's at a bar right now, in Shibuya. I'll ping you the address… His phone did ping off towers nearby where you were tonight… You might be right." There's a pause as Z types something into his computer. "I've sent an anonymous tip to the police. They're on their way to that bar now, according to dispatch."

"Okay good, I will check into the lab report and see if the DNA is a match for him. Thanks Z." I let out a shaky breath, my relief tainted with the weight of what I now knew.

"I'm always here to help you Elara... Let me know once everything's taken care of." He says in a softer tone than I'm used to. There's another brief pause before he asks, "Are you doing alright?"

"Yes… I'm fine. Good night." I end the call and hand Lius his phone back. I've always kept things between Z and I strictly professional. Never dabbling in each other's personal business. Ever since I met him, I've needed that to be the one constant in my life.

Lius furrows his brow. "What's that all about? Are you going after the guy who did this to you? Who is it?"

I refrain from giving the target's name as I know why I have all four ears leaning towards me. They want to know so they can handle this themselves… get revenge on my behalf. That's not how this will play out. That target is *mine* to hunt. "Not unless I have to. Police have been notified. His location is on your phone now."

Lius checks the address on his phone. "I see. The police will take care of it. But… what if they don't find anything or aren't able to catch him?"

"Then that's when I will hunt. As soon as I'm released from here and get word from Z. He will let me know one way or another." I suddenly became very interested in the shoes the nurse

315

brought me. Not wanting to see the look in anyone's eyes as I tell them I will go after this man. I know they don't approve.

Max's eyes widen just about as wide as Lius' at my declaration, uneasy glances fill the room. "Woah, hold on. You're seriously planning on hunting this guy down yourself? Even after what you just went through?" And there it is… Lius blurts out first before the others can protest.

"Lius, I've sobered up. I can protect myself now. Would it make you all feel better if you joined me on this one?" I look at Max. "I know *you* will."

Max meets my gaze, his expression thoughtful for a moment before answering. "Yes. If hunting this guy down will give you some closure, then I'm not going to stop you. But… I'm not letting the bastard touch you again… Understand…?"

I shake my head. "No… *I* have to take him down… You do what you normally do and just hang back-"

"Absolutely not." Max cuts me off.

"Max… please…" I pleaded with him. "I need to do this… for me-"

Max stands up abruptly looking down at me, rage filling his eyes. "No. I will not allow the piece of shit the chance to touch you *ever* again." My eyes widen at his sudden movement, but then they narrow to hold his gaze, showing him that I will not back down from this. Max's voice is firm, his stance unyielding. "Elara, you need to understand me: I won't let him hurt you again. I can't."

I stand up, stepping closer to him, my anger matching his. "Max, you can't protect me from everything. I need to face this. I'm strong enough to handle this."

His eyes soften slightly, but his voice remains steady. "I understand your need for closure, but there are other ways to get it. You don't have to risk your life to get it."

I shake my head, frustration bubbling over. "You don't get it, Max. This isn't just about closure. It's about reclaiming my power, proving to myself that I'm not a victim. I refuse to be!"

Max's jaw tightens. "And what happens if he overpowers you again? What then? I can't bear to watch that man do to you... what he's already done, Elara. I won't. I'll stand in your way if I have to."

Tears of anger and frustration well up in my eyes. "I won't let him overpower me. I'm ready this time. I can't live in fear, Max. I refuse to. You can't fight my battles for me!"

He steps closer, his hands gently gripping my arms. "I know you're strong. I've seen it. But this... this is different. I'm doing this for *me*. Let me help you."

I pull away, crossing my arms over my chest. "I need to do this on my own terms. I need to take back control. Please, Max. Trust me."

Max's eyes search mine, his internal struggle evident. I can see how he is determined to do this *one* thing for me. He takes a deep breath, his voice softening so as to not upset me further. He knows that when I am this hellbent on something, there's only going to be an argument. "I trust you, Ellie. I do. But I'm scared. Scared of losing you, scared of what might happen if you face him alone again."

My expression softens a smidge, my resolve unwavering though. "I'm scared too, Max. But I can't let that fear control me. I need to do this. For me."

He sighs, running a hand through his hair. "Fine. But I'm not staying behind. We'll face him *together*, even if it means just holding him down for you. I'll be there."

I nod, a mixture of relief washing over me as we compromise on this issue. "Thank you, my love. I appreciate it. But please, let me lead this. Let me prove that I can handle it."

Max's eyes hold a mix of pride and concern as he nods. "Alright, princesa. But if things get too dangerous, I'm stepping in. No debate." The way he says this final statement to our agreement, shows me it is not up for debate.

"Deal," I say, a small smile forming on my lips, as a signature on our agreement.

The tension in the room eases slightly as Max pulls me into a gentle hug. "We'll get through this. Together..." I can hear his heart thundering through his shirt. He's been my strength through this. My rock. "Thank you..." He whispers into my ear.

I lean into his embrace, my resolve stronger than ever. "Together." I can hear the others sigh with relief as I notice that Kai and Lius have moved closer in case things got out of control during our argument. They knew Max could fly off the handle and were afraid he'd lash out. He would never hurt me, I knew that. I see their surprise when it all smooths over so easily between us. They're seeing a whole new side to the mercenary Viper. That's all in great part, thanks to me. "Ok, so if the police can't catch him, then *we* will. I'll know by morning..."

18

Hours pass and I am finally released from the hospital as the early light begins to light the sky. As I am discharged, the guys all stand up and gather around me, ready to escort me back home. Lius steps forward as I ready myself to leave the hospital room once the nurse brings me my discharge and aftercare paperwork. Included are some papers and brochures on who to talk to if I'm having trouble coping with what happened to me. They have *no* idea how much I've been through... I set the information down on the sink counter in the room. Someone else may need that information in the future... who may not have formed a way to cope like I have over the years.

"Alright, doc said you can go home now. Let's get you home." Lius says as he opens the door to the room for us all to exit.

We return home and all walk through the front door, a sense of normalcy briefly returns to my life. However, there's still tension in the air, a sense that this is only the calm before the storm. Kai takes a deep breath and clears his throat. "So, now what? We just wait for an update from the police? Or Z?"

I raise a finger to quiet everyone. I looked around the empty and quiet house. The silence seems to be carrying something extra with it. Something that isn't normally here when it's empty for a period of time. There's the lingering scent of a man's cologne sticking to the walls. Nothing like any of the guys' scents. "Someone's been in the house while we were gone..." As soon as I raise my finger, the guys all immediately go on alert. Max moves to my side and places his hand on my lower back, looking around the house, his body facing my side in a protective stance.

Lius cuts through the quiet. "What makes you think that, birdie?"

"I can feel them. Smell a strange... yet familiar cologne." My voice is low in tone in case they happen to still be in the house. The guys all exchange a quick glance with each other, taut with tension. They all know that my senses are highly trained since they didn't pick up on that right away, and I seem to sense these things better than they can, given recent history.

Lius asks again, "Feel them... as in, you can sense their presence?"

"The remnants of it... They don't seem to be here anymore." I respond, holding still as I look around the house. The smell is very faint, my sensitive nose picks up on just about anything and the fact that it's very faint, for even me, means that they must have left.

Kai frowns, his eyes darting around the room. "Remnants... as in residual energy? How can you sense that?"

"I can't explain it... I just do." My head snaps towards the stairs, looking up towards our rooms as I run towards them. Although I can't explain it, residual energy is like a stream of white mist that shows the trail of where someone was, where they walked and where they touched. Like a trail left for just me to find.

Max darts after me as the others follow close behind him. I make my way quietly upstairs so as to not alert anyone, running lightly on the pads of my feet. I am approaching with stealth, just in case I am wrong, and they are still here. The other four follow suit, treading lightly and avoiding making any noise. All senses are heightened, all eyes sharp and focused, taking in every detail around them. Max's muscles coil, ready to react at a moment's notice, and even Ares seems on edge. The scented energy remnants lead me to stand in front of my bedroom door, which is still open from when Max bolted out of it late last night. The men can all sense what I sense—something is off.

Lius whispers quietly to the group. "I'll go in first… stay behind me." As the leader of the Vipers, he always walks into a potentially dangerous area, first. To be sure it's clear and safe for the rest of the team to follow suit.

I look at him and step back towards Max to allow him to pass me. He steps through the doorway and checks the room for any signs of an intruder or any other danger. After a few moments, he sticks his head from around the corner and waves us in, signaling that it's clear. "Coast is clear. It's safe to enter." He says to us in his normal tone.

I walk into my room as the others file in behind me, taking in the surroundings and searching for any signs of an intruder or any other evidence of what someone was doing in *my* room, but apparently nowhere else in the house. Lius crosses his arms as he observes me search my room for anything missing, or anything left behind. "So… you said you can sense they were in here. Did they take anything?"

I shake my head. "No… but their scent is stronger here. I think they've left something… I just have to-" I freeze when the mist trail I can see stops before exiting the room again. I see the corner of an envelope sticking out from under my pillow. I let out a sigh of aggravation as I realized who it was that was in my room. Where I know that scent and who broke into our house while we were out. "It was my father."

Max's expression morphs from serious to perplexed. "Wait, what do you mean your father? Why was he in here? How can you tell?"

I pull out the envelope from under my pillow and hold it up to show him and the others. It's a classic card envelope with my name written on it. It was my mother's handwriting. "Because he always leaves me notes like *this*. It's something he can't say out loud or verbally to me…"

Max tilts his head, fixating on the envelope pinched between my forefinger and thumb. "Your dad snuck in here and left an envelope under your pillow… and you know it's from him, for sure?"

"It's been our thing." I explain as I open the seal. "Wish he would've told me he was in Tokyo… *bastard*."

Lius rubs the back of his neck, looking a bit bewildered. "Wait, wait, wait… so you mean to tell me that your own father sneaks into your room and leaves you mysterious letters under your pillow as a form of communication?"

"Yes." I unfold the letter and begin to read the contents. "Only when it's something he's afraid someone will overhear."

Max begins to become suspicious at the form of communication. He's uneasy with the fact that someone was in my room that he didn't know. "That's… weirdly specific. Does he do this often?"

"Yes. He started it when I was working in... Arizona... What?!" I shouted as I read the letter.

Max moves closer to my side. "What is it? What's wrong?"

I take a deep breath and begin to read the letter to them:

~*~

My Dearest Elara,

I write this letter with a heavy heart, knowing that my words may not reach you as deeply as I hope. I've always believed that certain things are better left unsaid, but now I realize the importance of saying them, even if it's through these letters.

First and foremost, I want you to know that I am aware of your activities in Tokyo. I know what you've been doing, Elara. Your late-night escapades, your relentless pursuit of justice—all of it. There comes a time when you must know when to step back. And I am writing this to tell you, that time is now.

Your obsession with your uncle needs to come to an end. I understand your reasons, and we are aware of what he's done to you all those years. Your mother and I have always known... We knew you weren't lying all those times you came to us about what he was doing to you when he visited us. But sometimes we have to make sacrifices to take care of our family. Your uncle, as much as you may despise him, has been a pillar for our family. Since before you were born, he has shouldered burdens for us that you may never fully understand. Financially, he has supported us, ensuring we had a roof over our heads, food on our table, and opportunities for a better life. We had to pay a price to keep him happy... a price that you unfortunately had to pay.

I demand that you consider the bigger picture. Our family's survival, our well-being, hinges on a delicate balance. Your actions threaten to tip that balance, and the consequences could be devastating for all of us. Let go of this obsession, Elara. I beg you. Focus on building a future where you can be happy and comfortable. Leave the past where it belongs and stop chasing shadows. Your mother and I want nothing more than for you to live a life free from the chains of vengeance, and to come back home.

Please, my darling daughter, heed my words. You need to know when to let go, enough is enough. Come back to us, to the family that loves you unconditionally. We need you here to perform your duties as a Blake.

Father

~*~

As I lower the letter, the words swirl in my mind. How could they have known? All those years I spent being called a liar, gaslit into thinking I was imagining things... and now, this. The betrayal hits me like a tidal wave, leaving me gasping for air. The room falls silent as I let my hand down to my side, holding the letter as I place the other hand on my forehead in disbelief. Anger building in my chest at the audacity of my family.

Max places a hand on my shoulder. "Ellie..."

Lius grabs the letter and reads it over to be sure he heard what I said correctly. Ares and Kai look over his shoulder to re-read the contents as well. Once they all finish reading it, Lius' knuckles turn white from how hard he's clenching the paper in his hands. He looks ready to knock someone in the jaw. His expression turns grave, and his tone laced with fury. "What the hell?! This is *bullshit*!"

I scoff. "That's my family for ya..."

Kai gives me a thoughtful look. "So, your family has been covering up for your uncles' crimes this whole time? They *knew?!*"

"It appears so... and I guess they did know about my work in Arizona... and now here. You like that part where my dad said I need to let it go? Quit my *'obsession'* with my uncle?" My breath quickens as the weight of it all crushes my chest. Betrayed by the very people who were supposed to protect me. I try to breathe, but each breath is shallow, more panic than air. They *knew*. They *always* knew. And they let it happen! The rage boils up, faster than I can control it. I feel it rising, burning through every nerve. My fist connects with the wall before I even realize I've swung. The pain barely registers as I scream out, the sound of betrayal echoing off the walls.

All the men flinch, except for Max who rushes to my side. "Whoa... relax princesa... It's going to be ok..." He grabs my shoulders, turning me around and pulling me into an embrace. "Take it out on me, baby... let me carry some of that weight. You don't have to do this alone. His voice is steady, but his grip tightens, like he can feel the storm raging inside me. I cross my arms and lean into him. "Deep breaths now..." He whispers into my ear.

I take a few deep breaths. My phone rings, and I recognize the number. Of course. My blood turns to ice as I put it to my ear, barely able to control the fury in my voice.

"Hello?" Silence. Then the voice I never wanted to hear again. "No... *no*! I will not...! You two don't pay for anything as it is so I do *not* care...! Why do you say that?!" My expression goes cold.

"Thanks for sharing... Yes, I got it." I grab the letter from Lius in a rough snatch out of his hands, not caring if he got a paper cut from my actions. "You're wrong, you both are... Oh I *will* prove it. What good does it do for me to listen to you *or* father...? No 12-year-olds can't give consent, *mother*, nor go into that kind of graphic detail... That's besides the point! You *both knew*! *You knew*!" I screamed into the phone. "No... Then this conversation is over. Tell father to stay *out* of my house, and I *will* see him soon..."

I hang up the phone as the voice I referred to as my mother continues to speak, cutting her off completely. *"That bitch..."* I mutter as I shove my phone back into my pocket. After the call ends, the guys all wait in silence, watching me closely. They seem to all be trying to keep their own anger in check, but the tension in the room is palpable. As I pace back and forth, anger and betrayal twist in my chest. How could they have known all along and done *nothing*? My fists clench, and before I know it, I'm slamming my hand into the wall once again, pain radiating through my knuckles. But it's nothing compared to the pain of their betrayal.

Lius frowns as he works to keep his composure for my sake. "Are you alright birdie? What was that all about?"

"Just my mother trying to defend their decisions. Explain my father's letter and if I don't put a stop to my *'antics'* they are going to cut me off completely. But I did that already, I haven't used a *cent* of their money... Fucking Blake's man..." I run a hand through my hair as I shake my head and sigh. "She's been trying to reach me all morning... I had a lot of missed calls beginning at 6:00 AM... which must be about when my father dropped the letter off." I pieced together the timeline I was trying to put together once I saw the letter.

Max moves to wrap an arm around my waist, processing what I'm sharing. He, of all people, knows what that's like. "Your parents are trying to cut you off now? All because you're going after your uncle?"

"Yup... I need to find out how my uncle found out about my hunts in the night... my vigilantism..." A grin crosses my face. "But do you all want to know something...?"

They all perk up at the sudden change in my expression. More creeped out that I was smiling suddenly. Max doesn't seem to be creeped out though, since he's come to know me better and he knows that this isn't a smile of a sudden onset of joy. I've figured something out that benefits me. "What is it, princesa?"

"He's afraid..." I share cheerfully as this is the best realization I've ever uncovered in my life.

Lius blurts out as everyone's eyes show their confusion, I've lost them on that one. "Wait a minute. He's afraid? How do you know that?"

"Don't you see? What he's doing to get me to back off? Getting my parent's to try and force me to back down, otherwise he will stop giving them money? Sending thugs to capture me? He's scared..." My hands clap in front of my face out of joy.

Max's face brightens slightly. "You know what... I think you're right. He is trying to scare you into submitting to him... because he knows you're coming for him, and he's terrified." Max almost seems to be relieved as well. My greatest foe is afraid.

I look up to meet his gaze, full of excitement and pride. "And I just confirmed that I'm not going to stop, because of how that call went with my mother."

Max's grin turns sly as he chuckles out. "He's gotta be shitting his pants now. Thinking he just woke up a sleeping dragon or something."

"Okay... *Now* I really need your guys help... but understand this..." I address the room. All eyes are now on me. "I get the final blow... and I also get to toy with him a bit... I just think you all would be able to help keep his henchmen at bay while I get to him." I start thinking over the plan to get to my uncle, and what will happen once I find him. I have even more to prepare for now.

Lius grins wide, eyes filling with excitement. "Oh, you're speaking my language now, birdie. You want to drag this out? Make him suffer huh? Count me in!"

I grin wider as I keep my gaze on Max. He grins back at me, a dangerous gleam in his eye at the plan we have yet to unfold. Kai clears his throat, his own eyes filling with excitement, before he schools it to think it over rationally. "Alright, we're in. How exactly do you want to do this...?"

"Well first things first... I have to get back into training... I'm almost at 100% percent so Tatsuya will let me back in the ring soon. I have Z searching for my uncle's location... but maybe, one of you could do a little recon to put eyes on his movements. I will have to begin questioning my targets to see what they know." My phone pings with a text from Z.

Z: *"The DNA from your assault kit matches that of Tomio Kawachi, your most recent target. The cops did not apprehend him successfully."*

Me: *"Thanks Z."*

I wiggle my phone, after pressing send, at the guys. My grin grows even wider. "How about a family hunting trip first?" I smile with mischief.

All four faces smile as they understand what I'm asking. Max crosses his arms beaming at me. "Family hunting trip? I like the sound of a family hunting trip. I take it the cops failed to capture your assailant? ."

"Mmhmm…" I nod. "Awesome. Everyone else is in, I take it?" I look at the other three.

Lius grips the air in front of his face and pumps his fist down with excitement. "Hell yeah, I'm in. Sounds like a good time to me."

Kai crosses his arms as well, keeping his cool demeanor. "I'll come along as well. I'd like to get a few hits in on this man who mistreats women."

Ares, as watchful as ever just grunts, "Mmhmm"

I nod as I pull up the target profile that Z had sent me last night, which prompted my whole drunken charade of going out to hunt on my own. I gave a brief overview of what our target looks like and other information they will need to know about who we are hunting. I pass my phone around to allow the guys a closer look at the information that Z has gathered. They all take turns scrolling through my phone as they read about Tomio's background and past criminal activities. "He was last seen at a bar in Shibuya and the location is on Lius' phone. We can start there."

Lius nods as he reaches into his jeans pocket. "Right, so the first stop is this bar…" He pulls out his phone and brings up the pinned map point that Z sent to his phone showing it to all of us. "Here. Well, let's get going then."

~*~

We retreat to our rooms, knowing this brief rest is the calm before the storm. As the sun begins to set, I stand in front of my closet, my mind already shifting to the hunt ahead. I need an outfit that's not only alluring but also functional, allowing me to blend into the bar's atmosphere while keeping my movements unrestricted. I chose a fitted black leather jacket, its sleek lines and silver zippers adding a touch of edge to my appearance. Underneath, I wear a deep burgundy halter top that hugs my curves just right. Its rich color complimented my tanned skin and drew attention to my toned arms and shoulders concealed beneath the jacket.

My black skinny jeans I chose are snug but flexible, allowing for easy movement. The jeans have subtle distressed detailing, adding to the casual yet stylish look. I finish the outfit with a pair of ankle-high black boots with moderate heels, giving me a bit of extra height without compromising comfort or agility. For accessories, I opt for a silver necklace with a delicate pendant, catching the light just enough to draw attention to my neckline. I wear simple silver hoop earrings and a matching bracelet, adding a touch of femininity without being overly flashy. My makeup is bold but tasteful, with a smoky eye that enhances my deep green eyes and a swipe of deep red lipstick that ties the whole look together.

I style my waist-length black hair into loose beach waves, letting it cascade over my shoulders, framing my face. I take a moment to look at myself in the mirror, ensuring everything is in place before stepping out into the living room. The outfit is perfect. Alluring enough to attract my target's attention, but practical enough for any sudden movements or confrontations. I grabbed a small black clutch that contained only the essentials: my phone, some cash to pay the bartender, my I.D., and my blade. As I begin to walk out of my room. I look up and see Max leaning against the doorway, his arms crossed as he gazes over my outfit. His eyes flick back up to mine, I can see the approval in them.

Ever the epitome of calm and composed, Max is dressed in his Viper's fighting gear. The sleek, black jacket hugs his broad shoulders and tapers down to his waist, its design both functional and intimidating. The jacket is adorned with the Vipers emblem on the right sleeve—a coiled snake ready to strike, symbolizing their lethal efficiency and unity. Underneath the jacket, he wears a dark gray moisture-wicking shirt, its snug fit emphasizing his muscular build while allowing for maximum movement. The shirt's fabric is designed to keep him cool and dry, even in the heat of battle or during an intense mission.

His black pants are equally form-fitting, made from a durable yet flexible material that can withstand the rigors of their missions. The pants have reinforced knees and additional pockets, perfect for storing any small, necessary tools or weapons. The subtle details, like the zippers and stitching, give the pants a rugged look, enhancing his already imposing presence. Max's combat boots are sturdy and well-worn, the scuffs and scratches a testament to countless missions. They are designed for both comfort and protection, with thick soles that provide excellent grip and support. The boots are laced up securely, ensuring they stay put no matter how intense the situation becomes.

His belt holds several sheaths and pouches, housing an assortment of knives and tools essential for their missions. A tactical holster on his right thigh holds his sidearm, always within reach. Max's appearance is completed with fingerless gloves that provide grip and protection without sacrificing dexterity. His hair is slightly tousled, and his piercing obsidian black eyes scan my form with unwavering focus. Every part of his outfit is meticulously chosen for functionality, but the overall effect is undeniably striking, exuding both confidence and danger. And by the gods does he look really good…

One side of my mouth lifts as I admire how well he wears his uniform. A sly grin spreads equally across his face as he notices the way I roam my gaze over him admiring the view as I put the final bobby pin in my hair, pinning it to drape over my shoulder on the other side. He steps further into my room and closes the door, and walks towards me. I hold his gaze and straighten my stance as he closes the distance. "Damn babe. Trying to make me lose my mind tonight, are ya?" He grunts out.

I turn away from him and chuckle as I adjust my necklace while looking in my vanity mirror. "I have to bait the guy out somehow."

Max moves up behind me, his hands gently lay on my waist and rests his chin on my shoulder. "I guess you have a point. Though, I'm not a fan of this plan…" his eyes meet mine through our reflection.

"Well, that's the purpose of this outfit. This has been a lucky outfit when I'm out hunting and have to lure in my targets… That's why I wore it every time we went out to hunt together." I hold his gaze through the mirror's reflection.

Max's grip tightens on my waist, his brows furrowing slightly. "I guess you have a point. But, princesa… luring him out like this? You're playing with fire." His voice is steady, but there's a hint of worry underneath. His fingers still tight on my waist, his eyes darkening with desire as they meet mine in the mirror. There's something else in his eyes as well… concern. "You know this plan is going to drive me crazy, right?" His voice is husky, but there's an edge of protectiveness lingering in his words as he presses a kiss to my shoulder.

"I know amoré." I turn to face him. "I need hunting to be the exception. And you're not going to like it but, I need you to restrain yourself while we're hunting this guy, ok?" I take a deep breath. "I will have to let him touch me, more than likely. At least once... so that he lets his guard down enough for me to gain the upper hand. You have to restrain yourself because I only need you and the others for surveillance... to *only* jump in if you need to. Can you promise to do that for me?"

He clenches his jaw, the conflict in his eyes as he takes in my words, swarming like an angry hive at the very *thought* of this guy potentially touching me again. He doesn't like the idea of my targets touching me physically as it is, even if it is just part of my strategy. "You want me to just stand by and watch *this* guy put his hands on you again? You do know how much self-control that's going to take for me to restrain myself, princesa?"

"I know. And I know that it's not fair to ask this of you, and it's a lot to ask of you. But please, amoré... You can't blow my cover." I turn around and look up at him, pleading in my eyes. I rest my hands against his chest, which I know always soothes him from getting too upset.

Max clenches his jaw, the muscles twitching beneath his skin as he takes a steadying breath. His possessive instincts are screaming at him, but he forces them down, knowing this isn't the time for emotions to cloud his judgment. "*Gods dammit...* alright fine. I'll do my best to hold back. But just know... I'm not going to like it one bit. And if he steps too *far* out of line... the deal is off."

I run a finger along his chest as I look up at him through my lashes. "I know... tell you what. Once I get him all tied up and captured, you can get a hit in. Deal?"

A faint smirk appears back on his lips as I see him relax under my touch. He lets out a deep, shuddering breath as my finger travels across his chest. "You really know how to twist my arm, you know that? Fine, I'll hold off until you've got the target apprehended... I'm not making any promises once I get *my* turn with him..."

"Just make sure he stays alive, amoré. I have to– *unfortunately*–turn him in alive." I lift up on my toes to plant a kiss on his cheek. "Okay?"

He nods reluctantly in response. "Okay, we have a deal. I'm going to hold you to it. "

I wink at him as he brings a hand up to caress my cheek gently. I can sense that he's still bristling with jealousy, given his tone. "You're going to drive me insane, you know that? Now c'mon, the guys are waiting for us."

I step back and turn towards the door to exit my bedroom. "Someone better tie up Lius... He's bound to get in the way."

Max lets out a snort as he follows behind me, a rough laugh at my words. "Yeah, probably a necessary precaution. Lius is going to have a hard time restraining himself from ripping that bastard's arm off."

"Which is why I've already talked to Ares and Kai to let them know that you're going to have a hard time on this job, and for them to help you. I guess one of them is also going to have to keep Lius in check as well." I add in a breathy tone as we descend the stairs.

Max's smirk widens in appreciation for my efforts to anticipate and plan for any unnecessary issues that may come up in this mission. He gives a nod of acknowledgement. "Good thinking babe. You always know how to handle us. I have a feeling I'm going to need all the help I can get not to blow my top out there. I appreciate the back up." He grabs my arm to stop me in the stairwell at the halfway mark, taking my chin in his hand, tilting my face up towards his and gazes down at me intently. "Hear me when I say this, when this is all done, I better not find a single damn mark on you, you understand me? And you're going to owe me big time for this later, princesa."

I grin as my eyes roam over the features of his face. "Yes sir…" I take two fingers and do a mock salute.

We head down the stairs to meet up with the other three Vipers waiting in the living room, all dressed in similar uniforms as Max, awaiting the pre-mission briefing. Lius is lounging casually on the couch, while Kai stands near the door and Ares leans against the wall. All three of them look up as Max and I enter the room, eyes observing the outfit I've chosen to bait the target.

Lius chuckles as he leans forward to rest his elbows on his knees. "Oho, looks like someone decided to put the bait out tonight huh?"

"Hey guys. Yup, this is how I lure a creep in." I look at the three of them. "Okay, now down to business." All four men circle closer to me, Max standing behind me, hands in his pockets, which is what he does to control his urge to latch onto me and pull me towards him. "The game plan is, we will drive all together in one vehicle together to the bar. Then about two blocks away from our destination, three of you will get out of the car and the fourth will be disguised as my driver. Kai, that's you. I will enter the bar, and I should draw our target's attention right then, if I'm as successful with this outfit as I hope I am. That's the main part of this, getting his attention. Kai, you'll drop me off, then park two blocks away. Ares and Lius, you'll be positioned outside, keeping watch from the alleys. If I manage to draw him outside, that's when you act. Until then–keep your distance." I glare at Lius. "Be as stealthy as you've ever been in your lives guys. Does everyone remember when I said you were to interfere?"

I receive crickets from them as they take in the plan I have come up with. Lius lets out a huff of air before taking a step forward. "Yeah, yeah, we remember... We will stay in the shadows until you need our assistance..." His tone sounded annoyed. Ares and Kai nod as well, as they go over the plan I've laid out in their minds.

"Thank you. Yes. Kai, Ares, you all remember your separate agendas, right?"

Kai and Ares both give a nod in acknowledgement, their expressions serious as Lius' eyebrows rise in surprise that I've assigned separate agendas to those two and not anything to him. Ares speaks up. "We've got it covered, don't worry. You just focus on baiting that target out and protecting yourself. Let us worry about everything else."

"Perfect. Any questions before we head out?" I clap my hands together to bring our little pow-wow to an end so that we can head out. We have a bit of a drive ahead of us.

I see all four heads shake as Lius answers for the group. "No questions here. Let's get this show on the road."

"Ok. Let's go." The guys all nod at my command and I walk through the front door towards the car. Lius runs up to my side, slinging an arm around my shoulder. "Ooooh... you better get your arm off of me Lius..." I attempt to shrug out of his grasp. He snickers in response, glancing back at Max, being met with Max's sharp gaze.

Lius doesn't seem to be intimidated this time, his grin growing wider. "Ah, he always looks like that. I'm sure he doesn't mind a bit of contact among friends."

"If you value that arm… you will remove it. I can't have any of you distracted during this." I rejected his reasoning and pick up his hand with my own and remove it off of me.

Lius held his grin, but it was softer this time. "Okay, okay. You know I'm just trying to keep things light. But don't worry, I'll behave." He removes his arm from around my shoulders and Max quickly moves to replace where he was, snarling in Lius' direction.

Max glances at me, with a conflicted expression, doing his best to not hit Lius in order to save his energy for the mission ahead. For my sake. "Thank you for agreeing to this amoré… I know it's going to be tough for you." I wrap my arm around his waist and squeeze it for reassurance.

His expression softens as he squeezes my shoulders in return. "It's hard as hell, yeah. Probably harder than any fight I've been in. I'll do it for you though… Just… try to keep him from touching you? Please?" His eyes become dark and solemn. I know this is going to be harder for him. He has seen what happens when I lure a target out. But this one… *this* one is different. He's afraid of not protecting me again, for slipping up and this guy assaults me yet again. Under *his* watch.

"Okay… I will do my best." We load into the car. I am in the back seat between Max and Lius while Kai gets into the driver seat and Ares in the passenger. I adjust myself in the seat as I lift up my hips slightly to move my blade's holster on my waist so that I don't have to ride with it jabbed in my ribs the whole time. Max and Lius both try to inconspicuously look over as I reveal a bit more skin from my torso.

Max clears his throat and leans in, towards my ear to whisper. "Careful, babe. You're going to make me snap my restraint if you continue to do that."

I lower my top and grab ahold of Max's hand to bring it to rest on my knee. "I just didn't want to ride with the handle of my blade stabbing me in my ribs the whole time…" I pat the top of his hand. "Down boy." I smirk at him from the side of my eyes.

Max's breath hitches slightly as I grab his hand and place it on my knee. His fingers twitch against it, his possessiveness flaring up as he tightens his grip. "You're not playing fair…" he mumbles under his breath and looks out the window.

"Just trying to calm you. You can remove your hand if it's not giving the desired effect." I go to lift his hand. But his grip tightens to lock in place.

Feeling my touch is grounding him, in a way, and he shakes his head. "No, it is helping. Keep my hand there. It's giving me something to focus on." He keeps his eyes out the window watching the city blur by as Kai drives through the night. His thumb gently caresses the fabric of my pants covering my knee.

"Okay good…" I look out the front window, watching Kai maneuver around traffic. It takes us a bit to get there due to the volume of traffic. I take a deep breath as I see the car's GPS close in on the bar's location. I look over to Max, my voice almost at a whisper. "Amoré?"

He glances at me as if I snapped him out of a daze, and frowns as he notices my nervous expression. He gives my knee a light squeeze to reassure me. We come to a stop two blocks from the bar where the three are to exit and get into position. "Yeah, babe?"

"I love you." I whisper.

"I love you too. It's going to be fine. We will be right there, watching your back. Don't forget that." Under his soft expression, he says the most reassuring words I can ever hope to hear. He squeezes my knee again as the car comes to a complete stop, Kai unlocks the doors, and I hear three doors open as they all climb out of the car. Max lingers for a moment keeping his eyes on me. He gives me a small smile before exiting the car, leaning down and giving me a wink before closing his door, not wanting to leave my side. Once all the doors are closed, I watch as the three men take off into the shadows to get into their positions. Kai pulls away from the curb, towards the front of the bar. He puts the car in park and steps out of the car, walking around to open my door. Keeping up his facade as my "driver".

I step out of the car and see Kai's eyes scanning our surroundings discreetly, taking in the location and checking for any immediate threat. He closes the door behind me and whispers. *"We'll be waiting."* Before getting back into the car's driver seat. I nodded discreetly once without looking at him to keep up the mask of our plan.

In a normal and haughty voice, I say to him before he closes the door. "Pick me up in three hours please." Which is my code phrase for him to take his position and see him there. I turn and walk into the bar. Kai nods silently, as he watches me till I enter the bar. He waits for just a moment then quietly drives off to take his own with the others.

Once I'm inside the bar, the atmosphere is loud and lively. Music blares from the speakers, drowning out the noise of chattering patrons and clinking glasses. Couples and groups of friends are scattered throughout the dimly lit room, some occupying the small round tables with their drinks and others dancing in the middle of the dance floor. I smile as I walk in and look around for a brief second before going to the bar to order a drink. When hunting targets in bars, Z Group has set up that the bartenders will only make us virgin drinks under the mask of a real one to help us keep our cover as regular patrons. It's a made-up drink that he came up with to tell bartenders, so his agents won't get drunk on the job, and blend in better. I approach the bar and sit myself on one of the stools, catching the bartender's attention. He glances at me with a friendly smile in greeting, his eyes linger on my attire for a moment. "What can I get you, Miss?"

I ignore his gaze over me and ask. "A *Black Umbrella* please?"

The bartender's smile widens as he catches on to my request, recognizing the code word for a virgin drink, that I'm working undercover for Z Group. "Ah, yes, the *Black Umbrella*! Virgin, right? Coming right up for the lady." He begins to prepare the drink, mixing together the ingredients with practiced ease. My smile doesn't falter, but internally I'm seething. Rookie mistake. I sip the drink, careful to keep my cool as a couple of nearby patrons exchange glances. Z is going to have his ass for this. It only takes a few moments before he places the drink in front of me.

"I'm pacing myself..." I tell them as I raise my glass. Some of the other patrons chuckle at my response as they raise their own glasses in a mock toast, saluting my restraint.

"Pacing yourself, eh? Smart move." I feel his presence before I hear him, the weight of his gaze settling on me like a predator watching its prey. I take a slow breath, keeping my expression neutral as I turn to face him. "Can't enjoy the party if you can't remember it the next day, am I right?"

"Right?!" The music is so loud and mixed with the chatter of the other patrons I feel as if I am screaming just to speak to him.

Now that my target has been identified, my plan is put into motion. I'm pleased that he has taken the bait so early in the night. He smirks and takes a sip from his own drink, his eyes locked onto mine. I take a sip of my drink, keeping my expression light and friendly. The target, a man in his mid-thirties with a rugged charm, leans casually against the bar beside me. His eyes rake over my attire, clearly appreciating the effort I put into tonight's look.

"I'm Tomio," he introduces himself, extending a hand. His voice is smooth, but there's a hint of something darker beneath the surface.

"Arya," I reply, shaking his hand briefly before returning to my drink. Every hunt I make up a new name to give, never providing my real one. "Nice to meet you, Tomio."

"Likewise, Arya." He replies, his eyes never leaving mine. "So, what brings a beautiful woman like you to a place like this?"

I smile, leaning in slightly as if sharing a secret to keep from shouting so much. "Just looking to unwind a bit. It's been a long week."

Tomio nods, seemingly satisfied with my answer. "I hear you. Sometimes, you just need to let loose a little, right?"

"Exactly," I say, letting a playful edge creep into my voice. "And what about you? What brings you here tonight?"

He chuckles, glancing around the bar before returning his gaze to me. "Oh, just looking for some fun, you know? It's always good to meet new people."

"Absolutely," I agree, taking another sip of my drink. "So, what do you do, Tomio? For work, I mean."

"Me? I'm in the import-export business," he replies smoothly, though I know it's a cover for what he truly does for money. "Keeps me busy, but I enjoy it."

"Interesting," I say, feigning curiosity. "I've always thought that sounded like an exciting line of work."

"It has its moments," he admits, his eyes twinkling with mischief. "But enough about me. What about you, Arya? What do you do?"

"I'm a freelance writer," I lie easily. "Gives me the freedom to travel and explore new places. I guess you could say I'm a bit of a wanderer."

Tomio raises an eyebrow, intrigued by my fake profession. "A writer, huh? That's impressive. What kind of things do you write?"

"Mostly travel pieces," I reply, spinning the story further. "I love experiencing new cultures and sharing those experiences with others."

"Sounds like a dream job," he says, his gaze becoming more intense. "I bet you have some fascinating stories to tell."

"Maybe a few," I say with a coy smile. "But I'd rather hear more about your adventures. I'm sure you've seen some interesting places in your line of work." I need to get him to tell me more about his line of work… maybe it will connect with my uncle somehow.

Tomio laughs, enjoying the game he thinks we are playing. "Oh, I've seen a few things. Maybe I'll share some stories with you later, if you're interested."

"Definitely," I say, my heart racing as I feel the hunt closing in. The tug on the fishing line is becoming more strained as he toys with the bait around the sharp hook. "I'd love to hear all about it."

We continue to chat, the conversation flowing easily as I subtly steer it towards getting more information out of him. All the while, I remain aware of my surroundings, noting the positions of the other patrons around us. He leans in closer, his breath warm against my skin, and I fight the urge to recoil. His fingers brush over my arm with deliberate slowness, like he's savoring the moment as he whispers into my ear, "You know, Arya, there's a quieter spot upstairs. Maybe we could continue this conversation somewhere a little less... crowded?"

I smile, knowing this is the moment I've been waiting for. "Actually, what do you say we get out of here?"

Tomio's eyes light up at my suggestion, favoring the idea of getting me alone. He steps back slightly and sways his hand in front of us, "Sure, sounds like a plan," he says, his tone smooth and confident. "Lead the way."

I stand up and grab my clutch off the bar, giving him a playful smile. "Follow me." As we make our way through the crowded bar, I make sure to walk closely to Tomio, the plan is perfectly in motion. We exit the bar into the cool night air, the sounds of the city buzzing around us. I lead Tomio towards the alleyway that leads to the parking lot, the dimly lit area providing the perfect setting for what's to come. The guys are strategically positioned, hidden from view but ready to step in at a moment's notice.

"So, where's your car?" Tomio asks, trying to sound casual but clearly eager, as he wraps an arm around my waist and pulls me close to him. He sticks his nose in my hair and inhales its scent. My mind starts buzzing an alarm as I just *know* Max is going crazy from his hidden position right about now.

"Just over here," I say, pointing to a secluded corner of the lot. "It's a bit of a walk, but it's worth it for the privacy."

He follows me without hesitation, his excitement buzzing. As we reach my car, I turn to face him, leaning against the vehicle in what I hope is a seductive manner. "Here we are," I say softly, looking up at him through my lashes.

Tomio steps closer, his eyes darkening with anticipation. "You know, Arya, I've been thinking about getting you alone all night," he murmurs, reaching out to touch my arm. Running his finger lightly over the leather of my jacket, tracing a line towards my shoulder.

I suppress a shiver of revulsion at his touch, reminding myself to stay in character. "Is that so?" I reply, my voice low and inviting. "What exactly have you been thinking about?"

He smirks, his hand sliding from my shoulder down my side, and to my waist. He grips my skin firmly and pulls himself flush against me. His face inches from mine. "About how much fun we could have together," he says, leaning in even closer.

"Hmm... maybe some other time?" I suggest, my heart pounding as I prepare to spring the trap, gently pushing him away from me. "I just wanted to talk without shouting over the music." Tomio's grin widens at my resistance, a predatory gleam in his eyes. These creeps thrive on resistance to their advances.

He moves against my hand to kiss me, his hands roaming more boldly, his grip tightening on me. It's now or never. I push him back with all my strength, catching him off guard. He stumbles and grabs my waist in a bruising grip. In one swift motion, I pull the knife from my clutch, the cool steel gleaming under the dim streetlight. I press it to his throat, the sharp edge biting into his skin just enough to draw a thin trickle of blood. His eyes widened in fear, his bravado crumbling in an instant.

"Caught you now, Tomio," I say coldly, my voice steady despite the adrenaline coursing through me. My nausea builds in my throat after the feel of his lips on mine. "It fuels you when a woman resists you... tells you *no*. Doesn't it?" He tries to pull back, but I pull him roughly back to me, pressing the knife closer, the sharp edge grazing his skin. "You think you're so clever, preying on women who dare to say no to you," I continue, my voice low and dangerous. "But you messed with the wrong woman this time."

Tomio glares at me, his earlier confidence replaced with anger and fear. "You set me up," he growls.

"Yes, I did," I reply, my voice hard. "And now you're going to answer some questions."

He sneers, trying to mask his fear. "What makes you think I'll tell *you* anything?"

I press the knife a little harder, drawing a thin line of blood. "Because if you don't, you won't leave this parking lot in one piece. Now, tell me about your involvement with Nathaniel Quinn..."

His cocky grin falters, the fear creeping in as he pieces together my words. His breathing quickens, and his eyes dart wildly, searching for an escape that doesn't exist. "I don't know what you're talking about."

I apply more pressure, my voice steady and icy. "Wrong answer. Start talking, or this gets much worse for you."

He winces, the pain starting to get to him. "Alright, alright! I work for Nathaniel Quinn, okay? But I'm just a foot soldier. I don't know much about the big picture he has in store."

"Then tell me what you do know," I demand, my patience wearing thin.

Tomio swallows hard, sweat forming on his forehead. "I just handle the pickups and drop-offs. I don't ask questions. They don't tell me much."

"Who's in charge of you *foot soldiers*?" I press, needing more information.

He hesitates, but a quick flick of my knife makes him reconsider. "There's a guy named Kaito. He runs most of the logistics. He's the one you want, not me. He will know more, he works directly with the boss."

"And what does Nathaniel Quinn want with me?" I ask the most important question hanging in the air.

Tomio looks genuinely confused. "I don't know, I swear. They never told me anything about you. You do look a lot like a high-value target that we've been assigned to pick up and bring to him…" He immediately gave away that he wasn't supposed to say any of that to me.

I sneered as he just slipped up. He does know who I am and must remember me from the other night. I had no need for this whole ruse then. But I didn't know that prior to this moment… I growl as I flinch towards him, shifting my blade slightly against his skin. "So, you *do* know who I am…?" He flinches slightly at the motion and nods. Max and the others step closer within the shadows, keeping hidden, ready to take over at a moment's notice. I glance in Max's direction. I can sense that he is there, ready to help if things get rocky for me.

"Where is this Kaito?" I say, my voice leaving no room for argument. "And if you try to double-cross me or lead me into a trap. I assure you, you won't get another chance to walk away from me."

He attempts to maneuver an attack towards me. He pushes my blade away from his throat, gripping my wrist and spinning me in place so that my back is to him. One of his arms wraps around my waist, pulling me hard against his front. The other hand has my wrist and blade in its grip as he pulls my blade to my neck. Before he can make a move to slice my throat with it, I pull my wrist away from my neck and apply pressure to spin him back around behind his back and kick his legs out from under him. He fell to the ground with a thud, and I quickly straddled him, returning the knife to his throat. "Now, now" I say, panting as I lean in close to

346

his ear, "You're still going to pay for everything you've done. I want to hear you confess to what you did to me two nights ago…"

Tomio struggles beneath me, his eyes darting around wildly. But he realizes I have a firm hold on him. "I have *no* idea what you're talking about, you bitch!"

I tighten my grip as he tries to free himself. "Awww that hurts my feelings Tomio… you mean to tell me you *don't* remember me…? A drunk woman in a baggy t-shirt… in an alleyway in Tokyo. A woman who looks a lot like me—your target for Nathaniel." I coo as I lean closer to the back of his head.

Tomio's eyes widened at the realization. "Wha-What? I have… no idea what you're talking about!"

I press my blade closer to the major artery on his neck. "Yes, you do… don't play coy with me…" I jerk my grip closer as he grunts with pain. "Confess… let me hear you say it out loud…"

"Fine! Yes, I-!" I slam the butt of my blade to the nape of his neck, knocking him out. I release my grip on him letting his head slam to the pavement. The fight is over. Max and the others rush over, surrounding us. Lius, never one to stay serious for too long, starts mock-fighting with an invisible opponent, throwing exaggerated punches into the air. Kai scolds him for not taking things seriously, but a smile tugs at the corner of his mouth. Moments like these remind me that, despite everything, these men are my family.

"Nice work, baby!" Max says, his voice filled with pride and relief. He steps forward and ties up Tomio, ensuring he can't escape. Max's jaw clenches, his eyes locked onto Tomio, the anger barely contained beneath the surface. *"You're lucky she got to you first,"* he mutters, his voice low and dangerous, as he ties Tomio's hands with swift efficiency. As Max and the others secure Tomio and prepare to have him transported by the local authorities, I take a deep breath, the reality of what just happened settling in.

Max walks over to me, his expression softening. "You did great," he says quietly, placing an arm around my waist pulling me to him.

"Thanks," I reply, feeling a mix of exhaustion and triumph. "I have to call this in." I pull my phone out of my pocket and make my usual calls to the police to place an anonymous tip and to Z to announce that this target has been taken down.

Z answers after a few rings. *"Elara, how did the mission go? Did you capture the target?"*

"Target has been acquired." I replied. Then I remembered that new bartender, who messed almost everything up for me tonight. "On another note, that bartender at that bar gave away that he was serving me a virgin drink. May want to remind your bartenders that they can't say that out loud... It almost blew my cover tonight. Threw me off."

Z sighs, his annoyance coming through the phone in his voice. It's clear he's not at all happy with this information. *"Dammit... I'll deal with that. Thanks for the information. I'll mark the mission complete. Nice work, Elara."*

"Thanks." I press the *'end call'* button. With Tomio in custody, we head back to the bar once we see the authorities put him in the back of a squad car, the night's mission accomplished. As we walk, Max stays close to me, his presence a comforting reminder that I'm not alone in this fight. We walk behind the other three and laugh as we watch Lius goofing around as always and Kai giving him a lecture. These are the moments I'll remember most.

19

A few days pass and Lius and I are in a heated argument, one morning. His teasing and flirting antics have finally snapped my final straws of patience. Max is out on a *'personal business'* errand again and as always Lius decides to take that opportunity to pick on me. Kai and Ares are sitting at the kitchen table sipping their coffee and reading the paper as they listen to Lius and I argue.

"Hey, it's not my fault that you're so easy to rile up! You have targets ogle you every night! What do you expect me to do except to intervene?" We had gone on another hunt last night, searching for information on the whereabouts of Kaito–without Max this time. Lius had taken it upon himself to capture the intended target before I could have a chance to catch him in my trap. I'd *had* it with his antics, especially now with him getting in the way of my hunts.

"Lius! I can handle the missions on my own. Last night was supposed to be me taking the creep down! But *noooo*! Arelius Blackwood got too bored!" I shout, arms crossed in front of my chest as I tilt my head back and forth, rolling my eyes. "My own boyfriend stays out of it! He's the only one I'm not mad at right now for getting involved! Yes..." I direct my gaze at Ares and Kai at the kitchen table. "I mean you two as well! You failed your own agendas!"

Kai and Ares both look up at each other, but keeping their expressions stoic not wanting to get involved with whatever this big blow up is. Lius scoffs, "Oh, come *on*! It wasn't a complete failure. I still got to spend time with you, and we captured the target! That definitely counts for something doesn't it?"

"For *you*! You're being selfish *again*! I am not *your* girl, Arelius! I am with Max! Let it go already! It's pathetic..." I snarl, every ounce of my patience gone. Ever since Max and I have been together, Lius tries to force himself next to me and will wrap an arm over my shoulders or say sweet nothings to me in my ear. It's as if he's trying to show me, he'd be the better option, or maybe I'm being too self-centered. For a while I thought it was in my head, and then tonight... he's proving me right.

Lius' face contorted with frustration, his fists clenching by his sides. "You belong with *me*, not Max!" His voice echoed through the room, louder than he intended, causing even Kai and Ares to glance up from their seats.

My jaw drops. Is he seriously doing this? Does he really think by telling me this, by behaving the way that he does... That I will just drop Max and be with him? "Oh, my gods... you're deluded!" My blood boiling as I take a threatening step towards him. My knuckles turn white from gripping my fists so tight.

Lius holds his position, he grumbles as his jaw clenches in annoyance. "It's just a phase. You'll realize eventually that he's no good for you! He will only hurt you in the end. I can give you more than he ever could."

"He gives me more than I could ever ask for… from day one…" My eyes lining with tears at the frustration building in my chest, painfully. At this moment, of all the other times, I really wished that Max was here. I missed him terribly with all of his personal business trips that were keeping him away for days at a time in some cases.

Lius rolls his eyes, turning his expression sour as he adds a sarcastic tone to his words. "Oh, really? And what could he possibly give you that I can't? I bet I could give you a *list* of what he can't give."

"I'll give you *one*…" I lower my voice. "Peace. He gives me peace." I sniffle as I wipe my nose on the back of my hand. I should really keep tissues with me at all times, as much as Lius pisses me off. "He quiets my demons."

"That's a load of garbage. *Max* brings you peace…? Your demons would run screaming from me…" He snarls.

"You bring me *more* stress! Your cockiness and unforgiving *torment*! You're too conceited for your own good!" I fling my hands to my side out of anger.

His expression falters for a moment at the sight of my expression, in the face of my criticism. He scoffs to try and deflect the blow to his ego. "Excuse me? I'm not cocky, I just know my worth. And my worth is way higher than *his*!"

"That's *your* opinion…" I huffed out, panting from all of the shouting.

His expression turned petulant, "It's not just my opinion, birdie. It's a fact. I am Arelius Blackwood, the strongest elementals of the SP6 Vipers alive and their Lieutenant. What can Max claim apart from being a deadbeat dad." He scoffs as he turns away from me with a wave of his hand in a dismissive way towards me.

I freeze. The comment causes Kai and Ares to finally snap their attention to Lius, both men glaring at him for blurting that out. My eyes widen, my mouth agape. "A-A dad...? What are you talking about?!" The shock caused me to lose the restraints on the tears I was holding back.

Lius turns back to face me, the look of remorse on his face at the realization of what he just said. "Yeah, he has a son. He's not a part of his life–never has been. He left everything behind a long time ago when he left the Rossi family."

I turn and head up to my room without another word. Slamming the door behind me, I will have a discussion with Max when he gets home. Max has been going on frequent *'personal business trips'* more and more lately. Ever since I was attacked by the six rogue SP6 agents and I intend to find out why that is, along with the past he's been keeping from me.

Max finally arrives back home and heads upstairs to let me know he's back. He walks into my room and sees me sitting on my bed, hunched over resting my arms on my knees, waiting for him.

He walks slowly towards me as he sees I'm upset about something. "Hey babe... I'm back. Is... everything alright?"

I look up at Max, my eyes narrowing. "No, everything is *not* alright." My voice is steady but filled with barely contained anger. "We need to talk."

Max's brow furrows in concern. He's never seen me look at him this way. "What's going on, princesa?"

I take a deep breath, trying to keep my emotions in check. "Lius let something slip today. About you having a son. Is it true?"

Max's face pales, his expression shifting from concern to shock and guilt. "I... I can explain."

I stand up, crossing my arms over my chest. "I think you'd better. But more importantly, why didn't you tell me?"

Max runs a hand through his hair, struggling to find the right words. "It's complicated, my love. My past... it's not something I'm proud of. I left my family to protect *him*. Back when I was a hitman, I had a one night stand with a random woman. The next thing I know, she hits me up, saying she had given birth to a boy... *my* boy. I have never been father material, and I knew I never would be, not with the life I led. That's not the life I wanted for myself and I couldn't bring my kid into my mess." I glare at him, feeling a mix of betrayal and confusion as I wait for him to continue. Max shakes his head vehemently. "Protect him from the dangers that come with being an assassin–from the enemies I've made. I thought I was doing the right thing by leaving, by keeping my distance."

I let out a bitter laugh. "And you thought keeping this from me was the right thing too? You didn't think I deserved to know? For the two years we've been together? I didn't think we had any more secrets Max..."

Max's shoulders slumped as he struggled for words. "I didn't want you to carry my burdens. You deserve better than my past... my mistakes." His voice cracked, and for the first time, I saw real fear in his eyes–fear of losing me.

I felt a swirl of emotions–betrayal, anger, confusion. How could he have hidden this from me for so long? What else has he kept hidden in the shadows of his past? And yet... a part of me wanted to forgive him, to understand his reasons, but the pain was still too raw.

He sighs. "I've kept tabs on him—my son. I watched him grow up from a distance. Seeing how he's turned out, he didn't inherit anything but looks from me. I am proud of my decision to keep away from him because he's becoming a strong elementals. He will be stronger than me before I know it." He reaches out to touch my arm.

I take a step back, avoiding his touch. "Well ok then. But now, I don't know if I can trust anything you say. What else are you hiding from me, Max?"

Max's eyes widen, desperation creeping into his voice. "Nothing, I swear. That's everything you need to know about my son." He lies. I can see it in his eyes, hear it in his voice. "I know I've made mistakes, but *I love you*, Elara. I'm here now, please let me make things right with you."

I stared at him for a long moment, my mind racing. My voice trembles, "I need some time, Max. To think. To process all of this." I can sense that there's more to the story... There's something else he's keeping from me, and I will figure it out.

Max nods slowly, his shoulders sagging in defeat. "I understand. I'll give you all the time you need. Just know that I'm not going anywhere. I'll be waiting."

I watched as Max walked out the door, my heart sinking with every step he took away from me. The weight of our unresolved argument pressed heavily on my chest, and I wondered if I had just lost the one person who made me feel whole. As his car disappeared into the distance, an unsettling stillness settled over the house.

I lay down on the bed and curl into myself as I stare through my window into the night sky. If he could just come clean with me... then maybe, just maybe we can get through this. I can't think of that right now... I have to get back in the ring... I have to train, focus on completing my ultimate goal... And then maybe, Max and I will discuss things further, to fix this.

~*~

As I lay in bed, the weight of Max's absence pressed down on me like a heavy blanket. I loved him–I knew that. But love wasn't enough to erase the doubt gnawing at my mind. What else was he hiding? How could I fight for us when he wouldn't let me in? I can't seem to sleep after hours of trying... Max still hasn't come home, and I have a feeling that I won't be able to fall asleep until he does return. I make my way down to the kitchen for a glass of water. As I make my way down to the kitchen, I find Ares sitting at the kitchen table, nursing a cup of tea. He raises an eyebrow at the sight of me.

"Oh! Hey Ares... I didn't mean to disturb you." I look at the clock on the oven. "It's three in the morning, everything ok?" I grab a cup from the cabinet and fill it with some water from the tap.

Ares takes a sip of his tea before replying, his eyes study me carefully. "Everything's fine. Just couldn't sleep. I should be asking you that question. How are you?"

I take a sip of the cool water, leaning against the counter as I look at Ares. "I couldn't sleep either. My mind's been racing ever since Max left. I just... I don't know what to do."

Ares sets his cup down gently, his expression softening. "It's understandable, Ellie. Relationships are complicated, especially when there are secrets involved. Max cares about you though. I've never seen him like this with anyone before, but he's also dealing with his own demons. I know it's not easy for either of you."

I nod, feeling the weight of his words. "I just wish he would trust me enough to tell me everything. It feels like there's this wall between us now, and I don't know how to break it down."

Ares leans back in his chair, his gaze steady and reassuring. "Sometimes, people build walls to protect themselves, not realizing they're also keeping out those who care about them the most. Give Max some time. He needs to sort through his own issues before he can fully open up to you. You bring out a side of him none of us have ever seen before. He's more... *vulnerable* with you. More genuine. Max has had a tough life, and it's made him wary of people. But you've started to break that wall down, that's no small feat."

I take another sip of water, trying to find comfort in Ares's advice. "But what if he never lets me in? What if we remain stuck like this?"

Ares's eyes soften with empathy. "Then you'll have to decide what's best for you. You deserve someone who can be open and honest with you, someone who's willing to fight for your relationship. But don't lose hope just yet. Max has his own way of dealing with things, and sometimes it takes a while for him to come around."

I sigh, feeling a mix of frustration and sadness. "I just don't want to lose him. Despite everything, I really do love him. He takes care of me physically and emotionally."

Ares smiles gently. "Love is a powerful thing, Elara. It can overcome many obstacles if both people are willing to put in the effort. Just be patient and give him the space he needs to come to terms with everything."

I nod, feeling a bit more at ease. "Thanks, Ares. I appreciate you being here and listening. It means a lot."

He raises his cup in a small toast. "Anytime. We're a team, remember? We look out for each other."

I smile, feeling gratuitous for Ares and the support of my friends. "Yeah, we do."

We sit in comfortable silence for a few moments, each lost in our own thoughts. I let out a sigh and straightened up. "Now... Why are you still awake? Why can't you sleep?"

His gaze flickers over his cup to me, his expression contemplative. "Just restless, I guess. I've got some things on my mind, I suppose. Nothing too serious, just some thoughts I can't seem to shake."

I set my cup down and gave him a caring look. "Want to talk about them? I may not be very good at giving advice, but I am a good listener."

He considers my offer for a moment, his eyes studying my face. He seems hesitant to open up, but after a few moments, he relents. "Alright, I suppose I could talk about it. Just... Keep it between us, please?"

I nod. "You got it. If you respect my privacy, I will respect yours."

He nods, a smile of appreciation crosses his face. "Thanks. I appreciate that. So, where do I start? I guess I've just been feeling a little overwhelmed lately. Work has been exhausting, and I've been feeling a bit... stuck. Like I'm in a rut and I can't shake it."

I lean forward off of the counter and walk to take a seat across the table from him, giving Ares my full attention. "I get that. Sometimes it feels like everything just piles up and it's hard to see a way out. What specifically has been weighing on you?"

Ares takes a deep breath, his fingers tapping lightly on the edge of his cup. "It's a combination of things. The pressure from work, the constant vigilance we have to maintain, and... just personal stuff. Sometimes, it feels like I'm not making any real progress, you know? Like I'm running in place."

I nod, understanding exactly how he feels. "I've been there. It's tough when it feels like you're not moving forward. Have you thought about taking a break? Maybe doing something just for yourself to recharge?"

He chuckles softly, shaking his head. "Taking a break? In our line of work? That's a luxury we can't afford."

I smile sympathetically. "True, but even small breaks can help. Maybe find a hobby or something that's just for you, even if it's just for a few minutes a day. It might help clear your mind and give you a new perspective."

Ares considers my suggestion, his eyes thoughtful. "You might be right. I've been so focused on missions and responsibilities that I haven't taken time for myself. I'll think about it."

I reach out and place a hand on his arm, giving it a reassuring squeeze. "If you ever need to talk or need a break, just let me know. I've got your back too."

He smiles warmly, the tension in his shoulders easing a bit. "Thanks, Ellie. I appreciate it. Sometimes, just knowing someone's there makes all the difference."

I returned his smile, feeling a bit closer with Ares. Over the years I've done my best to bond with each member of my newly acquired family. "Anytime. We're a team, and that means we look out for each other, no matter what. Isn't that what you all always tell me? It goes both ways."

Ares nods, a renewed sense of determination in his eyes. "You're right. Thanks for listening, Elara. I feel a bit better now."

I stand up, giving him one last encouraging look. "Good. Now, try to get some rest. We've got a lot ahead of us, and we need *you* at your best."

He chuckles, raising his cup in a mock toast. "You too. Goodnight, Elara."

"Goodnight, Ares." I head back up to my room, after putting my empty cup in the dishwasher, feeling lighter after our conversation. It's comforting to know that they are all facing their own struggles, but they still show up for me when I need it most. As I lay down again, I feel a sense of calm wash over me. Whatever happens with Max, or with our mission, I know I have friends who will stand by me. And that's enough to keep me going.

~*~

I wake up early the next morning and head to the gym for my morning training session. I push myself harder than usual, trying to channel my frustrations and confusion into my workouts. My mind is plagued of this morning when Max leaves the house for another *'personal business'* trip, giving me a quick kiss on the forehead before he goes. I watch him as he leaves, a sense of unease growing in my chest.

Later that evening I returned home, exhausted from training. I eat a quiet dinner alone, my thoughts drifting to Max and our growing distance since our fight, we still haven't discussed what has caused this massive chasm between us. I call him, to try and just hear his voice, but it goes straight to voicemail. "Hey… it's me. Just checking on you… Haven't spoken in a while… Call me back when you get a chance? I love you..." I hang up the phone and set it down as I go back to my food, feeling the weight of sudden loneliness set in around me.

The next morning, I continued with my training–Max never called back, never came home. I don't think… This session I am focusing on sparring. My movements are sharp and aggressive, reflecting my inner turmoil.

As I continue my rigorous training, I focus on my realization that I've also not seen the others much since the fight with Max. I throw my weight into each punch, using my anger and feeling of being abandoned as fuel. The days ahead will be challenging and I maneuver around the sparring ring with Sensei Tatsuya, he can sense that there's a lot of pain behind my attacks and works with me to hone it into my movements. I'm still lost in my relationship woes as I give every hit filled with my sorrow, anger and frustration.

After today's training I spent some time with Ares, discussing strategies and techniques from today's session. I notice he's more distracted lately when we talk, but don't press him, assuming he's just tired. Later that evening, Max finally returns home, avoiding my gaze and questions about his day. We have a tense, awkward dinner together, he doesn't look at me even once, but I keep stealing glances at him as sadness and grief fill my heart. My frustration grows, but I decide not to confront him about it tonight.

I woke up that following morning to find Max already gone, his room vacant. He hasn't slept next to me since our fight. I feel a pang of loneliness but push it aside, focusing on my training. Something to distract my brain while I sit in this limbo with Max. I have to know why he's avoiding me completely. I've been going to the gym to train with Tatsuya every morning now for longer sessions, since I feel that's what I need to focus on more than yoga where I end up dropping that class and just doing it at home on my own. I barely make time to practice my yoga anymore.

I walk down to the kitchen and see the three men sitting with their laptops and phones, working on something important. I feel like I haven't really talked to any of them in a long time. I walk into the kitchen, my steps soft yet purposeful. I notice Lius, Kai, and Ares huddled over their laptops and phones, deep in conversation. The atmosphere feels thick with tension and secrecy, and the moment I speak, it becomes palpable.

"Good morning, guys. What are you up to?" I ask as I head to the sink for a glass of water.

All three men snap their heads up, startled by my sudden appearance. Lius quickly closes his laptop, trying to look casual. "Oh, hey, birdie. Just... some work stuff."

Kai gives me a forced smile, his eyes darting to the others before he responds. "Yeah, just catching up on some SP6 reports. You know how it is."

Ares, the most composed, nods in agreement but avoids eye contact. "Morning. How's your training going?"

Suspicion bubbles up inside me, but I push it aside, attributing their behavior to the usual secrecy of their line of work. "It's going well. Tatsuya has been pushing me hard, but I feel like I'm making progress." I fill a glass with water and take a sip, observing them quietly.

Lius clears his throat, attempting to shift the topic. "That's good to hear. You're really dedicated, Ellie. It's impressive." I'm stunned by the lack of humor in his tone as he speaks to me.

Kai nods eagerly as he notices my reaction. "Yeah, we're all proud of you. You've come a long way."

I feel the warmth in their words but also sense the underlying awkwardness, keeping my eyes on Lius as I answer. "Thanks, guys. I appreciate it. I just... feel like I haven't talked to any of you in a while. Everything okay?"

Ares shifts in his seat, glancing at Kai and Lius for a cue before he answers me. "Of course, everything's fine. Just been busy with work and all."

I narrow my eyes slightly, detecting the evasion but not pushing further. "Alright, if you say so. I'm heading to the gym. See you all later?"

Kai quickly responds. "Yeah, we'll be here. Take care, Elara."

As I leave the room, I can't shake the feeling that something is off.

I arrive at the gym, trying to push aside the unease from the morning's interaction with my roommates. I throw myself into training, channeling my confusion and frustration into each punch and kick. Tatsuya notices the intensity and pushes me even harder, recognizing the need for distraction.

"Focus, Elara. Let go of whatever is troubling you. Here, in the ring, you will find the clarity you seek," Tatsuya advises.

I nod, my determination sharpening. "Yes, Sensei." As I move through each motion, my mind keeps drifting back to the guys–to Max. The distance between Max and I feel like an unspoken black hole, and the secrecy of my friends only adds to my growing unease. But for now, I channel all my energy into becoming stronger, preparing myself for whatever truth awaits me.

Later in the afternoon, I'm in our home's backyard, the sun casting long shadows as it begins its descent. The air is filled with the sounds of leaves rustling and birds chirping, a peaceful contrast to the intensity of my training. Lius stands ready, arms crossed, studying my every move. The tension between us from the argument earlier in the week still lingers, unspoken but heavy in the air.

"Ready, birdie?" Lius asks, his voice unusually calm.

I nod, stretching my arms and legs as I prepare for another sparring session. There's an edge to him today, one that I can't quite place. It's like he's holding back something, but I shake off the thought, focusing on the task at hand. We've always had this push-pull dynamic, and today doesn't seem any different, at least on the surface. We begin sparring, the sound of our feet shuffling across the ground filling the air. Lius moves quickly, his strikes sharp and calculated, but something feels off. He's pulling his punches, not fighting with his usual intensity. I narrow my eyes, frustrated.

"Come on, Lius. Stop holding back!" I snap, throwing a hard punch that connects with his arm, but he barely reacts.

Lius meets my gaze, his expression softening, "I'm not holding back, Elara. I'm just... distracted."

I sense something is off but don't press him for details. Instead, I channel my energy into the training, using the physical exertion to clear my mind. As we continue, I can't help but notice the occasional glances Lius throws towards the house, as if he's expecting someone or something to happen.

I pause, lowering my fists, and take a deep breath. "Distracted? Since when does anything distract you? Lius, is everything alright?" I ask, pausing for a moment to catch my breath, lowering my fists.

He hesitates, his expression momentarily conflicted before he masks it with a forced smile. "Yeah, just a lot on my mind. Work stuff, you know."

I nodded, not entirely convinced but deciding to let it go. "Okay, if you say so." We resumed our training, but the tension between us is heavy. Every punch and kick felt heavier, burdened by the unspoken concerns lingering in the air. I push harder, trying to break through the barrier that seems to have formed between us. After an intense session, we finally call it a day. I wipe the sweat from my forehead and take a deep breath, feeling a mixture of satisfaction and frustration. "Thanks for the training, Lius. I needed that."

Lius nods, his expression softening slightly. "Anytime, birdie. You're doing great."

As we head back into the house, I can't shake the feeling that something is brewing beneath us, something that Lius and the others are keeping from me. But for now, all I can do is trust them and focus on my own goals. Back inside, I head to the kitchen for a glass of water. The house feels eerily quiet, the usual buzz of activity replaced by a heavy silence. I glance towards the living room and see Kai and Ares still engrossed in their work, their faces serious and determined. I join them, leaning against the counter as I sip my water. "You guys have been at it all day. What's going on?"

Kai looks up, his eyes briefly meeting mine before he returns to his laptop. "Just a lot of work. We're fine."

Ares adds, "Yeah, nothing to worry about. How was your training?" He does his best to redirect my focus.

I shrug, trying to sound casual. "Good. Lius pushed me hard, but I needed it."

An awkward silence follows, each of us lost in our own thoughts, mine is on them watching their every move and facial expression. I finished my water and decided to head upstairs to shower and change. As I walk past them, I can't help but feel a sense of isolation, a growing distance between me and my roommates. It's painful to feel so alone when I'm going through all of this with Max. I need my friends. Have they taken his side in this? Turned against me or thought that I was being unfair? Maybe I was...

Max returns home late, the weariness etched into his features as he steps through the door. He doesn't look up, his shoulders slumped under the weight of whatever burdens he's been carrying. I'm sitting on the couch, the TV on, but the volume muted as soon as I saw him walk in. The flickering images cast a soft glow around the room, highlighting the tension that has become almost tangible. As Max heads towards the stairs, I get up and intercept him. "Max, we need to talk."

He stops, his eyes meeting mine briefly before he looks away. "What part of *'I can't talk about this'* don't you understand?"

I feel a pang of frustration and sadness, as he calls me by my name instead of *'princesa'* like he used to. "The part where you stop being the man I trusted. You've shut me out, Max. I'm not just some bystander."

Max sighs, rubbing his temples as if trying to stave off a headache. "I told you, it's work. Things are... *complicated* right now."

I cross my arms, standing my ground. "Complicated how? You're not giving me any answers, Max. We're supposed to be partners, but it feels like you're shutting me out completely from you."

His expression hardens, a flicker of anger in his eyes. "You think I don't know that? You think I don't feel it too? I'm doing this for *us*, Elara. I'm trying to *protect* you."

"Protect me from what?" I demand, my voice rising. "You keep saying that, but you won't tell me anything! I can't keep living like this, not knowing what's really going on."

Max takes a step closer, his jaw clenched. "You wouldn't understand. It's too dangerous, and I can't risk you getting hurt."

I feel tears welling up, my frustration boiling over. "You're pushing me away, Max. Whatever danger you think you're protecting me from, it's tearing us apart. How can we face anything together if you won't let me in?"

He looks away, the anger draining from his face, replaced by a deep, weary sadness. "Elara, please... just trust me. I *need* you to trust me."

I shake my head, feeling a mix of despair and determination. "How can I trust you when you won't trust me with the truth of what's going on with you? If it involves me in any way, I have a *right* to know!"

Max opens his mouth to speak, but no words come out. The silence stretches between us, heavy and suffocating. Finally, he just nods, his shoulders sagging. "I'm sorry, Elara. I really am." Without another word, he turns and walks up the stairs, leaving me standing in the living room, feeling more alone than ever. I walk over and slump back onto the couch, staring blankly at the muted TV screen as I cross my arms over my chest, my mind racing as tears flow down my cheeks. Why won't he just talk to me? What is going on with him, and my roommates... I feel so alone for the first time in years, and *no* one will tell me why.

After I fix myself some dinner and take it upstairs, I sit alone in my room, the weight of the day pressing down on me. I hear the faint murmurs of conversation from downstairs, the guys still working late into the night. I can't help but wonder what everyone is so focused on and why they're keeping me in the dark–why Max has been avoiding me. As I lay in bed, staring at the ceiling, my thoughts drift to Max. The distance between us feels like an unbridgeable chasm at this point, each day pulling us further apart.

I think about our last conversation, the pain in his eyes, and the secrets that still linger between us. I begin to think over if I hadn't said what I did... pushed him like I had... would we still be okay? Would he be here holding me right now?

Sleep eludes me, my mind racing with questions and doubts. I get up and walk to the window, looking out into the night. The city lights twinkle in the distance, a stark contrast to the darkness I feel creeping into my heart. I know I need to stay strong, to focus on my training and my mission. But the uncertainty gnaws at me, and I can't help but wonder if I'm losing everything I hold dear in the process.

~*~

The next morning, I headed to the gym, feeling more isolated than ever. As I walk alone to the gym, my music plays sad melodies through my earbuds. I walk slowly, dragging my feet and looking down at the ground. My training is intense, my frustration evident in each hit I land on my training partner for the day.

I take a break from training to visit a quiet park, trying to clear my mind. I think about mine and Max's relationship and the secrets that seem to be piling up. I sit on the bench and watch the other citizens taking part in all that it offers the community. I want to stall myself from heading home right now. What's the point? I'm alone right now and I begin to think over everything I've done, that I've said, that could lead to my other three roommates to ignore me, to shut me out. They used to always tell me about their missions. This one is different though... and I hate that they won't tell me why. I stand up from the bench and head back home. I could really use a shower and a nap. Possibly some food too.

When I walk in the door, I see the three leftover roommates sitting in their new typical work spot in the dining room. They look at me as I enter the front door, and I think I finally see a few small smiles on their faces out of the corner of my eye. I glumly head up to my room without looking at them, I don't even greet them.

Max comes home late again. I waited up for him, but he barely acknowledged me before going to bed. I feel a deep sadness and betrayal as he just ignores me. I'm sitting on the couch watching TV with the other three, they all exchange sad glances mixed with concern as they all look over at me. My expression is stoic and emotionless as I lose myself in the show on the TV. Lius, who's sitting next to me, looks even more worried once he sees tears forming in my empty eyes.

As usual the next morning I headed to the gym, determined to keep pushing forward despite my personal turmoil. I trained harder than ever today, finally unleashing my anger towards Max, my body aching from the effort. I returned home from the gym and my now usual walk around the park afterwards–exhausted and emotionally drained. The front door closes behind me with a soft click, the sound echoing in the silence of the house. I drop my gym bag by the door and head towards the living room, my steps slow and heavy. As I enter, I find Lius, Kai, and Ares waiting for me, their expressions somber and serious.

I turn and look at all three sets of eyes. "Uh… hey guys."

Lius hesitates, glancing away for a moment before turning back to me. "Look, there's something we need to talk about. Something important."

My heart skips a beat, the weight of his words hanging between us. "What is it?" I ask, feeling a knot tighten in my chest as I walk closer to the dining room table.

Lius' eyes lock onto mine, the usual mischief in them replaced by a seriousness that sets me on edge. His voice is soft, "Ellie, this isn't easy to say. There's something going on with Max, and I didn't want you to find out like this... but you need to know."

My stomach drops. "What kinds of things?"

Kai exchanges a glance with Lius and Ares before speaking. "Follow us." He led me further into the dining room where I saw the table covered with photos, files, papers and Lius' laptop with a video ready to play.

Lius sighs, running a hand through his hair. "He's been working with Nathaniel, Elara. For longer than we thought."

The words hit me like a punch to the gut, knocking the breath from my lungs. *'Max? Working with Nathaniel? The very man who's haunted my life for so long? It can't be true. Max loves me. But the distance lately... the secrets...'* I take a step back, my mind racing, "No. You're wrong. Max would never..."

"I wish we were wrong, Elara." Kai interrupts gently. "But we've got proof. We've been tracking his movements, recording conversations. He's been in contact with your uncle's people, talking about you."

As I open the dossier Kai hands me, I'm greeted by a collection of photographs, documents, and printed transcripts of intercepted messages. My eyes scan the contents, my mind struggling to process the information.

The first photo is of Max, standing outside a warehouse on the outskirts of the city. His expression is serious, his posture tense. The next photo shows him meeting with a group of men, all of whom I don't recognize. There are photos of some of my most recent targets as well, out of jail. My breath catches in my throat as I flip through the pages, each one revealing more damning evidence of Max's involvement with my uncle. This can't be real. I trust him. But here he is... shaking hands with the very people I've sworn to take down. My uncle's thugs. Every photo is a stab to the heart—proof that I've been blind. That Max has been lying.

My hands shake as I try to process his words. Max? Working with Nathaniel? It feels impossible, like my world is suddenly tilting on its axis. "I don't... I don't believe it."

"I hate that this might hurt you, but I can't stand by and let you stay in the dark. You deserve better than lies." Lius steps closer, his expression pained as he clenches his fists, knuckles white. "I know it's hard to hear, but you deserve the truth. Max has been lying to you, keeping secrets, and it's not just about his past. This is happening right now."

Tears prick at my eyes, my voice trembling. "But why? Why would he do this? He loves me. He would never hurt me like that."

Lius reaches out, gently placing a hand on my shoulder. "I don't know why, but we need to get you out of this mess before it's too late. Nathaniel's plans involve you, and Max is right in the middle of it. He's been ordered to keep you close, to make you trust him."

I pulled away from his touch, my mind reeling. How could this be true? How could Max, the man I thought I knew so well, be part of something so dark, so twisted? "No," I whisper, shaking my head as I cross my arms tightly. My fingers digging into my sides, as though holding myself together. "There has to be another explanation."

Lius steps back, giving me space as he watches the turmoil play out across my face. "I'm sorry, birdie. I really am. But we need to be smart about this. Max isn't who you think he is."

I turn away, the ache in my chest growing with each passing second. This can't be real. My hand grips the back of one of the chairs as I struggle to keep myself together.

Lius's voice is soft but firm behind me. "We'll keep digging, find more evidence. But for now, you need to distance yourself from him. We can't risk you getting caught in whatever Nathaniel has planned."

I nod slowly, though the idea of pulling away from Max feels like tearing out a piece of my soul. "I need to talk to him," I mutter, more to myself than to Lius.

"Not yet," Lius warns. "If he realizes we're onto him, things could escalate. Let us handle this. We'll keep you safe."

I clench my fist, my emotions swirling in a chaotic storm. Part of me wants to fight, to confront Max and demand answers. But another part of me—the part that trusts Lius, Kai, and Ares— knows that rushing into this could be dangerous. "I don't know if I can just sit here and do nothing," I say to them, my voice barely above a whisper.

Lius steps forward, his tone gentle yet determined. "You're not doing nothing, birdie. You're staying safe, and that's what matters most right now. Trust us. We'll figure this out."

I turn to face him, searching his eyes for some sign of reassurance. His face is full of resolve, and though I'm not ready to fully accept what the three of them are saying, I know I have no choice but to trust them. "Okay," I finally say, my voice wavering. "But I need to know everything. Don't keep me in the dark anymore."

Lius nods. "We'll tell you everything as we find it. You have my word."

The sobs die in my throat, replaced by something colder. I straighten in my chair, wiping away the remnants of my tears with the back of my hand. I won't let this destroy me. He won't destroy me. I trusted him with my heart, but now... now I need answers. Answers only Max can give me.

"Thank you," I say, my voice stronger now, though the pain still lingers beneath it. "But I need to face him. I need to hear him say it."

I look at each of them who nod reluctantly in agreement, except Lius. He just looks at me with a sadness I've never seen in him before. As I turn to head upstairs to my room, the weight of the revelation presses down on me like a heavy fog. Every step feels like a struggle, each breath a battle against the rising tide of fear and doubt. If Max has betrayed me... what does that mean for everything we've built together? But deep down, another question lingers, one that I'm too afraid to ask out loud: *'Can I ever forgive him?'* As I walked into my room, the warmth of the space felt colder than it ever had before. The people I trusted, the man I loved, were now strangers hiding behind secrets. And somehow, deep down, I knew that my world was about to shatter.

20

Another week passes, and Max never makes an appearance. Either he's just not coming home, or he's been very carefully coming in when we are all asleep and leaving before we wake. I begin to become numb as each day passes that I don't see him. I continuously check my phone for any calls or messages from him. The last message I sent to him was letting him know that I need to talk to him, and he will not avoid it this time. I received no response, so he must be avoiding me completely.

One morning, I stand in the kitchen staring at my phone as the coffee brews. The smell of freshly brewed coffee fills the air, but it does little to lift my spirits. Lius comes down from his room, still sleepy. He's become a great friend in the past week, helping me with extra training outside of the gym and listening to me vent, being a shoulder for me while I cry, mourning the potential end of my relationship with Max.

"Hey birdie. Good morning," he says after a deep yawn.

"Good morning, goose," I say softly, sitting my phone down and looking at the coffee dripping into the pot snapping me out of my deepening dark hole of thoughts. I've adopted a new nickname for him over the past week as he's always saying something off-handed to try and cheer me up. Therefore, being given the name *'silly goose'* or *'goose'* for short.

Lius moves closer, noticing the dark circles under my eyes. "You look like you didn't sleep much. Everything okay?"

I force a smile. "Just thinking too much, I guess."

He nods understandingly. "How about I help you make breakfast for everyone? It might take your mind off things."

I appreciate the gesture and nod. "Sure, that sounds nice."

We start working together, moving around the kitchen in a comfortable rhythm. Lius chops vegetables while I crack eggs into a bowl. As we work, he glances at me, his eyes filled with concern and something else—something tender. "You've been really strong through all of this, Ellie." He says softly. "I admire that."

I shrug, trying to downplay my feelings. "I don't feel very strong right now."

He stops chopping for a moment and looks at me. "Strength isn't about not feeling pain. It's about moving forward despite it."

His words hit home, and I find myself blinking back tears. "Thank you, Lius. I don't know what I'd do without you, this past week."

He smiles warmly. "You'd probably have managed. But I'm happy to be here for you, whenever you need me."

As we finish preparing breakfast, Lius's hand brushes against mine. The touch sends a jolt through me, and I find myself looking at him in a new light. I'm beginning to see who he truly is under that fake playboy facade he gives off. Who's really in the heart of the Viper's Lieutenant. There's a gentleness in his eyes that I hadn't noticed before, and for a moment, I wondered if there could be something more behind those hazel eyes. But then I remind myself of Max and the unresolved feelings I have for him, the closure we still need. It's too soon to think about anyone else. Yet, I can't deny the comfort I feel in Lius's presence as of recent, whether it's just the feelings of losing Max, or if he's truly becoming someone important to me.

We set the table, and I find myself genuinely smiling for the first time in days. "Thank you, Lius. For everything."

He reaches out and squeezes my hand gently. "Anytime, birdie. *Anytime*, I mean that."

As we sit down to eat, the other two come down to join us after a while. We all spend the time eating and chatting about my training and what new moves we can try when I train with them. I can't help but feel a glimmer of hope. Maybe, just maybe, things will be okay. And maybe, in time, I'll find the strength to move on, with or without Max. For now, I'll cherish the support of the people around me, especially Lius, who has shown me a depth of care that I hadn't expected from him.

After breakfast I cleaned up the kitchen with all three of the guys' help, surprisingly. Once finished I decided I wanted to take a day off from training to spend time with my roommates. I've truly missed them while they've focused on their investigation of Max. "Hey guys, how about we just hang out today? Do you all have to go to work or anything?"

They all shake their heads, Kai responds for the group. "Nope, we're off duty today. What did you have in mind?"

As I dry one final dish, "Well I was thinking of maybe watching a movie or we can play a game. Or go out and do something. While you three were doing your investigation…" A solemn look crossed my face as I referenced the information that they've presented about Max. "I really missed you all. I know I saw you every day just about... but I didn't get to really hang out with any of you like we used to."

Lius smiles. "I think that would be nice, birdie."

I nod, pleased with their responses. As we move to the living room and sit, a thought crosses my mind. "Hey, how come I haven't seen you guys go out on dates or anything? Or have I just missed it?"

Lius and Ares both exchange a puzzled look at my sudden question before turning their attention back to me. Lius speaks up, "Well, you're not wrong. We don't have much of a dating life recently, if any at all."

Ares shrugs, "Yeah. Most women see us as too busy or unavailable. Or they're intimidated by our... status as Vipers."

"That's so sad guys! I'm sorry to hear that. Is it the same for you Kai?" I put the final dish I was drying back into the cabinet.

Kai nods in agreement, "Yep. Between work and SP6 duties, I don't have much time for dating either. Like Ares said, most women are intimidated or just not interested in dealing with our hectic schedules."

"You three just haven't found the right one then!" I walk into the living room and begin to flip through the TV channels to find a movie to watch.

The three men listen to my reassuring words, each of them contemplating the idea of finding the *'right one.'* Ares speaks up, his tone sounding thoughtful. "Maybe you're right. Maybe we just haven't found the right one yet. But with our schedules and the nature of our jobs, it's tough to meet someone who can really understand us and accept our lifestyle."

I look over to each of them. "Well, we're just chilling today. Is there anyone you want to invite over? I can make some snacks and prepare some drinks? If they turn out to not be a right fit and you're not interested, I can intervene as *'lady of the house'*." I chuckle at my self-given title.

Lius presents his usual sly smile. "Hey, that's not a bad idea. If we bring over some girls and we signal to you that they just, aren't it... You can help get rid of them. Like a dating bouncer, essentially."

"Right!" The three men seem to like that idea as I raise my coffee cup up to them.

Lius raises his hand in a mock toast. "To the lady of the house, protecting us from the wrong women for us."

"Here, here!" I laughed wholeheartedly for the first time in a long time.

The three of them settle into a seat in the living room, engaging in light conversation for a while. As the guys chat, I listen to their list of different ladies they may want to invite to our hangout session. I lean onto my knees, propping up on my elbows as I enjoy watching them converse. A sense of anticipation in the air as they narrow down the list. As the conversation progresses, Ares turns to me. "You know, we've been talking about inviting girls over, but what about you Ellie? Don't you have any friends you'd like to invite over?"

"Well... no. I don't have any friends here. They're all in America so I only talk to them via text or social media." I wave a hand in dismissal.

Lius' playful smirk softens as he recalls the details of my situation. "Right... I'm sorry that you don't have any friends or family here..."

"Oh, I have friends, Lius. You three! And that's plenty for me." I smile at him.

All three men were touched by my words, they each presented me with a sincere smile. "Of course we're your friends, birdie. We've got your back no matter what." Lius replies.

Ares has a tinge of red on his ears. "Yeah, you can count on us. We adore you."

Kai clears his throat into his fist. "We all have a special bond here, don't we?"

"I agree." I gave all three of them a warm smile. I truly am thankful that I answered the online ad to be their roommate.

While the conversation remains warm and friendly, Lius soon brings the topic back to the main subject at hand. "Okay, okay. As nice as this little bonding moment is, we were supposed to be talking about who to invite over. So… any ideas on who we should invite?"

"That's all you guys… I only know Sara and she's busy on a mission with Ren tonight so she's out." I add. "I do have a friend I talk to when I go to yoga class, but I don't have her number… Ares, you remember her right? I talked with her outside the studio? The day that rogue attacked us?"

Ares nods, recalling who I'm talking about. "Oh yeah, I remember her. She seems nice."

"She's really sweet. Not sure of what her type is though… I can find out! But Lius…" I point a finger at him with a serious look on my face.

"Uh-oh… I know that look. What…?" He asks as he straightens up.

"You will *not* grope any girls that come over here, you will *not* invade their personal space unless they want you to. Do I make myself clear?" I criticize him as I lower my finger.

Lius' smirk falls as he's immediately called out for his tendency to invade a woman's personal space. He lets out a reluctant sigh. "Alright, alright, I hear you. No invading personal space unless warranted... No touching unless asked, got it. I'll be on my best behavior like a *good boy*, I promise." He repeats with a hint of sarcasm. He rolls his eyes at being scolded like a child.

I chuckled. "Scouts honor?" I held up two fingers close together for the scouts salute.

Lius rolls his eyes jokingly this time, but still plays along with my request, holding up two fingers of his own in the scout symbol. "Scout's honor, I won't invade any woman's personal space without their explicit permission. Satisfied?"

I grin wide. "Very. Thank you." With the men now on board with the idea, trusting in my role as the dating bouncer to keep things in check and ensure everyone's safety, the guys start to brainstorm again, thinking up different options for potential invitees.

Lius claps his hands together in absolution as they come to an agreement. "Alright, so if we're inviting girls over, we need to make sure they're someone worthy of our awesome company. Any suggestions on who we should consider?"

Kai browses through his phone, thinking of who he'd be interested in inviting to our spontaneous party. "Well, we don't want anyone who's just interested in our status as Vipers. It has to be someone who's not just impressed by our power but can actually appreciate us for who we are as people."

Lius nods, adding his own criteria for potential invitees. "Good point, Kai. It's important to find girls who are interested in us as individuals, not just our SP6 gig. They have to be able to handle our insane schedules and understand what type of work we do."

Ares, being the more practical one in the group, offers a sensible perspective. "I agree, but let's also be realistic here.

We're all pretty busy people. We need to invite girls who have some level of independence and can handle having a partner who's often not available."

The men all ponder Ares' advice. Lius leans back in his seat, taking a moment to reflect on what they're looking for in a potential date. "Yeah, finding someone who understands our hectic lives and can still manage their own is key. It's not easy finding someone who can handle our unique situation."

I see the way the men are struggling to think of anyone to invite so I propose the idea. "How about this, you all just invite all the girls you know and just pin it on me. Say it's a long awaited housewarming for me, or a *'Hey, our roommate needs female friends'* kind of party? That way, we can eliminate as we go? I can invite that girl from my yoga class as well and even Sara to make it less obvious what we're doing? I'll see if she can make it if her mission with Ren ends early enough."

The guys pause as they ponder over what I've suggested. Lius replies, "Hmm, that could work... We could say it's a housewarming party, for you, and invite all the girls we know. That way, we can eliminate as we go without any pressure. I'm down for that. What about you two?" He turns the question to the other two, waiting for their opinions.

Ares nods, "Yeah, I like that idea. It gives us a chance to see who's truly interested in getting to know us as individuals, and who's just there for the wrong reasons. I'm all for it."

Kai also expresses his agreement with the party plan. "It's a practical approach. It allows us to assess potential dates in a more casual and relaxed setting." I knew he would appreciate the logic behind my idea more than the other two.

"Okay then! We should go ahead and reach out to the intended *'guests'* and get this party started!" I jump up and head into the kitchen to start putting together some snacks and drinks. This party will be something to distract myself from the heartbreak I've been experiencing with Max lately... even if it is for just a few hours.

~*~

Night time falls and we have all been in our rooms getting dressed for the party we are hosting. I stand in front of the mirror in my room, staring at my reflection. My hands grip the edge of the dresser until my knuckles turn white. I know this won't be easy. My heart feels like it's tearing apart inside me, but I won't let it show. When I look Max in the eye, I need to be stronger than I've ever been. I need to be prepared for the worst, even if it kills me to hear the truth from his lips.

We surprisingly had a lot of responses of 'yes' to our spur of the moment invites, well... the guys' invites since it was them who had to send out all the invites. I hear the doorbell constantly go off as people arrive. I am the last one to come downstairs and late to a party being hosted in my own house but... I was honestly nervous about this party. Meeting so many new people... watching all these women flirt with my roommates will definitely make me feel awkward. I truly hope Sara can make it, so I have *someone* to talk to who isn't interested in getting close to the guys. I don't understand why the thought of *Lius* being honed in on and swooned over, sends a pang to my heart at the idea . The house is filled with the chatter, music and laughter of our guests. The men have invited a mix of colleagues, acquaintances, and some friends from the gym. I invited my yoga friend and even managed to convince Sara to join us after her mission with Ren, if it ended soon enough.

Lius, Kai, and Ares are mingling with the guests already as I walk down the stairs, but I notice that Lius keeps talking with guests as if he was at a work function, professional and civil, it's an odd sight to see. Him being respectful and polite with females. No sign of his usual mischievous grin anywhere in his expression. The night carries on as I talk with different women from the SP6 headquarters. And I notice the Lius seems to find himself near me instead of doing what Ares and Kai are—talking with women trying to see which one will peak their interest the most. Whether it's to refill his drink, grab a snack, or just check in, he always seems to find an excuse to be near me.

"Hey birdie, having fun?" Lius asks as he leans against the counter next to me.

I smile, appreciating his company. "Yeah, it's nice to have a distraction. You?"

He shrugs, a playful smirk returning to his face. "It's alright. But honestly, I'd rather be training with you."

I chuckle, shaking my head. "You're hopeless. You're supposed to be finding yourself a date, goose."

His expression softens, and he gives me a look that makes my heart skip a beat. "Hopelessly devoted, maybe."

Before I can respond Sara walks in and instantly comes over towards me, her eyes bright with excitement as she glances around the scene. "Elara! This party is amazing! Thanks so much for inviting me."

I turn to her, grateful for the interruption but also curious about her take on things. "I'm glad you could make it. How was the mission with Ren?"

Sara waves a hand dismissively, "Oh, the usual. Nothing we couldn't handle. But enough about that. Are you enjoying yourself?"

I nod, feeling a mix of emotions. "Yeah, it's nice to have everyone here. And to see the guys trying to socialize for once."

Sara laughs, glancing around the room. "Speaking of which, are any of them making progress?"

I glance around, noticing Kai deep in conversation with a woman who seems genuinely interested in him. Ares is chatting with a group of girls, his usual *cool* charm on full display. But Lius... Lius is still right next to me. "Looks like Kai and Ares are doing well," I say, nodding towards them. "But Lius here doesn't seem to be interested in anyone tonight." I nudged him playfully with my elbow to his side.

Lius smirks, not even trying to hide his amusement. "What can I say? I have high standards."

Sara raises an eyebrow, glancing between us. "Oh, really? And what about you, Ellie? Anyone caught your eye?"

I look out at the mix of guests around our house. A few of the ladies invited to this fake housewarming party, brought a single guy friend as their welcome gift to me. I feel a blush creeping up my cheeks and shaking my head. "No, not really. Just trying to enjoy the party. I'm still involved with someone anyways... Wouldn't feel right."

Sara's eyes twinkle with mischief as she leans in closer. "Well, don't wait too long. Life's too short to miss out on opportunities." I confided in her about Max and mine's relationship and how it seems to have reached its end. She gives me a knowing look and moves off to mingle with the other guests, leaving Lius and I alone again.

I turned back to him, feeling a bit flustered. "You're not even trying to mingle, are you?" I accuse playfully.

He shrugs, his gaze unwavering. "Why should I? The person I want to be with is right here."

My heart skips another beat at his words, and I can't help but feel a mix of emotions. I quickly school myself as he has always flirted with me. So why is this any different? Is it because Max has been neglecting me for so long that any kind of flirting–even from Lius–makes me weak in the knees? Part of me is touched by his attention, but another part is still raw from the unresolved situation with Max. I force a smile, trying to keep things light and *friendly*. "Well, aren't you the charmer tonight," I say, trying to tease him in return. "But you're charming the wrong one tonight."

Lius chuckles, his eyes softening. "Just being honest, birdie."

As the night goes on, Lius continues to stay close to me, occasionally venturing out to chat with other guests but always returning to my side after a few moments. Especially when I was surrounded by the male plus ones. I share a few laughs with everyone, and I find myself relaxing more, the hurt from Max's absence dulling a bit in the presence of the party guests. At one point, Lius and I find ourselves alone in the kitchen again, refilling drinks. He leans against the counter, watching me with a thoughtful expression holding a few full cups to take back out to guests. "You know, Ellie, you don't have to put on a brave face all the time," he says softly. "It's okay to let people in."

I pause, the drink in my hand suddenly feeling heavy. "I know. It's just... complicated. Plus, there's a party going on right now. I don't need to ruin everyone's fun."

He nods, understanding in his eyes. "I get it. But just remember, you're not alone. We're here for you. I'm here for you."

I meet his gaze, feeling a warmth spread through me. "Thanks, Lius. That means a lot. Now get back out there before those three die of dehydration."

He reaches out an elbow and gently nudges me. "Anytime, birdie."

For a moment, we just stand there, the noise of the party fading into the background. In that brief moment, I feel a connection between us, something deeper than just friendship. But before I can fully process it, the doorbell rings, signaling the arrival of more guests.

Lius reluctantly looks towards the door then gives me a reassuring smile. "Looks like our housewarming party is a hit. Let's go see who's at the door."

As we head back to the front of the house, I can't help but feel a flicker of hope. Maybe, just maybe, there's a chance for something new to grow from the ashes of my heartbreak. And with Lius, Kai, and Ares back in my corner, I know I'll be okay no matter what happens between Max and me.

~*~

The party comes to an end, and the last of the guests have filtered out, leaving the house surprisingly quiet. Kai and Ares are still deep in conversation with the women they hit it off with, their laughter and chatter a pleasant background hum. Meanwhile, Sara and I are in the kitchen, tackling the aftermath of the festivities. She's washing dishes while I dry and put them away. Lius walks through the house collecting any stray dishes and trash.

"So," Sara begins, her tone light but curious, "What did you think of the party?"

I glance over at her, a small smile tugging at my lips. "It was fun. A nice distraction. I think the guys enjoyed it too."

Sara nods, her eyes twinkling with amusement. "They did. Especially Kai and Ares. It's about time they had a chance to relax and socialize."

I chuckle, glancing into the living room where Kai and Ares are still engrossed in their conversations. "Yeah, it's good to see them connecting with someone. They deserve it."

Sara hands me a clean dish, and I take it, wiping it dry. "And what about you? How are you holding up?" She asks.

I sigh, leaning against the counter for a moment. "Honestly? I'm still processing everything. Max hasn't been home, and it's been... hard. He *refuses* to talk to me..." I pause drying the dish, my face falls. "I think it's over between us, Sara."

Her expression softens, and she pauses her washing to look at me. "I know it's tough, Ellie. But you're strong. You'll get through this."

I nod, appreciating her support. Even though it's not at all what I want to hear right now. I know I'm strong–I have to be. Everyone seems to have come to expect that from me. "Thanks, Sara. I'm trying to stay positive. And Lius has been a great help too. He's been there for me, more than I expected."

She raises an eyebrow, a knowing smile playing on her lips. "Oh? Do I sense a spark there?"

I feel my cheeks heat up and quickly shake my head, drying the dish in my hand once again. "It's not like that. I mean, he's been amazing, but... it's complicated."

Sara laughs softly, handing me another dish. "Everything in life is complicated, Ellie. Just go with the flow and see where it leads." We continue our cleaning, the comfortable silence between us filled with the sound of running water and clinking dishes. After a while, Sara speaks up again. "You know, I saw the way Lius was looking at you tonight. He barely left your side."

I glance over at her, my heart skipping a beat. "He was just being a good friend. Keeping me company, that's all. He knows that strangers make me uncomfortable."

"Maybe," she says, her tone teasing, "but it wouldn't hurt to explore if there was something there. You deserve to be happy for once, El."

I don't know how to respond, so I focus on drying the dish in my hands. Deep down, I know she's right. But the thought of moving on from Max so quickly feels daunting. Is that even, okay? Is that a custom around here? Before I can dwell on it too much, Sara changes the subject. "So, what's the plan for tomorrow?"

I'm grateful for the shift in conversation. "I'm not sure yet. Probably just training with Tatsuya and trying to keep busy."

Sara nods, understanding. "Sounds good. Just take it one day at a time, okay?"

"Yeah," I agree, feeling a bit lighter. "One day at a time." As we finish up the last of the dishes, I can't help but feel thankful for Sara's presence. She's been a steady rock in the midst of my emotional storm, and I'm thankful for her friendship. It has helped to have a feminine point of view during all this. We put away the last dish, and I turned to her with a smile. "Thanks for helping me tonight, Sara. I really appreciate it."

She gives me a warm hug. "Anytime, Ellie. You know I'm always here for you." We part ways, and I head upstairs to my room once everyone has gone home, feeling a bit more at peace. As I lie down in bed, I can't help but think about the night's events. The party, the conversations, and Lius's unwavering support throughout the night and the past week. Maybe Sara's right. Maybe it's time to open my heart to new possibilities, but first, I have to talk with Max. With that final thought, I close my eyes and drift off to sleep.

~*~

My sleep is interrupted by the sound of my bedroom door opening. I jolted up, ready to fight the intruder. Once my eyes adjust to the dark, I see that it's Max, slowly walking into my room. I turn to switch on my bedside table lamp, the soft light illuminating his tired face. "Max…? Why are you coming into my room?" I ask, my voice laced with confusion and a touch of irritation.

Max stands there, looking hesitant. "Elara, we need to talk. I can't keep avoiding this."

I feel a mix of relief and anger bubbling up inside me. "You're right, we do. But you've been avoiding me for weeks, Max. What's changed now?"

He sighs, running a hand through his disheveled hair. "I know I've been distant, and I'm sorry. Work has been overwhelming, and I didn't know how to handle it."

I get out of bed, crossing my arms as I face him. "That's no excuse. You've left me here, alone, without any explanation. Do you know how that feels?" I know that it's not SP6 work that's keeping him… I replay the images of the dossier in my mind; the video on Lius' laptop. I want *him* to say it… I have to hear it from *his* mouth.

Max steps closer, his expression pained. "I know, and I'm sorry. But I've been dealing with some things… things I couldn't tell you about."

I narrow my eyes at him, the frustration boiling over. "What things, Max? What could possibly be so important that you couldn't talk to me? We're supposed to be a team, but you shut me out."

He hesitates, his eyes avoiding mine. "It's about your uncle, Nathaniel. I've been... involved with him. Working for him."

His words hit me like a punch to the gut, as I finally heard it from his lips. But I still need to hear his side of things. I keep my composure as my insides burn. "What do you mean, 'involved'? What are you talking about?"

Max takes a deep breath, his shoulders slumping. "I've been working with him. I didn't want to, so I walked away from working for him. But... he gave me no choice. He threatened to hurt you if I didn't cooperate with him again."

I feel a cold wave of dread wash over me, as I continue to play the part of an unsuspecting girlfriend. "You've been spying on me for him? All this time?"

He nods, shame evident in his eyes. "I thought I could protect you by doing what he wanted and by staying away from you. But I see that I've only pushed you away."

The betrayal cuts deep, and I struggle to keep my voice steady. "You should have told me, Max. We could have figured it out together. But instead, you lied, kept secrets and hid from me. How can I ever trust you again?"

Max reaches out, but I step back, shaking my head. "Please, Ellie. I didn't want to hurt you. I was trying to keep you safe."

I laugh bitterly, tears stinging my eyes. "You've broken my trust, Max! I can't do this anymore! You disappeared on me! Avoided me! *Abandoned me*! This could have all been avoided if you would have just talked to me sooner!"

He looks desperate, his eyes pleading. "Ellie, don't say that. We can fix this. We can work through it."

I take a deep breath, my heart aching. "No, Max! We can't. It's too late. I can't be with someone who hides things from me, who works with the enemy. *My* enemy!"

Max's face falls, and I see the realization sink in him. Trust was the biggest factor for me in a relationship. And he stomped all over it into the mud. "Elara, please. *I love you.*"

I shake my head, the tears finally spilling over. "Love isn't enough, Max. Not when there's no trust. It's over! You refuse to let me in! You've seen all of my darkest parts, and I have barely scratched the surface of yours! Two years, Max! Two *fucking* years! And you still don't trust me enough to handle my own emotions… to let me into *your* deepest darkest parts! You *saw* that I was suffering without you! You *knew* you were hurting me by staying away and you still continued to do it! You don't touch me, kiss me… We haven't had any *'intimate'* moments in *weeks*!"

His desperation snaps into anger, his voice rising as he interrupts my rampant list. "You think you know everything, Elara? You have no idea what I've been going through! And you know what? On those *'personal business trips'* I wasn't just working. I was seeing someone else as well. And *her* darkest parts aren't as messy to deal with!"

His confession stuns me, leaving me breathless. "What?! You've been seeing someone else the whole time?"

Max looks away, unable to meet my eyes. "Yes. I was weak, and I didn't know how to handle everything. I'm sorry."

The rage and hurt inside me boils over. "You're sorry?! Sorry for lying, for betraying me, for *cheating* on me?! That's not enough, Max! You've shattered everything I thought we had!"

Max steps forward, reaching out to me. "Ellie, please. I know I messed up, but we can still fix this. It's over with the other woman! I swear!"

I step back away from his reach, my voice trembling with fury and heartbreak. "No, Max. We can't fix this. It's over. You've broken my trust, and you've broken my heart. Possibly given me an STD from your *mistress*." Max stands there, looking broken, and I feel a pang of sadness. But I know this is the right decision.

I turned away from him, my voice barely a whisper. "Please leave, Max."

His shoulders slump as he realizes the finality of my words. He takes a last, lingering look at me before turning and walking out of the room, the door closing softly behind him. The sound of his footsteps fades into the night, leaving me alone with my shattered heart and the weight of his betrayal.

As the sound of his footsteps fades, I collapse onto my bed, the weight of the breakup crashing over me. I curl up, letting the sobs wrack my body, mourning the end of what once was; what I thought it was. As Max leaves the house, the sound of the front door slamming echoes through the quiet dark in the house. I sit on my bed, tears streaming down my face, feeling the finality of our breakup settling in. The pain is almost unbearable, but I know I made the right choice. Trust is the foundation of any relationship, and without it, we would have nothing. I wipe my tears, taking deep breaths to calm myself. I stand up and start collecting all of the things that belonged to him and chuck them into a pile on my bedroom floor, channeling my anger towards him. Just as I chuck his leather jacket to the floor, I begin to collect my thoughts. I slide against the wall of my closet and hear a soft knock on my door.

Lius, Kai, and Ares must have heard the commotion. I take a moment to compose myself before calling out from the floor of my closet. I watch the door of my room and call out with a shaky and weak voice, "Come in."

Lius enters first, his face full of concern. "Ellie, are you okay?" He steps in instantly once he sees I'm on the floor of the closet, stepping over the pile of stuff in the middle of my floor. He kneels down next to me in front of my closet door. "Birdie, what happened…?"

I try to smile, but it falters against my tear streaked cheeks. I feel even worse that now the others will see this side of me. "Not really. Max and I… it's over. He confirmed everything… and then some."

Kai and Ares follow him in, their expressions mirroring Lius's worry. Kai steps forward, kneeling down next to Lius, placing a comforting hand on my shoulder. They had heard the whole thing and already knew that I had ended things with Max before even entering the room. But they kept it to themselves. "We're here for you, Ellie. Whatever you need." Kai's words just confirm what I already thought. They had heard everything. That oddly comforts me as I don't have to repeat everything to them. The whole thing was replaying on repeat in my mind already, anyways.

Ares nods, his voice gentle. "You're not alone. We've got you. We will help you get through this."

I feel a surge of gratitude for them. "Thank you."

Lius sits down beside me, his presence soothing. "We'll get through this together. And if Max shows his face around here again, he'll have to deal with us before he even looks at you."

I chuckle softly, appreciating the protective nature of my friends. I pat Lius on the arm, "I think he got the message tonight." I feel a mix of anger and relief. "I just can't believe he betrayed me like that. But I'm glad you guys are looking out for me. He finally came clean to me." Ares steps out of my room and I hear his quick steps heading to his room. "Where is Ares going?" I'm concerned that he might try and take off after Max. I quickly climb up from the closet floor and walk towards my door when Ares re-enters with some shot glasses and a bottle of whiskey.

He holds the items up, "I thought this was necessary..." he smiles meekly and hands each of us a glass.

Lius grabs a hold of my other hand and squeezes. "We'll do everything we can to get you through this. I promise."

I nod, feeling a bit of my strength returning. "I know. Thank you." As the night wears on, we sit together, talking and supporting each other. The love I feel for the three of them grows even stronger, solidified by how caring they are to sit with me in another dark hour of my life. I may have lost Max, but I've gained a deeper connection with these three. We each hold our glass out as Ares pours some of the golden liquid into each glass. I press the glass to my lips and swallow the burning liquid quickly, instantly relaxing under the warmth it sends throughout my body. Eventually, the exhaustion catches up with me, and I can barely keep my eyes open. I'm sitting on my bed while the other three sit around me. Kai leaning on my bedside table, Lius sitting on the end of my bed and Ares reclined back against his arm on the floor. I rub both of my eyes, "I think I need some sleep," I say, stifling a yawn.

Lius helps me under my blankets as I climb towards my pillow. "We'll be right here if you need anything. Get some rest, birdie."

I smile, grateful for their presence. "Goodnight, guys. And thank you." As I grip onto my pillow, I feel the comfort of the whiskey coursing through me. I know I'll be okay, someday. But for now, I allow the liquor to lull me to sleep. I close my eyes, letting the exhaustion take over, and drift into a restless but deep sleep.

~*~

Days have passed and the grieving process after a bad breakup has its vice like grip on me. I focus on training, staying for even longer hours each day. Z has sent me some targets to hunt but the pain of knowing Max won't be there with me is too much and I ignore the messages that include the profiles of my intended hunts. I begin to cry as I think of all the hunts that Max and I have gone on and how proud he looked when I completed the mission. How we would go for an ice cream cone afterwards to celebrate. I become angry when I remember how gentle he was when he'd brush my hair out of my face, the fact that he was like that with another woman too tears me apart inside...

I've decided to seclude myself into my room more, only emerging when I have to go train or use the bathroom. Eating wasn't much of a thing for me, but the guys still tried. The three of them would take turns bringing me a tray of food whenever they made themselves something to eat. Everything I ate just came right back up anyways so I refrained from eating at all. I sat one night scrolling through my phone, planning a trip for myself. I can't bear this anymore... I need to get away for a while from all the memories in this house that Max and I shared. I knew I was beginning to worry the boys with how I just lay in bed and refused to eat. The circles under my eyes from crying and lack of sleep were profound, my clothes becoming noticeably looser.

One morning I was downstairs in the kitchen making some breakfast for the guys, my eyes swollen and my cheeks raw from all of my crying over the past week. As the others wake up, they make their way downstairs and walk into the kitchen. They're surprised to see me up and about, dressed for the day and for once, not in my gym clothes. They all see the puffiness and redness around my sunken eyes, indication of my nights filled with tears. None of them says anything at first, but the concern is evident on their faces. I look in their direction, "Morning." A solemn air about me. My heartbreak triggered depression seeping into the air around me. Max never came back, when I passed his room, I noticed that his belongings were gone as well. He seems to have moved out or gone away for a long time, but either way... Max was gone completely from my life.

Lius' initial surprise in seeing me up and about quickly fades at the sight of my somber demeanor. His eyes soften with concern, and he can't help but worry about how I'm handling the whole situation. He's been the most present during all of this. Listening to me repeat the same thing over and over about how badly Max hurt me. He would even lie in bed next to me when the dam would burst and I'd start crying uncontrollably, holding me close to comfort me. He would tell me funny stories to try and ease my mind and distract me; even if for a second. He slowly walks towards me, "Morning. You're up early." He hesitates for a moment before adding. "You okay this morning?"

"Yea. I'm going to go out of town for a while. I need to get away from here. I'm heading to Fujikawaguchiko for a few days." I point to my bags by the front door. "I just wanted to make sure you all had breakfast first before I left. And to tell you I was leaving."

The guys exchange another glance, silently communicating their surprise at the sudden announcement. Lius' expression turns more serious, his earlier concern deepening. "Wait... you're leaving? For how long exactly?" His tone moved into panic.

"I don't know. I booked a cabin for a week. So, at least that long." I flip over the pancake in the pan.

His concern grows even more at my vague response. "A week, huh? You've got everything packed already and ready to go?"

I nod. "Yep. I couldn't sleep last night so I made this plan and decided to pack while I was awake."

He takes a deep breath, feeling the need to broach a different topic. "Listen… before you leave, can I ask you something?"

"Sure." I turn to face him after putting the finished pancake on the plate that has a pile of them already made.

Lius hesitates for a moment, knowing this might be a touchy subject, but he decides to push through. "You've been through a lot with Max, and I know how tough it has been for you to go through this breakup. But, are you sure going off on your own like this is a good idea? I mean, you've packed a month's worth of things it looks like. You know you can stay here, we will keep helping you get through this."

"I know I am not handling this breakup very well. I loved him so much and now…" I sigh as my words become shaky, holding back more tears. How could I have any more to shed over him? "I need to get away for a bit. I'll be back in a week… this is home now. I just… I have to get away from here, goose… I have to."

His expression softens at the sound of my voice weakening as I attempt to hold back more tears. He can hear the pain and sadness in it, "But Elara… you know you have us, right? You don't have to go through this alone. And we're always going to be here for you, no matter what." I can sense that he's holding back what he truly wants to say, to beg me to stay here, with *him*. To let *him* soothe my pain and chase the demons away. But he stops himself even though his feelings for me are almost overwhelming.

"I know… I care so much about you all. But I can't hunt my targets while dealing with this. Tatsuya and Z agree with me. They want me to get my head on straight before I continue training and hunting. I'll become reckless and make mistakes… get myself killed, if not on purpose to put an end to this unbearable pain…"

Lius' concern turns into realization as he listens to me. He agrees that I need to have a clear head to get the job done, but he's still showing his reluctance to let me go. "I understand. You can't hunt your targets with your emotions all over the place. Still... a whole week alone? I just don't want you to be completely isolated out there all by yourself."

"I think that's what's best right now. I'm not going to trouble anybody else any longer while I try to heal what he destroyed." I turn off the stove eye and set the pan to the side to cool.

He lets out a sigh, his eyes still filled with worry. "That's not what I mean, and you know it. You're not a burden to anyone, especially not us."

"Arelius..." I place a hand over my eyes as I shake my head.

He walks towards me, cups my cheek with one hand, removing my hand from my eyes with his other. He pulls my face to look at him. He looks into my dark green sunken eyes, his expression firm but gentle. "I can't shake this feeling that you're making a mistake. What if something happened to you while you're alone in that cabin... I'd never forgive myself if you were hurt and I wasn't there to protect you."

My heart flutters under his caring touch, followed by guilt. "Lius... please... this is hard enough as it is. I can't... I can't let *you*, of all people, watch me go through this... I... I've started to have *feelings* for you Lius... so I have to be alone. I don't want you to watch me heal from heartbreak another guy has put me through..." I feel horrible that I've developed feelings for him, just before Max and I officially ended things. It felt wrong... and *so* not fair to him.

His eyes widened slightly at my confession. He looked as if he hadn't expected me to be worried about only *him* seeing me go through this healing process. He takes a moment to process my words, the realization hitting him. "Is that… why you're leaving? Because you don't want me to keep seeing you go through this process? From another guy? From Max?"

I nod. "Yes…" I whispered out.

His expression is a mix of surprise and disbelief. "You can't be serious. You're leaving, disappearing for a week, just to avoid me seeing you heal from this heartbreak?"

"Yes… I need to. I have to fix myself. Get my head on straight." I turn away from his touch and finish cooking breakfast.

He shakes his head and moves closer to my side, leaning against the counter, his eyes still fixed on me. "You don't need to fix yourself by being alone. Let me be here for you, even if it's just as a friend. You don't have to avoid me because you have feelings for me, and you want to be considerate of my feelings. Let *me* worry about that. Don't distance yourself from me, don't hide your emotions. Let me see all of it, I *want* to."

Lius gently cups my face with his hands, gently tilting it back up so he can look into my eyes again. He holds my gaze with intensity, his hazel eyes still full of concern and worry. "You don't have to hide anything from me, Elara. I've seen your darkness and that you're scared I'll judge you for it. That should be the *last* thing you need to worry about. I don't care about Max or what happened between you two and how recent it was. All I care about is *you*."

"Lius… it's too soon…" I stutter out.

He takes my hand into his, his grip firm but gentle. "Then let me go with you. Please. I won't push for anything more than what we already have right now but let me be there with you."

"It's not fair to you…" I am only able to mutter out that little bit. I can't give in on this, not this time...

Lius softens at my words, his expression turning tender. "You don't have to be emotionally perfect for me to help you through this. I just want to be there for you, to support you while you heal. And if that means waiting, then I'm willing to wait. Even if it takes months, or even a year, however long it takes I will wait for you as long as you let me be at your side. Please, birdie."

Tears fill my eyes, and I lower my head away from his gaze as they fall. He's so sweet and caring lately that it's overwhelming. Why have I just *now* seen this side of Arelius Blackwood? He gently cups my face with his hands, gently tilting it back up so he can look into my eyes again.

"Hey, shh. Don't cry, birdie. I mean it when I say I'm willing to wait for you. I don't care how long it takes. I'll be here for you no matter what. "His soothing words force the tears to continue to fall down my cheeks as I open my mouth to speak, but nothing comes out. He wipes away each tear that falls down my cheeks, his touch gentle and comforting.

"It's okay. You don't have to say anything. Just let me continue to be here for you. That's all I'm asking of you right now." He pulls me into his embrace and I sob a little harder against his chest. He wraps his arms around me, holding me close to his chest.

"Shh, it's okay. I'm here. Let it out, let it all out." He holds me tightly, his hands rubbing my back as I cry.

Kai and Ares have observed this whole ordeal, silent and solemn, their own expressions soft as they see just how hurt I truly am. Shocked at the interaction unfolding in front of them between Lius and me. They appear proud of Lius for finally starting to show me how he truly feels about me. Lius continues to rub my back gently and to whisper words of comfort as he holds me. After a few moments, I gradually started to settle down. He looks over his shoulder at Kai and Ares, catching their eyes. They exchange a silent look, a mix of concern and understanding. Lius returns his attention to me.

"Are you feeling a little bit better now?" His voice is soft and calming as he speaks.

I nod against him. "Thank you." I pull away and wipe the lingering tears from my face. "Okay. I need to get going. Check in is at four and the bullet train leaves in two hours."

Lius' eyes show how his heart aches a little as I pull away from him. His face gives away that he wants to say so much more, but he swallows his words, knowing it's not the right time. "Okay, just… be careful out there, alright? And if you need anything at all, don't hesitate to call me." Turning down his offer to go with me on this trip was hard for me. I just don't feel that it's the right time. It's too soon for me, even if he says he will wait. That fact makes my heart swell. But I can't ask him to do that for me, and I won't expect him to.

I nod and give a weak smile as I walk towards the front door and pick up my bags to head out. "I made you all some breakfast. Please eat up. I'll text you guys once I get to the cabin."

The guys watch as I walk out the front door with a wave.

End of Part 1.

EPILOGUE

Max's POV:

I knew it would come to this. Nathaniel made the threat weeks ago—offhand, casual, like he was talking about the weather. But I heard the weight behind it, the finality. *"If she keeps interfering, I'll take her myself."* That was the moment I knew I had to choose. Not between Elara and Nathaniel—that was never a question. But between saving her life my way, or watching Nathaniel destroy everything she was. So I offered a deal. I'd help him lure her in. Control her before she spiraled. Contain her before others tried to end her. If he promised no harm would come to her—if I stayed in control of how it unfolded. It was the only way I could protect her. At least, that's what I told myself.

Now here I was, boots on gravel, suited up before midnight even struck. The call from Nathaniel had come in earlier than expected. The lab was ready. The collar—Gods, even saying the word made my stomach twist—had been calibrated for her E-Level frequency. This was the night. Lius, Kai, and Ares stirred as the alerts lit up their phones. *Rogues spotted. Mansion perimeter. Urgent.* Right. Urgent for them. Planned for me.

I stood in the corner of the room, lacing my armor with mechanical precision. Lius kissed Elara goodbye without knowing it might be the last time he held her in peace. I watched, my chest tight. He looked back at her twice before walking out the door. Like part of him already knew she wouldn't stay behind. *She never fucking does.* She's fire wrapped in skin and willpower sharpened into a blade. And me? I'm the fool still bleeding from the last time I touched her flame.

I climbed into the SUV, keeping to the shadows. My eyes scanned the trees automatically, and sure enough, not long after we pulled out—I felt her. Of course she followed. She was always going to. The others didn't feel it, not right away. But I did. Because I never severed the bond. Not fully. I couldn't. It wasn't just guilt—it was her. Still in my blood. Still in my damn heartbeat. She was close. Watching. Like a ghost on the wind. Her scent drifted down the mountain minutes before I spotted the shimmer in the trees. Vivv's cloaking mist. Elara, no.

We rolled up to the mansion and disembarked. Lius's body language shifted immediately. His instincts were screaming, and I knew exactly why. He felt her too. I could see the questions forming in his eyes. Nathaniel's people were already here. Quiet. Efficient. Too many of them. Kai and Ares clocked it immediately. The tension in the air was thick enough to choke on. I hung back as they moved. Lius took point, jaw clenched, scanning the skies like he expected her to swoop down in flames. And she might've—if I hadn't planned this right down to the minute.

I pretended to check gear, adjusted my earpiece, and waited. Her scent hit stronger now. She was too close. Damn it, Ellie.

Then the intercom crackled. Lius's voice, low and lethal: "Why are you here?"

I froze. She answered. Said she was just observing. Classic. Always pretending not to care until she's already ten feet into the fire. And now the rogues were picking up her scent. Trained dogs, heads snapping toward the trees like they'd found blood in the water. This is what I was afraid of. This is why I worked with him.

I clicked into position, slowly pushing forward with the squad, flanking left. My job was to act like a Viper. Keep the rogues distracted. Let the trap close. Lead her right into it—but gently. No blood. No screaming. Just a quick hit with the tranquilizer if she got too close, and then the collar. Then... containment. Quiet. Controlled. Safe. Then I could free her and end Nathaniel for good. I could finally be free of all of this. But nothing about Elara is quiet. Or controlled.

I saw it then. That flicker of red behind the tree line. Vivv's pulse in the dark. My breath caught. She stepped forward. And our eyes met. Time stopped. Her gaze locked on mine—and I saw it all. Confusion. Betrayal. Heartbreak. And then—rage. It started in her shoulders, tightened in her fists. I felt it rise before she even took a step. I thought I could manage this. Thought I could control how much it would hurt her. But I was wrong.

She saw me. Not the mission. Not the plan. Just the man who left her... and led her right into the lion's den. This wasn't going to be clean. This was going to be war. And I just became her enemy once again. The moment I stepped into the clearing, I knew she was watching.

I didn't need to see her to feel her presence—like a phantom tether pulling at my chest, wrapping around my ribs and reminding me that even if I stood with Nathaniel tonight, it didn't mean I'd stopped loving her.

Elara was close. Too close. And judging by the sharp glint in Lius's eye and the subtle tension in his shoulders, he knew it too. I kept my expression unreadable, posture confident, even as the rogues around me fidgeted with barely-contained nerves. I unrolled the parchment in my hand—blueprints, real enough, though mostly a distraction.

"Tonight," I said, my voice laced with false cold conviction, "We reclaim what's rightfully ours. This mansion holds secrets. Power beyond anything SP6 ever let you touch."

Some of them bought it—wide-eyed, hungry, *stupid*. One asked if the place was haunted. I smirked. If only they knew. What I didn't say was that the power I was speaking of wasn't in the walls or foundations. It was in the woman crouched somewhere in the trees, burning with confusion and fury.

Elara.

She didn't know yet. Not really. Not that this wasn't about the mansion. Not about ley lines. This was about her. She *was* the power. And Nathaniel wanted her back under his control, whether that meant exploiting her, dissecting her, or turning her into a weapon. I was here to make sure that didn't happen. At least, that was the lie I told myself every night. Lius stepped into the open, SP6 agents fanning out behind him.

"Max Rossi!" he barked. "This ends now."

His voice cracked through the night like a gunshot. I felt the old itch stir under my skin—the need to move, fight, protect—but I didn't flinch. I met his gaze with a smirk and rolled my eyes.

"Vipers," I drawled. "Always so dramatic."

Kai sparked electricity at his fingertips. Ares shifted his stance, ready to lunge. The usual standoff—us versus them. *Me* versus them. Then Nathaniel emerged from the trees behind me like a ghost, and the tension ratcheted up tenfold. Elara must have seen him. I imagined the betrayal slamming into her like a physical force. The man who made her. The man who broke her. And me... the man who should've warned her.

When Lius demanded to know who told me about the mansion's supposed power, I answered truthfully in the only way I could: "A certain princesa of the estate."

It was enough. I knew the second I said it that she'd realize the truth. That it wasn't the ground beneath us Nathaniel wanted—it was her. The branch creaked somewhere above us, but the chaos of the moment masked it. Good. Stay hidden, Ellie. But of course, she didn't.

The second the fighting broke out—when a rogue lost his nerve and lunged—everything exploded. SP6 agents converged. Lius and the others tore into the rogues with terrifying precision. And Nathaniel and I slipped toward the back of the mansion, using the chaos as cover. Except we weren't alone. She landed in front of us with a gust of wind and a shimmer of crimson mist, wings out, eyes burning. *Vivv.*

"Elara," Nathaniel whispered, stunned.

I swallowed the lump in my throat. She looked like death and vengeance wrapped in something heartbreakingly beautiful. I couldn't stop the flicker of pride—even as I prepared to hurt her. "You've inherited some new tricks," I murmured. I let the smirk touch my lips, but my chest ached. I wanted to beg her to run. To *not* be here. To not make me do this. But it was too late. She shed her hood. Vivv came forward. Her voice—*their* voice—shook the night air as her staff hit the ground.

"You don't get to talk to me like that!" She growled out.

Nathaniel didn't flinch, but I saw the twitch in his eye. The guilt, buried under layers of ego and power hunger. He stepped forward, said something hollow about how much she'd grown. And then I made my move. A quick gesture behind her back. The agents Nathaniel had hidden among the trees triggered the collar, launching it onto her neck with pinpoint precision.

It clicked into place just as the needle pierced her skin. Her wings vanished. Vivv disappeared in a wisp of red smoke. Her body collapsed.

"Elara…" I whispered, almost too softly to hear.

She was on her knees, gripping the collar, panic in her eyes. Tears formed as she looked at me. She didn't understand. Not yet.

"We came to draw you out," I murmured, kneeling beside her. I hated the words coming out of my mouth, but I had to sell it. "You weren't as careful fighting those rogues in town as you thought…" I leaned in, my breath brushing her ear. "You weren't cautious enough, princesa."

And then I heard it. Lius. Screaming. I turned, just as he burst through the trees, rage and terror warping his face. He was tearing through the last few rogues like they were nothing, but he was too late. I pressed the detonator. The flashbang went off, swallowing the clearing in blinding white.

I scooped Elara into my arms as she slipped into unconsciousness. Nathaniel opened the back of the SUV. I stepped inside, cradling her limp body, heart pounding, stomach twisted. When the light faded, Lius dropped to his knees in the clearing where she'd stood. He screamed again. And I closed the door behind us, sealing my betrayal with it. But even as the SUV sped away, one thought repeated in my mind: *You'll forgive me, Ellie. One day. You'll see why I had to do this.* Because if Nathaniel wanted her, he'd have to go through me to get to the truth. And I wasn't done fighting. Not yet.

Read more in "Max: Rage Reborn"

If you or someone you know is living with borderline personality disorder (BPD), or if you think you might be experiencing symptoms, know that you are not alone. There is help available, and reaching out can be the first step toward understanding and managing your mental health.

If you suspect you may have BPD or are experiencing symptoms, it's important to talk to a healthcare professional for proper evaluation and diagnosis. Here are a few steps and resources to consider:

Speak with a Mental Health Professional:
Licensed therapists, psychologists, and psychiatrists can assess your symptoms and offer a formal diagnosis. Many clinics and mental health organizations offer screenings and assessments for BPD.

National Alliance on Mental Illness (NAMI):
Offers support and resources for finding local mental health professionals.
Website: www.nami.org
Helpline: 1-800-950-NAMI (6264)

Psychology Today Therapist Directory:
A helpful resource for finding licensed therapists and counselors in your area who specialize in BPD and other mental health issues.
Website: www.psychologytoday.com/us/therapists

Mental Health America:

Provides screening tools and resources for BPD and other mental health concerns.

Website: www.mhanational.org

Crisis Support

If you or someone you love is experiencing a mental health crisis, it is important to seek immediate help.

Suicide & Crisis Lifeline:

If you are struggling and need someone to talk to, the Suicide & Crisis Lifeline is available 24/7. Reach out to someone who cares.

Dial: **988**

Website: 988lifeline.org

Crisis Text Line:

Text **HELLO** to 741741 to connect with a crisis counselor 24/7 via text.

National Suicide Prevention Lifeline (US):

Call **1-800-273-TALK (8255)** for support, or visit their website for resources and online chat services.

Website: suicidepreventionlifeline.org

Support for People Living with BPD:

BPD Family: A resource for family members and loved ones affected by Borderline Personality Disorder.

Website: www.bpdfamily.com

DBT (Dialectical Behavior Therapy) Resources:

DBT is a proven therapeutic approach for managing BPD symptoms. Look for DBT therapy groups and resources in your area.

Information on DBT: www.behavioraltech.org

You Are Not Alone

Living with BPD can feel isolating, but there is support available. Reaching out for help is the first step toward managing your symptoms and finding the care you need.

You *matter*, and your life is worth *living*.